STONE CHALMERS AND ALIGNMENT WITH THE UNIVERSE

Other CV-2 Books by Raymund Eich

The Confederated Worlds
Take the Shilling
Operation Iago
A Bodyguard of Lies

Novels
The Blank Slate
New California
The Reincarnation Run

Short Novels
The ALECS Quartet
A Mighty Fortress

Collections
The First Voyages: The Complete Science Fiction Stories 1998-2012
Stage Separations: The Complete Science Fiction Stories 2013-2018

STONE CHALMERS AND ALIGNMENT WITH THE UNIVERSE

To All High Emprise Consecrated
(Stone Chalmers #3)
In Public Convocation Assembled
(Stone Chalmers #4)

Raymund Eich

CV-2 Books • Houston

This is a work of fiction. All the characters and events portrayed in this book are fictitious, and any resemblance to real people, living or dead, or any known events is purely coincidental.

STONE CHALMERS AND ALIGNMENT WITH THE UNIVERSE
© 2020 Raymund Eich
To All High Emprise Consecrated © 2018 Raymund Eich
In Public Convocation Assembled © 2018 Raymund Eich

All rights reserved. No part of this book may be reproduced or transmitted in any form or by any means, electronic or mechanical, including photocopying, recording, or by any information storage and retrieval system, without the written permission of the author, except where permitted by law.

Cover art: Jędrzej Tarkowski. Spy silhouette by Pixattitude | Dreamstime.com
Cover design, book design, and aircraft carrier logo are copyrights, trademarks, or trade dress of CV-2 Books.

First CV-2 Books trade paperback edition: April 2020

TO ALL HIGH EMPRISE CONSECRATED

Prologue

The Chairman of the High Council of the colony world Minerva faced the UN diplomat. The Chairman sat behind a curved conference table, flanked by the High Councillors and others.

To the UN diplomat's right, the tall, narrow windows let through and diffused a quarter of the afternoon rays from Minerva's bright yellow G1-type star. Despite the dimmed and indirect light, the diplomat's smile showed rows of gleaming teeth stark against his olive complexion. Behind and above him floated holographic lines of bullet-pointed text and a small UN logo in the lower right corner.

The hologram flickered, showed a new slide. The diplomat rested his open hand on his cocked hip. He spoke in a smooth American accent without looking at the words floating behind him.

"To summarize, when Minerva joins the Dubai Convention, multiple benefits will accrue to you. Instead of a four-month journey by warpdrive, you can instantaneously communicate with all of Earth's scientists, intellectuals, and content creators. You can export products free of tariffs—and the immense operating expenses of a warpdrive ship—to UN member states. The quick and easy travel only the wormhole can provide will give you an opportunity to recruit immigrants. Finally, you'll also receive the benefits of increased creativity when your society incorporates the vibrant diversity of the resettled."

The hologram flickered again, showed *Questions?*.

"Thank you. I'm sure you want to know more. I can stay as long as you wish to answer."

The Chairman of the High Council said nothing. He didn't need to.

To the Chairman's right, a blue-eyed man wearing a mustard-yellow blazer and a stubbly beard raised his hand. "What products does the UN forbid colonies to import to Earth?"

"Earth will accept a colossal variety of imports. Metals, fissionables, hydrocarbons, raw and processed foods, heavy machinery, consumer goods..." The diplomat made a juggling motion. "I can't list everything."

The man's blue eyes narrowed. "I didn't ask which imports are permitted. I want to know which ones are forbidden."

"Oh. *Forbidden.*" The diplomat folded his arms. "Very few imports are barred by General Assembly resolutions. Weapons of mass destruction. Fission or fusion reactors. Techniques for human genetic modification. Molecular fabricators. That's all." He held his gaze on the man in the mustard-yellow blazer, then turned to the only woman in the room, a statuesque blonde with hair piled high and a Big Dipper pin high on the bodice of her crimson dress. "You had a question?"

Her voice sounded huskier than the smooth lines of her face suggested. "Under the Dubai Convention, what rights would the Minerva government have to select or reject resettled?"

"You may be assured that the resettlement authority takes the cultural background of a colony into consideration, and strives to assign resettled from a similar background when possible. Of course, the crises that create situations where resettlement is appropriate do not always conform to colonial prejudices. Though I am certain the leaders of Minerva are free of such prejudices. I'm certain your heart is large enough to welcome hungry and homeless women and children to your world." The diplomat's brown eyes softened with the final sentences. He drew in a long breath. "Anyone else?"

"No," the Chairman said. "You've given us more than enough information to make our decision."

The diplomat blinked once, but the smoothness of his next words signaled mastery of any confusion. "I'm glad my presentation has been helpful to you. Of course, should you or any member of the High Council need any additional information, message or call me any time, day or night."

"Noted."

"Very well. I'll return to the UN base camp and await word from you. If you could reach your decision in four days, I and every UN employee, both here and on Earth, would be most grateful."

"We'll make our decision by then," the Chairman said, finality in his tone.

The diplomat bowed from the waist. He turned and strode through the hologram toward double doors on the far side of the room. Against the floor of polished, blue-flecked gray granite, the hard soles of his polished black oxford shoes struck like whip cracks.

The hologram's floating UN logo morphed into a magic lamp shape, sucked up the rest of the slide, then winked out of sight.

After the double doors closed themselves soundlessly behind the departing diplomat, the Chairman and Councillors rose from the curved table. Ceiling-high doors swung open in the twelve-foot wall of ceramic tiles behind them. Strong ventilation pushed robotic miniblimps into the conference room. The miniblimps bumped the ceiling as they dangled filters to scoop up any microscopic airborne sensors the diplomat might have left.

The ventilation chilled the Chairman's face as he led the Councillors down a corridor toward the executive offices of the Minervan government. Twenty feet from the conference room, they stopped at a door to what looked like a utility closet. The bearded man in the mustard-yellow blazer poised his knuckles to knock—

The door swung open. A dozen monitors and status boards glowed in a windowless room. In the doorway stood a lean-figured woman. Her eyebrows arched and her mouth formed a coy, closed-lip smile.

"He told us exactly what you said he would," said the man in the yellow blazer. "So what do you advise?"

Her lips parted in a wider smile. She rocked her head, setting her long blond hair rippling. A gleam filled her hazel eyes.

"Surrender."

1

The producer's office fit with the blue, cloud-dotted sky outside the windows. Potted plants turned waxy, deep green leaves toward yellow LED spotlights in the ceiling. Water dripped from microirrigation systems and fertilized potting soil filled the space with the rich smell of springtime.

Even better as far as Stone Chalmers was concerned, the warming weather meant girls in the streets of Manhattan wore short sheer dresses. He would get back out there soon. Just waiting for—

The producer hurried in. Tanned face and a feathered haircut. "Didn't mean to be late. My flight from Los Angeles got rerouted around thunderstorms in flyover country." He sat on an angular, black leather sofa, stretched his arm along the back, and extended legs crossed at the ankles toward Stone.

"Mr. Chalmers, Rolston—I can call you Rolston?—"

"Why not?" Stone said from a matching armchair facing the sofa.

"Rolston, glad to finally meet you. We've been trying to put together this project for, for—" The producer lifted his hand from the back of the sofa and rolled his wrist. "Tarquinia, how long has it been?"

The producer's assistant, Tarquinia, sat on the sofa six inches beyond her employer's extended hand. Plunging neckline, tight skirt hemmed above the knee, and a high heap of russet hair Stone would revel in for the five seconds he would need to loosen it. She gave Stone a look hinting she would revel in it too. "Five years ago, we acquired the rights to your great-grandfather's life story from his descendants from his second marriage. We didn't discover he had heirs from his first marriage until your—brother—?"

"Cousin."

"—until he heard about the project and threatened to sue."

The producer nodded. "We don't know what he told you, but, hand to God, from the start of this we wanted to play fair by everyone. We knew your great-grandfather had a son by his first marriage, but we had no idea your grandfather legally took his stepfather's surname after your great-grandmother remarried. Hand to God, when your grandfather's birth name disappeared from the public records, we assumed he'd died as a child during the Time of Troubles."

"Understandable."

The producer's lips clamped together. He looked away from Stone, toward the bright spring sky outside the windows. Probably subvoking to the auditory nerves of—

Tarquinia dabbed her lips with her tongue, then leaned her cleavage toward Stone. "Rolston—"

"Call me Stone."

"Stone. We know you might be unhappy about our mistake. Don't hold it against the project. Hold it against me. I'm the one who failed to dig deeply enough to ensure all your great-grandfather's heirs had the chance to buy in five years ago." She puffed out her chest. "How can I make it up to you?"

Five seconds to loosen her hair, then... an hour later he'd stroll the Upper East Side looking for his next conquest. Back on the treadmill—

Seducing women is a treadmill? What the hell has gotten into you? He forced a lazy smile. "I'll think of something."

"Glad you have no hard feelings," the producer said. "Let me tell you, we're excited as hell to bring Plutarco Blanco's story to the silver screen. It's got everything modern audiences are looking for. Romantic drama for women, action scenes for young men, and older men will love the political intrigue and the principled battle against racism."

Stone sagely nodded. "I was afraid that part might be neglected.

Mestizos—you know, Mexicans who look Mexican?—envied my great-grandfather's blond hair and pale skin." He glanced sidelong at Tarquinia with a faint smirk. Her lips parted in a shocked *o*, but she leaned forward, pulled by his magnetism just the same.

Fish. Barrel.

Treadmill.

"Well, yes, right," the producer said. "We were thinking more about the racism he faced from white Americans."

"Oh." Stone drew out the word and kept his poker face.

"Our working treatment so far doesn't play up the bigotry your great-grandfather suffered from other Mexican-Americans, but script development on a project like this goes on until the last day of shooting." He shifted against the black leather. "Now, Rolston, for licensing your rights to your great-grandfather's story, we're prepared to offer you—" He emphasized the next words. "—0.05% of lifetime net revenue."

Net meaning after a thousand vaguely-worded expenses added up to a few pennies less than the gross. "0.05%?"

"Rolston, Rolston, I know that might sound low, but let me walk you through some example math here. We're expecting a budget of half a trillion dollars—United States dollars—here, but this picture could bring a trillion in domestic box office alone."

At twenty thousand dollars to see a movie in Manhattan…. "Fifty million people will go see yet another costume drama set during the Time of Troubles?"

"Easily. And that's just domestic. Latin America will easily bring in another trillion. Another half trillion for merchandising—and, hand to God, from the novelization, the graphic novel, the action figures, the other collectables, that's a conservative estimate—anyway, your share works out to a cool billion." The producer spread his hands like a car salesman. "So we've got a deal."

If Stone received a royalty check for as much as a million, he'd be astonished. But no harm agreeing. The distant cousins he hadn't seen since his father's funeral would get an ego boost from their glancing contact with Hollywood, then return to their tedious lives, longing for fortune and fame never to come.

He opened his mouth to speak. A message appeared in his vision, green letters laid over the producer's tanned face and Tarquinia's buxom curves by electromagnetic stimulation of his optic nerves by a tracery of wires around his hair follicles.

Code 909. Minerva. Report to my office before close of business tomorrow.

909 meant a special detail. Which reeked of boredom. Bodyguarding some politician, likely. Minerva? A colony world so recently discovered by the UN that it didn't even have a sited wormhole mouth? And a mission so lacking in urgency Gray gave him over twenty-four hours to report?

A mission. After ten months—far longer than the inactivity period Gray had imposed at their last meeting, after his return from Trinity—after ten months, a mission.

Stone's heart beat a little faster.

"Rolston, Rolston, what's going on?"

Stone got to his feet. "An important project at work just came up."

"You mean you're leaving? I thought we had a deal here."

Tarquinia shifted her torso to give Stone a view straight down her cleavage. "I thought so too."

He kept his gaze at the level of their eyes. "Duty calls." He turned for the door.

"Rolston, Rolston, I get it." Humor with a manic edge sounded in the producer's voice. "You're playing the game. You're right, we're eager to close, but we can't give you the keys to the castle. We can go as high as 0.075% of net. Just for you. Provided you don't disclose your terms to the other heirs—"

The glass door made a faint mechanical hum as it swung toward him. "I'll be in touch," he said over his shoulder.

"Rolston!"

After an ear-popping elevator ride, Stone slipped out a revolving door from the building's lobby to the sidewalk. The noise of ten thousand cars and a hundred thousand feet reverberated off the glass and steel faces of skyscrapers. Through the press of pedestrians he glimpsed a low, faceted black shape amid dense traffic. He crossed the sidewalk to the curb. Men wearing neckties loose under unbuttoned collars angled around him. Neck-craning tourists ducked their heads and muttered "Excuse me" in cornpone Midwestern accents. Leggy young women fanned their short skirts and stared at him from wide, downturned eyes.

Imagine how much more these passersby would react if they knew how many women he'd bedded and how many men he'd killed.

His black coupe, faceted like a stealth fighter aircraft, pulled up to the curb. It popped open its door as he approached, closed it after he climbed in. In silence and cool dry air, he settled on the back seat. *UNICA HQ*, he subvoked to the car. *Priority.*

The black coupe pulled away from the curb, heading east. The message from its transponder compelled cars in front to change lanes and turned the red light at Broadway green.

North and east of Times Square, signs began to bear the logos of UN agencies and global charities. Cameras grew denser, like fungi expanding through a concrete and alloy forest.

In the mid 50s, between Lexington and the FDR, the headquarters of the United Nations Interagency Coordination Authority looked like any other eighty-story highrise. Perhaps the sidewalk in front held more anti-vehicle obstacles, concrete bollards and welded steel spikes, than some other UN buildings. The coupe turned into the garage.

Soon after, the elevator pinged at the 27th floor. The doors parted. Despite his hammering heart and churning emotions, Stone walked with forced casualness to Gray's office, rapped a jaunty pattern with his knuckles on the synthetic wood door.

"Come in."

Stone entered and shut the door.

At his standing desk, Gray looked like the upper-level bureaucrat of his job title, Assistant Director of Operational Planning. His three archaic monitors held scrolling text and a video from high altitude of dusty buildings exploding. Gray typed on a split, angled keyboard that clacked with every keypress. Not for the first time Stone wondered if the archaic input devices and displays were a cover, and Gray used the exact same transcranial magnetic stimulation hardware as everyone else.

The monitors went dark. "You're early, Stone."

And you're four months late calling me in. "I was in a meeting and needed an excuse to leave. You earned me an extra, let's see, one-fortieth of one percent of—"

"The film based on your great-grandfather Blanco's life and death?"

Stone's eyes blinked wide. How did he—?

Because he was Gray. Rivers of information from ten thousand sources flowed past his eyeballs.

"That's the one," Stone said.

"I'll buy a ticket to the premiere." Gray made a quarter-turn to his sitting-height desk and gestured at the visitor chairs facing it. "Sit, and tell me about Minerva."

Stone sat, faced a broad, glass-topped desk bare except for an in-box, an outbox, and a five-ball pendulum, all of which appeared to have never been touched. "A colony founded during the Time of Troubles. An Interstellar Transport Bureau scout ship reported the colony's discovery around the time I went to Trinity. An ITB diplomatic mission went out to bribe or blackmail the colony's leaders into acceding to the Dubai Convention." Stone subvoked up the diplomatic mission's departure date from Earth and the warpdrive flight time to and from Minerva. A date from the previous week appeared in his vision. "That mission just returned."

"And with success," Gray said, now seated across the desk from Stone. "Minerva acceded to the Dubai Convention. A wormhole is currently under construction at Hawking Station. The terrestrial end will be sited in the Mojave Desert 130 miles from Los Angeles. The ITB warpdrive ship that will tow the other end to Minerva departs Earth orbit for Hawking Station in five days. You will be on that ship."

Stone let out a long breath, and the stress of inactivity bled from his shoulders. "You suspect some ITB employees on the ship are saboteurs?"

"No."

"I get it. You want me to assassinate a Minerva politician or two."

"No."

Stone scowled. "Then what? I've been cooling my heels for almost a year and you're sending me on a mission I'm overqualified for?"

Gray peered down his nose with narrowed eyes. "You will go

where I order you. Unless you wish to move your hiatus from the temporary column to the permanent?"

The pattern in the carpet caught Stone's gaze. "Of course I'll go."

"Good. Your assignment is to gather intelligence on the Minerva government relating to any threats it may pose to the UN."

Blood drained from Stone's face. Reading public websites, maybe hanging out in bars where colonial government clerks drank together and vented about their bosses. His lips clamped together and he breathed heavily through his nose.

"Minerva is unlike other colonies." The way Gray said the words made Stone frown and look up. "Every other colony we've discovered to date was founded by people looking backward from the middle of the 21st century to some imagined golden age, typically comprising ethnocultural purity or monolithic religious belief. Minerva was instead founded by American scientists and engineers who believed their golden age lay in the future. Unlike other colonies, which settled on planets with native biospheres providing breathable air, the Minervans found a waterless and lifeless rocky world and terraformed it. Their economy is heavily roboticized and computerized. They have more molecular fabricators per capita than does Earth. To the best of our knowledge, they lack artificial intelligence, and if I were a praying man I would thank God for that."

"But Minerva acceded to the Dubai Convention—"

"My hunch is Minerva acceded too easily."

Stone felt more like himself. Through a smirking mouth, he asked, "A hunch?"

"If my job didn't require hunches, a computer could do it." A pause, then Gray said, "Your cover will be an employee for a UN import regulation agency. Under this cover, you will meet Minerva government officials and corporate executives. Find whatever you can, however you can, about possible threats to the UN, and return through the wormhole after ground transportation links are established."

A grin creased Stone's face. *However you can....* How many women worked for Minerva's government and large businesses? And how many of those would open their secrets to him as readily as they would open their legs? "I'll pick up the cover story packet from Jürgen right now."

"No hurry. The shuttle from Cape Canaveral to Hammarskjöld Orbital Port launches in three days. Fly to Florida the day after tomorrow."

A mission *and* two more nights in Manhattan. This day got better by the moment. Still, work to do before he left Gray's office. "You want regular reports?"

"Yes. Copy what you find to encrypted data devices and throw them in the UN's Earthbound diplomatic pouch—you'll learn the address when you hypnogogue your cover."

"What about our field office?"

"Our field office is not yet established. The team to do so will be on your ship, under a cover which I will not share with you. Even after they establish the field office, I don't want you generating sigint that Minerva counterintelligence might pick up."

Stone's nose wrinkled. "You're worried about colonial counterintelligence?"

"No," Gray said. The tone of his next words trickled a frigid feeling down Stone's spine. "I'm worried about *Minerva* counterintelligence."

2

Amid clouds of fruit-flavored nicotine vapor thick in zero-*g*, almost all of *Yassir Arafat*'s hundred-sixty passengers held onto straps and floated in front of the video walls in the ship's lounges.

On the video wall nearest to Stone, two parallel dark rings, their edges nearly touching, hung against a backdrop of thousands of stars. The closer to the rings, the more the background compressed. Crowded starlight haloed the rings' outer edges. Nanotube alloy filaments and electromagnetic grapples connected each dark ring to four space tugs. From experience, Stone read the tugs' interior schematics from their profiles. The dumpy vessels packed a life-support module smaller than a Japanese hotel room between propellant tanks and forward of a single drive nozzle in the stern.

In unison, the eight tugs fired. The dark rings drifted apart. Starlight slipped from the haloes into the growing space between the rings. Cheers and excited gasps came from the other eighteen passengers in Stone's lounge, and echoed down the curving plastic-walled corridors from adjacent lounges.

"Oh my," said a young white woman near Stone. Her pixie cut of purple hair drifted away from her face. The UN identification card clipped to her collar and naming her Merrill Mears rose and fell with rapt breaths. He'd seduced women far more gorgeous, but despite her dye job and unfeminine name, she would be in the top fifty. "It's so beautiful."

A puff of vapor smelled of rosewater and cardamom. "It would be even more gorgeous if we watched in virtual reality, alone in our room." The speaker was a swarthy male, about the same age as the woman. His soft face showed a trace of queasiness. Apparently the ship's medics underdosed his weightlessness drug. His sweatshirt hung loosely around his belly. Stone couldn't guess his ethnicity from either his skin tone or his accent—he could be from Mexico City, Marrakech, or Mumbai—but he knew the type. A man-child more at home in the interchangeable residential high-rises and international schools of the global political class than in the teeming streets of his birth city.

"In our room, just the two of us," the male repeated to purple-haired Merrill.

She turned her shoulder to him. Her rapt eyes soaked in the vista on the video wall.

A smirk touched Stone's lips. He leaned closer to the young woman. "No, you should stay here."

Her head swung around. Wide whites of eyes. Purple hair couldn't disguise black roots. "I should—" She glanced at the ID badge at Stone's collar. "—Edward?"

The man-child tried to sound tough. "Who are you to tell her what she should do?"

Stone kept his gaze on the young woman's brown eyes. "We're not on this ship alone, or even with one partner. We're on it to serve a higher purpose." He rested his free hand on her shoulder, then twisted her toward the video wall. "That."

Only one of the dark rings remained on camera. Though the ring circled the equator of the spherical wormhole, the tear in space remained invisible, except for flashing arcs along its perimeter, where gravitational lensing smeared the light of each background star into a brief, elongated blip.

"It glitters like a diamond," said the purple-haired young woman.

"I can buy you a diamond when we get back to Earth." Stone could hear the swarthy male's desperation. Which meant the young woman could too.

Stone smirked. Any time during the next four months, he could brush past the swarthy man-child at will. He slid his fingers down over her shoulder blade, then pulled them away. Merrill leaned a few millimeters back toward him.

Fish. Barrel.

Treadmill.

The four tugs pulling the wormhole drifted now, motors silent. The camera, mounted at the rotation axis of Hawking Station, zoomed out until a long, narrow ship came into view. The ship's greatest width came at two dark rings, one fore, one aft, joined by lattices and struts to the chunky modules making up the ship's elongated body. In the middle of the ship hung an empty cylinder with a diameter slightly less than the fore and aft rings.

Someone cheered. Then everyone followed suit, with the relaxing shoulders and relieved sidelong glances of people glad someone else had recognized what they saw: an exterior view of Nobel Peace Prize-class warpdrive wormhole transport *Yassir Arafat*.

Merrill stared wide-eyed at the screen. "We're going to carry the wormhole in the middle of our ship?"

"Well," the swarthy man-child said, "you know, I think so, but I'm not sure."

Her glance invited Stone into their conversation. "A wormhole inside a warpdrive cylinder? Is it safe?" she asked with a childlike tone. Subconscious or chosen, didn't matter.

Stone leaned toward her ear, deepened his voice. "Safety is overrated, isn't it?"

Over her shoulder, wide brown eyes regarded him. "You're joking. Aren't you?"

"I only joke when I'm serious." He looked past her to the video wall. "Keep watching."

A scale popped up on the video wall. The wormhole was now about two miles from *Yassir Arafat*. White vapor jetted from the tugs' forward attitude nozzles, slowing them. Changes in the glimmering of starlight provided the only sign the nanotube alloy filaments slackened. The wormhole's equilibrator ring drew abreast of the tugs, overtook them. Lateral attitude nozzles puffed. The tugs turned over, locked their orientation relative to the ship with bursts from the attitude jets. Very precise, well-practiced by the tug pilots.

How many tedious years did the tug pilots spend in simulators?

Stone shrugged to himself. They chose their career. Every man has his place.

The wormhole drifted closer. The camera zoomed in, tighter, tighter. Red squiggles on the ship resolved into the words UNITBS *Yassir Arafat DTTV-17*. The filaments holding the wormhole equilibrator ring to the tugs grew taut.

"Now," Stone said, softly enough for only the purple-haired young woman and the swarthy male to hear.

The tugs' drive nozzles blazed with light. The wormhole slowed its approach to the transport cylinder. Teasing, agonizing, the wormhole took thirty seconds to travel the last hundred yards. Merrill and the man-child watched the wormhole's progress. Stone kept his gaze on the tugs. Short puffs from their attitude jets, all four moving in unison, imparted to the wormhole course corrections Stone couldn't see.

The wormhole's equilibrator ring slipped into the empty cylinder amidships. Moments later, the tugs' drives cut out. A faint tremor ran through the ceiling, down the strap, into Stone's hand. The purple-haired pixie caught her breath. Her male companion looked even queasier.

The image on the video wall didn't change. Only a faint distortion of the stars visible through *Yassir Arafat*'s central gap showed any sign the wormhole had actually been sited.

Passengers drifted out of the lounge by twos and threes. The swarthy male tugged on Merrill's arm four times before she said a good-bye to Stone and followed her boyfriend. Stone was the last one to watch the unchanging image. Inside the module surrounding the wormhole, techs worked, locking the equilibrator ring into its cylindrical cradle. Labor as mind-numbing as the tug pilots', but again, every man has his place.

After an hour, the camera mounted on Hawking Station zoomed out. The entire length of *Yassir Arafat* fit on the video wall. The ship flashed multilingual warning texts across Stone's vision. Recorded voices spoke the words in all the UN's official languages. "Commencing acceleration in 5... 4... 3...."

Stone let go of the ceiling strap when the countdown reached 1. On the video wall, white-hot, wispy reaction mass poured out of the drive nozzles. The wisps thickened as the floor accelerated toward Stone's feet. He flexed his knees and an instant later landed at 0.25 g. He walked out of the lounge, the synthetic gravity of thrust increasing with each step. Fifteen seconds for *Yassir Arafat* to reach its standard acceleration of 1.0 g, equivalent to Earth's gravity. Except for a few minutes of weightlessness when the ship flipped in mid-flight for its deceleration burn, the ship would maintain 1.0 g for the four-month journey to Minerva.

Four months. Purple-haired Merrill crossed Stone's mind. He smiled to himself. He would keep busy.

But not simply with yet another seduction. Each night he practiced with his tool kit, shutting off the lights and pulling out spy equipment—an infrared camera disguised as a black onyx ring, a cloak of computerized fabric that wrapped infrared and UV around his body—from the canvas bag in the dark. Every morning he slipped past the elliptical steppers and recumbent stationary bikes in the gym's cardio section, and worked up a light sweat doing swings and get-ups with a ninety-pound kettlebell. He attended every thrice-weekly cultural sensitivity and diversity training session, and thus appeared to the others to be a typical white male UN employee collecting promotion points. In the sensitivity sessions, Stone struck his usual pose—aloof, sardonic, mildly flirtatious—and amplified it whenever Merrill attended. The women he flirted with responded with coy smiles, hair flips, fingers landing on his lean, solid biceps.

Merrill's interest in him rose with every sign other women desired him too.

When Stone judged she was receptive enough, he easily reeled her in, despite her half-assed resistance. "Eddie, I have a boyfriend."

"I won't tell him if you won't," he said, smirk on his lips.

Or in his cabin, still fully clothed but sitting side-by-side on the edge of the flipped-down single bed, when she said, "I really should go."

"No, stay." He put on a playfully stern look and jutted out a finger. "But you have to keep your hands to yourself."

Ten minutes later....

Fish. Barrel.

Afterward, she slunk away, blushing. Probably heading straight to her cabin to initiate sex with the man-child to soothe her guilt. She did the same after their second tryst, their third, fourth.... Each time after Merrill left his cabin, Stone shrugged. Data held in an encrypted storage device embedded in his armpit held everything Gray knew about Minerva. Might as well learn it.

Minerva. Originally, an arid planet orbiting a star hotter than Sol. After the colonists turned a hundred comets into a hydrosphere and an atmosphere, the planet's ancient impact craters acquired shallow seas, green and stinking with photosynthetic algae. Eight hundred miles south of Minerva's equator, the capital city, Euler City, straddled the banks of a freshwater river, the Strigidae, where it gouged a canyon through a crater wall and poured into the planet's largest body of salt water, the Wisdom Sea. The scout ship and the diplomatic mission both estimated Euler City's population at about eighty thousand, with another twenty thousand colonists living in smaller towns a thousand klicks or fewer from the capital. About three hundred people lived and worked at the base of a space elevator on the equator. The rest of the planet held no human life. No life at all, rather, except for mosses and fungi spread by the wind and algae seeded by the colonists from orbit.

Wait a minute. A hundred thousand colonists? In all Stone's missions, he'd never traveled to so populous a colony—and every other colony had been habitable from the moment settlers arrived from Earth during the Time of Troubles. Family sizes must be immense. A glance at the population distribution confirmed his guess. Half the colonists were under the age of eighteen standard years.

Stone frowned. He subvoked to his implantable. A map projected onto his view of his cabin's far wall zoomed out, showing all of Euler City. *Highlight schools.*

Seven red circles dotted the map.

He focused on one. *Zoom in. Visible light camera view.*

Two bright green lawns crisply lined, one for soccer, the other for ultimate flying disc. Three buildings with a cumulative footprint of about half a soccer field. The buildings' shadows showed each to have at most three stories.

This school might serve six hundred students. Nowhere near six thousand.

Maybe Minervans gave education a low priority—

—except Gray feared their high technology.

Perhaps the colonists had invented their own speedlearning technology. Squeeze a year's worth of school into a month. Not quite. Grind off the typical Earth school's busywork and ham-fisted propaganda, and you could squeeze that year down to two weeks.

The colonists might want to sell that technology to Earth.

Which is where his cover story came in. Edward Lavallette, newly-promoted to senior assistant manager in the acceded worlds division of the UN's Global Economic Cooperation Agency. Lavallette traveled to newly discovered colonies, helped business leaders navigate the mazes of red tape required to export advanced technologies to Earth, and helped Earth's superrich and superpowerful skim most of the benefit of those advanced techs. The speedlearning he'd done in his hotel on Florida's Space Coast, combined with the espionage skills grooved deep into his muscles and brain, would simplify his role as Lavallette on Minerva.

Too damn bad he couldn't end his in-flight fling with the purple-haired girl as simply. Firmly breaking it off, or simply ghosting her, could make her do something rash. Stalk him; go to ship's security with a false rape accusation; confess the affair to her boyfriend…. No. Better to carefully lower his value to her. Over the final month, he did just that. He acted needy and clingy, coldly gruff when she wanted emotional comfort, submissive to her whims when she craved his dominance.

His scheme worked. During the final week, the purple-haired girl stayed away from his cabin and rearranged her daily habits to avoid him in public spaces. Good. No distractions. Collect as much data on Minerva as he could and ride out on the first bus through the wormhole back to Earth.

Yassir Arafat dropped out of warp sixteen million miles from Minerva, far enough to dissipate the shock wave of ionizing radiation from the warp rings above the planet's atmosphere. Twenty hours of deceleration later, the passengers gathered in the lounges. Stone found himself near a gaggle of resettlement bureau site planners and wormhole placement engineers. Menthol vape clouds chafed the lining of Stone's nose. Rumor said the first two ships' ground parties complained of allergies their entire time around Euler City. More rumor said menthol vape juice would reduce symptoms.

The purple-haired girl came into the lounge at the opposite corner. Though the others partially blocked Stone's view of her, her eyes went cold. "Gautam. I want to go somewhere else." She tugged her boyfriend by his flabby upper arm back into the corridor to the adjoining lounge.

Minerva turned a narrow crescent of its dayside to the camera feeding the video wall. On the lighted crescent, crater seas lay like green-blue discs against the lunar gray surface. South of the planet's equator, two green-blue discs overlapped like the view through binoculars in some movie. Yellow-green fringed a quarter of the shore of the largest sea and cast filaments along jagged, hairlike blue lines. Near the edge of Minerva's dark face, a tiny cluster of lights along the coast of the double sea—

Text suddenly appeared on the video wall, labeling various features. A crewman remembered to turn on the labels for the less-savvy passengers, Stone guessed. The tiny cluster of lights marked Euler City, a few minutes before dawn. More words hung over the planet's lighted limb, attached to a computer-generated white line extending from the equator. *Space elevator*. The cable and any climbing cars would be too thin to see from tens of thousands of miles. The white line ended at a dot of the same color. *Stationary orbit station*.

Lines of text in the UN's six official languages popped up in Stone's vision. A voice induced on his auditory nerves read the words. "Prepare for reduced thrust in 30 seconds. Prepare for free fall in 60 seconds. *Préparez-vous à une réduction de la poussée*...." Most of the text vanished, except for one set of the numerals. The *30* shrank and slid into the lower left corner of his vision and counted down. The *60* did likewise to the lower right.

"Where are you going to put the wormhole?" a scrawny man with a short, woolly brown beard asked a leggy woman with a long raven ponytail. Stone easily read from the man's tone, and the hangdog look of his brown eyes against his pale skin, that he longed to bed her but had no clue how.

Her sharp Scandinavian cheekbones were like a castle wall, her Korean eyes like crenelations, her plucked eyebrows, like arrows in flight. "Twenty kilometers northeast of Euler City. Off the road and rail line to the surface station of the space elevator."

"How long will it take you to prep the site?"

The Eurasian girl waggled her vape pen. "The Minervans already did it."

Eyebrows knitted like crawling caterpillars. "They did?" the scrawny man said.

She puffed deeply on her vape pen. "You think that's odd?"

The scrawny man rolled his lips in between his jaws. "I mean, I've never been out before—"

Stone turned his rolling eyes away. *No kidding.*

"—but I heard it usually takes months after the wormhole transport arrives to place the wormhole." The scrawny man scratched his bearded chin.

Vapor streamed from the Eurasian girl's nostrils. "I was told that too. We'll be ready to place the wormhole in four days."

The lower left timer reached 0. Stone's weight faded, dropping six pounds per second. He crouched and eyed the array of looped straps hanging from the ceiling.

The scrawny man frowned at him. "Hey, man, what are you doing?"

The lower right timer counted down to 1. Stone rocked his weight upward. His feet left the floor and he curled his fingers around a strap. The scrawny man and his companions flailed their arms and ricocheted off each other. Stone smirked.

The Eurasian girl flapped her arms, struggling to swim in air. She grabbed a strap near Stone and caught her breath. Voice still ragged, she asked, "You've been on a wormhole transport before?"

"No," he answered, truthfully enough. His gaze meandered down her torso and long legs, then back up to lock on her eyes. His smirk sounded in his voice. "But there are a lot of places I know my way around."

Hours before a shuttle flight to the stationary orbit station. Over a day before a climber car touched down at the bottom of the space elevator.

"Oh?" Her eyes widened for an instant.

He smirked back. Fish. Barrel.

Treadmill.

3

Stone woke. His eyes shot open and his right hand reached toward the miniature plastic 9mm holstered at his ankle.

His hand stopped short as he oriented to his surroundings. He'd fallen asleep with bright sunlight outside the train windows and the tracks whispering underneath at three hundred miles per hour. He reclined in the same padded, auto-conforming seat he'd taken when he'd boarded at the space elevator; but shadow darkened the windows and the train no longer moved.

Outside the windows across the aisle to his right, a beige wall flecked with brown and yellow held a bright red e-ink sign.

Euler City
Main Station
  Ground Transportation
  Parking Garage

Somehow he'd slept through the train's deceleration into the station. Minerva's railroad engineers had great skill at slowing their bullet trains.

Or else four months of travel had dulled Stone's hair-trigger reactions.

The front and rear doors on the right side of the train car silently slid open. Currents of dry, hot air knifed through the air-conditioned car and rasped his face.

Under him, the seat moved back to upright. Stone rose, stretched his arms to the ceiling, stepped into the aisle along with the twenty other UN employees in the train car. Including—

Behind him, black hair and sharp Scandinavian cheekbones. Her Korean eyes narrowed even further than usual. The scrawny, bearded man stood behind in their row, craning his neck out the window at the sign.

Stone sniffed out a chuckle and turned his back to her.

His implanted computer pinged an incoming message notification into his hearing. Raised a red flag on a mailbox icon in the lower left corner of his vision. *From: Annika Kim.*

Who? The woman behind him. He hadn't remembered her name inside her stateroom their last night on *Yassir Arafat*.

He opened the message. Her voice burst onto his auditory nerve, louder than the shuffling feet and muttered conversations of the other UN employees.

You think you're God's gift to women, don't you, Ed? Trust me, you aren't. Jordan is ten times the man you'll ever be. I wish I'd seen that earlier on the trip here. But I see it now.

Female jealousy. What else was new? Stone kept his gaze on the door to the front of the train car. More and more hot outside air gnawed at his cheeks. *Enjoy your two kids with him in a house out in Queens.* He broke the connection.

The crowd flowed out of the train car. Stone stepped onto a platform under a curving roof made of a single sheet of some alloy. Hot, humidless air dessicated his nasal passages. He knew the term *dry heat*, but the temperature gauge projected next to the mailbox icon showed 105°F. An oven, not a sauna. A mission to Phoenix—the Arizona city, not the Dubai Convention world—would have given him the same miserable weather without an eight-month round trip. At least the surface gravity was a bit less than Earth's.

Three easy steps down the platform, a young Minervan woman in a short-sleeved sundress of pastel-yellow cotton extended her right arm toward the main station. Smooth skin, faint scents of body wash and floral perfume, blond hair held back by a plain stainless steel band the width of Stone's index finger. A Caucasian and casually dressed version of a Singapore Airlines flight attendant, the closest Earth's technology had ever come to building androids. Maybe the Minervans genetically altered her to not sweat.

Stone curled up the corners of his mouth and stared deep into her blue eyes. She met his gaze, unblinking. "Please keep moving. My colleagues will guide you to the bus to your residence."

"Will you be coming with us?" he asked with a lilt.

"No." Her blue eyes tracked back to the line of passengers exiting his train car and coming up the platform from the cars behind.

His smirk shriveled away.

The crowd carried Stone to a revolving door. He stepped in. Cold air bathed him. He inhaled deeply—the air smelled and tasted fresher than he expected from decades of experience in train stations, airports, office buildings, hotels—and tension bled from his shoulders.

A small concourse served the station's four platforms. Reflections of soft white LED lights glistened on a glossy tile floor and walls the same flecked color palette as outside. A rank of automated kiosks stood with their backs against the far wall and showed soft colors, curved edges, and antiquated icons for lockers, shoe shine, espresso drinks. Everything looked too clean, as if the station had first received passengers yesterday.

One traveller waited at a seating area near the farthest platform, sipping coffee from a mug and staring at the windows on the platform as if a computer projected data on them only he could see. He took no notice of the crowd of UN employees.

Stone made the solitary traveller instantly. He worked for Minerva's intelligence service. An amateur at spycraft: any normal person would turn his head toward over a hundred strangers from Earth.

The only other people in the station were more young women. Each wore a pastel-yellow sundress and a stainless steel hair band. Not a fashion choice, but their uniform. One waited directly in front of the revolving door and gestured the UN employees toward the center of the concourse. There, a guide with hair the same medium brown as the coffee kiosk behind her beckoned them down a corridor leading away from the platforms. Low conversations and hundreds of footsteps echoed off the corridor's high ceiling and smooth, windowless walls. At the end of the corridor, under a sign showing *Parking Garage*, a third young woman bade them descend an escalator. Another revolving door spun at the bottom, offering glimpses of a caravan of four tall, streamlined buses.

"We have to go back out in this heat?" complained Annika.

Jackson—or Jordan?—said, "I think we're underground now. It should be cooler than the train platform."

Stone went through the revolving door into the parking garage. A ceiling of gravel and larger rocks glistened with a thick coat of sealant. Underground, yes, but cooler? Maybe five degrees.

A strip of green light surrounded the open door of the lead bus. Another guide girl gestured Stone that way. Cool air from the open door wrapped him. Three quick steps up. Standard interior: a food and drink kiosk in front of him and above the nav and control computer. To his left, a center aisle ran between staggered rows of two seats on each side. A new car smell pervaded.

Stone took an aisle seat about two-thirds of the way back. Deep rows gave him enough space to cross his legs, jutting his knee toward the aisle. That should keep unwanted company away.

When his fellow passengers filled about two-thirds of the seats—fortunately, not the window next to him—the bus shifted into drive. Up a gently curving ramp, the bus emerged into dazzling daylight. The windows polarized a second later. From the sun's position in the sky, the bus headed east, toward the shore of the Wisdom Sea.

Stone turned his head. Forget orbital images and the photos snapped by the scout crew and the diplomatic mission. He would see Euler City with his own eyes.

Buildings between two and four stories, various shades of gray and white, all looking wilted by the heat. Stone soon realized why. Though essentially rectangular, the buildings' edges were rounded. The windows, all made from single panes of glass, had rounded corners. Adjoining buildings melded together in smooth curves and blended colors. Inefficient construction to build curved forms for glass and concrete—

He sucked in a breath. Concrete? He subvoked search terms to his implanted computer.

Not concrete. The dossier from the scouts and the diplomats referred to granular masses of quartz, feldspar, and mica formed and continually reformed by a framework of genetically engineered osteoblasts encoded with building blueprints. Specialized osteoblasts formed transparent regions of vitreous quartz.

Translating from tech-speak, the Minervans grew granite walls and glass windows like bones.

His gaze lowered to the street outside, dotted with aerodynamic cars whispering over blue-black fresh asphalt. Never had a street in Manhattan felt so smooth under Stone's wheels.

Stone shivered in the dense flow from the bus' air-conditioning vents.

If the Minervans grew buildings like bone, self-repairing streets should be easy.

Ahead on the left rose the tallest building he'd yet seen. Thick pillars of cream-colored granite jutted six stories upward to a broad dome. The granite pillars framed four broad, tall—murals? video displays? e-ink images?

No. Stained glass windows. Instead of a mosaic of single-color pieces of glass set in a framework, these were single panes holding regions of distinct colors. Each of the four windows showed a heroic image in an Art Deco style. Nine men in royal blue robes and three women in crimson dresses raised hands and rapt gazes toward constellations. A man in an officer's yellow dress uniform held a pistol in his right hand and a shield in his left, with a rank of similarly-equipped soldiers behind him. A man and woman faced each other, the woman handing over a green cornucopia while green 1s and 0s marched from the man's forehead, and impassive faces looked on from the background. Men in gray shirts worked at a long bench, each with a different gray antiquated tool—hammer, soldering iron, test tube, micropipettor, computer keyboard—

The bus drove on before Stone could make out more details in the stained glass. The last things he observed from the building were the words spelled by thick platinum letters jutting from the wall between the stained glass windows and three pairs of double-height entrance doors. *Center for Alignment with the Universe.*

A temple, one of about ten around the city and twenty across the inhabited part of the planet, Stone knew from reports. But to what god? The scout ship had provided no intel. The diplomatic mission had monitored traffic patterns in and out of this one. Roughly twenty cars per day trickled in and out of the parking garage. Three mornings and two nights per week, a thousand people thronged in for an hour at a time. The diplomats' informal inquiries about what happened inside the Centers met with vague answers and shifts in the conversations. Requests to attend an activity at a Center were politely rebuffed.

Stone shook his head. Months of forced idleness weakened his focus. Why care what rites the Centers practiced? Stone angled his head from side to side, working out crackles left by days of travel, loosening his thoughts in the process. The fanatics on Trinity hadn't threatened Earth with their Christian beliefs, but with their attempt to recover the last rogue warpdrive ship. Before that, the terrorists on New Moravia had acted on something like a religion—the belief that people with Czech ancestry deserved their own planet—but only their missiles aimed at the wormhole mouth on their planet required Stone to act.

Religions only provided motives. Motives didn't matter. Only actions did.

"Mr. Lavallette?"

Another guide girl stood in the aisle, twin to the ones in the train station. No—a brighter yellow colored her dress, and white piping lined her sleeves and neckline. A wider band of stainless steel glowing with pinpoint green LEDs at her temples held back dusty blond hair. High enough in rank to know the UN employees' names. And attractive enough, especially after four months of seeing the same stale faces…

Stone put on a lazy smile. "How can I help you?"

She shook her head. The ends of her hair brushed the back of her neck. "My name is Abigail. I'm one of the liaison officers assigned by the Minervan government to help you and the other UN employees settle in and get what you need to work smoothly. My fellow liaison officers and I will have rooms in your hotel. One of us will be on call at all times if you require assistance. The only question you need ask is, how can I help you?"

Stone put a smolder into his blue eyes. "For starters, you can tell me when you're off duty."

Her smooth forehead crinkled. "One of my fellow liaison officers would help you then."

He raised one eyebrow and shook his head. "You know I'm not talking about your professional duties, don't you?"

Abigail's voice grew cool. "Of course I do, Mr. Lavallette. It appears I must tell you that fraternizing with you is strictly forbidden."

With a slow lilt he said, "I'm sure that's what your handbook says—"

"I'm an unmarried young lady with a reputation to uphold."

Damn, she played aloof. Ah, the chase was half the fun. Stone's smirk widened. "I have a reputation of my own. Which includes never kissing and telling."

Abigail folded her arms over her chest. "We're nearing the hotel and I have more introductions to make. Good day, Mr. Lavallette." She stepped past him. Thin cotton rustled over her smooth pale legs. She didn't look back.

Losing your skill at the game? floated through his mind. From the Lavallette persona?

No. From himself.

Stone rubbed his eyes. Losing his skill? Couldn't be happening. Anywhere in the settled galaxy, women remained manipulable creatures. He would win the game. At most, playing it on Minerva might require different tactics.

Then into view on his left came something that put skirt-chasing toward the back of his mind. Two- and three-story buildings of stark white and classical styling rose from the middle of broad green lawns. Steel fences stood between the lawns and the sidewalks. Minervan government buildings, aping the style of United States government facilities in Washington. The Minervans were Americans, after all, and doubtlessly shared with most American-settled colonies a nostalgia for some well-governed golden age. Right down to the apparent lack of security. The cameras presumably hidden in the fencing wouldn't stop a truck bomb, let alone a thousand rioters or a squad of trained commandos.

A closer look beyond the little capitols and supreme courts revealed a pale blue wedge nearly invisible against the cloudless teal sky. Wait. Was that precise shade—?

His implanted computer copied sensory inputs from his optic nerve. His implant effortlessly performed an RGB analysis and mapped the location at the same time.

The results appeared in his vision as a glowing outline of the wedge with accompanying text. Stone read, then laughed.

Not pale blue. *United Nations* blue colored a thousand-foot skyscraper holding enough hotel rooms, recreation facilities, and office space for ten thousand UN employees. A skyscraper built sometime in the last eight months and towering over every other building on the planet. Towering over government facilities and Centers for Alignment with the Universe.

Maybe the Minervans could grow skyscrapers in hours, but they knew to bend the knee and build them for the UN.

Stone smiled and lolled his head back. He closed his eyes, able to relax. Gray worried about nothing.

4

The elevator slowed, lifting Stone's stomach back where it belonged. He swallowed to clear his ears as the doors opened on the one-hundredth floor.

Cocktail party chatter mingled with a muted trumpet soloing over piano and upright bass. Behind the short near side of the long, narrow triangular bar, robotic arms clattered ice inside shakers. Stone spoke three words to a parabolic microphone and ten seconds later a robotic arm lowered a glass of seltzer with a lime wedge in front of him.

He sipped. He'd been productive during his first full day on Minerva, despite fitful sleep from a stuffy nose and a mild headache dogging him most of the morning. Productive, and now time to play his favorite game.

Drink in hand, Stone sauntered to the right through a crowded mass of UN employees. Unlike his gray slacks and royal blue oxford shirt, the others dressed wildly, checked patterns, billowing sleeves, upturned starched collars. The trend for twentysomethings the week before *Yassir Arafat* left Hawking Station, now three months out of date on Earth. Many of the young UN employees were already drunk, and most others were well on their way.

A spicy vape, cumin and turmeric, wafted in Stone's face. "My maaaaan." Sweat plastered a pudgy fellow's black hair to his olive skin. Brown eyes looked down at Stone's drink, went wide. "Vodka tooooonic!"

Stone's nose wrinkled. "Sure." He slapped the man hard on the shoulder and pushed him aside.

Keep moving. Stone cut through the crowd. Rounded the corner of the bar. The riot of different checked shirts would bring back his headache before long. Where were the Minervans?

He pushed into an open area. The corners of his mouth lifted. Minervans in clusters of four to six, women in black dresses and diamond necklaces, gray-suited men with hair pomaded down and solid-colored ties knotted up. Only on a colony world could everyone in so stylish a crowd be white. The Minervans stood far from the bar, close to the glass wall lining this long side of the wedge-shaped hotel's penthouse.

Distance from the bar explained only a little why the UN employees didn't mingle with the Minervans. A glance down explained the rest. This uppermost level jutted outward from the main structure of the hotel. The glass walls behind the Minervans curved at the bottom to join the floor. While the UN employees kept their footing on the glossy granite near the elevators, the Minervans seemed to levitate in empty space.

Among the Minervans, Stone found a familiar face. Gaze straight ahead, he strode onto the glass floor toward a group of five. He extended his hand toward a man with a narrow, bulbous nose. "Mr. Ranta!" As part of the Lavallette persona's duties, Stone had visited Ranta's office four hours before.

They shook hands. Stone stamped the heel of his black wingtips against the transparent floor. "Is this one of yours?"

"I wish. My company can't grow glass both as thick and transparent as this floor. Not yet."

"If you can be the first to break in to the Earth market, you'll make huge profits you can plow into R&D." His gaze shifted a fraction, toward a dazzle of diamond on the upper slope of a woman's breast.

Ranta's eyes narrowed for a moment. "Let me introduce you to everyone."

The other man in the group, Yeardley, manufactured equipment for growing organs from a patient's stem cells. His equipment worked well for livers. "Looks like your colleagues might need it."

"All I can say in their defense is that they spent four months cooped up on a ship as spacious as two floors of this hotel."

Yeardley's wife angled her head to Stone. "So did you, but you haven't drunk yourself sloppy tonight."

Bleak memories of his dead alcoholic father stirred. Stone stifled the memories. Shrugged. A smirk touched his mouth. "I kept myself busy with—" He gazed into her wide brown eyes. "—Pursuits."

She quickly looked away, then leaned against her husband and wound her necklace chain in her fingers. Yeardley scowled. Ranta shuffled his feet forward, partially eclipsing his wife from Stone's view.

The fifth member of the party spoke in a husky yet alluring voice. "And what pursuits would those be, Mr. Lavallette?"

The woman stood nearly as tall as Stone. Blond hair billowed around her face. Crow's feet wrinkled the skin at the corners of her eyes. A long, crimson dress clung to her trim curves from collarbone to mid-calf. High on the left side of her chest, jewels woven into the velvet glittered in an image of a half-familiar constellation.

Identify, he subvoked to his implant.

Text popped into his vision. Diamonds as the Big Dipper and Polaris, the north star, in line above the Dipper's leading edge. His implant labeled a round yellow tiger's eye low to the left as *Unidentified*.

Stone returned his gaze to her blue eyes. She regarded him and the corners of her mouth curled up ever so slightly.

If he'd met her at a cocktail party in Manhattan, he'd consider attempting to seduce her. She might possess enough mature sultriness to make up for the faded bloom of her beauty. But here on Minerva, where single women fretted about their virtue and married men guarded their wives, he had no better prospects.

Plus there'd be an extra thrill at seducing a woman of her vocation....

"My pursuits on *Yassir Arafat*?" Stone put on a lazy grin while keeping eye contact. "I'm afraid they lacked any spiritual uplift—Reverend?"

"Facilitatrix. Sheila van Bentum." She extended her hand.

He bowed and kissed it. His lips felt the faint pliable ridges of veins on the back of her hand. The crisp floral scent of her perfume lifted his eyebrows. He straightened his back and slowly pulled his hand away. His fingers slid over smooth skin.

"Fa-cil-i-ta-trix," he said. "Not Reverend? The Centers don't provide guidance in spiritual matters?"

"Not in the manner of a church or temple on Earth. You see, Mr. Lavallette, when one lives in alignment with the universe, all one's actions are equally spiritual. And profane."

"An intriguing perspective. And please call me Edward."

"Edward." She tasted the name.

Time to neg her a little. "Just how much can you know about religion on Earth?"

Her eyes blazed like sapphires. "I was born there."

Stone's jaw fell. "Born? You… you tell a good joke." He glanced to either side. Ranta and Yeardley's faces showed no humor.

"I'm ninety-seven," Sheila said.

Stone regained his poise. He gave a lazy smile. "You don't look a day over seventy."

Angled head, arched eyebrow. She looked like a fit fifty-year-old from the era before longevity tech, and she knew he knew that.

Longevity tech. More advanced than Earth's. The Lavallette persona darted around his subconscious, wanting to make calls, schedule meetings, bring that tech home—

Tomorrow. As for tonight… did he still want to seduce a woman nearly three times his age?

Oh yes.

Stone touched her elbow. "I'm curious how a young woman on Earth became a priestess of a colony world's state religion." He applied gentle pressure in the direction of the window wall.

"I would love to tell you my story. But I don't want to bore these well-aligned people." She murmured good-byes to the Rantas and the Yeardleys, then stepped backward on thick black heels.

A few seconds later, Stone squeezed her elbow through the velvet sleeve, stopping her feet six inches from where the floor curled up to the wall. In the window, the lights of Euler City glowed through the party's blue-white reflections. Three hundred yards below their feet, the waves of the Wisdom Sea spumed up the crater wall.

"The twenty-first century was an era of social upheaval," Sheila said. "In all such eras, the traditional beliefs and rituals that assure us—all levels of *us*, species, society, and individuals—of our place in the universe shrivel. Many perish completely. But our need to know our place in the universe remains, like a seed craving a patch of dirt and a trickle of water."

"Poetic," Stone said.

"During my college years, that need was in me. But the dominant culture only wanted young people to seek meaning by...." Her gaze knifed past Stone. Slashed across the drunken and horny faces he'd pushed through to get here. Her face showed the tracks of dark thoughts behind it.

"The profane only, without the spiritual."

"Exactly." Sheila smiled. "I lacked alignment with the universe and would have been miserable the rest of my life without knowing why. Then I met the First Facilitator."

"How?"

"He lived and worked in a warehouse in a neighborhood of the city still half in ruins from the street battles between Chicanos and Bantu-Americans in the '30s and '40s. He was a theoretician who knew what a future where everyone lived in alignment with the universe would look like, and wise enough to know that many practical and detail-oriented people would have to get their hands dirty to build that future."

A cult leader. Probably surrounded himself with young women with daddy issues. "You were one of those people?"

"I had a few of the needed skills. Enough to take my place on the team. The First Facilitator provided some money and equipment to start us on the work. Doing the work brought me toward alignment with the universe for the first time in my life."

Stone trailed the backs of his fingers down her right arm. "How did you come to Minerva?"

She brushed a blond strand behind her ear. "Zachary Euler had graduated many years earlier from my university. Many of my team members were my classmates, graduate students, or had recently finished their degrees there too. Euler heard of our work through the alumni network and came to visit. He had profited handsomely during the Crisis of the Twenty-First Century, but still he craved an alignment with the universe that his trillions could not buy.

"After two days talking with the First Facilitator," Sheila added, "Euler took up our cause."

"A trillion here, a trillion there, and soon you're talking real money."

"Euler opened his checkbook, yes, but he did much more. He publicized us. His name alone gave us credibility. And despite his prominence, Euler deferred to the First Facilitator on everything. With one exception."

"Stay on Earth," Stone said, "or colonize a distant planet."

"You have it. Euler commissioned an exploration ship months before he met the First Facilitator. He said in hindsight it was a fumbling attempt to align himself with the universe. Then the ship returned to the solar system and reported finding a world meeting Euler's criteria." She spread her arm to indicate the night-dark portion of Minerva visible from the window.

"The First Facilitator wanted to stay on Earth," she said. "The team could focus on the work, instead of putting most effort into constructing a biosphere. The team could recruit more people and would have access to more infrastructure, and could achieve the final stage faster. The main reason he wanted to stay, though—I grasped it right away—was because he wanted to bring everyone on Earth into alignment with the universe. If he could do that, all Earth's problems would be solved, and there would be no need to flee."

Solve all Earth's problems. Sure, any millennium now.

"How did Euler win the debate?" Stone asked.

Her tone of voice shifted, clashing with cool jazz trumpet. "US government agents raided, arrested the First Facilitator and several team leaders, and confiscated much of our equipment. Almost everyone sided with Euler after that."

Except for the few who realized Euler had pulled strings to get US agents to eliminate his rival for control of the cult. "Then you came here."

"I was on the first of three ships. We worked hard those next years, some of us sending comets to graze the planet while others perfected the techniques of alignment with the universe. We survived a second great loss when Euler died on Earth recruiting a fourth shipful of colonists. But we persevered. We built a habitable world and gave purpose in life to all its inhabitants. And I am humbled to have played and continue to play my small role in our adventure."

Sheila didn't look humble. Quiet pride filled her mature features and her sapphire eyes. She leaned closer.

Time to close. "Your life has been an intricate tapestry," Stone said. "Let's add a new thread to it. Twenty floors down. My room."

Her features remained open, yet: "No."

Stone flicked his gaze down and up her torso. "Your mouth says one thing, but the rest of you—"

"Not your place. Mine."

UN employees could leave the hotel at any time in a car checked out from the motor pool. A Minervan counterintelligence officer would trail him, would gather evidence of his tryst with her, but that would be Sheila's problem. "Sure. I haven't been inside a Minervan house."

She moved her mouth close. Her breath smelled of one vodka drink. Her husky whisper filled his ear. "You were so curious about alignment with the universe, I thought you might like to see a Center from the inside."

His interest immediately rose. "Talk about the sacred and profane."

Eyes suddenly tight, Sheila glanced about. Her facial expression eased but a hunch in her shoulders revealed unease.

"Send me the address," he murmured. "You leave first. I'll take a different elevator to the garage and ride in my own car. No one will see us leave together. I know how important her reputation is to a lady of Minerva."

She smiled wryly. "You have no idea."

5

His borrowed blue coupe rolled to a stop under a granite buttress as stout and curved as a rib of leviathan. The coupe popped its door. Blue-white light washed over the space under the buttress. A spotlight shone on dappled steps leading up to an automated sliding door. A sign above the door read *Enter, and Know Yourself.*

Stone climbed out of the coupe, a smirk on his lips. Know himself? His interest lay in knowing Sheila van Bentum. In the biblical sense.

The coupe shut its door and drove into the main part of the subterranean parking garage to wait for him.

He took the steps. The sliding door opened. Cool air cloaked him as he entered.

At the head of a broad spiral staircase, he came to a long hallway. Signs pointed left and right to meditation rooms. Straight ahead, down a short passage, waited the auditorium. And Sheila.

Stone strode vigorously forward. Another door slid out of his way.

He entered a cavernous space. Dim accent lights glowed where sandstone-colored walls met a floor of a slightly darker shade. From the street outside to his left, the lights of downtown Euler City cast swatches of gray, green, yellow, blue, and red across the upper portions of the walls and the lower reaches of the vaulted ceiling. High on the deep indigo vault, a familiar pattern of lights twinkled like bright stars. He'd entered the auditorium from the east. The Big Dipper's leading edge pointed to Polaris at his right. Which meant the bright yellow disc low in the vaulted ceiling opposite him represented Venus as the evening star.

"Welcome," Sheila said. She stood ahead to his right, in a center aisle between ranks of oaken pews. She came toward where the pew nearest him would lead him to the aisle. Thick carpet muffled the falls of her black heels.

He went to the aisle, glancing at the pew backs to his right. Dense hardbacks showed titles *The Way of Virtue and Other Books* and *Music Aligned with the Universe*. His fingertips brushed along tight-packed pages, jumped up to a smooth oak beam atop the pew backs. Jumped to Sheila's elbow.

Enough light filled the vaulted room to show the sapphire-blue in her eyes. "For a non-religion, you've got a regular cathedral." He flexed his eyebrows upward. "Vaulted ceiling, stained glass windows...."

"The First Facilitator studied psychology and comparative religion in college," Sheila said. "Even though he knew establishing true alignment would require scientific insight and technical skill, he also knew that symbolism and group ritual would help people accept their place in the universe." She broke eye contact.

Stone squinted at the ceiling. "Sure, but why Earthly constellations? Polaris almost certainly isn't your north star—south star from this hemisphere—and if you could even see the stars of the Big Dipper, this far from Earth they'd draw a totally different picture." He nodded toward the evening star on the far side of the auditorium. "And Venus?"

"The astronomical symbols reflect our origins on Earth, in the northern hemisphere, in Western civilization. They also provide metaphors for alignment with the universe: Polaris, a lodestar; the Big Dipper, a vessel for the bounty of the universe; the evening star, a sentinel that observed our labors in the day just finished and lights our rest in the evening just begun."

There would be some alignment between the two of them this evening, but hopefully not too restful. Stone brushed his upper arm against hers, then turned his head toward the stained glass. "You also use colors as metaphors."

She shifted her weight against him. "Colors have borne symbolic weight since before the dawn of Western civilization. Blue evokes logic, objectivity, constancy, and dispassion; red evokes passion, subjectivity, lability, and partisanship."

The headlights of a passing car sent a wave of brightness across the male and female clerics raising their hands to the heavens. "Blue is masculine, red is feminine?"

"Close. Blue represents masculine energy, red, feminine. Both energies are at work in each person at all times, though the proportions differ from person to person and time to time."

Stone cupped her ear. Ran his fingers through her blond locks toward the back of her head. "Your feminine energies are running strong right now." He pressed his fingers together, grasping strands of hair, and faintly tugged.

"Much as masculine energy runs through you." She moved her head forward and he released his grip. "Come with me."

Sheila turned away from the stained glass and walked toward the front of the auditorium. The carpeted aisle ended at a dozen ivory-white steps as wide as the space. The steps ran up to a dais. Lectern to the left, an altar of white granite at the center. Behind the dais rose blank walls, e-ink displays, he guessed, with a choir loft above them.

He sped his pace, caught up with her. Put his arm around her waist. She leaned against him.

At the foot of the steps, she pulled to the left. He followed, puzzled for a moment, until he saw why. Thin seams in the ivory-white steps marked a rectangle as wide as the altar and as high as the stairs. Another seam down the middle divided the rectangle in half.

A retractable, not-so-hidden doorway.

What secrets lay within?

Sheila led him up the steps to the left of the retractable doorway, and across the dais between the altar and the lectern. The back wall held a plain door, not even with a knob. The door swung open soundlessly as they approached, revealing a hallway running straight away before bending to the right.

After passing a meditation room and offices with hers and other facilitators' names embossed on closed doors, they entered a study. Ceiling lights came on automatically. Nailhead trim decorated brown leather armchairs. Ten chairs surrounded an oak conference table with scenes from the stained glass windows carved in the wide upper portions of the legs. Gray would approve the decor.

Sheila gestured to a loveseat matching the armchairs, far from the room's curtained windows, then went to a cabinet nearly her height. The cabinet opened its doors. Interior lighting glinted on glasses, bottles, a steel sink and faucet. "What will you drink, Edward?"

His forearm on the arm of the loveseat, Stone said, "Sparkling water with a citrus wedge, if you have it."

Bottles thunked and thudded as she rummaged inside the cabinet. "We do."

Carbonation hissed into a glass. A machine hummed. Ice clattered. Sheila pulled a cork with a *thwoom*, cracked open a twist cap, and poured twice.

Stone guessed her state of mind from experience. A stranger, a one-night stand, second thoughts. And liquid courage to numb her fears.

She settled next to him on the loveseat. He took a highball of sparkling water from her, raised it, and drank.

He winced. Bitter with minerals and too much sour lemon.

"Not what you're used to?" she asked.

"Nothing on Minerva has been, so far." He fortified himself against the taste of the sparkling water and drank deeply.

"Good," she said. She sipped a pallid red drink, then fixed her blue eyes on his. "I would hate to think you've ever met a woman like me."

Stone extended his arm along the back of the loveseat, behind her. "A non-priestess of a non-religion? Who's three times my age? Never had the pleasure, till now."

Sheila arched her eyebrow. "You mean two and a half."

"Let's not quibble." He poured the rest of his sparkling water down his throat, set the empty glass on a side table.

"My age doesn't bother you?"

"No. Does it bother you?"

"Prove it doesn't bother you," she said. "Kiss me."

Normally he would have strung the tension out longer, but when she put it like that, time to seize the moment. He leaned forward. Her lips pressed full and soft against his. The tart taste of cranberry juice, the aseptic scent of vodka. Her sapphire blue eyes remained open, peering at him.

He took her gaze as an invitation. Lifted his hand to cup her breast. His hand felt too heavy to move.

Sheila moved her head away from him. "Sit back."

She wanted to be the assertive one at first. Fine by him. He would pay her back with interest.

Later. He sat back, hands on his thighs, a lazy smile on his face. "Empty your pockets onto the side table."

His hands moved to his hips before he could think about complying. "I don't carry erectile dysfunction tablets because I don't need them."

Sheila's eyes looked cooler all of a sudden. She said nothing. His right hand pulled out a pocket computer, backup to his implant. His left retrieved a flat, supple stick as long as his little finger. An encrypted memory stick. He had more in his hotel room. The memory stick's transparent, antistatic wrapping crinkled in his fingers.

He watched his hands set the three objects on the table as if he watched an actor on a video screen. A frown furrowed between his eyes. The hell?

"Send no messages and acknowledge the receipt of no messages through any computer. Stop any recording of audio or video data to any computer. Delete any stored audio or video data you recorded after you arrived at the party from any computer."

"What's going on?"

She rose and took two long steps away from him. "Stand. Walk to the conference table with your arms at your sides. Put your hands on the table, move your feet wider than shoulder width. Stare at the table between your hands. Do not move."

His body lifted itself from the loveseat. Walked to the table. Stopped at one of the short sides, between carved priests and a shield-bearing soldier. Set down his hands and shuffled his feet as she'd ordered. His mind had no choice but to go along.

"You dissolved a drug in my drink." She'd left him enough free will to speak.

"Thirty seconds to figure that out? I expected better." Sheila crossed the room. Her hands patted down his shoulders, arms, pits. An amateur's hands, knowing the theory of how to frisk but lacking practice. He might have a chance.

His hands felt bolted to the tabletop. "You didn't have to. I'm man enough to act out any woman's kink."

Velvet rustled. Her hands ran down his legs. Stopped at his right ankle. Pulled the compact 9mm from its holster. A second later, plastic clattered on leather.

She knew he was more than a UN bureaucrat. How?

His heart slammed inside his immobile chest. Not how.

From whom?

She untucked his shirt and reached inside his waistband with hands as cold and clinical as a nurse's. Then she stepped back. "Hands to your sides."

His hands swung like sides of beef on a slaughterhouse's hooks.

"Turn around."

He did. The crimson velvet of her dress contrasted with the blue ice of her eyes.

"Walk at a medium pace out the door. I will direct you where to go after that."

Stone's body moved moderately. His insides writhed like trees lashed by storm winds. He managed a deep and calming breath.

Keep your mind clear and you might walk out of this. The drug would wear off eventually. Don't eat or drink anything she offers.

The door opened. He went through and paused in the hallway. She followed. Gave instructions. Left. Another left. Through a door under an exit sign. Stone's mouth dried. A stairwell down. To the parking garage or the outside of the building, either way, a chance to escape....

At the next landing, the stairwell continued downward into shadow. "Through this door."

Still inside the Center. Why? A non-religion wouldn't perform human sacrifices. Right? And she wouldn't want to spill blood on the beige carpets or the crinkly pages of secular scriptures.

His thoughts raced while his body plodded at her command further into this level. His internal compass still worked, she ordered him somewhere under the dais. Not far from—

To his left, the floor of a short hallway ramped up and curled to the right.

Stone rounded the corner. Light spilled from an open door. Machinery hummed inside.

"Enter."

A trusswork of metal shelving and sliding racks filled the back and side walls with a squared-off horseshoe of computers, e-ink displays, and other equipment. Some appliances reminded him of hardware in the genomics lab at UNICA headquarters, but most he couldn't identify. Generic boxes of off-white plastic, green LEDs, cooling fans. Conditioned air spilled from a vent. Stone tucked his arms against his sides.

In the center of the horseshoe, a chair swivel-mounted to the floor showed its back.

"Sit," Sheila said.

His body moved. He noticed black vinyl covered a padded seat, back, and armrests. Hope surged for a moment, no straps…. but with the drug, she didn't need straps. He sat, just as some nameless drudge from the outer boroughs might in a barber's chair near a train station, or a chair in a dentist's office in Queens.

Except a dentist's office would have a light mounted on a pivoting arm from the ceiling. Not a hemispherical helmet, descending with a whir.

He jerked his head around. The helmet paused.

"Sit up straight with your arms and head still."

Stone's body did as she ordered. The helmet descended the rest of the way. Folded over the tops of his ears, let them flick back up. A soft inner lining snuggled his head. Two e-ink displays formed a sterograph.

```
Alignment with the Universe.
Initial consecration. Adult subject.
```

A thud of binaural beats ping-ponged from ear to ear.

"What are you doing?" Stone asked.

"In this place, in this moment, we work together, to all high emprise consecrated." Despite the helmet's padding and the binaural beats, Sheila's words came to him, clear and solemn. A priestess intoning a phrase from ritual.

"Edward Lavallette. The time has come for you and us to find out who you truly are."

6

Edward Lavallette? She hadn't pierced his cover….

In 3d appeared an inverted L assembled from cubes, most white, two black. Two white cubes held black circles in their faces closest to him. The inverted L slowly rotated. A different white cube showed a black circle, and one of the black cubes, a white one. Rotation showed another slightly varied pattern on the third face, the fourth.

Duplication. The second inverted L differed slightly, more contrasting circles on one side, fewer on another. More rotation. Another duplication. More variation, but the pattern—

An IQ test of visuospatial reasoning. A set of four more inverted Ls popped up, one of which would complete the pattern of variation.

That's all this was? Why lure him, why drug him?

Piss on her. He looked away. The stereograph inside the helmet followed his gaze. He shut his eyes. The four possible answers remained in his vision. Of course the third was correct, but he wouldn't give her any satisfac—

A prick in his right ring finger. His arm tried to lift off the chair but Sheila's command locked his arm in place.

Pairs of words shot by. *Activate Actuate. Consign Condign. Instigate Investigate.* Don't play her game—his mind darted over the meanings anyway. The next pair appeared before the definitions fully formed in his mind.

The hell kind of IQ test was this?

Verbal analogies followed. Algebra and geometry problems. Like his senior year of high school, taking the college aptitude tests—

Green paint peeling off concrete block walls. Cops at their desks outside the holding cell, sipping oily-smelling coffee from white foam cups, glancing through the bars. Through him.

Adolescent indignation burned Stone's eyes. You can't do this to me! My parents come from families you've heard of! You'll write parking tickets in the Bronx if you don't let me go!

Later, unease nibbled at him. The girl—Melanie? Melody?—lied. The sex had been consensual.

Consensual enough. They'd both been drinking at the hall party in the dorm. But just because her inhibitions were down didn't make it rape.

Hours in the cell. A hole expanded inside his gut. Mom cavorted with her latest boyfriend on a Mediterranean beach. She wouldn't come. Dad? The hole's crumbling edges exuded bitters. Too drunk in his study to answer a call.

—*Christ damn it how does Sheila know this?*

Out of Stone's sight, a door creaked. Measured footfalls.

A cop looked over the thick rim of his cup. Freckles surrounded a once-broken nose. "Whaddaya want?"

A brisk and formal voice. "Your prisoner."

Stone didn't know the owner of the voice. But the diction, the tone. Maybe Mom from six timezones away had called—

"You frat boy's lawyer?"

"No."

The cop scowled. "If you ain't his lawyer, boyo—"

A faint snick of an attaché case unsnapping itself. The rustle of heavy paper.

The cop leaned forward, squinting. Then he jerked his head back. "Hey, why din't ya tell me?" He rose so fast his chair spun its cracked vinyl arms. He waddled to the cell door, fumbling with keys on a handheld computer.

Stone stood up. He wanted to reach for the bars, but resisted the urge. He wouldn't show weakness in front of some cop. If not his lawyer, who came to rescue him?

More measured footfalls brought the owner of the brisk voice into view. Two piece suit, complete with a diagonally-striped tie impeccably knotted at a fully buttoned collar. Wavy hair, brown going gray; high forehead; and a pair of piercing gray eyes.

In an instant, the hole in his gut vanished. Filled with warm jitters.

In an instant, Stone knew his destiny had changed.

The memory froze. Rewound the cop back to his battered swivel chair, Gray back out of Stone's life. The hole reopened in Stone's gut. Its jagged edges burned with bile.

Sight, sound, smell, mood swirled, reformed. The scent of carpet shampoo wafted up from the maroon carpet under his stomping feet. A familiar painting, Model T cars clogging Times Square two centuries ago, its oil paints textured with brushstrokes, near the apartment door. The reddish-brown door, trim and proper like the rest of the hallway, hiding the shambling mess inside.

Sheila couldn't know this. The helmet and all the computers around the room tapped his memories.

Stone shoved his thumb against the doorknob's reader. The goddam biometrics better work or he'd stand in the hallway for hours.

The door snapped back its latchbolt. Stone pushed harder than he meant. Not really. Stone stepped through and the door bounced off the coiled-spring doorstop. He slammed the door shut behind him and stalked toward the study.

Dad sat at his workstation. A spiraling screensaver gyred over the angled touchscreen. The old man—

How old was he when I graduated? Fifty-five? Christ he looked like hell.

—turned sunken eyes out the window to the French curlicues on the building across 47th. Morning light pitilessly revealed four days' beard and a white salt crust under the armpit of his shirt. A wheezing grunt rocked his upper body. Wait eight seconds and he'd grunt again.

"Dad." No response. "I said, Dad!"

The old man's head wobbled around. "Stone. Glad you came by. Let me show you what I'm working on. I haven't programmed a movie this good since *New California*." His left hand shook as he touched the screen. The spiral vanished, revealing a litter of icons and a dozen overlapping windows. "Where the hell is it?" Another grunt. "I'll show you later."

He reached for a stainless steel tumbler in the cup holder at the lower right corner of the touchscreen. His jittering right hand cradled the lid. He didn't lift it. A frown carved deep lines from the sides of his nose past his mouth. "What brings you by?"

"You didn't come yesterday."

"Come? Where?"

"My graduation. From high school. Where I've gone the last four years."

"Graduation?" Dad lifted the tumbler. "It's on my calendar for next week." He brought the tumbler to his mouth.

A decade before, when Dad's last two photorealist computer-animated movies had underperfomed compared to his earlier hits, he'd poured a cup of orange juice over two fingers of sextuple-distilled vodka every afternoon at five. When Mom left him four years later, he'd mixed equal parts of orange juice and a cheaper vodka, starting at two-thirty or three.

Now Stone would bet the tumbler contained only vodka from the empty plastic bottle lying on its side next to the overflowing trashcan.

"Commencement happened last night," Stone said.

Dad squinted at the tumbler's lid. "It was last night?"

"Do you even know what day it is?"

"Friday." Another grunt. "Right?"

He locked his body as a boiling sensation welled up his chest. Stone's eyes flicked to the window. Push the old man through the glass and to the sidewalk four flights below. Finish the job alcoholism started.

A chill shivered over his arms. He'd loved his dad, not just as a child, but as a young teen, living with Mom and beginning to understand just how badly Dad ruined his own life. If he'd shown up just once to a game, just once….

Damp warmth pushed from behind against his eyes. No. He wouldn't show Dad how much he hurt.

"Today is Saturday? Commencement was…." The hole in the tumbler's lid pulled down the older man's attention. His hand trembled, sloshing vodka against the tumbler's walls. He lowered his hand. Looked up. Red filled his eyes. A tear flowed down the wrinkles in his right cheek. "Jesus, Stone, I'm sorry, how could I have forgotten, how can I make it up to you—"

Stone's voice choked. "You can't." He yanked his gaze away, hurriedly stumbled out of the study, across the living room. Grabbed for the door.

He touched the knob and everything shifted. Night sky hemmed in by skyscrapers. Ranked white orbs of the field lights. Breathing hard, inhaling the taste of dirt, grass, chill autumn evening. So few boys had come out for football he had to play both sides of the ball. Defense now, playing free safety on the strength of his great-grandfather's name and hips.

Stone knew the play before the snap. His high school led by two with two minutes left. Ball near midfield, the other team would run out routes, its receivers instructed to get out of bounds after making each catch in order to stop the clock.

The receiver cut for the sideline and the cornerback slipped. The quarterback threw. Stone broke toward the pass. Ball high. The receiver jumped, stretched arms overhead—

Stone extended his arms. Shoved the receiver in the small of the back, bending him into a C, flinging him at an awkward angle toward the opponent's bench. The ball thumped the cold ground somewhere behind Stone. Red lights on the receiver's sensor display, a well-timed touch, clean and legal.

The receiver writhed on the ground. "Muh fuh-ing back!" His teammates gathered around.

Stone stared at his wincing brown eyes. Stone's teammates bounded up, slapping his helmet. Fingertips smudged his visor. "Good touch!"

Stone barely heard. His stare left the receiver and slashed through the visors of the receiver's teammates. Most flinched. Hell yes.

The back judge moved toward him, pudgy middle-aged authority in no mood to tolerate taunting. Stone's teammates tugged him away, still cheering his play.

High-pitched voices squealed in the bleachers. The girls would talk about him in the hallways tomorrow.

Hell yes.

Stone's senses shifted. The whites of the injured receiver's eyes faded last. Girls flowed by. Cheerleaders wearing short dresses met him at their apartment doors while their parents traveled for the weekend. College girls stinking of cannabis vape pens. Melanie, confusion and panic in her eyes. A blur of fun fearless females out to change the world, grinding away their twenties and early thirties in the heartless maw of Manhattan. Women on missions on Earth, dark skin, choppy accents, sweating stinking Third World cities blaring outside the windows, crumpled wads of US currency, thousands and five thousands, dropped on the chipped veneer of particle board nightstands. Colonial women, fresh-faced and naive on newly-rediscovered worlds, prematurely aged on planets long acceded to the Dubai Convention.

Teresa Benavides in his hotel room on New Moravia, posing as the former.

A woman he'd never bedded, the keyhole kop, Caitlyn Fredriksen. Long blonde hair and hazel eyes sparkling like agates. They climbed out of *Lady Lux* canted by the uneven melting of orange rock under its engines. His left arm ached and the floor's angle made his gorge rise. The hatch opened. Australian desert air assailed him. Caitlyn gripped his forearm and helped him out. Even hotter than the air, the melting rock below poured out heat like a vent of hell.

At the horizon, a line of red hills swirled. His stomach clenched. He shut his eyes.

His nausea vanished. Cool air, dry, late winter or the first days of spring. But not New York. He opened his eyes.

A crowd gathered in front of the limestone steps of a medieval palace. Men and women in ragged wool thronged the street. Near the steps, velvet and silk replaced wool, and leather replaced bare feet. Each step held a rank of men-at-arms, swords scabbarded, shields point-down on the stone, steel chestplates and arm pieces and open-visored helmets gleaming in midday sun. On the landing above the steps, priests and priestesses, robed in blue and red, flanked a tall man, broad-chested, a yellow tunic draped over his polished armor, and a plain golden circlet on his head.

STONE CHALMERS AND ALIGNMENT WITH THE UNIVERSE

The helmet induced the logic of a dream. He was both Stone Chalmers and a common laborer, come to hear the king's speech as crisis stirred on the realm's borders.

Stone inhaled. The stench of a thousand unwashed bodies made him gag. *Push forward to the merchants. They can afford perfume. Maybe even soap—*

An eyeblink found him among the merchants. He glanced down at a jacket of green velvet and ruffled silk sleeves emerging from the jacket's cuffs. His belly strained the ample waistband of his pants. Agates adorned gold rings half-swallowed by pudgy fingers. The gem-cutters and goldsmiths in his employ, now somewhere behind him in the throng, did fine work.

He looked up. The men-at-arms' shields bore a starry device: the Big Dipper's leading edge pointed at Polaris, while Venus hung low in the western—

Another eyeblink. He stood tall despite the steel mail and plate weighing him down. Uneasy looks from the nearby merchants glanced off his armor like the swings of ill-trained swordsmen. The merchants knew how much they owed the men who protected their interests. Guilt gnawed them at how little they paid. He didn't just guess from their expressions. He knew from being born among them.

Behind the merchants crowded the poor. He had trained with some of their sons, in skills that seemed dreamlike in the light of the cool spring morning, in parachute insertions and long-range marksmanship in fanciful places named Al-a-ba-ma and Ken-tuck-ee. Simple folk who worked hard to afford bread for their children and cups of watery beer. Simple folk who worshipped unexamined gods—

Blue robes draped over his stooped shoulders. The backs of the ranked men-at-arms dominated his view. No doubt Car-ter next to him studied the curves of their thigh armor with great interest. Live and let live. Car-ter kept his perversion hidden and spared the priesthood public embarrassment.

Enough of his fellow priest. His thoughts ranged to the other side of the landing. Priestesses in red robes, and smooth pale skin beneath, and all the ways a priestess could remain a virgin and a priest could get no woman with child….

The king's voice turned solemn. Rote prayers flowed from the king's mouth.

If the gods heard human prayers, they never showed a sign. But if invocation of divine favor made commoners work harder, merchants provide greater value, and soldiers fight harder, pray on.

He blinked and sniffed out a breath. Perhaps invocation of divine favor made kings more kingly—

"—and we beseech Thee, o Lords of Heaven and Earth, to guide us according to Your will, all the days of all our lives. So be it."

His final words echoed off the wall of the temple to the side of the square. He held his back straight and his jaw firm for a long moment, then turned for the front gate of the palace.

Even then, the guardsmen at the gate could see him. He kept his face and posture resolute. They couldn't see how tired he was. Barbarians to the south, civilized but inscrutable kingdoms to the east. Defeating one only meant another shrieking tribe or another foreign dynasty would rise up and raid or invade one of his provinces. And whatever policy he chose would cut at the livelihood of someone among the four estates. Schemes would enmesh him like spiderwebs, all cloaked in stirring words about the good of the kingdom, all seeking to enrich one of his subjects at the expense of others.

If only he could abdicate and take the green of a common soldier.

He strode through the gate. Everything around him lost color, lost sound.

His mouth went dry. *What's happen…*

Lost consciousness….

Stone woke in darkness. Cooling fans whirred nearby. Padded seat under him. He thought about lifting his arms from the armrest but they refused to rise.

Still under the influence of Sheila van Bentum's drug. Still in the chair.

Three-d text coalesced in front of him.

```
Name: Rolston Wentworth Gridley "Stone" Chalmers
```

```
Aliases: Edward Lavellette
Tobias Becker
Jasper Jezhek
```

The list scrolled on. Had the procedure pulled out of his brain every cover identity he'd ever used? He couldn't remember them all.

```
Sex, anatomical: Male
Sex, chromosomal: XY

++++++++++
Genetic markers of personality traits
++++++++++
Androgen receptor CAG repeat length: 15
ADRA2b deletion: no
5-HTTLPR variation: long
```

Hundreds of lines of gibberish raced up his field of view. He couldn't understand it even if he had time to read it.

Sounds. Somewhere outside the helmet. The padding of soft-soled shoes. A rustle of fabric, bodies shifting position.

The lines of gene-marker gibberish scrolled out of his vision. New text popped up, swimming for a moment until his eyes adapted to their fixed position in front of his eyes.

```
Gender identity: Male
Sexual orientation (modified Kinsey): 0.1 (exclusively
heterosexual)
Lifetime sexual partners (female): 200 est.
Lifetime sexual partners (male): 0
Monogamous relationship suitability: very low
```

He sniffed out a chuckle. Sheila van Bentum's black box delivered accurate results. So far.

The words slid to the left, out of sight. New text filled in.

Stone's smirk softened. His eyebrows crinkled.

```
++++++++++
Personality parameters
++++++++++
IQ: 112±3

Five Factor Model:
    Openness to experience: very high
    Conscientiousness: low
    Extraversion: very high
    Agreeableness: low
    Emotional stability: high

Myers-Briggs type: ENTP

O.S. Card life stage assessment: Adolescent (seeks power
and freedom, rejects belonging)

    Likelihood of advance to next stage (Adult (seeks
power and belonging, rejects freedom)) within
five years: very low

V. Frankl loci of meaning:
    Faith: 0%
    Family: 14%
    Work: 81%
Overall sense of purpose: 83%
```

In the room outside his helmet, someone drew in a long, sharp breath. A murmur. "So low?" Sheila's voice.

"For a man from Earth today," muttered a reply, "be surprised even one of the loci is so high."

A woman's voice. Had he heard it before? Where? Whose?

A third page of text appeared. Stone read. His eyebrows crinkled more. Varna?

```
Placement in Four-Category Social Alignment:
```

```
    Hindu varna: Kshatriya
    Western estate of the realm: Nobility
       Substate: Knight
Leadership suitability: medium
Follower suitability: low
++++++++++
Suggested careers: policeman, soldier, spy.
Likelihood of fulfilling marriage: very low.
```

The words hung in front of his eyes for ten slow, pounding beats of his heart.

```
Protocol complete.
You may wish to discuss your results and their
applicability to your evolving quest for
alignment with the universe with a facilitator.
```

A voice came to him. Sheila's. "Do you grasp what this means?"

"No."

Sheila sighed out a breath. She muttered something Stone barely heard. Perhaps "You're sure?"

If the other person in the room answered verbally, the words didn't penetrate the helmet.

Sheila spoke again, much louder. "There is another person in the room with me. You will follow this person's instructions exactly as you follow mine."

A motor hummed above him. The helmet rose, squeezing his ears against the side of his head. White light flooded his eyes. He blinked and squeezed his eyes shut. Cooling fans sounded on three sides. A delicate floral perfume trickled into his nose. Not Sheila's scent. Whose?

Stone reopened his eyes. He could tolerate the washed-out brightness now. "Turn the chair."

Servos under him slowly rotated the chair to his right. Sheila van Bentum came into view. Her eyes still showed him sapphire ice, but her tongue darted nervously between clenched lips. Her blue eyes darted to her left.

Dark pride welled in him. Not agreeable at all. Edward Lavallette turned out to be more than she expected.

The chair spun further. He forgot Sheila in an instant. A lean woman, smartly dressed in navy blue pants. Blond hair brushed the shoulders of her white blouse. Her hazel eyes appraised him.

Caitlyn Fredriksen.

How? Not a fellow passenger on *Yassir Arafat*. She must have journeyed here with the diplomatic mission, and stayed.

Forget that. Caitlyn. Once a rival, once a partner, but now…?

"Key—" He cleared his throat. "Keyhole kop. What do you want from me?"

"Stone Chalmers," she said, "I want you to help me save the human race."

7

He kept his voice calm. "I save the world every day."

"Stand." Her words yanked him out of the chair. "Exit the room…."

His mind raced while his body trudged through the Center at her commands. What was Caitlyn's game? Some operatives ran side hustles, smuggling, gun-running, the like. But from their first meeting, he'd viewed her as a straight arrow who would never abuse her position.

A rogue operative wouldn't try to enlist him in a side hustle by telling him joining her would save the human race.

Stone stepped through the revolving doors. He halted on the landing under the swooping granite buttress. Although the mass of rock held traces of the day's heat, a chill ran down his back.

A black coupe with rounded lines, standard issue from the UN motor pool, pulled up and parked itself. The door on the near side popped open.

"Get in the car," Caitlyn said from five feet away. "Sit on the back seat. Do not move."

Stone climbed in, sat on gray leather. He caught his breath. Did every vehicle on Minerva have a new car smell?

Caitlyn took the front seat, facing him, and crossed her legs. Her top foot dangled six inches from his knee. Her blond hair brushed the ceiling as she looked up and spoke to the coupe. "Travel plan A."

"Where are we going?" Stone asked.

The coupe whispered out of the buttress's shadow. Stone squinted against the parking garage's stark white light. A moment later, the coupe's windows polarized. Darkness enveloped them.

"A place to talk."

"Meaning you'll talk and I'll shut up and listen."

Caitlyn raised an eyebrow. "Have I ordered you to be silent?"

He tried to roll his wrists in a shrug, but they wouldn't move. When would the drug wear off?

Wrong question. How much intel could he gather until he regained his freedom to act? "Why does the human race need saving? And what makes you the one to save it?"

"*Now* I order you to be silent until the car stops."

The coupe climbed the ramp and turned right onto the dark and quiet street. Away from the UN tower. Midrise structures loomed above empty, clean sidewalks.

After a few minutes the coupe drove through a neighborhood of single-story buildings, coffee bars and boardgaming parlors, unlit in the late evening. His implantable couldn't radio the UN tower from this range even if he were free to try. Caitlyn took him further out of range every second.

The city thinned out. To the left, a golf course undulated under the wan light of Minerva's small moon. Bunkers looked like misshapen yin-yang symbols, gray-white sand contrasting with moonshadows. Lampposts behind the golf course lined the railroad line to the space elevator. On the right, the roofs of houses on acre lots peered over a wall of grown granite facing the road.

The last neighborhoods of Euler City fell behind the coupe. Hundreds of rows of potted evergreen saplings, about five feet tall, ran perpendicular from fences along the highway into the night-shrouded distance. A sign clipped to a fence wire marked the nursery as property of Berglund Ecoseeding Company. The company's logo was a blue tree bisecting a yellow sun.

Ten minutes later, the coupe slowed. The bluish-white headlight beams showed the highway curved around a rocky mound and out of sight. The coupe left the highway, turned right onto a two-lane road. The headlights glistened on blue-black asphalt and crisp yellow dashes down the center line. Evergreens eight to ten feet tall blurred by. Pines, maybe, or firs planted by the ecoseeding company. Not potted, but wild, digging roots into thin soil. The road climbed into a range of low hills, sliced through the hills' knife-edge ridgelines.

The coupe slowed. On the left, a gravel road cut through another low hill dotted with evergreens. The car turned. Gravel crunched under the wheels as the coupe slowly continued its journey to wherever they were bound.

Five more minutes and the coupe turned left, onto a narrow lane consisting of two dirt strips separated by tufted grass. The grass brushed the coupe's undercarriage. They must be approaching their destination.

Fourteen breaths later, the coupe rolled to a stop. Muffled by the coupe's closed doors, a hundred crickets chirped outside.

Stone's body stiffened. Enough space separated the pines or firs to fit a shallow ditch, six feet long and two and a half wide. But if she wanted to kill him, why claim she needed his help to save the human race? To dull his resistance to her killing strike? Sheila van Bentum's drug did that ten times better.

Unless it wore off soon.

He tried flexing his fingers. They refused to budge. Do not move, indeed.

At least his eyes could turn to right, then left. Unless the drug disrupted his sense of direction, the future wormhole site should be no more than five miles to the left. No sign of it reached the corner of his eye through the evergreen forest, not even a light glow in the distance. His gaze paused on a small metal sign on a post along the dirt track. Blue evergreen, yellow sun, letters *BEC*.

The headlights blinked off. Darkness surrounded the cabin. A dome light in the ceiling angled toward him. Caitlyn remained in shadow. Faint sounds came from near her right hand. Assume she'd pulled a handgun from a storage cubby.

But no sound of a slide racking. She hadn't chambered a round. If he could leap across the cabin, he could strangle her before she could fire.

"Societies have life cycles," Caitlyn said, "just like people, from youthful vigor to decline and death. The ancient Hindus, Greeks, and Levantines all imagined a past Satya Yuga, a Golden Age, an Eden, that devolved to the present fallen world. Ibn Khaldun and Oswald Spengler created qualitative frameworks for thinking about societies' life cycles. Peter Turchin's innovation over a century ago lay in applying quantitative analysis to the problem. Other cliodynamicists—quantitative historians—since then have expanded on Turchin's foundation and brought in other ideas, such as James Grier Miller's living systems theory and—"

Stone's voice crackled from disuse. "Enough background."

"You don't need it. Here's what we know about society life cycles. At an early stage, a growing society has a high degree of group cohesion. As a result, the society's leaders perceive that their greatest personal gain will come if they work together to exploit their society's skills and resources. By working together, they start their society on the path to greatness."

Strangle her, but then what? Locked in a car with a dead woman until he died of dehydration. Assuming the car didn't drive him to the UN tower or Minerva police headquarters. Edward Lavallette would cool his heels in jail until long after *Yassir Arafat*'s engineers landed the wormhole mouth on Minerva.

"The Romans conquered neighbors who were too poor to defend themselves and rich enough to make worth conquering. The Americans swept aside primitive indigenous peoples and turned the temperate half of a continent into the workshop of the world and the arsenal of democracy. Perhaps it's like winning football games?"

Memories of high school practices and his coach's pep talks drifted up. Stone tested her words against the memories. Her words rang true. "I see what you're saying."

Besides, you can't gather much intel from a dead woman. The more she talked, the more she might reveal.

Especially if she meant to recruit him to her cause.

"Next question. Why don't great societies continue on an upward path forever?"

"Another society with more ruling class cohesion comes along."

"A good guess." She shook her head. "Invaders are a symptom of social decay. Not a cause."

"And the cause is…?"

"The time of greatness contains the seeds of decay. The society's leaders think the growth phase will last forever. What they don't realize is the founders built the time of greatness by plucking low-hanging fruit. Sooner or later, the low-hanging fruit runs out. The Romans ran out of easy, rich conquests. The barbarians to their north and northeast were too poor to be worth conquering, while the advanced societies of the Near East were rich enough to defend themselves. The Americans ran out of frontier and inefficient social sectors they could easily reorganize."

"Wouldn't their group cohesion make them agree to lower their expectations? Or—" How had she phrased it? "—learn new skills and find new resources to exploit?"

"Group cohesion is difficult to maintain. It's similar to preventing symbiotic organisms from becoming parasites, or normal cells from becoming cancerous. The first to defect from the group's cohesion can reap huge gains. We're getting into the indefinitely iterated prisoner's dilemma discussed by Robert Axelrod—"

"I'll take your word for it."

"Back to the society's leaders when growth becomes more difficult. The inheritors of the founders were usually born with a silver spoon and lacked the drive to work as hard as their predecessors, let alone work even harder to extract the same amount of growth. So they don't. But they still want personal gain. Where can they find it?"

"You tell me."

"Since it's too much work to find personal gain outside the society, they seek it within. Group cohesion gives way to faction and intrigue. The principles the society's founders held themselves to become empty slogans. Government goes from raising the tide to lift all boats to picking winners and losers within the society. The rulers focus on persuading the government to maintain their perks. Elites who lost out when perks were granted seek to seize the government. Both factions of the elite use the masses as pawns, then ignore them. The society rots from within."

" 'Rots from within'? Sounds melodramatic."

"You'd like concrete examples." Caitlyn ticked them off on manicured fingers. "The elites prop up the profits of their business enterprises by importing cheap labor. This threatens the livelihood of the masses, who are mollified by an ever-expanding welfare state and taxpayer-funded stadiums. The military's budget grows, but elites divert most of the increased funding to themselves and their cronies, and military effectiveness collapses. To pay for all its programs, the government increases taxes, inflates the currency, and imposes draconian economic regulations."

"Are you talking about the Romans or the Americans?"

In the dim cabin, her hazel eyes became dark pits turned on him. "Both."

Stone smirked. "So your faction is the one that lost out when the UN granted perks fifty years ago?"

"No." Her tone lacked any taking of offense. "We intend to found a new society better able to maintain group cohesion."

"The revolutionaries always say that when they grab for the brass ring."

"You think the leaders who turned the UN from a debate club into a world government founded something. No. I glossed over a stage that frequently appears in the societal life cycle. It's similar to the point in a human life cycle when a person gets over his midlife crisis. Some societies have an elite faction attempt retrenchment and restoration of the society's founding spirit."

"Meaning?"

"The Romans suffered a civil war five decades long, with twenty-five different warlords proclaiming themselves emperors. Diocletian restored order, by making the Roman government more authoritarian, more bureaucratic, and more repressive than it had been before the crisis. When Diocletian's policies and the rise of Christianity didn't solve Rome's problems, Julian the Apostate attempted to restore paganism as the state religion. The Americans about two centuries ago went through economic and social upheaval and the loss of China and Eastern Europe to Communism. The conservative masses turned to

Reagan, who defeated Communism but failed to restore the former American way of life. As a last attempt to restore their way of life, the conservative masses then turned to Trump."

Stone's eyelids drooped at the history lesson.

"I'll sum up," Caitlyn said. "In both Rome and America, the restoration attempts failed, because conflict between factions proved too strong."

"The men who remade the UN as the world's government succeeded," Stone said.

Caitlyn angled her head in an *oh really?* look. "They had good luck. So far."

"Luck?"

"They seized control of the exotic matter factory—what we now call Hawking Station—and found a physicist from a small town in North Dakota, of all places, who provided the stroke of genius needed to turn exotic matter rings into semi-stable wormholes. This allowed the heads of UN member states to exile troublesome minorities to colony worlds."

"Even without the Dubai Convention—"

"They manipulated public opinion in the United States to turn a still-formidable military into a peacekeeping force ready to suppress dissent at a moment's notice anywhere around the world. They built the most pervasive spy agency in history to maintain a watchful eye on every threat they could imagine."

"You're welcome."

Caitlyn sniffed out a breath. "It won't be enough. The Dubai Convention colonies will soon be overwhelmed by the resettled."

"So what?"

"The demand for resettlement slots is increasing."

"...Increasing?"

"You didn't know that? I shouldn't be surprised. Few do."

Stone said, "The rate of colonies acceding to the Dubai Convention has slowed."

"Yes. Minerva will probably be the last one ever. But the number of UN member states wanting to exile undesirables is increasing. Originally, resettlement had some justification. Five to ten thousand people from each of six countries suffering intractable civil disorder, voluntarily moving to new worlds without the baggage of the past. But now, two hundred UN member states want to ship out up to forty-nine percent of their populations. Call it two billion people divided among almost fifty worlds."

"Forty million each…" Stone's eyebrows jumped. On a typical Dubai Convention world, the resettled would outnumber the colonists fifty to one. No colony could feed that many resettled, and would itself starve if it tried.

"Resettlement will cease before two billion people are exiled from Earth. Instead, those two billion people will suffer the same fate as billions before them. Oppression, ethnic cleansing, genocide."

A cynical thought came to him, cloaked in leftover words of the Tobias Becker cover story he'd used on Trinity. "The poor you will have with you always."

"Don't get cute. Now, a small group with an ion exchanger, a mass spectrometer, access to seawater, and electricity from a shantytown's roofs covered with solar panels can isolate enough enriched uranium to build a twenty-kiloton atomic bomb smaller than a shipping container. A larger group with ten competent nuclear engineers can use that atomic bomb as the primary for a twenty-megaton hydrogen bomb and deliver it at optimal burst height over any city on Earth. Another small group with a protein synthesizer, a nucleic acid synthesizer, and computer software to predict interactions of viral coat proteins with cell surface proteins differing between ethnic groups can unleash a genocidal plague. Unlike the Time of Troubles, these small groups may emerge not just from the slums of Earth, but from the resettlement camps and original colonies of almost fifty worlds. Forget the Time of Troubles; the human race risks apocalypse."

Even if her dire prediction were accurate, "What can you do to stop apocalypse?"

She stared at him from deep shadow. "Our best chance is for the Minervans to spread Alignment with the Universe through the settled galaxy as rapidly as possible. If a critical mass of people learn who they truly are and where they truly belong in their society, group cohesion will emerge naturally."

"How did they ancient song go? 'You could say I'm a dreamer'?"

"It may not be a good chance, but it's our best chance. Which is why we need you."

Stone clamped down on a smirk. There were four main ways to recruit a humint asset or turn an opposing operative, known by the acronym MICE. Money? He had more than enough for his lifestyle. Ideology? Caitlyn didn't need Sheila's mind-reading tech to know he wouldn't respond. Compromise? You can't blackmail a man for sexual indiscretions when he brags about them.

Only Ego remained. Flatter the target into thinking he could outsmart the recruiter.

"What can one man do for you? Even if that man is me?"

"Keep Gray from blocking the Minervans."

Stone gave one slow blink. Gray didn't conspire with Caitlyn. Or she wanted him to think that. "Why would Gray care about the Minervans' state religion enough to stop its spread?"

"He worried enough about Minerva to send his best operative here, didn't he?"

She didn't need to know Gray sent him here to build up credit in the UN bureaucracy's favor bank. He let himself smirk. "Good point."

"You're in?"

Of course he would say he joined her conspiracy. He could only leave the car alive and free to act if he did. But she knew that too. If he agreed too quickly, she would suspect he lied. "I've struck out with every Minervan woman. If Alignment with the Universe spreads, I'll strike out with every woman on Earth."

"Don't worry. The kind of women you pursue will still throng Manhattan for decades yet."

"They're aligned with their inner sluts?"

A breath in, then Caitlyn said, "You could put it like that."

Another objection arose, carried by images of Euler City's quiet streets and the truths revealed by the Alignment protocol. "If every human being in the galaxy is aligned with the universe, no one will need a policeman, a soldier, or a spy."

"A fit and healthy person still has an immune system. Policemen and spies are a society's analogs. Even Minerva suffers from crime and disorder."

"A kid throws a rock through a window once every week?"

"Even if everyone were aligned with the universe, the settled galaxy would suffer from crime and disorder too. And don't worry, the process of aligning every human being with the universe will not end until after you've retired. You will have many more chances to ply your trade even if you join us."

He still couldn't record her treacherous words to his implantable, but after he got back to his room in the UN tower, he could record an encrypted report he would send to Gray in the first diplomatic pouch back to Earth after siting the wormhole.

Stone peered into the gloom on her side of the cabin and put on the most sincere expression he could manage. "I'm in. If I could move my hand, I'd shake on it."

8

Yellow light flared on the western wall of Stone's hotel suite living room. He blinked bleary eyes and squinted to the east. A limb of Minerva's sun peaked over the horizon and its reflection dazzled off the gray-green surface of the Wisdom Sea.

"Close the blinds," he said to the suite. No harm would come if Caitlyn Fredriksen or a Minervan counterintelligence officer overheard those words. He'd swept for bugs and cameras, of course, both after first arriving at the room and when he'd staggered in late the night before. He'd found no spy devices hidden nearby, but the Minervans might have longer range monitors about which he lacked intel.

The motors hummed until the rectangle of yellow light on the far wall shrank to nothingness. The floor lamp near the wood-grain plastic desk seemed dim in contrast to the stark daylight.

Stone lolled his head back on the plush, boxy armchair and shut his eyes. A hidden camera would show a man who'd partied late and couldn't sleep. A hidden microphone would fail to pick up the dictation he subvoked to one of the encrypted memory sticks in his pocket synced with his implanted computer.

Extent of conspiracy is unknown. Subject Fredriksen multiple times used 'we,' though she might have been suggesting she has numerous supporters to increase my chance of joining her. Her travel with the diplomatic mission and assignment to that mission's stayover team suggest one or more ITB personnel are coconspirators.

Threat does not appear urgent at this time. An analyst can model spread of Alignment based on some math I don't care to understand, but my hunch is we have years before it gains enough converts to disrupt social structures on Earth or any Dubai Convention world.

I will continue to pose as a coconspirator and gather intel on Subject Fredriksen, other conspirators, and Alignment. Codename Hybrid, out.

He subvoked the command to encrypt the report on the memory stick, the one with a red stripe and raised blue bumps. The other memory stick had a turquoise band around the middle. For that one...

Spoken with heads of Minervan companies developing building materials and techniques. Scheduling meetings with heads of longevity tech companies. Numerous opportunities for profit for our agency's business partners....

A thought tripped up his subvoked dictation. To what estate of the realm did the business partners of the UN business development agency belong? And how low were their agreeableness and emotional stability?

He pushed the thought away. *In summary, visit is on track for high success. Signed, Edward Lavallette.*

Stone locked the report on the turquoise-banded stick. He would drop both sticks in the diplomatic pouch when the communications office opened in—he checked—ninety minutes.

Catch some sleep? He could use it, but last night's events kept his nerves taut. Shower, dress, eat breakfast? His stomach soured at the thought of food. Suckered by a woman three times his age—

Flip your perspective. Sheila van Bentum's trap gave him an opportunity to gather intel on a conspiracy that almost certainly reached back to New York. How wide through the UN bureaucracy? How high?

He couldn't answer those questions from here. But other intel he could gather. Stone ordered bacon and a spinach and tomato omelet from the commissary's delivery service, then called up a map to his mind's eye.

Euler City to the east, arid evergreen forests and irrigated farms to the west. The rail line to the space elevator base ran straight from downtown Euler City for about twenty miles, then curved to the northwest. Another track ran abreast of the space elevator line for about twelve miles out of the city before curling north and terminating at a meteor crater in the middle of farmland. The crater, about a quarter-mile across, was the wormhole site.

He zoomed in. According to lidar—laser rangefinding—data from the crater floor and rim, the crater floor lay about two hundred feet below the average elevation of the surrounding terrain, and the rim rose about fifty feet above. As of yesterday's date stamp on the map, the railroad track and a parallel two-lane road ended five hundred yards outside the crater, at the start of a narrow north-south cut through the rim.

Unlike New Moravia's wormhole mouth, if the equilibrator ring on this one lost containment, billions of tons of rock would shield the colony's capital city from the brunt of the gamma ray burst.

Had Caitlyn told the Minervans to do this? Or had they figured it out themselves?

He shook his head. Someone else could answer that question. He zoomed out and retraced his path from the night before. The black coupe had turned off the main road here. Turned onto the gravel road there.

The map omitted the narrow dirt track. Only a few pale pixels on the verge of the gravel road in a satellite photo revealed its existence.

Sixty or ninety seconds at five to fifteen miles per hour. Stone's eyes drew a circle on the map projected to his optic nerve. Caitlyn had taken him somewhere in that circle to invite him into treachery.

Why there?

Because she knew no one would eavesdrop.

On Earth, a handheld lidar unit could pick up the vibrations of a window caused by people speaking inside a building—or vehicle—and decode their speech from half a mile. Assume the Minervans had technology twice as capable.

How could she have known no one hostile to her cause lurked within a mile of that circle?

Stone subvoked, *I need Minervan public records of ownership and license to access—* He drew a larger circle with his eyes, radius—he made it a mile and a half.

Breakfast arrived on a wheeled robot's tray. Stone crunched crispy bacon and wripped apart wilted spinach while the search worked through Minerva's planetary network. For a society so technologically advanced in most things, the search seemed very slow. Probably an interface delay between the UN's computers and the local servers.

Results appeared as tooltips overlaid on the map in his mind's eye. Three thousand acres of the evergreen forest belonged to the Berglund Ecoseeding Company. No other legal entity or person held rights of access. Droplet Farms LLC owned thirteen thousand acres of eggplant, sunchoke, and tomato fields at the southern end of the circle, extending all the way to the north end of the wormhole crater.

A link indicated Droplet Farms contracted out ecosystem maintenance. Stone followed the link with an expectation.

Another tooltip popped up. A knowing smile curled his lips.

The farm's ecosystem maintenance was performed by the Berglund Ecoseeding Company.

Plans hatched in Stone's mind. The company's CEO would probably agree to a meeting request from Edward Lavallette. But he might know Stone's true identity and ask Caitlyn why their recruited agent had gotten curious about the evergreen forest near the wormhole. Stone would face tough questions from Caitlyn. *The UN elite don't need ecoseeding tech, do they?*

That's if she didn't write him off as a recruit to her cause and try to kill him.

Stone munched more bacon. He liked his odds in a fight to the death against her, but she could still land a lucky blow before he killed her. Especially since he'd last seen his 9mm at the Center's conference room.

And if he killed her now, his best trail into her conspiracy would die too.

He sipped ice water and an idea came. Berglund's CEO almost certainly lacked any knowledge of Stone's identity. Caitlyn possessed enough skill in tradecraft to only share knowledge with her co-conspirators on a need to know basis.

But that didn't matter. If Berglund's CEO told Caitlyn about a meeting with Edward Lavallette, then back to tough questions or a fight to the death.

Stone remembered the mission to New Moravia. The head of an organization could be ignorant of what his underlings did. Reconnoiter Berglund Ecoseeding's facilities for intel? Or drive back out to the evergreen forest and scout the site yourself?

No. Assume those blue tree and yellow sun signs held embedded cameras. Assume the same signs guarded the perimeter of each of the company's facilities. Again, tough questions or worse.

And odds were he'd find nothing worth the risk of being spotted while reconnoitering in person. Caitlyn would know the UN's standard procedures for wormhole placement included subtle but pervasive monitoring of the area around the site, both from orbit and by low profile, high endurance drones able to look deep into the infrared and far into the ultraviolet. He could ask for drone data from the photorecon team, but even if he reviewed that data, he'd probably see nothing amid the evergreens and the rows of sunchokes and tomatoes.

Reconsider Berglund Ecoseeding. Why would Caitlyn want to include a bioseeding company in her plans? Genetically engineered pines and advanced drip irrigation techniques would be useless as weapons against the UN.

What other people or entities did Berglund work with?

Stone leaned his head against the chair back and composed a search request for Minerva public records. Business associates, fellow volunteers, and family members of Berglund Ecoseeding as a company and of the company's principals. He adjusted settings to anonymize the request, then subvoked *Send*.

A 3d hourglass popped into the lower right corner of his vision. Sand slid down. The hourglass flipped. More sliding sand.

He sniffed out a breath. Even if a bottleneck lay between Minerva's network and the UN's, the search should be faster than this.

A chime pinged his auditory nerves. The hourglass vanished, replaced by a text notification. *8324 results. Select report options?*

He grunted. Eight thousand results? Most of them trivial, but he had to review them all.

His wristwatch showed 0806. At 0900, the Lavallette cover had to meet with the first of today's ten Minervan technoloqy leaders.

Stone saved the search results to his implantable. He rose and stretched wiry limbs to the ceiling.

After showering and dressing, he zipped down the elevator to the UN communications office on the third floor.

His wristwatch showed 0835, yet no one waited behind the window in the opaque wall of milky glass at the comms office. He tapped his foot on milky granite and glanced around at extruded plastic tables, boxy armchairs, framed videoloops of Iguazu Falls and the tide rising around the island monastery of Mont-Saint-Michel. The vistas of World Heritage Sites didn't fit with the utilitarian decor in the room.

Footsteps behind the glass wall. A scrape as the window slid open. Glimpses of brown face, black hair. "May I help you?"

The voice sounded slightly familiar. Stone went to the window, composing his face to cover his annoyance at the delay. "Something for the first outgoing pouch. Outbound in two days?" He dug in his pocket for the first of three items. Found it. Froze.

The swarthy boyfriend of Merrill, the purple-haired pixie, scowled at him. He spat out his words. "What do you want?"

Damn her, had she confessed to him her shipboard affair? He pulled a smooth memory stick from his pocket, glanced long enough to confirm a turquoise glint. "For the first outgoing pouch."

"You stopped flirting with other men's girlfriends long enough to do some work?"

Stone exhaled. Flirting? Merrill had kept her dirty little secret. His faith in the predictability of women returned. "Sorry?"

"The party on the *Yassir Arafat* when we all watched the wormhole dock at Hawking Station?"

Stone rolled his shoulders. "I try to be friendly with everyone. Did I make your girlfriend uncomfortable?"

The swarthy man puffed out his chest. "Yes."

"My apologies to her. And you. You know, I never caught your name."

The swarthy man's scowl softened, but distrust remained in his eyes. "I am Gautam. Put the memory stick on the counter."

Stone did. Gautam's flabby arm groped to his right and pulled into view what looked like a glue gun on an articulating arm. He touched the tip to the memory stick's turquoise band, then pushed the gun back out of sight. Only a tiny black bump against the turquoise revealed the RFID tracking chip.

"Your name?"

"Edward Lavallette." Stone preemptively spelled it.

"Addressee?"

Stone made up a name and the general incoming mail stop at the Global Economic Cooperation Agency's headquarters. No special handling, no delivery confirmation. Stone stifled a yawn. Did Merrill know her boyfriend's position in UN communications meant he worked as a postal clerk?

After the final question, a hatch in the counter dropped open. Red LEDs rimmed the opening. Gautam swept in the memory stick by hand. The LEDs flashed green. The hatch closed with a faint click.

"If ITB does its job correctly, it will return to Earth through the wormhole in four days."

"Four? The wormhole drop is scheduled for tomorrow, isn't it?"

"It will take four days for the colonists to connect the transport links to the Earth side," Gautam said. His tone made clear he believed he knew everything aboout the capabilities of the Minervans. "Is this all?"

A tingle ran down Stone's arms and legs. If Caitlyn had compromised Gautam, Stone's next action would tip her off that he still spied for Gray. But to inform Gray as quickly as possible, he had no other choice.

"One thing more." Stone slipped two items from his pocket and covered them with his hand all the way to the counter. "Another stick." He requested a private connection between their subvocal microphones and their auditory nerves.

Gautam opened the connection. His expression gave little hint that they would speak without an observer noticing. Enough to fool an amateur poker player. Would it fool Caitlyn if she watched through hidden cameras?

Pick a different sender's name. Anyone from the mission directory. Odds were the random choice probably wouldn't be another member of Caitlyn's conspiracy.

What are you asking me to do?

Tag the stick with a different name. That's all.

A ponderous shake of Gautam's head. *Such a thing is contrary to proper use of the diplomatic pouch.*

Stone lifted his index and middle fingers from a corner of a US $5000 bill.

Gautam's eyebrows jolted. He inhaled deeply and set his hands flat on the counter as if steadying himself. He lifted three fingers and slid his hand until his raised fingers almost touched Stone's.

The heel of Stone's hand shoved the bill and the memory stick under Gautam's raised fingers. *This one has a different destination.*

A curt nod.

Stone subvoked over the address provided by Gray four months earlier. The glue gun added a fourth dot to the memory stick's red stripe. "It is quite simple when the same person sends two items to the same address," Gautam said.

Hamming up for any microphone that might be hidden nearby. With luck, Caitlyn and her conspirators didn't monitor audio feeds from the communications room.

Red flashed, then green, followed by a faint click.

Would knowing he was a noble or a peasant, or that he derived more meaning from faith or family, reduce Gautam's tawdry corruption? Even if the human race could be saved, Caitlyn deluded herself that Alignment with the Universe could do the job.

"Yes," Stone said. "Quite simple indeed."

9

Stone returned to his suite late that night. Finally he could shuck the Lavallette persona for the day.

Not as easy as changing clothes, though. Eleven Minervans—Bradley dell'Angelo, CEO of a drone company called Light Flight LLC, had asked to move their meeting up a day—blurred together, one twenty-minute meeting after another about technologies ranging from solar-electric films to software for more rapid and more photorealistic animation. The software wouldn't have saved his father from an early, vodka-soaked grave, but Gray could use it to fill the worldnet with a hundred videos by a cover story, adding to the layers of forged digital verification UNICA's cover stories branch already knew how to assemble. On some future mission, that software might save Stone's life.

After normal working hours, maintaining the Lavallete cover sent him to dinner at a steakhouse on a bluff overlooking the Wisdom Sea, where thick glass and whispering air conditioning kept the green stink of algae from overwhelming the tang of bleu cheese and the bite of peppercorn sauce smothering his vat-grown filet mignon. Forty locals, already abuzz about the wormhole placement scheduled for the next day, came for a pitch session, taking thirty seconds each to persuade Edward Lavallette that their technologies would be valuable to Earth. Eleven made the cut for a second round, three minutes apiece, where they spoke in smooth voices and projected uncluttered slides onto the wall behind them about how their technologies could change Earth for the better.

He'd waste half the next day speaking with the second round's five winners.

He dimmed the lights, opened the blinds onto the deep dark sky over the sea. A far cry from the glowing arrays of lighted skyscraper windows visible from his apartment back home. At least the view wouldn't distract him.

Stone rubbed his eyes. Opened the results of the morning's search of Minerva public records relating to Berglund Ecoseeding. Over eight thousand documents.

He winced. Hours of tedious work. Caitlyn could write a script to search for keywords and find any needle that might hide in this haystack.

A damn shame Caitlyn wanted to destroy civilization.

Thoughts nipped at him like a pack of stray dogs. How long had she conspired against the UN? The only answer that made sense was that she'd been sent to Minerva with the diplomatic mission by her co-conspirators. Eight months ago, and even before she, or her coconspirators, or anyone else on Earth could know what Alignment with the Universe involved. After arriving with the diplomats, she must have conspired with Alignment on her own initiative.

She held a high position in the conspiracy. How far back did that push her induction into it? Before Trinity?

Before New Moravia?

He shook his head to clear the thought. Time to dig in.

First, he sifted the results to pull up names of the Berglund company's principals. Three members of the Berglund family, among them Gerald Berglund, the company's founder and CEO for decades, plus six others who were either sons-in-law or strangers.

The company name appeared in over six thousand documents. Each of the nine individuals appeared in thousands. Many duplicates. Probably most duplicate hits were company records naming one or more of the principals.

An insight pushed up his eyelids. He knew at least one other Minervan conspired with Caitlyn.

Search these results for name Sheila van Bentum.

In a blink, a summary page superimposed itself on Stone's view of the seaside window. *16 records.*

He rubbed his palms together. *Open all.*

The documents leaped out of the summary page and stacked themselves. His heart picked up its pace. He expanded the first one and read.

```
Record of Alignment with the Universe
Subject: Berglund, Eliana H.
Minerva Citizen ID: 4855364938851
Date of Birth: 2092-11-01
Date of Consecration: 2105-11-02
Facilitatrix: van Bentum, Sheila L.
Date of Convocation: 2110-11-05...
```

Something like a Catholic's first communion record, if Catholics still practiced their faith somewhere in the settled galaxy. Sheila had pressed the buttons and spoken the ritual words when Caitlyn Fredriksen had been in diapers.

Useless.

At least there were only fifteen more documents...

...of which the next dozen proved equally useless. Sheila facilitated secondary consecration protocols when Eliana Berglund married, gave birth, and entered middle age. Next.

Eliana's father, Gerald, had served on a neighborhood association with Sheila four decades before. A scintillating document approved water slides in homeowners' private swimming pools. Next.

A company's certificate of formation. Gerald Berglund and Sheila van Bentum were two of the five owners of a company called High Emprise LLC.

Stone yawned. The intent to flip to the next document pushed toward the muscles of his throat. His eyes flicked over the document.

And widened at the company's date of formation. He stayed on the page.

Berglund, van Bentum, and the others had formed High Emprise LLC seven months earlier, less than a month after the diplomatic mission returned to Earth.

Stone studied the docoument. High Emprise LLC named its founders. Its stated purpose was *Any venture permissible under the law of Minerva*. Standard boilerplate, presumably. The certificate of formation listed a primary place of business at—Stone called up a map centered on the address—a lowrise office building on the south side of the river.

Reconnoiter High Emprise's office? Stone zoomed in on the map. The names of twenty companies smothered the building's outline like mushrooms growing on a fallen log in Central Park. At most, a shared office; more likely, a mail drop. Like any illicit enterprise on Earth, High Emprise gave the government a primary address that was an empty shell, three data sticks half-buried under dust in a corner. A site visit would garner him minimum intel for a high risk of being spotted.

What could the names of the other founders tell him?

Stone prepared another search for Minerva public records naming the company's other three owners. What were the names?

He blinked at the first one. *dell'Angelo, Bradley.* Where had he heard that name?

Earlier that day. The CEO of the drone company.

The other two names—Simon Bale and Matthew Thomas—lacked significance. Stone subvoked them and added *Search* while the back of his mind turned over what he knew.

He'd met with Bradley dell'Angelo at Light Flight's R&D facility five miles down the shore of the Wisdom Sea. In the distance, clouds of steam billowed from the cooling towers of a fusion power plant and a molecular fabrication facility. Sea breeze fluffed dell'Angelo's fine, light-brown hair and almost muffled his soft voice.

Translucent quadrotor drones darted, barely visible in the pale blue sky. They flocked like birds, wheeling together in seeming chaos but never colliding. One descended and dell'Angelo raised his hands and caught it while his upper arms stayed at his sides. A dark gray sheen of solar-electric film failed to obscure an on-board controller, lightweight batteries, and a storage compartment, now empty.

"It can stay airborne for three weeks," dell'Angelo said, "while carrying a two pound payload."

Two pounds? Enough to fit a surveillance suite of cameras and microphones. "Does it scale up?" Stone had asked as Edward Lavallette.

"Our largest model can carry two hundred pounds, remain in the air for six days, and cruise at ninety miles per hour. If you need something that big."

Back in the hotel room, Stone rubbed his fingertips on his forehead. Alignment with the Universe. Long duration drones. A bioseeding company's close access to the wormhole site. How did they fit together?

Caitlyn and her Minervan allies could launch a drone a few miles from the wormhole. Avoid detection for five minutes or less, and that drone could slip through to Earth.

A two hundred pound payload could carry a person. At ninety miles an hour, a drone could fly from the Mojave Desert end of the wormhole to New York City in a day and a half. A drone small enough to have at least a slim chance of sneaking through Manhattan airspace.

High Emprise LLC wanted to send an assassin to kill the Secretary-General?

No.

High Emprise LLC wanted to send a facilitator to—what did they call the Alignment protocol?—consecrate the Secretary-General?

Stone chuckled. Deluded colonists. Even if the Minervans could make the SecGen see himself as he truly was, the SecGen only held his figurehead position at the suffereance of dozens of power brokers. The Minervans couldn't know who those power brokers were—

Unless Caitlyn told them.

But she couldn't know all of them. Gray she knew, but the others? Stone only had hints. Someone as young as Caitlyn would know even fewer names than he did.

He chuckled. Even if the Minervans facilitated Gray's consecration, Gray already knew who he truly was. A remorseless spider in a dark wool suit.

And even if they knew all the names they needed, the Minervans would need a dozen drones to fly unseen over a continent and the most secure city on Earth. Fat chance.

An hourglass in the corner of Stone's vision stopped spinning. Simon Bale and Matthew Thomas. Results.

He swept the business documents aside and called up information on the remaining two individuals.

Simon Bale. A photo showed calculating blue eyes. Brown scruff over his jaw and around his mouth clashed with the yellow shoulders of a suit jacket.

Stone's heart slammed as he read the dossier. Bale held the post of High Councillor of Security in the Minervan government.

The Minervan government worked with Caitlyn to overthrow the UN. Deliver that proof to Gray, and the Security Council could invoke Article 37 of the Dubai Convention, which allowed the UN to remove a rebellious colonial government from power.

He called up the next set of documents. Frowned at the photo. Did he have the right person?

Yes, Matthew Thomas. Wavy black hair, brown eyes in a light brown face. Maybe an Indian whose family took on Christian names centuries earlier.

Then Stone's eyes tracked Thomas' occupation, and thoughts of where the man's ancestors hailed from fell away.

Matthew Thomas served as Chief Scientific Officer for a company called In Vivo Biolectronics LLC, which developed nanotechnological delivery systems for implantable medical devices.

A drone developer, a med-nano guru, a Minervan government official, and a priestess of the Minervan state religion. What the hell were they up to?

More importantly, could he find out undetected by Caitlyn and her Minervan allies?

Search Minerva public records for High Emprise LLC. Real estate ownership and leases. Employment records.... Who worked for the company, and where. All he needed right now. More data would flood him with too much information. *Search.*

The hourglass reformed in the corner of his vision. A hunch told him it would spin for a long time. He crossed the suite's living room, pulled a bottle of sparkling water from the minifridge, twisted the cap. Plastic crackled, carbonation hissed. Then he grabbed two encrypted memory sticks from his stash in the desk drawer. Time for today's reports by Edward Lavallette and Stone himself.

...investigating company, High Emprise LLC, owned by Subject van Bentum and CEO of bioseeding company owning site of my meeting with Subject Fredriksen. Other owners include High Councillor Simon Bale of Minervan government....

He finished his report to Gray, then quickly ginned up a report from Edward Lavallette to the interstellar trade bureaucrats. He would drop the reports in the diplomatic pouch in the morning.

Ping.

He opened the search results. Scanned the data. His heart beat faster and the suite's beige walls seemed a little brighter. He knew where to go for more intel. High Emprise LLC leased a warehouse in a complex on the south side of Euler City, across the Strigidae River.

Stone threw the encrypted sticks into the suite's safe. Before he locked the safe's door, he pulled out his toolkit with energized hands.

Enough computer searching and investing time in a cover story. Time to do his real job.

Stone slung the toolkit over his shoulder and strode to the door. A chuckle bubbled between his lips.

His work gave his life its primary source of meaning? Maybe Caitlyn knew who he truly was after all.

10

Stone's car from the motor pool rolled out of the garage and into Euler City's cloudless night. He had ten minutes before he would arrive at his first destination. He peered out the window, but as he expected, saw nothing.

With the naked eye, at any rate.

He unzipped his tool kit. His hand went unerringly to the onyx ring. Glossy black glimmered as he passed a street light. He slipped it on his right ring finger, then leaned back against synthetic leather and rested his forearm on the bottom frame of the car window. A subvoked command instructed the ring to feed a false-color overlay of its inputs to his vision and a tone to his hearing if it saw something.

Nothing. He rolled his wrist to sweep the ring's camera over the sky on the right side of the car. Still nothing to that side.

He stretched his hands toward the ceiling. Cradled his hands behind his head.

Nothing.

Yet.

Stone reached his hands down to his shoulders and dug his fingers in like a desk jockey rubbing tight muscles.

Ding.

He slid over to the left side of the back seat and laid his right hand between the headrests. The ding returned. He turned his head a fraction to the right. A bright red line sliced through his view of the ceiling.

One ring couldn't provide binocular vision, but he didn't need to know the precise range at which the drone followed him. He only needed to know that one did follow.

He smirked and sniffed out a breath. The Minervans thought they were clever, didn't they? But even if they built drones transparent to the human eye and miserly with power, even the most efficient drone motors would still radiate waste heat.

Did the Minervans trail all UN motor pool vehicles leaving the tower? Or just his?

Stone looked out the window. The streetscape looked familiar from the night before. He checked a map of the city to confirm.

Six minutes till the car would arrive in the parking garage underneath the Center for Alignment with the Universe.

His hands returned to the tool kit. Pulled out a cardboard carton with the logos of a playing card brand and a casino in Atlantic City. Deft fingers opened the carton and pulled out its contents.

The armory techs called it a *Harry Potter cloak* for reasons unknown. Stone crouched on the floor, unfolded it, slipped it on. The fabric clung to the bare skin of his arms. Heat-absorbing rods bumped against his thigh. A message box popped into his vision. *Connecting.... done. Self-test.... done. Active mode: visible.*

He looked down at his arms and legs. Thin, transparent sleeves, rough and plasticky to the touch, hung loosely past his fingertips. A hem like an Amish woman's dress brushed the floor. After a minute, and despite being lightly dressed in jogging shorts and a moisture-wicking T-shirt, the smothering fabric already brought sweat to his armpits.

Just wait until he walked two miles across Euler City.

The car descended into the parking garage under the Center. If the nearly-invisible drone belonged to the Minervan government, and not to Caitlyn and the conspirators, the Minervan government would think that Edward Lavallette sought more spiritual guidance from Sheila van Bentum.

And if the drone belonged to the conspirators, he would at least have a chance to escape their surveillance.

The car reached the main level of the parking garage. Completely empty. The car turned left, toward the entrance to the building. Stone glanced back. Should be out of sight from any person or drone at street level.

"Stop. Open the door."

The car did as he ordered. He climbed out. Long enough since sunset for a pleasantly cool feeling to trickle under the cloak's hem and over his bare legs.

"Park and wait. Listen for further instructions on—" He named a radio channel and the car replied with a confirmation tone.

Stone shoved the door closed. The car rolled toward the nearest parking space.

Full invisibility, he subvoked to the cloak. He glanced down. Where he knew his arm to be he saw only concrete.

Maybe the armory techs knew what they were talking about for once. He slowly swept his arm in front of his eyes.

Streaks of distortion outlined his sleeve.

Stone sniffed out a black-humored breath. The armory techs always overpromised and underdelivered. Not the complete invisibility they'd promised, but it would have to do.

And more concerns than visible light faced him. A temperature gauge appeared in the corner of his vision. A standard icon, a pillar with a bulbous base. Green filled the lower fourth of the icon.

The cloak trapped infrared radiating from his body. Too much time inside and he'd suffer heat stroke.

Get moving. He activated one of the heat absorbers near his right thigh with a subvoked command, then lowered the hood over his face and walked up the ramp toward the street.

The fabric passed light inward through the hood to his eyes. The cloak's folds distorted what he saw, but Stone easily observed the streets lacked pedestrians. Infrequent cars passed without slowing.

Somewhere in the sky, too small and transparent to see and too quiet to hear, the drone undoubtedly waited for his car to emerge from the parking garage. He kept his gaze at street level and turned south at the next intersection. Above him, balconies bulged from mid-rise apartments. Drawn curtains glowed in pleated oranges and yellows.

White brightness bloomed nearby. A rectangle of light at street level. Boisterous conversations and a band playing some old rock standard.

Stone drew a breath. The open door of a bar.

Two silhouettes emerged. Streetlights resolved the silhouettes into a couple, hands intertwined, leaning against each other.

They strolled toward him.

Stone padded sideways on rubber soles. Stood rigid against stippled granite. Held his breath.

The woman squinted in Stone's direction.

Adrenaline surged through his limbs. Did she see him? His hands clenched around non-existent weapons. His eyes widened, seeking the vulnerable strike points on their two bodies, eyes and necks and kidneys. His mind raced, how to dispose of two bodies—

The woman's squint turned into a self-deprecating shake of her head.

"You good, babe?" the man asked.

She leaned her cheek on her companion's shoulder. "I am now." The folds of the invisibility cloak obscured her face on the dim street, but her voice carried a smile. The couple ambled within a yard of Stone without another glance.

He waited ten seconds, then went on, past the pub's closed door. His legs shook for a dozen steps from adrenaline hangover. The near miss soured the sweat his body generated under the stifling cloak.

Inside a pocket, the activated heat absorber softened against his right thigh.

He strode toward the river. Euler City's streets remained quiet, like a small Midwestern town after nine at night. Under the cloak, though, sweat soaked his armpits and glued his shirt to his back. Yellow floated on top of green, halfway up the temperature gauge. The rod couldn't absorb all the heat his body generated, and it neared its limit.

A gap appeared ahead between the city's midrise buildings, just as the softened rod of heat absorber sloshed into liquid inside his pocket.

He strode with purpose toward the gap ahead. The Strigidae River rustled along hard surfaces somewhere beneath street level, rising up like an overture from the orchestra pit. A wisp of cooler air leaked up from under the cloak's hem.

Even so, the temperature gauge climbed faster, through the yellow. The first sliver of red sliced across the gauge.

Stone came to a bridge. An arch sprung from the sidewalk and climbed over the river. The arch's black alloy blotted out both slices of streetlight reflections off the granite fronts of buildings across the river and a handful of stars bright enough to shine through the light-polluted night sky.

He stepped over an expansion joint between the sidewalk and the bridge. A breeze from his right, from upriver, curled over a railing and pierced a chain link fence between the walkway and the drop to the river. A suspension cable, braided metal as thick as his upper arm, plunged from the arch into a stanchion bulging from the roadway.

Sweat streamed down his face. A salty taste trickled over his upper lip.

Stone stopped even with the cable stanchion and jutted his right hip toward the railing. *Vent.*

The melted heat-absorbing rod gurgled from its pocket and out a valve in the cloak. The liquid splashed and hissed against the railing. A stink of stripped paint curled his nose.

The temperature gauge plummeted back to green.

Stone caught his breath for a moment, then activated the second heat absorber and kept going.

Fifteen minutes later, under the fluted dark green foliage of an irrigated cypress, he vented the second heat absorber across the street from his objective.

Staggered slats about eight feet high and a foot wide formed a fence around the warehouse complex. The roofs and upper walls of the warehouses peeked over the fence. The roofs slanted to the north, aiming solar panels toward the track of Minerva's bright sun. Clerestory windows ringed the warehouse walls just under the roofline.

Stone gulped at fresh air. Made a decision.

He jutted his right hand out of the cloak's sleeve. A risk, but he had to take it. He panned the onyx ring across the sky to his north.

No sign of the drone.

He resisted the urge to shed the cloak immediately and scanned the sky in other directions. Only when his scan showed the drone had not followed him from the Center's parking garage did he shed the cloak. He folded it up, laid it down under the cypress, nudged a rock over it with his foot.

Two deep breaths. A shiver ran down his back as sweat evaporated into the cool desert night. Pleasant, but he could relax after he finished his mission. Stone shrugged to reseat his toolkit on his shoulders and set out like a local on a stroll.

He studied the fence around the warehouse complex with his peripheral vision. Cameras and microphones embedded in the fence had to be watching him but were too small for him to see.

A tendril curled in his gut. Could the Minervans have a facial recognition database complete enough for the cameras to determine he wasn't a local?

As slow as the local network seemed to be, he could make it back to the UN tower before any Minervans noticed.

He circled the warehouse complex. Two hinged pedestrian gates in opposite corners. A single roller gate for vehicles stood in the middle of one of the complex's long sides. Next to each pedestrian gate, a small black box mounted on the fence looked like a biometric access control panel. A similar black box appeared to be an override for the vehicle gate control.

Trying to get in through any of the three gates would fail, and reveal his intention to the invisibly small cameras.

In his toolkit he carried a few cubic inches of shape-memory alloys and thin fabric. A parasail. Glide over the fence... if he could find a high ledge to leap from.

Where?

Stone turned away from the vehicle gate onto a side street. Even quieter than the rest of the city. Empty pavement to his left, dark windows of a kettlebell gym and a testosterone clinic to his right. Above, yellow lamps glowed behind the drawn shades of apartment windows. In this neighborhood, the apartment windows lacked balconies.

He could make it work. Find an apartment whose occupant was

out for the evening. Break in without triggering an alarm or a security camera. Open a window and crouch on the sill. Jump off with enough upward force to parasail into the warehouse complex.

He winced. He could try if he had to—

A bluish-white glare bobbed against a cultured granite wall in front of him. Brakes hissed and a clattering sound followed.

A hunch fired his limbs before he could think. He sprinted across the street. Pressed his sweaty back against the granite wall of an alcove.

The light came from a vehicle approaching an intersection ahead of Stone. The vehicle's headlights swept across the clinic's windows, across where he'd stood seconds before.

He peeked out of the alcove. Sweeping curves, blue-black in the night, riding on tall tires, and an open cargo area to the back. A pickup truck. Three shadowy figures crowded the cab.

Another clatter sounded. A trailer bounced along behind the pickup's tow hitch. A rectangular cage twenty feet long, silvery and gleaming, with thin horizontal gaps near the roof, at about head height on cattle or horses. The Jezhek persona he'd used on New Moravia poked into Stone's consciousness like a corpse exposed by wind scattering the fill dirt over a shallow grave. A livestock trailer.

What brought a farm vehicle into the middle of the planet's only city?

He sniffed. The trailer smelled only of clean metal. Lacked any scent of hay or manure.

The truck slowly picked up speed.

Another hunch struck.

The cone of headlights passed Stone's hiding place. He ran toward the trailer. Eyed the end of a running board visible at the back corner. Jumped.

Stone landed deftly on the running board at the trailer's rear. His grip clamped on horizontal slats and he pulled himself against the trailer's back gate. Inches below his feet, the running board held the embedded discs of radar sensors.

He sucked in a breath, held it. The radar must have picked up some reflection as he ran and jumped, but the pickup had smoothly accelerated, a sign the pickup's autopilot had dismissed his radar reflection as noise. Unless one of the figures in the pickup had happened to glimpse him as he jumped on, he could ride the trailer wherever it might go.

The pickup slowed, turned onto the street running along the warehouse complex's long side. Yet even after making the turn, the pickup didn't accelerate.

Ahead of the truck, metal and hard plastic rattled.

Stone stole a glance around the corner of the trailer.

In the middle of the slatted fence, the vehicle gate rolled open.

11

The pickup veered left across the center of the street and made a wide right turn into the warehouse complex. It turned to the right. Tires whispered on fresh asphalt. Up came the welcome smells of tar and rubber. On Stone's right, a strip of grass ran along the driveway. Just beyond the grass, streetlights flared and vanished as the slatted fence flowed across his gaze. Warehouse buildings with high, dark windows slipped by on the left, like cargo ships docked in moonlight.

A growing brightness came from ahead and the left. The pickup slowed. Stone leaned away from the trailer's back gate and peered in the direction of the glow.

Stark white light glowed through a warehouse's clerestory windows. Halfway down the wall, illuminated by a spotlight, an e-ink sign named the warehouse's tenant as High Emprise LLC.

The pickup slowed further. "Truck's here!" called a man's voice outside the warehouse.

Dammit. If someone saw Stone now—

Stone jumped off the trailer to the right. Sprinted three steps over smooth asphalt toward a vehicle charging station. Crouched on the strip of grass between the charging station and the complex's outer fence.

The pickup and trailer rolled forward. Spotlights glared over a loading dock. More light spilled out from the warehouse interior through a rolled-up door in the middle of the wall. A man with a sharp nose and messy hair stood on the dock, hands in the back pockets of his pants and his gaze on the pickup's cab.

Record optic nerve input, Stone subvoked to his implantable. He peered past the man on the dock. Spindly racks of plastic or alloy receded into the warehouse interior, blurring like the stripes of a zebra herd.

He squinted. Just inside the door, two men draped black cloth over each shelf. What cargo did the racks bear? If he read the shape of the covered object or objects through the black cloth, not a man-sized drone.

Then what?

The pickup stopped. White lights on the trailer's back end flared. The pickup beeped monotonously and backed the trailer to the center of the loading dock. A man hopped out of the pickup's cab, from the side nearest Stone's hiding place, and puffed on a vape pen before the trailer's running board thudded against a rubber bumper embedded in the vertical face of the dock. The pickup's headlights whitewashed the asphalt in front of Stone's hiding place.

He froze. The men in the pickup and at the loading dock might not see him, but the glare pinned him behind the charging station. Move and they'd spot him immediately.

Stone squinted against the headlight glare. The pickup and trailer blocked most of his view of the warehouse door and the path between the door and the trailer's rear gate.

The pickup's door opened. Two men climbed out. The first, with a clipped black mustache, bowed his long neck when the second hopped down to the asphalt.

The second man looked past the other, his eyes like security cameras. The second man hadn't shaved his brown stubble for a week.

Stone's eyes widened. Simon Bale, one of High Emprise's owners and a councillor in the Minervan government.

What would the company load into the trailer?

How could he find out?

"You knew we were coming! Why aren't you ready?" Bale shouted.

Muffled voices responded. Indistinct words, but weak excuses judging by their tone.

"No more standing around!" Bale called. "Load up!"

Motion at the open warehouse door. Two human figures walked fore and aft of a spindly rack rolling under its own power. Both the black cloth and the narrow slice of his view past the trailer, he still couldn't tell what Bale's men loaded onto the trailers.

While he watched the men load the next rack, Stone slipped the toolkit off his back and rummaged inside. Muscle memory and sensitive fingers told him each item he touched. Flare gun. Rotary cutter. Flash bang grenade. A coiled forty-foot rappel line with an adhesive anchor—

Those would have to do.

Stone set the coiled rappel line on the grass near his left foot. Picked up the flash bang grenade. Small, the size and weight of a jar of hair pomade. A double activation, two buttons on the top and bottom. A slider on the side to select the effect. Four ounces, easy to throw….

He slid the switch to noise only. With his left thumb and forefinger, he pressed the activation buttons at the same time. Counted one thousand one. Threw the grenade in a high arc over the corner of the warehouse to his right. Picked up the coiled rappel line. Drew in one breath.

A *crack* echoed.

Stone ran soundlessly to his left along the grassy strip.

Men shouted behind him.

He glanced over his shoulder. Torsos twisted and necks craned away from him. He ran past the unlighted warehouse next to High Emprise's, then cut across the asphalt on nimble feet.

When the unlighted warehouse blocked the light from the loading dock, Stone slowed to a brisk walk. He caught his breath before he reached the back corner. He turned, then strode forward until he could peek at the rear side of High Emprise's warehouse.

The strip of windows at the top of the long wall gleamed with light. The pickup's headlights illuminated the charging station. Near the pickup, voices called to one another in strained tones. Simon Bale barked out commands to his men.

At the moment, no one patrolled on this side of High Emprise's warehouse.

Bale's men would need many seconds more to investigate the area on the far side. The flash bang grenade would have disintegrated, and the explosive residue should be odorless. Fifteen seconds, maybe thirty, before they reported negative findings to Bale.

Five seconds more before Bale would decide the noise could have been a diversion. Ten seconds from then for his men to follow his order to circle the warehouse.

Stone took the adhesive anchor with his right hand and held the main coil of the rappel line in his left. He padded across the gap between the warehouses. Activated the adhesive. Flung the anchor to the roof. The rappel line trailed behind, uncoiling from his left hand.

A faint splat above.

Stone tugged once. The adhesive held its grip.

He raced up the rope, pulling with his arms and walking his sneakers up the cultured granite wall. Arms only as he passed the windows—pounding the window with his feet would attract attention.

He clambered over the edge of the roof onto a black carpet of solar film. His arms ached.

No time for that. He whipped the line up from ground level. The rope burned between his palms. He winced and kept going until the line lay in a heap on the roof next to him.

From the back of the warehouse, noise. Footsteps. Low voices.

Stone lowered himself to the roof, head near the edge. He pressed the fingertips of his left hand hard against the smooth sunlight-absorbing film to keep from sliding forward and clutched the rope six inches from the adhesive with his right. He breathed cold night air deeply but quietly through a wide mouth.

Two pairs of footsteps came closer. "You seen anything?" one man muttered.

"No. What the hell made that sound?"

"Maybe a circuit blew the next warehouse over."

"You think so?"

The footsteps halted. "You got a better guess?"

The question hung for a moment, then the two men below walked away.

Once silence returned, Stone wriggled forward and peered over the edge. Nothing disturbed the space between warehouses. Out of sight to his left, men shouted and equipment rattled at the loading dock.

He ducked his chin toward his chest but only managed a steeply slanted view through the clerestory windows into the warehouse. Judging from the color, sheen, and number of roller racks inside, the warehouse held many more racks than would fit on the trailer. But what was on the roller racks?

He needed a better look. Simple to climb down ten feet of rope and look through the windows. Did he dare while Bale's men were active outside the warehouse?

No need. If they shipped out everything tonight, more trucks would come. He would only need a minute between trucks, when the men loading the vehicles would visit the toilet or the break room, to peer through the windows. If they didn't ship everything tonight, he would wait until the workmen went home and break in. Even if he tripped an alarm, the Euler City police or the Minervan equivalent of the FBI would likely conclude one of the workmen activated it improperly.

Stone sat cross-legged and coiled the rope around his ribcage.

"That's it!" boomed Bale's voice. Aluminum rang and scraped. Moments later, headlights swept across the fence. The truck rolled into view, heading for the vehicle gate. The trailer bounced along the asphalt. Even if the trailer's cargo filled its interior, its cargo weighed little.

A silence followed from the loading dock, broken by a rattling sound and the clang of metal against a hard surface. Bale's men had closed the loading door.

Thirty seconds, then Stone stood and unwound part of the rope. He peered over the edge, estimated lengths. When he had enough rope unwound, he backed his heels to the edge of the roof and jumped.

The rope jerked a grunt out of him. His feet thudded against the cultured granite a yard below the window, bounced off. He settled his feet and shifted his hands up the rope. Double-checked that his implantable recorded optic nerve data and had enough storage. Leaned forward. Looked in.

A rack stood alone in the middle of the floor with its long side facing Stone. Its shelves lacked any black cloth. A perfect view. The items on its shelves finally revealed themselves.

Drones. Translucent and small, no bigger than the one Bradley dell'Angelo had caught in his hands mere hours earlier. Each payload compartment held a tiny canister as blue as the sky over Central Park.

Drones. Four on a shelf, three shelves to a rack. Stone swallowed and turned his head to take in the entire warehouse. A hundred and twenty racks, maybe a hundred and fifty could have fit before Bale's men started moving them.

Drones. Roughly fifteen hundred of them.

Stone's arms ached. He climbed the rope and lay down on the roof to gulp more cold air from the desert night. He replayed the video his implantable had just captured from his eyes.

The cold air entering his lungs failed to dispel a burning at the base of his mind.

Fifteen hundred drones. Bound for the wormhole. Fifteen hundred drones heading to Earth. They could traverse the wormhole tomorrow, within minutes after the wormhole was sited, before work crews on Minerva and Earth could complete the road and rail links between homeworld and colony.

He zoomed in on the payloads. Cans of peaceful, restful blue, camouflaged against a sunny Earth sky.

What the hell did they carry?

The burning inside him turned to a chill stippling gooseflesh on his arms and legs.

One of High Emprise LLC's owners had expertise in medical nanotechnology.

The small canisters carried nothing good.

Stone bolted to a sitting position and rapidly unwound the rope from around his torso. Any wasted second could be fatal.

To billions.

12

Stone stalked down a thickly-carpeted corridor in the UN tower. His toolkit bounced against his back with every step. Doors along the beige walls, shiny aluminum numbers in an art deco font. Room 4841… there. He halted, rapped his knuckles on brown synthetic wood, angled his ear toward the door.

Ten seconds, no sound. He rapped with quicker tempo, greater force.

Ten more seconds. Inside the room, footsteps shuffled closer. A woman's voice, soft and sleepy, clashing with the memory image of Annika Kim's high cheekbones and slitted eyes. "Who's it?"

"Edward."

As if she'd never spoken the name before: "Edward?"

Despite his hurry, old habits kicked in. Can't let a woman see you out of control. He smirked and enunciated, "La-va-lette."

"What are you doing here? At—Christ, it's 0200?"

"It's important. Very."

"In the morning."

"No. Now. Every second counts."

The magnetic locks released with a thud. The door swung open. A disheveled lock of jet-black hair dangled in front of Annika's left eye. She sniffed and her nose wrinkled. Stone realized how much he stank of sweat from his time under the invisibility cloak.

She nodded at a yellow, floral-printed couch. The color summoned up the dossier photo of Simon Bale. "Take a seat," she said.

Stone perched himself on the edge of the cushion. He splayed his hands and tapped his fingertips together in a quick rhythm.

Annika sat in an armchair covered in matching fabric turned at a right angle to the couch. She pulled her disarrayed hair back into place and tied a ponytail with an elastic band. "If every second counts, start talk—"

A faint whine of a turning hinge, and a vertical sliver of darkness widened at the bedroom door. Her skinny, bearded boyfriend, Jordan, was it? studied Stone with narrowed eyes. "Anni, what's going on?"

"Nothing important. Go back to bed. I'll be back soon."

Jordan nodded but stayed in place. He eyed Stone with a mix of anger and fear. Not the first time Stone ever encountered that reaction.

Annika said, with emphasis, "Go back to bed."

Finally, Jordan backed out of the doorway. He swung the door most of the way closed, but a sliver of darkness remained. Eavesdropping.

Stone lowered his voice. "Thank you for talking with me. I don't know anyone else who works for ITB and I couldn't think of how else to get word to whoever needs to know."

"Know what?"

He took a breath. "ITB must abort tomorrow's wormhole placement."

She folded her arms over her chest. Her eyes turned into arrow slits. "You woke me up at 0200 for some practical joke?" She whispered harshly through clamped lips. "I thought you were man enough to not be petty that I found Jordan."

"I'm more than man enough for that. Why I'm here is a billion times more important. ITB must not place the wormhole until someone checks out what I've seen and says it's safe."

Annika squinted. "Nothing's unsafe about the wormhole site. We checked for seismic issues—"

"Not a risk of wormhole containment failure. Much worse."

"Nothing could be wor—"

"The Minervans are going to release a plague."

For a moment, her eyes flashed wide. "A plague. Really?"

"Hand to God." He chuffed out a breath, amused at the line. The producer's office seemed to lie years, not months, in the past. And he'd never reeled in Tarquinia....

Annika shook her head, bringing him back fully to the present. "But the rail and road lines will take days to connect to Earth. Without trains or buses, no disease carrier—"

"They don't need rail or road connections. They're going to deliver the plague through the air by drones."

"Drones." She rubbed her eyes, then suddenly scowled. "I said, no practical jokes."

"I'm seri—"

"How did you, some tech transfer bureaucrat whose main talent is talking to drunk women until they say 'yes,' discover this dastardly Minervan plot?"

He'd precooked a lie while parasailing from the warehouse's roof over the complex's slatted fence. "I visited a medical nanotechnology company. I took a wrong turn coming out of the restroom and stumbled into a storage facility full of drones in biohazard bags."

The bedroom door creaked. Annika scowled that direction. "Jordan, I *said*—"

"Too thirsty to sleep." He shuffled across the living room, boxers and a wrinkled tee shirt draped over his slender frame. "Don't mind me," he said through a yawn as he entered the kitchen.

Stone said nothing. His splayed fingers tapped each other more rapidly now. How long did the man need to pour a glass of water? Finally, water gurgled from the tap. Jordan emerged from the kitchen, scratching his beard, his gaze down on the glass of water in his hand.

This time he shut the bedroom door completely. Rather than guard his mate, however feebly, by eavesdropping, he preferred to go back to sleep.

Neither one of them would be happy together with two kids and a house off the Van Wyck Expressway in Queens.

Stone inhaled, focused his thoughts. An unhappy marriage lying in the future of some woman he'd seduced didn't mean a damn compared to what the Minervans threatened.

"Drones in biohazard bags?" Annika said.

"Hundreds."

"At a med nano company?"

Stone nodded.

"You uncovered their plot and they just let you walk out?"

"They were so nonchalant and they lied so smoothly about what I'd seen that they had to be up to something." Frustration ran through his voice.

She raised a stylus-thin eyebrow. "That's it? You want to call off the wormhole placement because you have a hunch the locals are up to something?"

"Not permanently. Keep the wormhole in orbit until someone can investigate."

Annika's gaze roved his face, clearly looking for a waver in his confidence. "Are you crazy? I can't go to my supervisor based on your hunch. Never mind him going to his supervisor, then her to hers, before wormhole placement ops can even tell you no."

He held out his hands. "Please. You have to. If there's even a one percent chance I'm right—"

"If."

"—how many people on Earth would die?"

She let out a breath in seeming exasperation. "Let me think on it."

"Don't think. Act. You can go to your boss based on my hunch. You know how to persuade him."

Her eyebrow sliced upward like the edge of a knife. "I do? And how would you know that?"

Stone put on a leer. A shame Jordan couldn't see it. He lowered his voice. "I've seen you up close."

Annika scowled. "I'll think on it. Now you have to go."

He blew out a breath and stood. Something in his toolkit clanked. "Don't let the deaths of billions ride your conscience."

"I'll think on it."

He read her tone of voice. A slim chance Annika would bring his request to her supervisor, let alone that it would reach the head of wormhole ops in time.

What to do? Find someone higher in the ITB hierarchy and make the same desperate pitch to them?

Stone's heart slowed and pounded like a gong. A smirk touched the corners of his mouth.

He still had ten hours to save Earth.

Stone left the room and turned toward the elevator bank. On his right, UN employee rooms along the outside of the tower. If this floor had the same layout as his, the sporadic doors to the left led to utility spaces. Exit signs marked emergency stairwells down the building's interior. Out of hard-learned habit, he kept the exit sign locations in mind, updating them as he traveled the hallway.

He mapped out his next steps. Down to the motor pool. Out to the Berglund Ecoseeding site. Find the trailers full of airborne death. He could improvise a weapon from what he carried on his back—

Around the corner ahead and to the left, an elevator door dinged. A short yet thickly-muscled man ambled around the corner, rubbing his eyes with stubby fingers. More casual than business: all the buttons of his polo shirt hung open and its tail rode over his pants. He smelled of sweat, not alcohol. He gave an amiable grunt when they passed.

Stone turned the corner to the elevator bank.

Another man waited. Despite the late hour, his gray eyes regarded Stone at full alert. He wore his polo shirt tucked and the right hip pocket of his tactical pants bore the unmistakable print of a handgun.

The hallway suddenly seemed colder. A chill shivered down his back. He'd seen the two men on *Yassir Arafat*. Security officers.

Who now stood between him and the nearest emergency exits.

"Evening," Stone said. He continued walking on a line toward the elevators, as if he disregarded the gray-eyed man.

The man sidestepped across Stone's path. Stone halted. The man asked, "What are you doing on this floor at this hour, Mr. Lavallette?"

"Calling on a lady."

"To stop tomorrow's wormhole placement?"

Stone put on a squint. His thoughts roiled. Why would Annika have called security—?

Not Annika. Jordan, eavesdropping from the bedroom. Too meek to throw a romantic rival out of his girlfriend's suite. What a pathetic, spineless—

Forget him. Talk your way past *them*.

"Stop? I tried to make the placement." He grinned sidelong. "Two foreign bodies coexisting in one spot, know what I mean?"

The man's gray eyes remained as flat as a river rock. "We heard different. Didn't we?"

"Sure did." Behind Stone, the shorter man's voice squeaked incongruously with his muscular build. He'd come closer, but not too close. About twenty feet away. Far enough to give himself time to react to any sudden attack or feint Stone might make against him.

"Here's what we're going to do, Mr. Lavallette." The first man's gray eyes glimmered. "You're going to come to our facility in the basement and you're going to stay there overnight. After the wormhole gets sited, then we'll have a talk. You'll tell us who put you up to disrupting our whole reason for coming here, and we'll check out your story. If it corroborates—" He enunciated the word. Mockery danced in his gray eyes. "—then you can go about your business."

Stone licked his lips. He could probably take them—the gray-eyed man would find it impossible to draw his pistol in time. Stone could crush his trachea and use him as a shield until he could take out the pocketed pistol and shoot the shorter man.

Did they deserve to die? Two men-at-arms, doing the king's duty according to their station?

Where did that thought come from? He'd killed better men than them on flimsier grounds.

Another thought elbowed into his mind. How long would Gray sideline him for killing two poor bastards who were only doing their jobs, when he had another option? Six months? A year?

The rest of his life?

But the other option would reveal—

—assuming Caitlyn had ever trusted him? Come on—

With a smile, Stone shook his head. "Here's what we're going to do instead. You two are going to activate Protocol Eleven-J. Then my implantable will transmit the encrypted authentication and yours will receive and decrypt it. After that, I'll walk away and you'll tell no one about our little transaction."

"Eleven-J?" squeaked the shorter man.

A head shake accompanied a roll of gray eyes. "We'd know if Lavallette were authorized to invoke it."

"Then my encrypted authentication will fail," Stone said. "Activate."

The gray eyes blinked. Through his pants' fabric, his right hand patted his pistol's grip. "Done."

"Me too," came from behind Stone.

Stone subvoked. A green checkmark appeared over the head of the gray-eyed man and a cheerful *ding* sounded. A moment later, a second green checkmark joined the first and there came another *ding*.

He tensed like a coiling spring. If these two belonged to Caitlyn's conspiracy—

The gray-eyed man's torso rocked. "Mister—Lavallette?—"

"Keep calling me that."

"We, uh, we didn't know—"

"Obviously."

The gray-eyed man raised his palms in a double stop gesture. "We'll scrub the call from our records and we'll tell wormhole ops to abort—"

"Don't bother. They won't believe you. There's nothing more you can do for me."

Their silence would prove useless. The protocol Eleven-J activation left a trail in the tower's computer network. Even though the activation record would anonymize Stone's role, if Caitlyn or her cronies received a notification that someone had invoked the protocol, she would infer that only he could have requested it.

"Excuse me, gentlemen." He strode toward the elevator. The gray-eyed man stepped out of his way. The door opened as Stone approached.

"Motor pool." His voice echoed off the walls of the elevator car. The doors slid toward each other. "Wait!"

The doors stopped, half-closed. Through the space, he called, "You *can* do one more thing for me."

"Yes, Mr. Lavallette?" said the gray-eyed man.

"Give me your sidearms."

Whispered debate ensued between the two security men. The debate ended with them both extending their pistols butt-first toward Stone. He took them one by one, studied them with a single glance. Standard UN rent-a-cop issue, plastic and stamped steel, 9mm with a fifteen round magazine, and heavy triggers designed to keep improperly trained men with fingers habitually inside the trigger guard from accidentally shooting.

He double-checked the safeties, then dropped the pistols in the loose pockets of his jogging shorts.

Thirty rounds and ten hours to save the Earth.

More than enough of both.

13

Twenty minutes found the golf course and the last houses of Euler City receding behind his sedan from the UN motor pool. Instead of turning right at Berglund Ecoseeding's evergreen nursery, Stone headed down the highway past the intersection. "Slow."

The car obeyed. Stone studied a map projected into his visual field, then blanked it with a subvoked word. The headlights tracked the highway's curve to the right around the rocky mound.

He glanced out the rear window. The mound blocked from his view the intersection and the side road leading to his meeting site with Caitlyn—and, presumably, also leading to the staging site for High Emprise's plague drones. No glint of headlights behind him. He took another look. Nor in front.

"Pull over."

The car rolled to a stop on the highway's wide, paved shoulder. It cut its headlights, plunging the terrain into a moment of extreme darkness. Stone crouched on the floor in the center of the cabin, as far as he could get from the infrared eyes of any Minervan drone that might have followed him, and slipped the invisibility cloak over his head and arms.

Just an ITB employee, heading to the wormhole site on some last minute errand, stopping for some embarrassing purpose. That's what the Minervans should think if they matched this car to the motor pool request Stone had forged.

He told the car to open the door on the right side, away from the main lanes of the highway. Five thousand stars shone as clear and cold as Siberian diamonds in the cloudless sky. The cloak's stifling interior would be pleasantly warm, at least at first, in the desert night.

Stone lifted his toolkit from the rear seat, then slipped out of the car. His sneakers padded on smooth asphalt until he turned for the rocky mound. As he climbed, pebbles skittered from his sneakers and trickled downslope.

He took one step over the crest and sat cross-legged next to a thorny bush. He draped the back of the invisibility cloak onto stunted branches, careful to keep the fabric from tearing. Chill night air lifted sweat from his back. The next-to-last of his heat absorbing rods remained firm in its pocket against his hip. The temperature gauge visible in his mind's eye still showed green. For now.

The cooling provided by the night would extend the time he could wait.

He opened the toolkit. The fingers of his right hand found the object he sought. He squished a soft one-inch cube, stroked his fingertip over the activation button. Starlight cast a sheen on the cube's shrinkwrap.

Stone slowly breathed pine-scented air and kept still. He looked past the potted evergreens across the side road. His gaze hovered on the diffuse smear of light rising from Euler City above the eastern horizon.

Twenty minutes passed before blue-white light glinted behind a roll in the terrain half a mile away. Headlights came into view. The array of potted trees diffracted the glow. A distant, bouncing rattle reached Stone's ears.

The vehicle slowed. Stone ducked his head. Excess fabric from the cloak's cowl slid down his face and pooled over his breastbone.

The vehicle turned to its right, his left. The cloak distorted the vehicle's outline and its headlights blue-white glare. A moment later, the glare began to diminish.

He snapped his head up. Whipped the cloak back with his left hand. An extended cab pickup pulled a trailer twin to the one he'd ridden into the warehouse complex.

Stone squeezed the activation button on the cube with his right index finger. Tossed the cube in a low arc onto the trailer's roof.

The truck and trailer proceeded to the north. Stone scrambled over the crest of the mound and jogged back to his car. He climbed in and shucked the cloak while his implantable projected a map into his vision.

Three-eighths of a mile to the north, out of sight behind the first of the parallel ridges crossing the side road, the truck and trailer drove onward.

The tracking beacon in the small cube functioned properly.

Stone tossed the invisibility cloak into a corner of the cabin. He panted three, four breaths of cold air from the vents. No more time to waste.

"To the wormhole site," he said.

The car's headlights illuminated the empty blue-black asphalt ahead. The electric motor engaged and the car pulled from the shoulder onto the main lanes.

Five minutes later, the car took a flyover ramp suspended above empty desert onto the highway to the wormhole. The ramp descended to a divided highway, pristine and empty of traffic, like a freeway leading to one of the planned-cities-turned-ghost-towns that dotted the Third World. Five minutes after that, a concrete barrier narrowed the carriageway to one lane. The car coasted to a stop at a robotic arm extending across the road. The concrete barrier held the arm's pivot and connected at the back side with a mesh fence eight feet tall and topped with coiled razor wire. A sign on the fence next to the concrete pillar read *United Nations Interstellar Transport Bureau Wormhole Infrastructure Division. No Trespassing.*

A robotic camera on a telescoping arm emerged from behind the barrier and extended toward the car window. Stone opened the window and stared at the microphone.

"Name?" asked an artificial female voice.

Stone grinned. Robots had one advantage over human security officers. Robots didn't question when an operative invoked Protocol Eleven-J.

The arm swung up. Stone drove in.

Construction trucks and stacks of alloy trusses loomed on both sides of the highway. Plastic zip ties as thick as his arm lashed the trusses together and secured backhoes and front end loaders to the main bodies of their vehicles. Battening down the hatches before fusion exhaust descended half a mile ahead, beyond the reach of his headlight beams.

After the last parked construction vehicle, the highway continued toward the crater. To the right, a wide strip of dirt, gouged from Minerva's thin topsoil and grooved by hundreds of knobby, man-high tires ran perpendicular from the highway. "Turn there."

The car stopped on the highway like a skittish donkey. The electric motor turned off.

The hell? Ah. "Turn off transponder assistance. Switch to full self-driving."

Transponder assistance required formed in his vision, red letters against a black box. *Full self-driving mode disabled.*

Stone squeezed his forehead. Dammit. The UN limited its personnel to only routes it had mapped.

He grinned. *Most* of the UN's personnel. He spoke again to the car.

Double dammit. The UN's cars failed to respond to Protocol Eleven-J.

So be it. He exited the car and slung his toolkit onto his back. Tapped the pistols through the fabric of his shorts. Both there. Then he scanned down a mental checklist, nodded to himself. Nothing else he needed from the car. "Go home."

Travel without you? Please confirm.

"Confirmed. Go."

The car backed into a three-point turn. After the headlights turned away from him, Stone pivoted to the north. A faint breeze sighed over rocky ground, heightening the night's chill over his bare arms and legs. Beyond nearby clumps of cactus and thorny brush, the crater poked its jagged rim toward the stars.

He checked the map in his mind's eye. The truck and trailer had stopped moving, somewhere up the gravel road five miles beyond the wormhole site.

Time to get going.

Stone took loping strides onto the dirt track. He aimed his feet at the deepest ruts, the ones most traveled by the heaviest vehicles. Compacted dirt gave firmer footing and reduced the impress of his shoes. He passed stacked drums labeled *bioasphalt - biodegradable packaging*. The smell of tar wafted through the cool night air.

The dirt track curved to the right, where stood the main formation of parked trucks. He turned left, onto hard ground, toward the wormhole.

His destination might be five miles as the crow flew, but on foot lay even more distant. Near the wormhole and the construction site, an area both UN personnel and Minervans would pack in the morning, he wound his way around tufts of brittle grass and thorns jutting from cactus. Someone skilled at bushcraft could track him like a Cape buffalo if he blundered across the terrain.

Half a mile north of the wormhole, low to the ground, a haze shimmered faintly in the starlight. Stone moved closer. The haze resolved into a six-foot chain link fence crossing his path. Beyond, narrowly-packed stripes of darker ground ran from the fence into distant darkness.

The farm between the wormhole site and the evergreen forest where the Minervans staged their drones of death.

Stone stopped at the fence and kneeled on dusty ground. He spat on a link and listened for a sizzle. Silence.

Good. Not electrified.

He dropped his toolkit off his back and reached inside. Pulled out shears with diamond blades. Snipped a link at ground level.

More silence. No alarms. At least, none here. Perhaps in a security office or police station miles away, where a bleary-eyed dispatcher would send an officer out in the morning.

He cut more links. Shook his head. Most colonies had ramshackle law enforcement. Minerva bore little resemblance to most colonies.

Could he get across the farm in time to avoid a local policeman?

The pistols tugged down Stone's pockets. A local policeman wouldn't stand a chance. Some poor bastard doing his job, ignorant of the evils that Caitlyn, Simon Bale, and the others prepared to unleash, would have to die if he did his job too well. A shame.

Stone finished cutting a flap in the fence, then pulled it back and crawled through. He yanked his toolkit through, strapped it to his back, and stood.

Rows of slender plants crowded him. The highest leaves blocked swathes of stars. Only a pulsing red target projected onto his vision by his implantable showed the direction to go. He pushed forward between two rows and rough leaves brushed his bare arms. A humid smell drifted up from the bases of each stalk, where green LEDs pierced the shadows cast by the leaves and made irrigation pipes, drip valves, and data cables glow as if seen in night vision.

He couldn't identify the plants and didn't care. He pushed on.

The rows veered to the right and climbed a contour in the rocky terrain. The target crept to the left across his vision until it lined up with his shoulders.

Stone peered ahead. The massed stalks denied him a view of the end of the rows. His low-visibility passage between the rows would have to end.

He sidestepped up sloping ground to his left. A leaf's point scratched his upper arm. Fortunately the stalk straightened back up when he entered—

Another space between rows. He sidestepped through again. Again. Again—

He broke through into a clear strip about eight feet across. The clear strip ran lengthwise along the sharp edge of a ridge, a feature of Minerva's pre-terraforming not eroded by a few decades of wind and rain. Rows of the same plants followed contour lines on the opposite, downslope side of the ridge.

Stone's gaze snapped up. Thousands of stars blazed. He glanced north, west. Part of him sought the Big Dipper, Polaris, and the evening star. Failed to find them.

He shook his head. Sheila van Bentum and the icons of her non-religion didn't matter a damn. He had work to do. Billions of lives to save—

You don't care about those lives and you know it.

Stone squinted into the darkness. A cover story flashback. Maybe traces of the Jezhek persona from New Moravia, or the Becker one from Trinity, had survived removal after their missions and leaked out of his subconscious now while adrenaline and lack of sleep distracted him.

He shrugged and crossed the ridgeline. He did care; those lives were useful to him.

A bubble of disdain burst on the surface of his subconscious.

He snorted out a breath as he sidestepped across the first row of plants on the downslope. People were useful to him. The women in their twenties, yes, for the obvious reason, but many more. The techs in the armory and cover stories branch who equipped him for missions. Gray for providing a fig leaf for his naked pursuit of the thrill of action.

Hell, even Manhattan's teeming millions were useful. The kettlebell trainer at his gym. The wizened old Korean man who ran the hotdogs-with-kimchi cart on the corner. The men and women who maintained his building, hauled away trash, cleaned the streets.

Beyond that, how many billion people contributed to the economic web supporting him in First World luxury?

He pushed aside stems that sprung back at him, swatted rough-edged leaves at his face.

And how many of those billions would become even more useful to him if they found their varna, their estate of the realm?

He stopped between two rows of plants and stretched his arms to the sky. Eyes closed. Head leaned back. Breathe in. Breathe out.

Stone opened his eyes. The stars above glittered coldly.

Earth's billions couldn't grow more useful if Caitlyn and her fellow conspirators killed them.

Forget all this philosophy. How much and why he wanted to stop Caitlyn and the others paled compared to his purpose in life. He was born to kill people and break things.

Partially veiled by the rows of plants in front of him, the red target pulsed about three miles away.

Make it to the target and he would have a chance to fulfill his purpose.

14

The eastern sky still lacked any hint of dawn as Stone crawled between pines up a slope. Needles brushed his face and an evergreen scent filled his nose. A cone fell nearby, hitting a rock and sending a crack echoing through the trees.

He froze, listened. Only insects and small animals made noise nearby. From ahead came far more interesting sounds. The clang of equipment. The calls of men to one another.

He reached the crest and peered over.

The ridges in the landscape ran parallel and about two hundred yards apart. Beyond the next one, a red arrow aimed downward at a valley hidden from his sight. Red glimmered over the pines beneath the arrow, like the glow of a forest fire.

Target marker off, he subvoked to his implantable. He no longer needed directions to the drone launch site.

The red arrow vanished. The glimmer remained.

Not from fire. From worklights scattered around the launch site, to give Bale's men light enough to work by while still keeping their night vision.

So much for strolling into the launch site unseen.

Stone glanced to the east. Checked his watch. An hour before dawn. Perhaps thirty minutes before twilight would render moot the night vision of Bale's men by exposing him to the naked eye.

Had Bale's men already detected him with augmented senses? No sign of it. According to the onyx ring on his finger, the sky lacked the heat signatures of airborne drones and the forest around him lacked active sensors. He'd listened for armed men patrolling the woods and heard only the hoots of owls and the skittering of small creatures in the undergrowth. He seemed to be secure here.

But from here he couldn't see the drone launch site in the valley. Let alone stop Bale's men.

He eyed the next ridge. Just a hundred yards from the site. Could he make it there while remaining unseen? And stay unseen while he reconnoitered the site?

In his mind he ran through the items in his toolkit. An idea erupted. He smiled to himself in the starlit gloom, then crept downslope.

Three minutes to the bottom of the valley. A gully wound across his path. Dry but for the black splotch of a nearby puddle shadowed from starlight by tree cover. He kneeled in the gully with a thick-trunked pine providing further cover in case Bale's men looked his way from the ridgeline.

A mosquito bit his neck. Stone swatted at it, but broke off before his hand smacked against his skin. The mosquito buzzed away from the motion.

Stone rubbed the bite against his shoulder and silently cursed. For all their advances, the Minervan ecological engineers couldn't omit mosquitoes from their artificial paradise.

Back to work. From his toolkit he withdrew the folded invisibility cloak. Only two heat-absorbing rods left, but he wouldn't need them. He pulled from another pocket the parasail. Now, a compact mass of collapsing spars folded into eight-inch lengths and sleeved by thin strong sailcloth. But soon....

Soundlessly he straightened the spars length by length. He found his toolkit knife and sliced the sailcloth off the spars, hunched over his work with his back to Bale's men to muffle the sound of fabric tearing. More knifework gave him strips of sailcloth. He tied the strips around the spars to form a low wedge shape about three feet wide and four long.

Next, he draped the invisibility cloak over the wedge, tied it to the frame of spars, and crawled underneath. With luck, the open end of the wedge would let in enough cool air to keep him comfortable if his observation lasted long after sunrise.

He snaked his binoculars' fiber optic stalks over the frame crosspiece and under the cloak at the wedge's point. Tightened the strap cinching the binoculars' cups to his eyes. The pines upslope from him formed deep shadows against the red glow suffusing from the launch site.

Stone activated the cloak's invisibility and infrared blocking functions and crawled upslope. He pushed the frame by the crosspiece and slowly picked his way over grass and pine straw, avoiding rocks that might clank and brush that might rattle with his motion. The ground jabbed the pocketed pistols into his hips.

He cocked his ear for sounds from over the ridge, checked the binoculars for Bale's men. Nothing to see. Only the sounds of men and equipment working in the next valley.

Ahead, a dwarf pine sprouted from a crevice in the ridgeline, a yard from a scruffy shrub. He nudged the left corner of the wedge against the pine's roots and stopped. The right corner nestled soundlessly under the shrub's coiled branches and needle-like leaves. The lenses on the fiber optic stalks peeped over the crest. Through the forest on the next ridge, twilight paled the eastern horizon.

He raised his hand to his temple and worked controls. The fiber optic stalks peered downward into the valley.

A camouflage net hung taut over a clearing of sparse grass and pebbly dirt. Red globes dangled from the net, providing light. The net covered the truck and trailer, which were parked next to a canopy about twenty feet square and eight feet off the ground. Some of Bale's men guided roller racks down a ramp from the back of the trailer to the ground. More men unloaded drones from the racks and carried them away from Stone and up the far slope of the valley. Closer to his observation post, a large number of empty roller racks leaned against trunks or lay sideways on pine straw.

Stone quickly counted a rough fraction of the empty racks and multiplied to get a full estimate. A hundred-twenty-five, give or take ten. Which meant the trailer had likely made its final trip from the warehouse.

He panned over two men who looked like security personnel with holstered pistols at their hips standing at an SUV's open cargo hatch. They looked to be watching monitors set up inside.

Stone's heart beat a little faster. Checking the perimeter, but they hadn't found him yet. He aimed the fiber optics at the canopy.

Another red globe hung from the center over a sitting area of folding chairs. The red globe yielded enough light for Stone to identify four people, seated, conversing. Simon Bale stroked his beard. Bradley dell'Angelo ran one hand through his feathery hair, then dropped his hand to join his other in his lap. Despite khaki cargo pants and a matching shirt, Sheila van Bentum's mound of blond hair identified her.

Caitlyn Fredriksen crossed her long legs and listened to the Minervans with a thoughtful look in her hazel eyes. Her conscience wrestling with the cognitive dissonance of believing she would save the world by killing billions?

He shook his head, refocused. He pegged the distance to the canopy as seventy-five yards. Three times the effective range of his pistols. He would have to get closer. At twenty yards he could charge in, put two rounds in each person's chest, and sprint upslope before Bale's men reacted.

He panned around the clearing. Enough predawn light percolated through the pines for him to count Bale's men. Fifteen workers lacking visible weapons, and five armed men, the two at the SUV and three others patrolling the clearing. Get out of the perimeter, stay twenty-five yards ahead of the guards, and sneak into the wormhole site where he could invoke Protocol Eleven-J.

The plan might work.

A bird chirped. Another of its species answered. A sliver of sunlight touched the tops of the tallest trees on the far slope of the valley.

But how to infiltrate without camouflage in daylight, with two dozen pairs of eyes and ears in the area?

A diversion? He'd used his only flash grenade the night before.

Wait till the wormhole tugs descended through the atmosphere? The roar of spaceship engines and the distorted sphere of the wormhole itself just five miles away would attract everyone's attention. Bale and the others wouldn't launch the drones until the wormhole mouth rested on Minerva's surface. He had time—

One of the security men from the SUV, his hair sandy blond and his tactical pants wrinkle-free, came into view under the canopy. He stopped in front of Bale with his back to Stone. Presumably the sandy-haired man spoke to his superior, words inaudible from Stone's distance. Bale looked up and a sour look scrunched his mouth. He nodded once. The sandy-haired man tugged his earlobe and hurried from the canopy.

Stone's mouth turned dry. He tracked the sandy-haired man back to the SUV. The man said something curt to his comrade. The two returned their attention to the monitors in the cargo space. The same low alert level as before, the only change being the sandy-haired man's toes now tapped the dusty ground. Zooming out showed the other guards continued to patrol at the same level of alert.

Stone zoomed in on the canopy. There things had changed.

Bale, on his feet now, towered over Caitlyn. His fists pressed against his hips, his elbows jutted out. His shoulders and head bobbed from vigorous speech. Stone saw his mouth from too sharp an angle to read his lips.

Amusement danced in Caitlyn's hazel eyes.

Bale leaned toward her. Spoke again.

Her hazel eyes turned cold. Caitlyn uncrossed her long legs and stood. She twisted her lithe upper body over Bale's jutting elbow and moved her mouth close to his ear. She gestured toward Sheila, who replied with an uncertain series of quick nods.

Bale pivoted to Sheila. His body language suggested brusque speech.

Sheila flinched, then lifted her chin and stared in the direction of Bale's eyes. Her mouth moved in what might have been *Yes*.

Bale held his position for a second, then shrugged. His hands opened and fell down his sides. Everyone returned to their seats.

What the hell just happened? Stone studied each face, but the argument seemed to be over.

He zoomed back out. The guards continued their patrol, their monitoring.

All normal. In front of his position.

Stone pulled the binoculars off his head and rotated his body in a half-circle under the invisibility cloak. Pebbles nibbled at him through his clothes. When his head poked out the back of the wedge, he darted his gaze around, then held still and listened. Only animal sounds. Only a small black bird moved, winding among the pines.

He swept the onyx ring across each patch of sky visible between trees. Bale's men failed to observe him from above.

Stone turned back around and watched the site through his binoculars while he listened for the motion of men behind him.

Minerva's sun climbed the eastern sky. Flying insects buzzed under the invisibility cloak, drawn perhaps by the trapped heat from his body. Something crawled along his nape. He reached back and pinched. A carapace crackled and goo squirted onto his fingers.

He continued to watch. The workmen guided the last empty roller racks into the heap amid the trees downslope. Three racks leaned together against a pine just twenty yards from the canopy. The racks left a space at the base of the tree large enough to hide a man. The guards patrolled. The two security men watched their equipment inside the SUV.

Stone's gaze tracked a path from his location to the three racks, by way of broad tree trunks, a lumpy gray boulder, and shrubs within the undergrowth. If he went quickly when the wormhole descent distracted the security personnel and the workmen, he could reach the hiding space under the three racks. Close enough to sprint to the canopy and kill Caitlyn and the others within ten seconds. He only had to wait for the descent.

From the east thumped metal and rubber. A car door.

He turned the lenses that direction. The forest and an intervening ridge or two hid the vehicle.

Who drove up? One or both of Gerald Berglund or Matthew Thomas, the other two owners of High Emprise LLC? No. Their car would have rolled to a stop next to the canopy. More security men to block the dirt track leading to the clearing? Or the car might carry some fun-seeking Minervans driving toward the wormhole site to get a better view of the descent, who ran into a roadblock Bale's men might've set up hours ago.

Stone clenched and relaxed the muscles in his arms and legs to loosen stiffness. His body handled stakeouts better in previous years. No help for that. He had to wait until the wormhole provided a distraction.

The morning warmed. Animals made less noise in the brush around his hiding place.

He waited. And waited. And—

Men in the clearing stopped work and looked high in the western sky. The guards did the same. Their hands dangled past their holsters.

Stone craned his neck. Despite the blurring effect of the cloak, a pinpoint of light reached him. He angled his ear that direction but no sound came. The wormhole tugs approached but had not yet entered Minerva's atmosphere. A thought flavored by traces of the Becker persona told him he had thirty minutes before the wormhole reached the crater floor.

The corners of his mouth curled up. Bale's men milled about with bent-back heads. He wouldn't need to wait that long.

Bale rose from his camp chair and cupped his hands around his mouth. "We're not spectators! Get to work!"

Workmen lurched up the far slope, toward where the unloaded drones must be waiting. The guards drifted after the workmen like sheepdogs behind and flanking a flock. Apparently they only expected a threat to come from the UN personnel crewing the wormhole site.

Stone turned the lenses toward the SUV. The two security personnel still watched their monitors, except when they stole a glance at the descending wormhole.

Bale's men wouldn't know what hit their boss, Caitlyn, and the others until long after Stone fled into the surrounding forest.

Binoculars back to the canopy. Bale stood, watching the workmen, his back to Stone's vantage point. The other three joined him and looked in the same direction.

Stone's heart thumped. A predator poised to pounce. You could shoot a person in the heart and lungs from the back as easily as the front.

He glanced over his shoulder. Nothing but trees, shrubs, and rocks.

Stone uncinched the binoculars. Slipped the pistol from his right pocket and worked it between his chest and the ground. A stamped steel corner poked his pectoral muscle. He chambered the first round with his left hand controlling the slide backward and forward. A faint click muffled by his body's mass. He thumbed off the safety. Returned the pistol to his pocket. Repeated with the other firearm.

Final scan of his path. All clear.

Go.

He crawled backwards from under the invisibility cloak. Still on his belly, he went to his right, behind the shrub.

He grasped a coiled, woody root with his left hand, then reached his right hand past the shrub, over the crest—

A semicircular chorus of semiautomatic rifle slides jacked cartridges into chambers behind him. A crisp male voice said, "Chalmers. Freeze."

15

Stone froze. His gaze remained over the crest, and the thick-trunked pine he'd planned to crouch and run to. Twenty feet away, but might as well be twenty miles.

How the hell had they detected him? How had he missed seeing them when he'd checked the area behind his hiding spot?

One breath pushed the questions away. How they found him didn't matter. Only completing the mission mattered now.

He lay prone, his outstretched right hand about four feet from the pistol in his shorts pocket on that side. His left hand still gripped the root near his shoulder, much closer to his other pistol.

Draw with his off hand, roll over, aim, and fire at five, six, seven men who would fire back at any sudden movement? He'd be lucky to hit one before multiple rounds punched through his chest. Gray didn't pay him enough to die for no reason.

Did Gray pay him enough to die for any reason?

New thoughts. The men behind him wanted him as a prisoner, not a corpse, or else they would have killed him already.

A gleam tightened in his eye. He would have his chance to complete the mission.

"Hands slowly to the top of your head," said the crisp voice.

Stone palmed his scalp with his right hand, then overlaid his left.

"Stand."

He propped his head up on his elbows, rose to his knees, climbed to his feet. Amid the trees below, motion at the canopy. Caitlyn and the other three watched him. Bale spoke to her, words inaudible—

"Face my voice."

Three steps with each foot turned him around. His face fell and his eyes darted over pine trunks and undergrowth. Six men, at most ten yards away, but where?

A camouflage-patterned mannequin suddenly appeared. Bodybuilders might think his build was undermuscled, but if they did, they'd be fools. Its right hand kept the muzzle of rifle shape of the same pattern trained on Stone's chest while its left lifted a pliable mask from its face. Wide-set green eyes regarded Stone from a face smooth yet rigid as a marble statue of a youthful demigod.

Stone cursed inside. Military concealment must be yet another technology where Minerva had overtaken Earth.

"Pat him down."

Movement glimmered to his left. One member of the squad suddenly turned blaze orange, like a hunter entering the woods in deer season, and slung his rifle over his shoulder. The orange figure moved silently over the rocky ground. He topped the crest and approached Stone from behind.

Tension fired in Stone's legs. Grab the orange figure and use him as a human shield? Then what? At least four or five other armed men stood in front of him... and how many others had sneaked behind Stone while he'd faced the unit leader?

Let them take you where you want to go. Then take your chances.

The orange figure pulled the pistols from Stone's pockets and tossed them to the pine straw near the unit leader. He did the same with the toolkit. Then he patted Stone down further, pulling his buttocks apart and tracing the outlines of his genitals through the jogging shorts.

Stone winced. "At least buy me dinner first."

The orange figure and the unit leader stayed silent. Not just well-equipped, but disciplined too. But had they ever fought an actual battle? Unlikely.

The blaze orange figure stepped back, faced Stone. The leader nodded. The blaze orange figure returned to his place in the semicircle.

Suddenly, at what Stone presumed came as the leader's unvoiced command, everyone's coloration transformed to camouflage. The unit leader and four soldiers. Four of them, their faces still masked, formed a diamond shape around Stone, two flanking, one ahead, one behind. Close enough from Stone to contain him, far enough away to have time to react to an attack.

The unit leader's wide-set green eyes drilled into Stone. "Turn around. High Councillor Bale and the woman from Earth are going to talk to you."

Stone turned. He glanced up at the blazing dot. So distant that the drives of the individual tugs blurred together. Twenty-five minutes till wormhole placement. Not that placement would provide him with a diversion anymore. Now, placement was a time bomb. The moment the tugs detached from the equilibrator ring, Bale and the others would release the death drones.

He walked down the slope toward the canopy. His gaze roved the woods and the clearing for clues he could use. The workmen could be ignored. The security guards too—they looked relieved when they saw the soldiers in the camouflage body suits.

Stone couldn't ignore the soldiers. Well-armed and well-trained, they surrounded him like camouflaged phantoms. When he walked to put a tree between him and a flanking soldier, the soldier would adjust his pace to keep Stone in view as much as possible, and the other three watched him every moment their comrade didn't.

They entered the clearing. The unit leader stalked through the last undergrowth and across patchy grass. He saluted to Bale, who stood just outside the canopy, wearing sunglasses against a patch of bright Minervan sunlight.

Bale returned the salute. "Have him come forward."

The unit leader tossed the toolkit under the canopy, then gestured to Stone like a traffic cop. The soldier in front of Stone moved to the side and covered him with his rifle muzzle. Stone stopped in front of Bale.

The High Councillor smoothed his beard and chuckled. "You misjudged him, Ms. Fredriksen."

Caitlyn emerged from under the canopy. A broad-brimmed, camouflage-pattern hat shielded her fair skin and blond hair from the sun but failed to obscure her hazel eyes. Her gaze measured Stone while she replied to Bale. "He's a talented and ruthless operative. He was worth recruiting."

"It was a security risk. I only allowed it in the spirit of cooperation." Bale's sunglasses made his expression unreadable.

"Not much of a risk, was it? Your men caught him." Her gaze swung to Stone's face. "He failed to alert Earth."

Stone kept his poker face. If she didn't realize he'd thrown a report into the diplomatic pouch, he would leave her ignorant.

"True enough." Bale smoothed his beard. "It doesn't change what we must do."

"No," said Caitlyn. "A regrettable waste of talent."

Stone's heart pounded. They were going to kill him. His mind grasped at sounds. Where was the nearest soldier? Could he wrest a rifle from one and gun down Bale and the others before the other soldiers finished him?

Stall. Distract. "Congrats," he said to Bale. "You passed the test."

"Test?"

"Every pack of colonists resisting the UN have been amateurs. I had to prove to myself that you were professionals. You are. I still haven't figured out how you detected me observing you just now."

"And we haven't figured out how you found this location." Bale grinned. "Answer me that and I'll return the favor."

Would answering Bale reveal any of the UN's capabilities it would need to fight the Minervans? No. Bale had already taken his toolkit and his men would bring in the invisibility cloak and the parasail pieces soon enough.

"I accessed public records and found the paper trail of High Emprise LLC. I hitched a ride on your trailer to enter the warehouse complex on the south side of Euler City. My flash bang grenade—"

"I'd surmised."

"I climbed to the roof, observed your…."

Who stalled whom? In twenty minutes the tugs would detach the wormhole. The hundred and fifty plague vector drones would traverse to Earth maybe ten minutes after that.

The soldier at Stone's four o'clock breathed slower than the others and shifted his weight more. Eight or ten feet. Could he do it?

"…drone fleet, parasailed off the roof. I assumed your men brought the drones out here, so I put a tracker on the trailer, then came out here by car to the wormhole site and on foot the rest of the way." With his hands staying on his head, Stone pivoted his elbows from the sides to the front, both to keep his arms limber and to accustom the soldiers to believe his motions remained harmless. To Bale, he said, "Your turn."

"My turn?"

Before Stone replied, Sheila van Bentum emerged from the canopy. She wore the same style of hat as Caitlyn and it looked out of place on a priestess of the Minervans' state non-religion.

What was she doing here? Blessing of the death drones?

Shriving the sins of the captured spy before his execution?

"You agreed to tell me how you detected me just now."

Bale chuckled, a cold sound in the warm morning. "I shan't play 'before I kill you, Mr. Bond.'"

Stone's mouth turned arid. "You swear to me you can save the world and you expect me to take your ability to do so at face value? Dammit, you're amateurs after all." His gaze darted to Caitlyn. "Now's the time."

"Time?"

"To get me the hell out of this."

She laughed, like a Valkyrie might at a mortal man. "You haven't figured it out? Stone, I almost killed you in Kovar's empty garage on New Moravia. I almost killed you in your sleep in the pilot's stateroom in *Lady Lux*. I would have killed you within minutes of your arrival at the UN tower if I hadn't realized what the Minervans offered us." She lifted her chin. Her hazel eyes regarded him with a trace of sadness. "We consecrated you. You had your chance to live in alignment with the univ—"

Stone lunged toward the soldier at his four o'clock. Two sprinting strides. He grabbed the rifle before the soldier responded. Swung up, wrenching the rifle from the soldier's grip, clocking the soldier under the chin.

He pivoted. Moved the barrel handguard to his left hand, the trigger to his right. Like women's bodies, each unique in a thousand subtle ways, but all conforming to the same template. Safety off. Raise the sights to his eye. Sunglasses and trimmed brown beard. Squeeze the trigger.

The trigger didn't budge.

He pulled the trigger even harder.

Nothing.

Jammed. Dammit. His left hand worked the charging lever. Brass flicked out of the chamber. Another round snapped home. He aimed again at Bale.

The trigger still refused to move.

What the hell? A setup—

Pine branches and blue sky wheeled across his vision. His back slammed hard ground. A line across his calf muscles throbbed.

The soldier he'd disarmed had swept his legs—

He looked up at a semicircle of rifle muzzles aimed at his chest. The unit leader's wide-set green eyes regarded him impassively. "Our weapons are biometrically and cryptographically locked to the individual soldier."

Stone laid the rifle on the ground and caught his breath. He'd faced death before, but never this close. If even one moment remained, he had a chance.

"Here?" the unit leader said.

"Good as anywhere," Bale's voice replied.

The unit leader nodded. "Ready."

Adrenaline drove Stone's elbows into the ground for leverage, pawed his heels for purchase. His shoes sent pebbles skittering.

"Aim."

No—

Sheila van Bentum's husky voice cried, "Convocation!"

16

A crown of hot pain ringed Stone's head.

Delight bubbled up his chest. He lived. He would take any amount of pain over oblivion.

Why hadn't the soldiers shot him yet? And what the hell was convocation?

He levered himself onto his left elbow… and the ring of pain around his head tightened. His upper body collapsed to the ground.

Agony squeezed his skull, his brain, his mind. Under the pressure, emotions long unfelt, memories long buried, jetted into his consciousness. Guilt, shame, hate, love, joy, tagged with times and places. People he'd wronged. People he'd done right. The emotions flowed over his consciousness like viscous liquids spilled on a smooth table, then dribbled off the sides, into his body.

His face contorted, eyes twitching, mouth lopsided and pulled open. His limbs trembled. Nausea clenched his stomach.

Stone gasped breaths. His limbs flailed, pounded the dusty ground. Sweat drenched his clothes and trickled down his temples and neck. Inchoate noises burbled from his mouth. His eyes misted at the memories of unnecessary killings and lies that lured women into his bed. A warm nodule in his chest reminded him of the few good things he'd done, coaching boys in football, accompanying his mother when she needed an escort to her charity events. Then his eyes cleared and the warm nodule vanished. *You never asked dad to get therapy for alcoholism* lashed him with guilt, then blew away in the emotional gale.

The pain around his head transmuted into a snug presence seemingly gluing him to the ground. Through the storm of emotions he sensed the hot, sun-dappled clearing; Caitlyn, Bale, and Sheila van Bentum standing together sharing expectant looks; the soldiers shifting their weight and letting their rifle muzzles drift away from Stone's chest; a faint roar somewhere in the western sky. His perceptions were amplified, as if he heard through high-gain microphones and saw through an immense telescope at maximum magnification, yet at the same time the people around him seemed infinitely distant.

"Why isn't the facilitatrix doing something?" muttered one soldier. His shoulder-slung rifle pointed skyward.

"A woman is never supposed to facilitate a man's convocation," replied another, muzzle aimed at the ground.

"But she's the only facili—"

"Quiet," came the unit leader's low, crisp voice. His green eyes cast a sharp glance at his two subordinates.

The emotional storm subsided to a gale. Stone's muscles relaxed. His face unwound its contortions. The torrent of emotions drained, leaving shards of memories like the clutter of leaves and branches and garbage left behind when floodwaters receded. He still couldn't move. If only he could run—

A black rectangle ringed with a thin gray bezel appeared in the center of his vision, like a computer monitor in Gray's office overlaid against the cloudless blue sky. Bright red words in the middle read *Convocation complete.*

Convocation. Obviously the soldiers knew what it meant. In his hotel room half a day ago, Stone had learned Sheila facilitated Gerald Berglund's daughter through it. A ritual Minervans underwent in a Center around their eighteenth birthday. But what the hell had he gained by undergoing it?

What had Caitlyn and the others gained by subjecting him to it?

The red words scrolled to the top of the window. New ones appeared in the center.

STONE CHALMERS AND ALIGNMENT WITH THE UNIVERSE

```
Rolston Gridley Wentworth "Stone" Chalmers
Public-facing profile (algorithm: esb-2078.34.113;
block: 6814044)
++++++++++
```
Adventurous, courageous, and extremely cynical.

Spy and assassin employed by [United Nations Interagency Coordination Authority]/[UNICA].

He kills with minimal conscience. His killings are excused by his employment. Persons he has killed include [Paul Ulrich], [Teresa Benavides] <remainder of list omitted for brevity, [fullest known list] accessible>. He has negligible interest in political justifications for his actions.

He also seduces with minimal conscience. Sexual encounters include [Teresa Benavides], [Melanie (surname unknown)], [Annika Kim] <remainder of list omitted for brevity, [fullest known list] accessible>. Sexual encounter with [Melanie (surname unknown)] involved mutual alcohol-impaired consent.

In professional settings, others consider him "highly skilled" and "sexist."

Insufficient information regarding how others consider him in social settings.

[Detailed profile] and [consecration profile] accessible.

Reputation score: 4

    The words hung over him while he caught his breath. Public-facing profile? What did that mean?
    How did these words appear in his vision? Had the Minervans hacked his implantable? Fed signals to the fine mesh of transcranial

magnetic stim leads woven around his hair follicles?

He could move now. He propped himself on one elbow. Damn, the morning had grown bright. He squinted, shaded his eyes with his free hand. Looked around.

His gaze landed on the unit leader. A black window appeared to the side above the soldier's head.

```
g3kexQM4Tm (pseudonym <Minerva Security Directorate request>
<validation: reputation scores: 5x1000>)
Public-facing profile (algorithm: esb-msd-2081.88.37;
block: 6814044)
++++++++++
Sergeant in [Minerva Security Directorate]/[MSD]
[Ground Force]. Training score 98/100. Training completed
2132-04-27. Operations score 97/100. Full compliance with
[Minerva Code of Military Justice] smart contract.

Civilians encountering him during course of his duties
consider him "respectful," "disciplined," "a man any
enemies should fear."

[Detailed profile] and [consecration profile] accessible.

Reputation score: 204
```

Stone sat up. Looked around. Black windows appeared near the other soldiers. Corporals and one private, all pseudonymous at MSD request. They scored below their leader, had one or two minor violations of the military justice smart contract, and civilians found them less praiseworthy.

Enough of them. He peered at Bale.

```
Simon Bale
Public-facing profile (algorithm: narrat-2107-11-03;
block: 6814044)
++++++++++
Simon Bale is the [High Councillor] of the [Minerva
```

```
Security Directorate], holding office since 31st January
2126. Prior to his current office, he worked as a senior
investigator for the [Euler City Police Department] and
deputy commander of the [MSD Colonial Police]. The
[MSDCP] foiled an attempted 51% attack on the [Center for
Alignment with the Universe] convocation blockchain
during his tenure. His leadership is considered by
knowledgable persons of high reputation <[link]> to have
been a key determinant of [MSDCP]'s success.

Bale is highly reputed <[link]> to be honest, diligent,
patriotic, and pious. He is married with three sons....
```

Stone skimmed the rest. The profile omitted "plotter of genocidal pandemic." Which meant all the data forced into Stone's vision was a lie.

Right?

He rose on wobbly legs. The soldiers brought their muzzles halfway to Stone's chest. He looked past them, to Bale, Sheila, and Caitlyn. "What—" His voice seized up like an unoiled gearbox. He cleared his throat. "What have you done? How? Why?"

Caitlyn raised slender fingers toward the two Minervans. "I should be the one to explain. This is part of your culture. Stone wasn't raised to expect this. Just like me."

She came closer. A black window opened over her shoulder.

```
Caitlyn Fredriksen
Public-facing profile-
```

Stone swiped his left hand at air. He knew her already. The black window vanished. So did the others. The way they disappeared told him he could reopen any of them with a thought.

The soldiers parted for her. She stopped six feet from Stone. Her hazel eyes glittered like onyx. "Stone, you've put it together, haven't you? I've worked to save Earth from its corrupt and incompetent government since before we met."

"You and who else?" She might slip some intel. How the hell to get it to Gray he'd figure out later.

She dismissed the question with an arched eyebrow. "I've worked to forge alliances with colonial forces that could help us achieve our goal. On New Moravia, we thought the Benavides family could lead a guerrilla war against the UN, which would erode popular support on Earth for UN peacekeeping policies. Not a killing blow, but the first slash in a death of a thousand cuts."

"You only joined forces with me because your attack dogs slipped the leash."

"Teresa Benavides' plan to destroy the wormhole, if successful, would have ruined all sympathy for the New Moravians among the average person on Earth. She had to be stopped. Your interest and mine aligned at that point."

Stone sniffed out a breath. "You seriously thought fifty thousand New Moravians could resist Earth?"

"We had to play the hand dealt to us."

He thought of their joint mission. "You didn't try to turn Ulrich's people into a guerrilla force."

"On Trinity," she said, "we thought whoever stole the interplanetary ship plans would wish to use *Lady Lux*, the missing warpdrive ship, to flee somewhere outside the UN's jurisdiction and start a new colony. Given decades to build up a technological and industrial base, during decades when Earth's decline would steepen, a new colony could resist Earth and eventually fight back."

"If you wanted Ulrich and the others to lead their followers on a ten thousand light year exodus, you never told them that."

"My plan was to strangle you in your sleep," Caitlyn said, "then tell them everything. I would have had to join them on their trek and never return to Earth. Not ideal, but a price I would have paid. Then Laclede invaded our cabin with the only firearm on *Lady Lux* and, well, you know the rest."

Stone's gaze flicked over the camouflaged soldiers and Bale's hardened face. "The scout ship report on Minerva made you think they had the technological and industrial base to fight back."

"The report was promising enough to bring me out here with the diplomatic mission," Caitlyn said. "But when I discovered what the Centers did, and how they did it, I saw a chance to free Earth from the UN without an interstellar war."

"If ships and soldiers can't bring down the UN, how the hell can—" He touched his aching forehead. He expected a mushy strip of softened bone, but his fingers found throbbing muscle and warmth like hot wires under his skin. "—convocation do it?"

"As the Minervans say, consecration allows you to truly know yourself. Convocation allows everyone to truly know everyone else."

Stone pictured himself strolling down Lexington Avenue. Every pedestrian on the sidewalk reading the open book of his public profile and cringing.

Not just because they saw his secrets. Because they knew he saw theirs.

Bah. His public profile revealed things he'd rather hide? A simple fix: edit it. Just like everyone else would. He lived in Manhattan, where everyone cultivated a public persona and kept their true selves hidden. He nodded toward Bale and Sheila. "You believe them?"

"I'll tell you how the Minervans do it, and you'll realize why I believe them and why you should too."

"I'm listening." Not just to her. The wormhole tugs' engines rumbled like far-off thunder. How could he stop them from launching the drones?

A glance found Bradley dell'Angelo seated under the canopy. His slack face showed his attention lay on data projected to his sensory nerves. Get past the soldiers, get past Caitlyn and Bale, kill dell'Angelo with bare hands before he launched the drones….

"Decades ago the Minervans developed brain/computer interfaces. Like the transcranial magnetic stimulator wiring we have, but better. They use medical nanotechnology to grow a quantum computer within our skull bones and to wire that computer into many parts of the brain. Their wiring even accesses the subconscious and the emotions. Convocation requires that access."

Stone touched his forehead again. "My head hurts because your nanomachines grew a computer inside my skull."

"Nanomachines did that, but they didn't cause your headache."

She grinned. "I'll get to that soon."

"Get to it now."

"Aren't you curious how those nanomachines entered your skull?"

Stone's brow creased. Two evenings ago with Sheila in the Center, part of consecration? He remembered a fingerprick. To draw blood for DNA profiling, he'd assumed, but had they injected him with nanomachines then?

He rubbed his forehead. His head hurt worse than it had from that sinus headache his first morning in the UN tower....

A dry swallow, then he said, "You aerosolized the nanomachines."

"Not me," Caitlyn said. "You found the name Matthew Thomas, I take it?"

The UN tower... Despite the warm morning, a chill ran down his legs. "You infected everyone who came dirtside from *Yassir Arafat*?"

"Yes. It's dormant for everyone. Except you."

His eyes widened. His gaze swung to the parked trailer, then up the far ridge. Under the shade of the trees, sky blue points swathed in gossamer dotted the pine straw.

"You aren't unleashing a plague on Earth," Stone said. "You're unleashing convocation."

A nod dipped the brim of Caitlyn's broad hat. "Each of the drones carries enough aerosolized nanomachines to wire the brains of—" She turned her hazel eyes to Bale and Sheila. "—ten thousand people?"

Bale spoke. "They'll average twelve thousand, says Dr. Thomas."

Stone did the math in his head. "You'll infect a million and a half people." Then he chuckled. He might not need to kill dell'Angelo after all. "It won't work, keyhole kop."

"Based on my briefing, Bradley dell'Angelo's team targeted the drones to key locations—"

"Not that. You put a computer in my head that learned all my deep dark secrets and broadcasts them to the world. All I have to do is edit what it broadcasts."

Caitlyn laughed like tinkling crystal. "We've come to why you should believe the Minervans can free Earth from the UN."

"Which is?"

"Because your public profile is impossible to edit." Her cheeks tightened. "I'm sure you never heard of blockchain."

"Oh but I have. Watch out for those 51% attacks. They're a doozy."

"You did read High Councillor Bale's public profile." A chuckle flavored the words, then dried up. "Be serious."

He vented tension from his shoulders. The UN would survive the drones reaching Earth. Playing along with her gave him more time to plan his escape. "Enlighten me."

"I hadn't heard of blockchain either before I made contact with Sheila and Simon Bale. The concept arose a century ago but the UN suppressed it before I was born. Maybe even before you were." A teasing smile revealed straight white teeth.

"Skip the cheap shots."

"Blockchain is basically distributed record keeping. Instead of, say, a bank keeping the only ledger of who owes how much money to whom, all the debtors and creditors keep a copy of the ledger and periodically update it. Blockchain has some drawbacks. One is that at the time of convocation, your computer downloads the entire existing blockchain. Even with data compression and exponential decay of transactions of deceased people, we're still talking about petabytes of data in a couple of minutes. Even quantum computers handling that workload generate noticeable waste heat."

"That's a hell of a drawback."

"Blockchain has one huge advantage over a bank that outweighs all the drawbacks."

Stone winced and rubbed his forehead. "It better be huge."

"A banker can falsify a ledger. A blockchain can only be falsified if a majority of its ledgers are falsified at the same time. The 51% attack you read about but didn't understand."

"What do financial ledgers have to do with…." Stone's hands juggled air.

"The convocation blockchain is a ledger of reputation," Caitlyn said. To the side, Sheila van Bentum smiled like a stained glass saint.

"Ledger of reputation…. Like customer reviews on the worldweb? Like gossip?" A breeze rustled pine branches. The engines of the wormhole tugs roared a little louder.

"And more," Caitlyn said. "The computer in the skull picks up memories you associate with guilt, shame, embarrassment, and the like. Memories of the wrongs you know you've committed. And memories of your actions that violate social norms. Those too are added to the ledger."

Gooseflesh stippled Stone's cheeks. The drones still posed a risk to the UN. He would still have to break dell'Angelo's neck.

Stone squinted up at the descending wormhole tugs. Blue-white exhaust plumes knifed across the sky. In formation between the tugs, a night sky from Earth showed as a black dot.

Caitlyn said, "You see what the convocation blockchain can do."

"You're going to infect a million and a half key people on Earth. When you activate convocation, they'll broadcast all their secrets. To everyone?"

"No. Only to everyone else who's undergone convocation."

Stone sloughed out a breath. "Then it still won't do what you hope. The UN's high and mighty already know each other's dirty secrets. A web of blackmail makes the world go around."

"Mutual blackmail only works if everyone agrees to play that game. If one person comes clean to the public, the game is over. We think the drones can spread the nanomachines widely enough to reveal the insiders' transgressions to everyone in the settled galaxy."

"You *think*."

She shared a glance with Bale. He flicked an icy gaze to Stone, then nodded.

Caitlyn nodded in reply, then said to Stone, "Nothing is certain, but we can increase our chances."

"How?"

"You can join us."

The soldiers in unison moved their rifles to ready positions, firing finger on the outside of the trigger guard, other hand on the barrel handguard.

"Or," Caitlyn said, "you can die."

17

"Sign me up!" Stone said.

Neither the soldiers nor their leaders near the canopy moved. On the far slope, men spoke indistinctly to one another and rustled through undergrowth and pine straw. A bird tweeted somewhere amid the pines. Then Bale barked out a laugh.

"It won't be like when you 'joined' us after consecration," Caitlyn said, fingers air-quoting.

"Because I mean it this time. You convinced me."

"*They* convinced you." She gestured at the soldiers ringing Stone.

"We're quibbling."

"You're right. Because if you join us, even if you intend to play double agent, you will be bound to us."

Stone said, "I'm not usually into kink, but when I am, I do the binding."

Caitlyn's face turned humorless. "Do you have one of the soldier's public profiles open?"

"No."

"You figured out how to close them on your own. Good. Open one. Doesn't matter which."

Stone found the green-eyed leader, still the only one with face exposed. An intention to open the man's public profile formed in Stone's mind before he could put into words. The profile reopened. His gaze went to the gobbledygook pseudonym, the validation entry about reputation scores....

"Sheila and the other founders of the blockchain understood that secrecy is at times required. Now that Minerva needs soldiers, for example, their identities need not be exposed to any enemy that might access the blockchain. Accordingly, the founders set up mechanisms to allow agencies that need secrecy to request pseudonymous transaction logging, time-limited gray blockchains, or both for personnel who need it."

More jargon, but one thing stuck out. "Request? So instead of a banker who can forge a ledger, you have a judge who can issue a secret warrant."

"The request is to a set of decentralized, highly-reputable people selected by a—what do you call it, Sheila?"

"A Venetian election," the Minervan woman said. Her eyes crinkled at him. "Stone has too much on his hands for me to pile the details on him."

"I would ignore them anyway," Stone said.

"We know," Caitlyn said. "And there are checks and balances to reduce the risk of abuse." She waved her hand as if wiping away the details. "Our organization—High Emprise LLC and Friends—requested a gray blockchain and smart contract terminating ten years after—" She pointed over her shoulder, to where the tugs' fusion drives threw the shadows of pines over Stone and the others. Only minutes to go. "—placement of the wormhole."

"Meaning?"

"Now, the things we do are shared solely among ourselves. After ten years, they will enter the full blockchain."

"I take it you just described a gray blockchain," Stone said. "What the hell's a smart contract?" A sinking feeling in his gut hinted at the answer.

"A contract implemented by a blockchain. A breach of contract is immediately alert every other party to the contract." She raised her chin. Her hazel eyes peered down her nose from under her broad-brimmed hat. "If you join us, you must enter into a smart contract. Divulging the existence of High Emprise LLC and Friends or any information about our private club's goals or actions to anyone not connected to the full blockchain will be punishable by—?" She looked to Bale and Sheila.

Bale turned frosty blue eyes on Stone. He enunciated his next word. "Death."

Sheila winced. "I wish I didn't...." Her husky voice trailed off.

"You do," Bale said.

"Yes. When I joined you, I knew I might have to grasp the nettle. I agree with the High Councillor. Death."

Caitlyn glanced down and to her left. "Matthew and Bradley agree."

Under the canopy, Bradley dell'Angelo lifted a hand in their direction, while his gaze drilled into a sight only he could see.

Caitlyn looked at Stone with eyes like onyx. "I agree too. And before you think you've found a loophole, yes, by the terms of the contract, you may divulge the existence of our private club to people who are connected to the full blockchain. But divulging the name of any member, or our goals, or actions, to anyone will also be punishable by death."

Bale grunted. "If you attempt sabotage, death." His blue eyes peered at Stone. "You're not the type to sacrifice yourself, but if you were, and after revealing our secrets tried to cover your tracks by suicide, your embedded quantum computer stores enough power to transmit your treachery to us."

"You're right that I'm not the type."

The blue eyes turned icy. "Don't waste your breath telling us what we already know."

Death if he didn't join them. Death if he joined and double-crossed them.

But death how? Could the quantum computer in his skull destroy his brain? Or did *death* only mean a death sentence, to be carried out by.... His gaze took in the soldiers, the unit leader, Bale. Caitlyn.

If he could slip away from them, then fight his executioner when he—or she—hunted him, he liked his chances.

Stone lifted his chest. "I understand what I'm getting into. Sign me up."

Caitlyn bowed her head to Sheila van Bentum. "Facilitatrix?"

"You don't need me to bless his entry into our, what did you call it, private club," replied the Minervan woman in her husky voice.

"I don't. He doesn't. But…." Caitlyn nodded at the soldiers, looked up and down the group of workmen scattered through the forest. "Many others do."

Sheila stepped forward. Despite wearing khaki outdoors wear instead of her red dress embedding a constellation of diamonds, she bore herself like a priestess. The soldiers stepped back for her and bowed their heads. Even Bale dipped his chin.

"Stone Chalmers, do you knowingly choose to join High Emprise LLC and Friends, to further its goals, to settle all conflicts of interest in its favor, and to keep its secrets for the duration of the contract, with any breach by you of this contract punishable by your death?"

His heart thumped like a gong. "Yes."

A trickle of warmth ringed his head. On flexed knees and with held breath, he braced for emotional impact.

Nothing.

Stone exhaled, inhaled. Looked around. Thought open the private profile windows for every member of High Emprise LLC and Friends in and around the clearing. The same black rectangles appeared over each shoulder, but now their bezels were thick bands of deep red, pulsing like a heartbeat. In the bezel above each window hung crisp white lettering.

Private Blockchain - High Emprise LLC and Friends - Private Blockchain

The soldiers' private profiles indicated the men all tested high for genetic and personality markers of loyalty and secrecy. The Minerva Security Directorate had assembled this unit solely to assign it to High Emprise. The men were all Level 2 members with 0% voting rights.

A glance around the clearing showed the other security guards at Level 1, and the workmen at Level 0. Security clearances? Likely: Bale and Sheila held Level 4 membership and 18% voting rights each.

Caitlyn—

A chill ran down Stone's bare limbs.

```
Caitlyn Fredriksen
```

```
Level 3 member
10% voting right
++++++++++
Recruited by her mentor, [Robert Holbrook] of [United
Nations Interstellar Transport Bureau], to overthrow the
UN, she contacted High Councillor [Bale] and Facilitatrix
[van Bentum] 2131-12-29. After undergoing consecration
2132-01-03 and convocation 2132-01-06, she joined High
Emprise LLC and Friends 2132-02-09 in planning [Operation
Sunlight]-
```

Stone blinked. Holbrook wielded great power. He had to relay this intel to Gray. But how?

Caitlyn's profile shrank down to a tab at the bottom of the rectangle. New text took its place.

```
Operation Sunlight
++++++++++
```

Ah, by blinking he'd clicked on a hyperlink in brackets.

He read more.

```
Motto: Sunlight is the best disinfectant.
Drones will be dispatched to Earth. The drones will bear
medical-grade nanomachines configured to construct
quantum computers-
```

He knew all that. He skimmed, clicked on *Next Page,* and skimmed more.

```
-targets include:
Secretary-General Abdullah Sayyid
Fatimah Sayyid
UNICA Director Karlheinz Kroebel
Luise Kroebel
UNICA Assistant Director of Operational Planning
Martindale Gray
UNITB Assistant Director of Security Robert Holbrook-
```

Gray actually was the old man's surname. Widowed, divorced, or never married? From Gray's mentions of grandchildren, probably never married and throwing a smoke screen.

Stone squeezed shut his eyes, not believing the next line. Yet when he reopened them, he still read Holbrook on the list of targets. Why had Caitlyn chosen to target him?

The list continued. Pages of *UN Ambassador from*; US President Kwame Goldbaum and the prime ministers of twenty European and Far Eastern countries, plus their domestic political rivals; administrators and faculty members at fifty universities; the CEOs of the Global-Fortune 500; a hundred influential pundits on the worldforum; a hundred prosecutors and law enforcement officials.

And their spouses. Perhaps that was High Emprise's plan. All the wives and the few husbands at the highest social stratum who were ignorant of how their spouses amassed wealth and power—or pretended to be ignorant—would get the truth shoved in their plastic surgery faces. A dream for gossip bloggers and divorce lawyers.

Not enough to topple the UN.

Still, he had to get this intel to Gray. Somehow.

Stone noticed the Minervans' gazes on him. He thought closed all the windows.

Bale rubbed his beard with his palm. His blue eyes darted over something over Stone's left shoulder. "The new recruit has his first assignment."

"I agree," said Caitlyn.

Sheila opened her palms. "I trust your judgement."

"Me too." Bradley dell'Angelo's soft voice barely emerged from the canopy.

Stone scowled at Caitlyn. "My first assignment?"

"You didn't read your profile?"

"I know my own mind. Now you do too." He spoke with banter.

"We know you composed two reports about our private club to Gray," said Caitlyn flatly. "One is in the safe in your room at the UN tower. The other is in the diplomatic pouch waiting for transport to Earth."

All traces of levity vanished from Stone's face, like water in a gully under the midday Minervan sun. "I subvoked those before I joined you. I can't be in breach of contract for something I did before I signed the contract."

Bale's voice cut the air between them. "We are honorable people. This isn't Earth, Mr. Chalmers."

"What's my assignment?"

"You must retrieve those reports and hand them to Ms. Fredriksen for destruction before the road and rail links to Earth are constructed. If you fail in that task, then you would be in breach."

"I will succeed." Stone didn't need the encrypted sticks to pass intel to Gray. He could read aloud the profiles stored in his node of High Emprise's gray blockchain. "If someone can give me a lift back to the UN tower—"

"Not yet," said Sheila van Bentum. "The roadway and rail line to Earth won't be connected for two days."

Caitlyn stepped closer to Stone. Her hat's brim nearly brushed his cheek. "I've never seen a wormhole placement. Have you?"

"Only from the Earth side."

"Seen one, seen them all, I'm sure. But I haven't seen one and I want to. And I'd like you to join me. Doing so will show your team spirit."

"A team I had to join or else get a rifle round through my brain?" He shrugged. "Sure. I've got nothing else to do."

"Follow me." She strode away from the canopy, up the southern slope of the valley. Her lean legs, smooth and lightly tanned between her shorts and hiking socks, should've allured him, but didn't. Amazing what getting press-ganged by fanatics could do to his mood.

They wound their way past drones lying on the pine straw. Workmen crouched with instruments, running final diagnostics. A bright light from the south doubled the shadows of the trees. Near the crest of the ridge, the pines grew short and twisted, and bare rocks poked through a thin cover of scree and fallen needles.

She reached the top first. "Wow. What a sight."

Visible between pine trunks, The wormhole was a night-black circle half the size of a full moon. It contrasted with the pale blue sky, and the four exhaust plumes of the tugs framed it like a golden setting for a black diamond. The tugs' engines screamed now, a sound that should be inflicted on some poor bastard in Queens, living under the flight path of suborbitals into Kennedy. The wormhole crept down the sky as the tugs holding it by invisible cords matched their descent with their dance partners lowering the Earth end toward the Mojave Desert.

"Could the Minervans have shot down the tugs?" Stone asked. "Or *Yassir Arafat*?"

"I don't know, but I believe so."

"Why didn't they? Ah." He saw the answer before she put it into words.

"*Yassir Arafat* and the tugs are in continual contact through the wormhole with Earth. The Minervans couldn't make it look like an accident. The UN would launch a punitive expedition to slag Minerva back to lifeless rock."

"Minerva might be able to fight them off."

"The UN is still strong enough to break direct resistance. And Minerva is too precious to squander as cannon fodder."

Stone raised an eyebrow. "Precious? How much of their koolaid did you drink?"

"I've been consecrated and joined the convocation almost nine months ago. I'm the most focused and at the same time the calmest I've ever been. And I would be even if the Minervans couldn't help us save the human race."

"Oh, yeah, from that UN tyranny." Sarcasm thickened his words.

The broad-brimmed hat amplified a gentle shake of her head. "Worse. From UN incompetence."

The wormhole's slow descent finally carried it below the tops of the trees on the nearest intervening ridge. The tugs followed the wormhole out of sight ten seconds later. The engine scream filled the air, frightening birds and the small animals of the undergrowth into silence.

"There's a camera feed from the top of a tree about a quarter of a mile away," she said. She pushed a link to him from her implantable through his. After interfacing through the Minervan blockchain quantum computers, using the older Earth tech seemed like writing a letter with pen and paper.

He opened the link. A magnified image filled his mind's eye. Fusion exhaust softened the rocky ground in four spots outside the crater. Harder boulders slumped like empty vape cartridges littered on melting snowpiles. The equilibrator ring around the wormhole's equator shone like a platinum wedding band in dazzling sunlight. The black sphere of the wormhole itself swallowed the daylight.

The bottom of the wormhole dipped below the crater wall. The softened ground melted. Lava like brown and red pus oozed across the ground, rippling under the downforce of the drive exhausts. The tugs descended, engines burning furiously to control the placement of the wormhole's tons of exotic matter in sync with their partners on the Earth side.

Presumably the tug pilots derived great meaning from their work. Or feared the crushing notoriety of failure.

The tugs hung in the air atop pillars of fire for long seconds. Then in a blink they shot upward. Traces of the Tobias Becker persona from Trinity tried estimating the acceleration of their ascent.

Stone shook away the useless thought. The tugs rose because they'd released their cables in unison. "Wormhole in place," he said. A link to a different camera popped up and he subvoked to it. A camera in the road and rail cut in the crater rim, looking downward. The equilibrator ring rested on the crater floor. A hemisphere of desert night rose above it.

Caitlyn stared at the tugs rising through her naked-eye field of view. "I know."

The roar of the tug engines reverberated through the trees around Stone. Another sound joined them, high and faint, as if he strolled through a park along the East River and every weedwhacker in Brooklyn fired up at once.

Stone looked over his shoulder.

A hundred and fifty drones rose from the sun-dappled pine straw and filed between the trees, heading south.

18

They returned to Euler City in a black coupe Caitlyn summoned from the UN motor pool. The air conditioning reached full power just as the coupe turned off the gravel road onto the paved road slicing through the parallel ridges.

After turning left at the intersection with the main highway, they passed a steady stream of oncoming vehicles, mostly pickup trucks bearing the logos of Minervan construction companies. Workmen heading west to the wormhole site to finish the road and rail lines to Earth.

Even with their advanced tech and a round-the-clock schedule, they would need about forty-eight hours to finish construction. Given the venality and petty ineptitude of Gautam, the mail clerk at the UN tower, Stone could add another dozen hours to the window of time he had to retrieve the report to Gray.

The wormhole's placement impacted the lives of more Minervans than just the construction crews. As they approached downtown Euler City, conversation bubbled under the sunscreens over sidewalk cafés. The locals raised demitasses of espresso and quart steins of beer with warm smiles.

One woman's gaze, brown eyes in a pale face framed by long auburn hair, landed on the coupe's window while it waited for pedestrians to cross the street. Stone sucked in a breath.

"Her quantum computer can't identify you through the window tint," Caitlyn said. She sat next to him on the rear seat, her legs together and crossed at the knee. "That means she can't see your profile on the public blockchain."

"Good." He spoke with forced casualness. "Wouldn't want to scare the locals."

But his embedded quantum computer could identify the woman's. He skipped past her name—not relevant—and found the great shame of her life; at the age of sixteen, one cloudless evening in a riverfront park, she'd let a boy run his hand up her skirt. Since then—

The coupe drove on. The window shrank away before he could read the woman's attempts to redeem herself. Not that she'd done anything wrong in his mind. "The Minervans won't let anyone live down anything, will they?"

"Childhood is private. The quantum computer won't push to the blockchain anything embarrassing, unethical, or illegal you did before age thirteen."

"What's the point? Twelve-year-olds can't get into any real trouble."

Caitlyn raised an eyebrow. "Even you?"

"I wasn't that precocious."

She ignored his comment. "Also, parent-child relationships are private until the child turns eighteen. Same for intimate relationships after the couple gets engaged."

Stone laughed with an edge of nervous disbelief. "Everyone's a virgin until they get married?"

"Pretty much." She shook her head. "Don't worry. Even if everyone on Earth joined the convocation, pre-marital chastity won't become the norm for decades yet."

The windows of the Center for Alignment with the Universe glowed blue, green, and gold in afternoon sunlight. "I thought Operation Sunlight targeted a million people, not five billion."

"That's right." Her hazel eyes betrayed nothing.

Which told him what he needed to know. The voting members of High Emprise LLC and Friends at levels 3 and 4 of the security hierarchy could change the plan without him knowing. At least they'd assigned him to level 2, a notch above the workmen launching drones in the forest, and on par with the soldiers in their advanced camouflage bodysuits.

A red glint from a stained glass facilitatrix' dress caught Stone's eye as the coupe drove past. A question came to mind. "If you have a plan that doesn't need me, why did you bring me into your conspiracy?"

She nodded. "As soon as I identified you among the arrivals from *Yassir Arafat*, Bale argued for killing you. Sheila and I believed you might be more useful to us alive than dead."

"I have that effect on women." Stone smirked. "Especially two at once."

Caitlyn rolled her eyes. "You and I have at least one thing in common."

"Oh?"

"Like you told me on the flight to the Trinity wormhole, I too don't shit where I eat." She went on. "Sheila's argument was that we needed a test subject to confirm that unfacilitated convocation could work. In my view, setting aside your many flaws, you are effective at tradecraft. Even though we thought we could win enough tricks to make our bid, recruiting you was drawing an ace in the hole."

"Are you playing bridge or poker?"

"I'm mixing metaphors?" She gave a tinkling laugh. "Bridge, then. We aren't bluffing."

Stone eased back in the seat. They passed the Minervan government buildings in silence. The coupe turned left, onto a boulevard with only a guardrail between their travel lanes and the bluff overlooking the Wisdom Sea. The crash of waves reached them from the shore below as the UN tower loomed in the distance.

Minutes later they reached the tower. The coupe rolled into the parking garage entrance. The entry gate lifted and the coupe pulled into the nearest gap in the row of parked vehicles. Behind plexiglass windows in the motor pool office, cups of cold coffee rested on a desk strewn with smartpaper. Lifts held an orange sedan man-high above the concrete floor of the maintenance bay. Stone climbed out. Caitlyn handed him his toolkit and the 9mm pistols.

As they crossed to the elevator, their footsteps echoed in the empty space. "Where is everyone?" Caitlyn asked.

"Wormhole party."

"At 1400?"

"Any excuse to start drinking. For half of them, their mission is over and they're attitude is screw-it-got-my-orders."

Caitlyn's lips mashed together.

"Weren't you the one," Stone said, "who told me UN employees are corrupt and incompetent?"

She forced a chuckle. "The reality of it still surprises me. It doesn't surprise you?"

They neared the elevators. Stone arched an eyebrow and subvoked *Up.* "No."

She switched to subvocal through their embedded quantum computers. [Yet you still hold back from believing in us. Don't lie.] The elevator car hummed down the shaft toward them. [I know you signed the smart contract to avoid getting shot. I'm sure you're scheming about how to report us to Gray.]

The elevator opened. Stone gestured for her to enter. He gazed at the blond locks flowing down her graceful neck. How easy to snap it…

…and how easy for the soldiers to hunt him down?

He followed her in. [What's your point?]

The doors slid together. [You know how corrupt and inept the UN is. Why fight for it?]

To the elevator, he said, "Eighty." To Caitlyn, he rolled his eyes. [Because your Minervan friends are equally incompetent. What, you think they know what they're doing?]

The elevator zoomed upward. She pinched her nose and exhaled. [They have the cohesion of a group of founders, and the blockchain to maintain their cohesion. So, yes.]

Stone worked his jaw against the pressure of the rising elevator. The car slowed and stopped at his floor. Music and the chatter of a crowd trickled down from the top of the shaft.

[Almost everyone will be partying in the penthouse,] he said.

[Good. That will make it easier to get the second encrypted stick.]

She nodded out the open elevator doors. [Now we get the first.]

He led the way around the corner and down the long hallway leading to his suite. The door opened for him. After the dark hallway, daylight glared through open blinds. He strode in and beckoned her to follow. Her footsteps padded into the suite and the door swung closed with a whisper from the hinges and a quiet thud.

The safe opened for his thumbprint and retina. He reached in for the stick with last night's message to Gray. Tossed it to Caitlyn with an easy underhand motion.

She plucked it from the air and shoved it in a pocket of her cargo shorts. "We're done here."

One hand on the safe door, Stone put on a lazy grin. "What about the other stick?"

"The one you wrote as part of the Lavallette cover story? I don't need it." She gave a knowing smile in return, then turned as a motion in khaki for the door.

"Wait." He gestured at his jogging clothes, then hooked his thumb toward the bathroom. "I'm going to change. You should to."

She faced him, palm on her hipbone. "Why?"

"Everyone else will be in desk jockey clothes until they change to party wear. We'll look out of place. Like we spent last night and all of today outdoors."

Caitlyn weighed his words, then said, "Good call."

"You're still quartered with the diplomatic mission holdovers?"

"The Minervans moved us all to rooms here in the tower. Sometime yesterday. I'm on 37, apparently."

"I'll come by with the stick from the diplomatic pouch."

She shook her head. "I'll meet you back here and we'll head down together. Understood?"

"You do outrank me."

A moment later, she left. Stone went into the suite's bedroom. A spritz of cologne and a change of clothes? Wait, he was waiting for a woman to get dressed. Forget the French bath; he had time for soap and hot water.

While he showered, he searched for the current location of Gautam the mail clerk. Upstairs, probably drinking, certainly far away from the transparent floor hanging over the crater rim. Stone wondered if Merrill had found out how low Gautam ranked and moved on, then filed the irrelevant thought. The communication office was empty.

Who else worked on the third floor? His implantable found offices, found names, searched for locations. Most everyone was upstairs, except for one woman in her room on the sixtieth floor. Even better. No one would see him and Caitlyn sneaking around the communication office.

He cut the water, toweled off, dressed in a V-neck shirt and tight pants. After he retrieved the encrypted stick, he would join the party. Drunk women giddy in the afterglow of the wormhole placement. Fish, barrel, and one of his last times on the treadmill before Caitlyn tried to play him as an ace card—

Knuckles tapped the door. He opened it to find Caitlyn in a red blouse and a skirt with a beaded hem. Bare toes and sandal straps peeked under her skirt.

[You're casual,] he said through his embedded quantum computer.

[Playing the part. Ready?]

Stone slipped into canvas loafers and slung the toolkit over one shoulder. He pulled the door shut. After the latch clicked closed, he led her to the elevator.

As they descended, she asked, [Can you cut off security camera feeds in the hallway?]

[Don't need to. I invoked Protocol Eleven-J on tower security.]

The elevator slowed. The doors opened with a ping. No trace of sound from the party a thousand feet above. Stone headed out of the elevator and rounded the corner toward the communication office.

He stopped in front of the office's closed door. Pulled a scanner from his toolkit. Cameras in the hallway didn't worry him, but sensors on the door did. If Gautam had rigged the door to alert him if someone went into the office wanting to add something to the diplomatic pouch, he might barge in and force Stone to kill him.

Imagine the paperwork.

Stone ran the scanner along the door frame.

[What's that?] asked Caitlyn.

The scanner's electromagnetic field strength display hovered around zero. [You ever do any breaking and entering on the job?]

[I'm trained.]

He passed the scanner over the top corner of the door above the handle. [Just say *no*.] The needle in the display bounced up. He continued the sweep. No other items. Just a pair of proximity sensors, one on the door and the other on the frame, forming a circuit that would alert when broken.

Stone tapped the scanner's display, called up the *mimic* function, and held the scanner up to the corner of the door. [Open it. Go in.]

Caitlyn did. He followed her, sliding the scanner over the frame as he went. On the inside, the sensor on the frame showed a round black bump.

[Close the door.]

She eased the door shut. A telltale on the scanner showed the sensor on the door closed the circuit. He pulled the scanner down, turned it off.

The waiting room looked as shabby as it had the previous morning. In the video loop, a high tide isolated Mont-Saint-Michel. The closed window in the opaque glass wall shielded the workroom from view.

Beside the window in the corner of the room, a door of the same milky glass stood flush against the opaque wall. One handle, one deadbolt, both with key locks.

Pick the locks later. He scanned again. Two alarm circuits this time, one formed of prox sensors like the front door, another a motion sensor. From the scanner signal, it looked like the motion sensor's beam formed one side of a triangle, with the glass wall forming another and the grown bone side wall of the office forming a third.

Stone smiled to himself. Easy. [Same door as the first one, but after you go in, step over the motion sensor cutting the corner.] He pointed at the glass wall on the outside of where the motion sensor stood, then bent his arm to indicate the beam path.

She nodded.

He picked the locks, foiled the door's prox sensors, then lifted the handle. He high-stepped over the motion sensor beam into the workroom.

Easy so far, but if he failed to find the encrypted stick, Caitlyn would still try to kill him.

19

Blinds on the far wall smothered Minervan sunlight. A tang laced the air from the glue gun mounted on its telescoping arm near the front glass wall. Plastic shelves neatly arrayed with office supplies jutted from the bone wall on the right. A thin plastic desk in the corner. A dozen black boxes about one foot by one by two long, stacked three-high along the wall to the left, each sealed with a round UN logo sticker.

Stone switched the handheld scanner to RFID reader mode and crossed the room's tan carpet.

[There's a diplomatic pouch in each box?] Caitlyn asked.

[The box is the pouch]. He scanned the first. *UN mission, UNITBS Yassir Arafat*, dated three months earlier.

[Ah. The term must date back a few centuries. They used to send messages written on paper in a bag or pouch.]

Stone went to the other end. Knelt. Scanned the top box. *UN mission, Euler City, Minerva*. Today's date.

Second box in the stack. Dated yesterday.

A grin pushed up the corners of his mouth. He set aside the top box of the stack. Lifted yesterday's. Put it on the floor in front of him. With his gaze on the UN sticker on the lid and sidewall, he reached into his toolkit for a small knife. [I need another sticker.]

[Where? —I see a carton.] Caitlyn padded on her sandals to the shelves on the far wall. The carton of security stickers stood next to some antiques for handling paper mail: a block of wax, a seal, a set of letter openers.

He sliced through the sticker. Even if she couldn't find one to cover his tracks, he still had to get the encrypted stick out of the box. On discovering a compromised sticker, Gautam would just scrape it off and slap a new one on. The time and date stamp generated when the sticker unpeeled from its backing would differ from the date code readable from the box' RFID chip, but the mail clerk would hope none of his superiors would notice.

Stone sniffed out a chuckle. His superiors were UN flunkies too. If they noticed a discrepancy, they would bury it and hope *their* superiors never found out.

A sobering thought trickled down his chest. A Minervan would never do that.

He inhaled and pushed out a breath. Refocused, he opened the lid. Scores of memory sticks jumbled together, a riot of garish colors like the bin of toy cars his father had been too busy to play with in Stone's childhood.

Another focusing breath. Dump the box of memory sticks. Ping the one he needed through his implantable. In the middle of the pile.

Stone spread the sticks on the carpet. A red stripe. Three blue bumps. No, four; Gautam had added an RFID address label. There— no, two red lines, not one stripe. Was that—? Only one bump. There? Maroon, not crimson.

There. Right color, right width. Stone ran his fingertips over the red stripe. Four bumps. One bump uneven from excess glue. He pinged it through his implantable to make sure. He didn't recognize the sender's name, but he'd burned the destination address into his memory four months earlier.

[Here you go.] he said. Caitlyn, one hand behind her back, watched him with her hazel eyes. He tossed her the stick.

She slipped it into a pocket hidden in her skirt, then grinned and revealed her other hand. A round UN logo on a square white backing.

Stone scooped up two handfuls of sticks. [Help me get these back in.] He dumped the sticks into the box. Plastic clattered on plastic, thunderous in the dim silence. Caitlyn kneeled on her skirt and cupped her hands around more sticks—

Noise at the front door. Stone's hand shot to her wrists. He gave her a warning look, then turned to the opaque wall.

The frosted glass muffled a squeaky voice. "If someone wants to put something in the outbound pouch, your office should be open, right?"

"The alarm did not come from here," said Gautam. "It came from the workroom."

Stone tightened his grip on Caitlyn's wrists. [Looks like we tripped an alarm. No problem. Mail clerk called in tower security.]

[No problem!?]

[I invoked Eleven-J on them. I'll talk us out of this.] He stood and faced the door with open palms. She released the sticks from her hands to the beige carpet and mirrored Stone's pose.

The door from the waiting room swung open. The short and muscular security officer burst in. His partner followed. Gray eyes darted around the room, frowned at Caitlyn, then landed on Stone. "All clear."

Gautam's voice came from behind the opaque glass. "That cannot be. I test the alarms every day. It is not possible for there to be a false alarm." Black hair appeared behind the short and muscular officer. Gautam pushed the officer's shoulder and the officer chose to move out of his way.

Gautam stepped through the motion sensor beam. He regarded Stone and Caitlyn and rage boiled in his dark eyes. "Two criminals have broken into the communications office—broken the seal on a diplomatic pouch—and you issue an all clear?"

"They're here on vital UN business," the gray-eyed security officer said.

"How do you know this?"

"I'm not at liberty to say."

Gautam puffed himself up, a Third World bureaucrat asserting authority, either to make a threat or ask for a bribe. Or both. "*I* am here on vital UN business."

The short and muscular guard spoke in his squeaky voice,

"Mr. Lavallette, ma'am, whatever your business, wrap it up soon so we can all forget about this—"

"I said vital UN business." For a moment, Stone didn't recognize the communication clerk's voice. He'd flattened it, given it a tone of dry menace.

Gautam went on. "I invoke Protocol Eleven-J."

Caitlyn sucked in a breath. The security officers shot nervous looks from Stone to Gautam and back.

"Here is the confirmation code," Gautam said. A moment later, the gray-eyed security officer pressed his lips together.

Caitlyn's face regained its usual poise. With a glint in her hazel eyes, she said, "And for the record, here's mine."

The security officer nodded, face pale. Sweat beaded on the short, muscular guard's forehead.

Stone kept his face calm. His mind raced behind it. Who could have Eleven-J clearance other than Caitlyn or him?

Gray's comment on that last spring morning in UNICA headquarters came back. The team to establish the UNICA field office on Minerva traveled under cover on *Yassir Arafat*.

This officious, forgettable Indian was Gray's man on Minerva.... A grin bared Stone's teeth. An excellent cover—

The grin froze. If Gautam checked the manifest of the diplomatic pouch, he'd realize that Stone had stolen the real message to Gray. Then he'd report Stone's action to the old man. Then....

Stone's heart pounded like a gong, loud yet slow. He could still come clean. Enlist Gautam's help to kill Caitlyn and reveal the plot to Gray.

Except Caitlyn's embedded quantum computer would betray him to Bale and the others even after her death. Five soldiers had sneaked up on him before. Even in the tower, could he and Gautam and the encrypted stick all survive to alert Gray?

No. [He's UNICA field office,] Stone said. [We have to kill him.]

[Agreed,] Caitlyn replied.

"Gentlemen," Stone said to the security officers, "this is above your pay grade. You should wait in the hall."

The gray-eyed security officer tapped his partner's shoulder. "Good idea." Both men slipped out. The short, muscular one pulled closed the frosted glass door. The front door to the communications office shut with a click sounding around the edges of the opaque door and window.

"Who the hell are you?" Gautam asked.

"She's ITB. As for me... you and I have a mutual employer."

"What? I'm a communication clerk."

"With Eleven-J authority? Don't blow smoke up my ass and tell me it's a nicotine enema. You're head of the UNICA field office."

Gautam rocked back on his heels. "You're an operative? Which one? Phantom? Hybrid? Sharpshooter?"

"That's not important."

"Yes it is," Gautam said. "I have to include it in my report." His brown-eyed gaze dipped to the heap of memory sticks near the opened box. "Along with why you compromised a diplomatic pouch."

"Gray had evidence that someone with inside knowledge was bringing schematics for the exotic matter factory at Hawking Station to Minerva on *Yassir Arafat*. We're pulling the report he wanted to send to co-conspirators on Earth." A good story to come up with in a few seconds.

Gautam considered. "That would explain her presence. But yours?"

"We're on a joint task force. Someone from ITB to identify the evidence. And a UNICA operative to do good tradecraft."

Through their embedded quantum computer interface, Caitlyn sent Stone an image of her sticking out her tongue.

Gautam sounded like he believed the story. "Where is the pulled report?"

Stone kneeled. Shrugged the toolkit off his shoulder. "In here." The toolkit thumped on the flimsy carpet. Stone reached in.

Gautam leaned forward.

Plastic and stamped steel touched Stone's fingers. He slid the safety off. One smooth motion brought the pistol out, sights to his eye, finger squeezing with extra pressure the heavy trigger.

The pistol roared and kicked against Stone's hand. The tang of propellant filled the air.

Gautam toppled backward. Blood oozed out of a pit in his face where his eye had been. The air stank of blood and brain. Crimson soaked the thin beige carpet.

His body trembled under the last commands of his mangled brain. You have to hit the brain stem to kill a man instantly.

Poor bastard. Doing his job.

Just like I'm doing mine.

Slender fingers touched Stone's shoulder. He got to his feet. Caitlyn kept her mouth shut. Speaking wouldn't work, her ears must ring as loudly as his. [What's our story for the security officers?]

[Nothing.]

[They heard the gunshot!]

Stone's gaze dropped to Gau—the comm clerk's ruined face, then shied away.

What's wrong with you? He's not the first man you've killed.

```
[Stone Chalmers has killed 204 people, of whom 191 were
adult males-]
```

He swatted the reminder away. The embedded quantum computer shoved facts at him like a hypnogogued cover story? Dammit.

```
[Adjusting settings.]
```

[Hey.] Caitlyn's hazel eyes studied him. [Answer my question!]

Her question—

[How can we tell the two men in the hallway that nothing happened?]

[We don't have to. We invoked Protocol Eleven-J. Follow me.]

They carefully went around the dead man's pooling blood. Stone grabbed his toolkit like a wino clutching a bottle in a paper bag. His foot disturbed the heap of memory sticks around the open box. Stone led Caitlyn through the opaque glass door without deactivating the alarms.

In the hallway outside the waiting room, the security officers looked up from a tight huddle. "What happened?" asked the gray-eyed one.

"I can't tell you. For your own protection." Stone reached into the toolkit. "Thanks for loaning me your sidearm." He handed the 9mm to the gray-eyed security officer. "And you can do the UN a great favor. Go to your office, scrub all audio and video from the entire building for the last hour, and leave the cameras and microphones off until we contact you. All should be clear by 2200."

The gray-eyed security officer slipped his pistol into a pocket of his tactical pants. His lips mashed together like he wanted to spit out a mouthful of foul options. "We can do that."

Stone clapped his hand on the security officer's shoulder. In his own ears, his voice sounded brittle. "You two are a credit to the UN. I only wish I could write a commendation."

"Doing a good job is all the commendation we need."

"That's right," echoed the short, muscular one.

"Words to live by," said Stone. He gave the security officer's shoulder an extra squeeze. The man took the hint. The two security officers shuffled down the hall and around the corner to the elevator lobby.

[Now we have to clean up a crime scene in eight hours,] Stone said.

[I'll ask for help.]

[Wait. You're going to bring your Minervan friends into the tower?]

[UN employees are inviting their local contacts to the party. But we don't need my colleagues. Just some items that can help us. Carpet cleaners. Deodorizers. Large scan-proof bags. One of Bradley dell'Angelo's heavy cargo drones.]

[Okay. Go make arrangements. I'll stay here.]

An eyebrow arched over a hazel eye. [Why?]

[I missed a sensor in the workroom. And if that's the UNICA field office, there are recording devices in there too.] Dumping the corpse twenty miles out to sea wouldn't help if Gray found out Stone had killed his field officer.

[Take care of them. I'll contact my friends when I get in the elevator.] Caitlyn set off down the hallway. The slap of her sandals against the carpeted hallway sounded carefree.

Stone went back into the waiting room. He left the outer door unlocked. On the slim chance someone came with a dropoff for the diplomatic pouch, they would expect to enter the waiting room. But when the mail clerk failed to answer at the window, and they tested the locks on the frosted glass door—

He opened the workroom door. The stink of blood and brain hit his nose. Stone slipped in. The door thumped closed. A thumbpress locked the handle; a turn, the deadbolt.

The stench assaulted him more strongly. Stone ignored it as best he could. Secure now, he pulled the scanner from his toolkit. Perhaps they'd stepped on a pressure sensor under the carpet. With his back to the dead man, Stone scanned the carpet along the path they'd taken.

The scanner beeped as soon as he started, where their first steps over the motion sensor beam had landed. Clever placement.

Now to find the recording devices hidden in the room, and the computer saving those devices to memory. He worked methodically, passing the scanner over a foot-wide swathe of the walls, starting next to the ceiling near the door.

He paused with his sleeve brushing the window blind. First pass clear. One foot lower, back toward—

A handle clanked. Hinges sounded. Light from the hallway entered the waiting room and blurred when it hit the frosted glass window.

Stone lowered his arms. He rested the scanner on the floor near his feet, then stood immobile.

A pad of footsteps. The handle to the frosted glass door rattled.

[Caitlyn, is that you?]

[I'm two miles across town.]

[Then who's in the waiting room?]

The deadbolt shot back into the door. A key scraped the tumblers in the handle lock.

The handle turned. "Gautam, you here?"

The door opened. A shock of purple hair. Eyes as white as full moons fixated on Gautam's corpse, then regarded Stone.

20

Four strides across the room. At his third, Merrill reacted. She shuffled back and pulled the door toward her.

Far too late. Stone's left hand clamped the door. His right hand shot to her neck. Lifted her. Squeezed.

Her eyes seemed even larger now. Gurgles came from her throat. She swung her fists sideways at his face, kicked black canvas sneakers at his shins. His longer reach held her at bay.

He pivoted. The door fell shut. Still strangling her, he shoved her against the shelves. The box of security stickers tumbled to the floor, unrolling a dozen copies of the UN logo. He jammed his left hand past her frantic fists. Plowed his fingers through her hair. His fingernails scraped her scalp, pulled hair, drew blood.

A growing mass of minuscule wires lodged under his nails.

She grabbed his right arm, tried pulling it away from her throat. He squeezed harder. Her face turned blue. Sweat matted her hair to her forehead and stank of her panic.

He kept scraping the transcranial stim wiring from her scalp. It looked like black thread, finer than the purple-dyed hair and blacker than the red droplets of blood coming with it. Had to get enough to block her from making an emergency call.

Her blue face turned purple. Her eyes bulged. She scratched her nails on his arm, acceding to his strength, trying to break his grip with pain. Soaked with adrenaline, he felt only the pressure of her fingers, no pain.

She kicked like a trapped rabbit. Her foot slammed the inside of his right knee.

His leg wobbled. He grunted. Despite his adrenaline pain throbbed.

He grunted and squeezed harder.

The muscles of her throat worked but no sound came. Her eyes rolled back. Her arms fell to her sides.

Stone lowered her feet to the floor, but his grip remained strong. Unconsciousness comes quickly, but her heart had to stop for strangulation to kill.

He looked away, then forced himself to look at her purple, eye-bulged face. A viscous black liquid seemed to run down his spine. He kept looking.

He'd killed women before, even women he'd previously bedded. Granted, those had all been like Teresa Benavides, subjects of his investigation who'd ended up in the UN's crosshairs. Part of the game.

Not like this. Merrill had been doing her job, in a sense. She'd come looking for her boyfriend. The fool had given her a key to a UNICA field office. He'd brought this on her—

Don't. Sure, lie to other people. But don't lie to yourself. You're the one killing her. Yes, you have a good reason. Kill a witness to a crime you committed while committing another crime....

You have a reason, at least. If she lives long enough to get a message to Gray, you die. Either at Gray's hand or those of Caitlyn's Minervan friends. Now, you live one more day.

There was never more than that to his life.

His right arm ached. He checked her pulse with his left. Nothing.

His knee almost buckled under when he moved. He laid Merrill's limp body on the carpet near Gautam's corpse, outside of the crimson splotch of blood-soaked carpet. He checked her wrist, her neck, her chest. No pulse, no breath. Dead.

Stone rocked back with his backside on the floor. Three messages from Caitlyn waited for him. He skipped them, went straight to a call.

She answered in a moment. [What happened?]

[Bring a second body bag,] he said. He expected to hear black humor in his voice yet heard none.

A forest green sedan from the motor pool crouched with its headlights off near the guardrail of the scenic overlook off the coast highway. A hundred yards down the sheer crater wall, the Wisdom Sea crashed waves. Euler City glowed over the horizon, washing out the lowest tiers of northern stars.

Stone limped back from one of the two heavyweight drones. He'd shoved Gautam's stiffening body into the drone's cargo bay despite his swollen, unbendable knee. Caitlyn had offered to let him handle the lighter of the two corpses. He'd declined. Hopefully she accepted it as a gesture of manliness, and didn't see the chasm opening inside him at the thought of handling Merrill's body.

Fool. The same gray blockchain bound them together. She already knew.

"Ready?" she said over the rustle of waves.

"I'm glad Sheila didn't come to facilitate their funerals."

Her face showed as a pale oval against the night. "Me too. She's a good person who knows in her head what we must do. But not in her heart."

The drones' motors hummed. She must have sent the command to them by a thought. The drones rose, unimpeded by their lifeless cargoes, their warning lights turned off. Over the guardrail they flew and headed east over the sea. Night veiled them within seconds.

Five miles out, the drones would open their cargo hatches. The depth and prevailing current would carry the corpses fifty miles further, through habitats of sharks and carrion-eating wolffish. Even if their remains washed ashore in months or years, investigators would write it off as a murder-suicide, strangulation followed by a gunshot to the forehead.

"Sheila's a good person," Stone said. "Unlike us."

Caitlyn stared out to sea. "We do some evil things."

"But the goal justifies them?"

"No. It just makes it easier for me to sleep at night. I didn't think that was a problem for you."

"It's not. It wasn't."

"What do you mean?"

He blew a breath into the chill desert night. "I tell myself I play the greatest game in the settled galaxy. A game where the loser dies. But unless I win every round, I'll end up like them." He looked up in the direction the drones had flown. "Meat to be disposed."

Wind gusted over the crater rim. "You'll end up like them even if you do win every round," Caitlyn said. "You're good at the game. You could be great if you had a reason to play."

He leaned against the sedan and let the pounding waves below set the rhythm of his thoughts.

After a time, a faint buzz over the sea heralded the return of the drones. They emerged from the night and descended over the guardrail. Gently they touched the asphalt. The motors silenced.

Caitlyn reached into the sedan and handed him a spray bottle. He limped over to one of the drones. With one hand, he tilted the drone onto its side rotors. The drone's cargo hatch dangled open. He sprayed a foam of nanomachines on the underside of the hatch and on every surface of the cargo compartment. Caitlyn did the same.

They'd used the same foam in the communication office. For five minutes the foam hissed like a glass of sparkling water. After that, the hissing faded. The foam hardened, then crumbled into powder carried off by the wind.

Caitlyn handed him a can of compressed air. He chased stubborn flecks of the powder from the hatch hinge and corners of the compartment with sharp puffs. One puff jetted bitter grit into his mouth. He winced and spewed breath between tight lips.

"Final check," Caitlyn said.

"I can do this."

"You've done enough. Rest your knee." He limped back to the sedan. A scanner display threw a sickly green light over her as she ran the scanner's wand over the hatch and interiors of both drone cargo compartments. "Clean."

"Send them home," Stone said, but their motors had already spun up. Seconds later they climbed into the sky, heading north toward

Bradley dell'Angelo's shoreline facility. Their silhouettes showed briefly against the glow of Euler City before vanishing into the night.

"Our turn," Caitlyn said. The forest green sedan opened its near-side doors. "We should be back fifteen or twenty minutes before the security officers restart the cameras." She stooped to enter, then halted.

"I need to say something," said Stone.

She straightened her back. "Go."

He swallowed. "Earlier, when I agreed to join you, I didn't mean it."

"I know."

"I mean it now."

The night was too dim to make out her agate eyes. "I know that too."

Epilogue

A thunderstorm threw rain like pebbles at Gray's windows. Inside, warm lights, plush chairs, and the peaty aroma of whisky formed a bubble of comfort.

Stone drank sparkling water. Tart juice from a lime wedge mingled with the bitter edge of minerals as he prepared to lie.

Gray angled his head toward one of the monitors on the standing desk behind him to his right. "Minerva isn't the threat I feared."

"I realized that even before the wormhole placement. High technology combined with complete innocence. We'll roll the Minervans before they know what hit them."

"How did you acquire such detailed intelligence on the Center for Alignment with the Universe?"

Stone shrugged with a smirk. "Minerva's ruling class is like any other. They insist on a strict moral code, while underneath they're corrupt as hell."

"You refer in particular to Facilitatrix van Bentum? A woman three times your age?"

Stone's smirk widened. "The things I do for the United Nations."

"Spare me the details." He sipped whisky. "You failed to see a live consecration. Convocation?"

"Consecration is the psych testing they inflict on thirteen-year-olds. Myers-Briggs, enneagram, something like that. Convocation is a form of verbal hazing, like the lemon sessions sorority girls use to make each other conform, or what Third World dictators call struggle sessions, where the capitalists or the communists or whoever publicly admit their crimes. Standard cult stuff."

"So it sounds." Gray picked up his whisky glass. With the shimmering brown liquid near his mouth, he said, "Setting aside your report, what do you know about the double disappearance?"

"The—? Oh, the mail clerk and the girl? People were whispering about it my last three days on Minerva."

"What do you think happened?"

Stone sipped. "The day of the party, the UN staffers were giddy after the successful wormhole placement. By late night, they were hammered drunk as well."

"You observed your father often enough in his last years to know 'hammered drunk' when you see it."

Who the hell was Gray to bring that up? Stone kept the thought off his face. "Anyway, I'd guess they went up on the tower's roof and fell off."

"Both of them?"

"Drunk and giddy? Sure. Why do you care?"

Gray's eyes reminded him of shotgun barrels. "The tower's security systems happened to fail near the start of the party and only resumed working at midnight."

"Hmm. I never heard that." He gazed past Gray at the painting of a sailboat race and looked thoughtful. "No surprise. Those security officers struck me as inept from the day *Yassir Arafat* left Hawking Station."

Gray sipped, then set his whisky on his cherrywood desktop with a thud. " 'Never attribute to malice what can be explained by stupidity?' "

"Exactly." Stone sipped mineral water. Gray would soon hint he should leave. Time to bring up what Caitlyn had instructed him to ask. "I won't take more of your time, but before I go, I want time off."

One eyebrow arched. "How much?"

"A month." Stone read the older man's face. "Is that a problem?"

"It's an unexpected request. At the end of your previous mission, you recoiled at an enforced leave of absence."

"That was for six months," Stone said. "And it wasn't my choice or yours."

"True. But why?"

Stone yawned from the red eye flight from LA and the body clock reset from Minerva's shorter day. "I spent a week pretending to be Edward Lavallette, gathered intel from public sources, and no one tried to kill me. It was easier work. I could get used to it. I want to think about it. Make sure before I request reassignment."

Gray blinked once, then nudged at the knot in his necktie. "There are times you surprise me, Hybrid. You have your month. Use it well."

"Thanks." Stone threw the rest of his sparkling water down his throat, then rose from the plush chair.

"Wait."

Stone stood, left hand like a crane holding the empty glass. "Yes?"

"I only learned after your return that Caitlyn Fredriksen had journeyed to Minerva with the diplomatic mission and stayed until after the wormhole placement. Did you know that?"

"No." Stone shrugged.

"Would you have sought her out if you had known?"

"Sought? You mean ask her out on a date?" Stone laughed. "No. Never. My relationship with her is purely business."

IN PUBLIC CONVOCATION ASSEMBLED

Prologue

Forty-seven stories above Manhattan, a stiff wind lashed the man in the plaid tan suit. Ahead of him, a ventilation shaft like an aluminum pagoda jutted four feet above the roof of UN headquarters.

Wedged between two of the shaft's horizontal slats hung a slumped gray smear. A man clad in pale blue overalls, with a tool belt on his hip and a UNHQ maintenance department patch on his chest, accompanied the suited man. The maintenance worker said, "I was about this far away when I saw the thing. Thought it was a plastic bag at first. Stuff like that blows up here sometimes, you know?"

A gust rippled the suited man's pants leg and whipped the end of his necktie below a gold tie clasp as he strode on.

The maintenance man kept talking. "Even though plastic bags are regulated. I was going to pull the thing off and hand it to NYPD so they could scan the chip and figure out who dropped the thing instead of throwing it away...."

The man in the plaid tan suit stopped at the ventilation shaft. He knelt and peered at the object. A translucent gray skin, torn and snagged on a gouge in one of the horizontal slats, covered a palm-sized frame of clear plastic. From the frame's corners rose propellers formed of the same clear plastic and secured within clear plastic rings.

"When I saw the thing was a drone," the maintenance man said, "I figured it was some toy a kid let loose from a balcony on the other side of First Av." He waved the back of his hairy hand toward the skyscrapers rising above their heads to the west. "I was just going to toss it—"

"You were going to throw out an item that violated UNHQ airspace?" The suited man had a gravelly voice. "Toy or not."

The maintenance man blinked repeatedly. He mouthed air before words came in a rush. "I know I'm supposed to report every last little thing that's out of whack but I'd just be wasting your time with distractions that keep you from what you're supposed to be doing, am I right?"

"In that case, why didn't you throw it in the trash?" The suited man cleared his throat. "Why are you wasting my time?"

"No, swear to God, I'm not wasting your time. I was going to toss it, but when I got as close to it as we are now, I saw a flash. Lit up the inside of the shaft like a strobe. White so light it looked blue. I've never seen or heard of a kid's toy drone that would do that. And then it put out a burned electrical smell. A spy drone would self-destruct like that, am I right?"

"A spy drone?" The suited man ran a finger along his mustache. He then reached into his suit jacket's inner pocket. Out came latex gloves and a rolled-up case of brown leatherette.

He slid the gloves over his hands, then set the case on the roof, opened the hook-and-loop closure with a *scritch* momentarily louder than the moaning wind, and unrolled the case. Pockets held tools and evidence bags in straight rows.

The man in the plaid suit slid large tweezers from their pocket. With a pinch of his fingers and a flick of his wrist, a gallon bag unfolded. The bag's opening gaped.

He moved the tweezers toward the snared drone. "If this is a spy device, we'll find out."

1

A woman's voice in his head woke him. [It's time.]

The light of an overcast day seeped through the vertical blinds and softened the clinical lines and grayscale palette of Stone Chalmers' bedroom. Instead of rain, Manhattan's incessant background noise sounded on the windows.

Alone on his king mattress, Stone stretched his arms. His knuckles bumped the headboard. [Let me sleep, Caitlyn.] The quantum computers embedded in their skulls on Minerva were too damn invasive.

[There's a lot we need you to do today. Get up.]

We? Caitlyn Fredriksen—hazel eyes, long blond hair, an Interstellar Transport Bureau operative with three years of experience in spycraft, and despite her youth trusted with great responsibility—ran the Minervan conspiracy's operations in New York alone.

Didn't she?

Stone swung his legs over the side of the bed. Clad only in pajama pants, he shuffled toward the bathroom. [Where do you want me to start?]

[The Iron Horse Gym. On 94th between 1st and 2nd. Your retina scan is in their system under the name Galen Heinrichs. Your retina scan will allow you in. It will also open men's locker 19.]

[And then?]

[I'll let you know. Out.]

After taking a leak, he went to the kitchen of his apartment and prepared a pre-workout shake. A soprano's aria trickled to him through the wall from Mr. Leipziger's place. Stone drank bitter greens incompletely masked by the flavor of chocolate.

In the living room, he slid the coffee table on its plastic feet across the hardwood floor, then ran through five Tibetan yoga exercises. He took a step toward the eighty-eight pound kettlebell on the corner rack, then stopped.

If he had to go over thirty blocks north to a gym, why not work out there?

By the time Stone changed into workout clothes, packed an outfit to change into after a shower, and descended the elevator, his coupe waited for him at the curb. The coupe's black finish and faceted angles alternatively absorbed and reflected the sickly light of an autumn day. A far cry from the curved lines of the cars the Minervans had given to the UN motor pool. The two-door in which he'd ridden with Caitlyn to the pine forest two nights before the wormhole placement. The sedan carrying two corpses out of the UN tower—

Stone pinched the bridge of his nose. If the plot he'd joined with her succeeded, in ten years, all his crimes would be revealed.

If the plot failed, he would be dead.

His black coupe popped open its curb-side door. He climbed in.

The car's nav computer decided that the FDR would be quicker than 3rd Avenue. He soon traveled north along the East River. Choppy gray water like the scales of a rotting trout lay between him and Roosevelt Island. Behind him, teeming skyscrapers blocked the view of UN headquarters a mile to the south.

In the neighborhoods around UN headquarters, a million people worked for official agencies and affiliated international non-profits. A million people imposed the UN's will on Earth's five billion survivors of the Crisis of the Twenty-First Century and the inhabitants of almost fifty colony worlds.

Five Minervans, Caitlyn, and he would somehow depose them.

Stone exhaled. He'd faced long odds when he'd worked to impose the UN's will on others. He'd deal with the long odds now the way he had then: take one action at a time.

His coupe pulled up in front of the gym. Tinted glass covered a three-story building. Stone got out and went to a door under a flat awning while the coupe drove off to the nearest parking garage with an open space. He turned his eye to the retina scanner, pressed his bare forearms together in front of his chest.

A buzz. A green light. He pulled open the door and went in. Across an open space the width of the building, black and cushy interlocking mats covered the floor. The far wall held racks of kettlebells, black cast iron cannonballs with integrated handles. In one corner, an obese man huffed through swings with an eighteen-pound kettlebell. A man whose deep wrinkles and wispy white hair indicated years of missed rejuvenation treatments wobbled on his knees while he pressed a thirty-six-pounder above his head. A woman with frazzled hair and postpartum jowls lunged across the gym, holding in each hand a kettlebell so small Stone couldn't even guess the weight.

Quick glances told Stone these weren't counterintel operatives tipped off to who he was and why he came here.

He followed a sign for *Locker Rooms* and went toward the back. Down open stairs came the whiskings of a stationary bike class. Flashes of color from upstairs suggested a video wall depicted a jungle full of ruined stone temples blurring past the cyclists.

The door to the men's locker room creaked open when he neared. A musty scent and the aroma of a citrus cleaner battled in his nose. The musty scent won. Cobalt blue subway tiles covered the floor. The lockers stood two-high along the sidewall. Silence from the showers and no one else about.

A retina scan lock you could buy at a bodega sealed locker 19. Stone lifted it to his eye. A green LED soon flashed. He tugged the lock open and used it as a handle to swing out the locker door.

An unlabeled memory stick lay in the back corner, as if it had fallen out of someone's hip pocket. A plastic sack, twist tied by its handles, looked—and smelled—like it held last week's socks.

Stone shoved his gym bag in and locked up.

Twenty minutes later, breathing slowly while his straight left arm held eighty-eight pounds of iron above his head, Caitlyn's voice barged into his mind. [What are you doing?]

[Putting legs under my cover story.] Gaze on the black kettlebell above him, he bent his knees and blindly reached for the floor with his right hand.

[You have to be in Turtle Bay in two hours.] She referred to the neighborhood around UN headquarters. [With one stop along the way.]

His right hand flattened on the padded floor. He sat, kettlebell still held straight up. [I'll make it.]

[You're planning to shower after your workout?]

[Yes. Wait, do you have a thing for sweaty man smell?] He lowered his back to the mat, reached his right hand across his chest to set the kettlebell down with two hands. [I didn't realize you were nearby.]

She drew out the word [No.]

[You aren't nearby? You know enough tradecraft to hide your interaction with me. Say, what's the wireless comm range on our embedded quantum computers?] He'd guessed a few miles, but would love to know for certain.

[You don't need to know. Take a shower. But don't shave.]

After rinsing off body wash and leaving a day's stubble on his jaw, Stone changed into a long-sleeved light blue polo, a sweater of darker blue, khakis, and leather sneakers. He tossed the plastic sack and the memory stick on top of his workout clothes in his gym bag. Moments later, the front door of the gym opened for him. A gust off the river swirled around him. His black coupe waited at the curb and opened its door. Stone threw his gym bag onto the seat and climbed into comfortable warmth.

[Where's my stop before Turtle Bay?]

[Go to a parking garage on 58th between 5th and Madison,] Caitlyn said. [Open the plastic sack after you park.]

Stone spoke his destination aloud. The car pulled away from the curb and he asked, [What's in the sack?]

[We'll get to that. On the way, I'll tell you what's on the encrypted stick.]

[I'm listening.]

The coupe slid into the lane to turn left onto 1st.

[It contains intel you gathered about the Minervan exotic matter factory and fleet of warpdrive ships being prepared for a mission against Earth.]

Stone squinted at the tower on the Queens side of the Triborough Bridge a mile across the East River. [I'm feeding someone false intel. —It is false, right?]

[Of course it's false,] she said. He couldn't tell if she lied. The coupe turned north on 1st. But she must have lied. When they towed one end of a wormhole to Minerva, the crew of *Yassir Arafat* would have turned their cameras toward the rest of Minerva's solar system. Judging from the tens of thousands of square kilometers of photovoltaic panels visible on his approach to the UN's exotic matter and wormhole factory at Hawking Station, an exotic matter factory would be impossible to hide. The rumor mill would have spread news of a Minervan exotic matter factory to every UN employee on the ship before *Yassir Arafat* entered orbit.

The coupe turned left onto 95th. [Who are we lying to? Why?]

[Your assignment is to make contact with a woman named Nina Irani.] Caitlyn sent a dossier to his mind that felt like a large pill stuck in his throat. [She's a senior security affairs advisor for Secretary-General Sayyid. When you have achieved rapport, give her the false intel.]

[How did I get this intel? Why aren't I letting it reach her through the usual channels?]

[Tell a partial truth: you're an operative sent out on one of the first missions to Minerva. Don't say who you work for. And as for the usual channels, hint to her that they're compromised.]

[Don't say who I work for? No, I have to.]

[Why?]

He shook his head. It should be obvious, even to an Interstellar Transport Bureau operative, a keyhole kop. [I'll have a lot more credibility if I drop an agency name. And if the usual channels are compromised, she'll know not to inquire about me to my superior.]

After a pause, she said, [Good call.] Her tone of voice matched her relative inexperience in tradecraft.

[I know.]

At 2nd, the coupe turned left through a break in the flow of pedestrians through the crosswalk. The car accelerated south toward Midtown. [You haven't told me about our objective.]

[Our objective is straightforward. We want Secretary-General Sayyid to call for military action against Minerva.]

[You've lost me.]

[Good.]

He drove downtown with silence in his head. The clotted flow of traffic gave him time to skim the dossier and form an impression of Nina Irani. A summertime video shot through a telephoto lens was a study in earth tones: deep brown hair coiled at the back. Large amber sunglasses. Olive skin. A low, wide mouth with lush lips painted ochre. A lightweight blazer of oak-brown linen over a pastel yellow silk top and soft trim curves.

If he could see her eyes, he would know how to play her. He would just have to improvise in person.

He skimmed her biography. Born in Mumbai, the largest and richest city remaining in the Republic of India after the secessions and civil wars of the twenty-first century. Irani graduated *summa cum laude* from the Nehru School of Public Administration in New Delhi, and had worked for the UN ever since. Fifteen years in New York. Married two years back in her late twenties, divorced. Childless.

A strategy seeded itself in his mind. Still, he would have to meet her in person before committing to that angle of attack.

The coupe turned left on 57th to loop back to the garage on one-way 58th. Stone closed the dossier and opened the false intel report. The mythical Minervan exotic matter factory supposedly shared the colony world's nearly circular orbit, half a revolution behind Minerva and hence hidden by Minerva's sun. Schematics showed a gigantic cyclotron, a vast array of solar cells to power it, and a comparably vast set of radiators to dump waste heat toward interstellar space. A schedule purported to show how the exotic matter factory avoided detection by the UN wormhole tug: selectively turning off scattered solar cells, to send reflections matching the starfield behind the power array to the UN ship. Crew lists and resupply ship manifests rounded out the story.

But exotic matter alone failed to threaten Earth. The airdocks for assembling the battlefleet masqueraded as mining facilities on a rocky moon of a gas giant a billion miles from Minerva. The ships matched the typical design of warpdrive ships throughout the settled galaxy, with fore and aft warp rings at the ends of a long, skinny cylindrical hull. The battlefleet's crews trained—Stone chuckled—in the basements of Centers for Alignment with the Universe.

The false intel implicated not only Minerva's government, but also the colony world's official pseudo-church in preparing for war with Earth.

Why?

The coupe turned left into the parking garage on 58th. It avoided the lane for *contract parking only* and climbed the ramp to a gate and a payment kiosk of blobby blue plastic. *Use same card at exit* and who still used bits of plastic to charge things? *$4,000 per 15 minutes. All day $100,000.*

[Pay for all day,] Caitlyn said.

Twenty-five blocks to UN headquarters under blustery weather. [You want me to walk to meet Nina Irani?]

[No. Pay for all day anyway.]

Stone subvoked to the computer implanted under a flap of skin on his chest—old Earth tech that felt obsolete compared to the quantum computer embedded in his skull on Minerva—and his implantable relayed his instructions to the kiosk.

"All day parking on levels 15-19," announced a synthesized feminine voice. The gate lifted.

[Level 18. Back corner,] said Caitlyn.

[Why?]

[You'll see.]

The coupe spiraled up a concrete corkscrew. The ramp reminded him of the long descent in Ulrich's secret tunnel from the inhabited plateau to the lowland launch site on Trinity. Headlights snapped on against the dark passageway. Faintly queasy, he shut his eyes. Ears aching, he pinched shut his nose and tried to exhale.

When his car straightened and leveled its path, Stone opened his eyes. A giant *18* in an ugly decades-old typeface slipped past his headlights. He rode past a knot of cars near the elevator bank. Empty parking spaces lay on both sides of the drive lane. Ahead stood a nondescript sedan, four doors, tinted windows, metallic blue paint on a thin aluminum skin faceted like an old-time stealth aircraft. One of ten thousand clones plying the streets of New York. [There,] Caitlyn said.

[Thanks for the tip.] His coupe parked next to the sedan. [Now what?]

[Switch cars. It will unlock for you.]

Stone slung his gym bag over his shoulder and climbed out of his coupe. He grabbed the handle of the sedan's nearest door. It hesitated, then opened. Cloth seats and a chill interior, the sedan had waited hours for him. He sat and rubbed his hands together. He inhaled new car smell. [You bought this for me?]

[Use this car from now on when you meet Irani or do other things we might ask of you. It has a transponder for the contract parking entrance to this garage so payments won't be charged to any account in your name. For all your other expenses, look in the envelope tucked in the pocket behind your lower legs.]

Stone pulled out the envelope. Two credit cards in different names and a sheaf of US dollars in small denominations, $5000s and $20,000s. He slid the credit cards and about a quarter-million in 20Gs into his wallet. He buried the envelope with the rest of the cash under rustling plastic deep in his gym bag.

With a hunch forming, he fished the plastic sack from the locker out of his bag. [And this—?]

[You've figured it out, I think,] Caitlyn said. [Your disguise.]

2

Stone untied the handles, reached in. Pulled out a fake beard the same dirty blond as his hair except for a few grays along the sideburns.

He flipped it over. Frowned. For all the skill at tradecraft Caitlyn and the Minervans had shown, they thought this amateurish nonsense would fool anyone?

[Just when I think you aren't the usual keyhole kop, you hand me this? This beard doesn't even have adhesive on the back.]

[It doesn't need it.]

[Like hell—]

[You didn't shave at the gym, right? Press it against your face.]

Stone raised it toward his jaw.

[Stop! Flip down the visor and use the makeup mirror!]

He rolled his eyes but lowered the beard. He crouched, took a step, flipped down the visor, then flipped up the flap over the makeup mirror. LED strips flanking the mirror illuminated his face with strong white light. When had he gotten those fine wrinkles around his eyes?

Stone set that thought aside. Carefully he lined up the beard, then starting next to his left ear he pressed it three inches at a time to his face.

A sensation like tiny insects crawled from left to right over his jaw. The urge to jerk his head away from the fake beard struck him, but he resisted. His head stayed still as he pressed the last portions of the fake beard to his face.

[The artificial beard tied itself to individual facial hairs,] Caitlyn said.

When the crawling insect feeling went away, Stone pinched the end of the beard between his fingertips and gently tugged. The fake beard held. He tugged harder. The fake beard held and he winced.

He checked his appearance from three angles, then snapped the visor back against the headliner. [A good disguise, as far as it goes. But it won't fool anyone who knows me.]

[Yes. But we have more for you. Look in the sack.]

Stone looked and pulled out an object. A clear plastic zippered sandwich bag held a yellowish folded item and a smaller clear zippered bag. The smaller bag held eight dollops of a thick gray material sandwiched between sheets of transparent plastic.

[Put on the gloves first,] Caitlyn said, [or you'll get elf fingers.]

The yellowish folded item was a pair of latex gloves, he saw now. [Elf fingers? Sounds serious. Can I cure it with an antibiotic?]

His attempted joke made no impact. [Don't even open the inner bag until the gloves are on.]

[Understood.] He slid on the latex gloves, then withdrew the inner bag. [What now?]

[You remember Matthew Thomas?]

Through the reputation blockchain, shared by every adult on Minerva, and recently including Caitlyn and Stone, a public profile came to Stone's mind. Matthew Thomas, medical nanotechnologist of South Asian ancestry and high ratings for skill and safety.

The High Emprise conspiracy's private blockchain, shared only by Caitlyn and a handful of Minervans—and recently, and unwanted, by Stone—confirmed that Matthew Thomas had purchased ten sets of osteomorphic nanomachines for topical application from a Minervan company with excellent ratings for quality, safety, and value.

[How could I forget?]

[How a convoked person's embedded quantum computer interfaces between the blockchain and the person's brain can vary between individuals,] Caitlyn said.

More information rushed into Stone's mind. Simon Bale, the Minervan government's highest security official, had placed the osteomorphic nanomachines in the diplomatic pouch sent through the new wormhole to Minerva's mission to the UN.

Osteomorphic... topical application....

[Thomas selected some nanogoop that will penetrate my skin and change bone?]

[Exactly. Facial recognition software running on a public camera feed would see through your beard in seconds. The software looks for distances and angles of brow ridge, cheekbones, jawline, and chin. This will fool it. You'll need the makeup mirror in the visor again.]

Stone's muscles tensed to cross the cabin. Headlights washed over the concrete wall in front of him. A tiny car, a two-seater box on wheels, parked three spots away. Stone dropped his gloved hands below the windows and blanked his face like someone reviewing text or video projected to their optic nerves by Earth's standard tech, transcranial magnetic stim. He in fact watched video, live feeds from cameras mounted on the sides and rear corner of the sedan.

A scrawny beanpole of a man emerged from the tiny car like a jack springing from a box. He peered at a fitness monitor strapped to his wrist and headed for the stairwell instead of the elevator, ignoring the sedan and Stone inside. A man trying to reach his 10,000 steps early in the day. The stairwell door clanged shut behind him.

Stone sat on his knees on the seat in front of the visor and opened the makeup mirror. He pulled the sandwiched dollops of nanomachines out of their bag. The transparent plastic sheets flexed slightly in his hands. His fingers hesitated at a corner of the upper sheet of transparent plastic.

[It will hurt some, if that's what you're worried about.]

[I can handle pain. How will it know to stop in time?]

[I used a programming unit that received a 3d picture of your face and simulated randomized settings until the output fooled a panel of facial recognition software. Put the *nanogoop* in about the right spots on your face and it will know what to do.]

Stone nodded and yanked free the top sheet of plastic. His gloved fingers pulled one of the gray dollops off the backing. Warmth trickled into his fingers. [Where?]

[The outer end of one of your eyebrows. Close your eye until the material fully absorbs. Press hard.]

He shut his left eye and squeezed the material in place. Warmth flashed into heat. His skin reddened as the gray material permeated it, crawling into it with a feeling like insect larvae burrowing into a host's flesh. Pain throbbed along the upper rim of his eye socket. Stone breathed raggedly through gritted teeth. *Some?* he thought, but didn't bother sending the word to Caitlyn.

The gray material completely entered his skin. The pain spread in waves like a rising tide, around the eye socket, toward his temple, up his forehead. At least its intensity remained constant. He opened his eye. Pulled up the second glob of material. Raised it toward the outer end of his right eyebrow—

He glanced at his left eyebrow in the makeup mirror. His stomach suddenly turned queasy. The bone under his left eyebrow flowed like putty, stretching and slackening his skin.

Stone shut both eyes and inhaled three slow breaths. He opened his left eye and focused on the spot where the next dollop would go.

Twenty minutes later, a hot feeling faded from the sides of his chin. He looked into the makeup mirror and saw a stranger. Sunken eyes in wider sockets; a face more oval; a jutting lower jaw and thicker chin. If people who knew him by sight happened to pass him on the street, they might double-take but would end up walking away.

He gave the face in the mirror an overall look. Less handsome than he really was, not that it mattered. His confident demeanor remained. Persuading Nina Irani that he had real intelligence and she should take it would pose no challenge.

Red splotches on his skin marked where the osteomorphic nano-goop had penetrated. He looked like a victim of a medspa malfunction. [I've got to do something about those red spots.]

[Pull open the storage drawer under the rear seat.]

Stone did. A sealed pouch of insulated plastic held cold, moist cloths. He lay on his side on the back seat, knees curled up to fit, and pressed five cloths to his face, one across his eyes, one to each cheek, and one on each side of his jaw.

[After the mission, we'll use that same 3d image of you to program the reversal.]

[Generous.] He yawned, then readjusted the cloths on the side facing up. [The osteogoop is off-the-shelf tech on Minerva?]

[Yes.]

[Which means in half an hour a prospective criminal can fool facial recognition software?]

He imagined her smiling when she sent her next words. [A Minervan citizen can only buy the material if they've undergone convocation.]

The reputation blockchain, implemented by quantum computers interfacing directly with human brains, made Minerva a world where no one would become a criminal because their own mind would betray them to everyone else.

Could Caitlyn and her allies truly transform Earth the same way?

Stone turned the question over in his mind. No answer came before she said, [That should be long enough.]

He sat up. Smooth skin with a uniform healthy tan tone covered his strange face. [Looks good.]

[Two more things. Look in the sack.]

Stone pulled out a small bag containing two elongated ovals on a plastic backing, then a dropper bottle the size of his finger. He held the small bag next to his face and looked in the visor mirror. [You matched my skin tone. Do I need to prep these before I put them on?]

[No. Just peel off and press to the front of your ear. Wrap the excess around. It won't rebuild the cartilage inside your ears, but the recontouring will fool—]

[Got it.] Ears were like fingerprints, except that a traffic cop or a customs official could note a difference in ear pattern between a subject and a matching photo ID with the naked eye.

Stone applied the elongated oval stickers. A hundred ants seemed to crawl over each ear. His face scrunched until the ants returned to their nest.

He checked the mirror. His ears looked different but he couldn't put the difference into words. Presumably the difference would fool facial recognition software.

He reached for the dropper. [This will change my eye color?]

[Exactly. It helps that yours are naturally blue. Just three drops per eye.]

[Why three?]

[One drop won't change the color much. Two drops, the volume of each can vary enough that you might get noticeably different colors between your eyes.]

[Three it is.] He opened the bottle. Pulled up his eyelid with one hand. Squeezed out three drops with the other. Repeated on the other side.

Expecting burning or itching, he shut his eyes. Seconds ticked by and he felt nothing. [It isn't working.]

[Look in the mirror.]

He did. Blinked. He could discern himself behind the face of the brown-eyed stranger, but would anyone else be able to?

More to the point, would Gray?

[Enough with the narcissism. It's time to make contact with Nina Irani.]

3

The blue sedan pulled up to the curb on 2nd around the corner from his destination. Stone climbed out and assisted the door's closing mechanism with a shove. A faint whiff of rotting garbage from a dumpster in an alley clashed in his noise with the smell of impending rain.

Ten steps down the sidewalk, the overcast sky spat raindrops at him. At least they washed away the dumpster odor. The blue sedan melded into traffic heading downtown.

He hunched his shoulders. As he walked, he scanned the pedestrian swarm for anyone who might be tracking him. Sidelong glances at mirrored glass revealed only New Yorkers hurrying against the thickening rain.

At 44th, a panoramic camera bulged like a wart from the bottom of the street sign. The Minervan bone-shifting tech had better work. He turned right. He wound his way through a mass of pedestrians who hurried by holding umbrellas and briefcases overhead. Clouds tumbled above highrises where the logos of UN agencies and national missions adorned flat faces of steel and black glass. One of those agencies was ITB, the Interstellar Transport Bureau. Caitlyn could be watching him from a window even now.

The rain pelted him now. Stone stalked toward his destination. Three Eyes Open stood on the ground floor of a skyscraper. One of a hundred meditation lounges in Manhattan. The door to the sidewalk opened and Stone slipped in.

A color scheme of pastel yellows, oranges, reds. Four rows of six beanbag chairs crossed the floor, with a horseshoe of padded knee-high wall backing each chair. Above each seat hung a helmet on a flexible arm. Five customers sat with helmets pulled down over their ears and eyes. The helmets lacked visors, reminding him of the one he'd been forced to wear in the basement of the Center for Alignment with the Universe on Minerva.

His implantable computer fed the time 10:58 to his optic nerve. His chest tightened. What if Nina Irani had arrived early today? He checked the customers. Two men. One woman's long blond hair spilled out from under a helmet. The backs of another woman's deep brown hands lay folded on her scrawny ribs. The final woman's chubby form sank deeply into her beanbag chair.

Stone's upper body relaxed. As he went to a gleaming, underlit counter, a soft and slow duet of a jangly string instrument and a hand drum trickled from hidden speakers. A man in his twenties with $250 coins stretching his earlobes waited behind the counter. Three oxygenators jutted from the wall at his back like vegan beer taps.

"What do you want?" the barista asked in a thin voice. A menu icon pulsed at the side of Stone's vision.

He blinked at the icon, skimmed the menu. Uncarbonated mineral waters from fourteen US states and seventeen countries. "What do you recommend?"

"The Redshift Cavern Select, Webster County, Missouri. Bottled from an underground lake. Strong limestone notes. You simply must try it."

The most expensive domestic water on the menu. Stone grinned and sniffed out a breath. "And how much oxygen?"

"Four pulses will maximize the mental boost and complement the acidity of the water." At two thousand dollars per pulse, this drink of cave water would cost him twenty-five grand. No: it would cost Caitlyn and the Minervans.

Stone grinned again. "Make it a double."

The barista reached under the counter and cracked open the cap of a glass bottle. Stone's gaze rested on the barista's actions without watching. Pouring, pulsing oxygen. The burble of compressed oxygen jetting into the glass almost drowned out an eruption of street noise from the front door.

The barista set a bubbling glass in front of Stone. Stone pulled cash from his wallet while the barista turned to footsteps clacking on the concrete floor. "Nina. Your usual?"

"Yes." The voice sounded melodious, reminding Stone of an opera singer from a fling a decade past.

He turned. Drops of rain dotted Nina Irani's nut-brown suit jacket and trickled down the amber lenses of the sunglasses riding atop her head. Her large brown eyes betokened self-assurance, under narrow, arched eyebrows meant to inform any man he was unworthy.

Stone read right through his first impression. She was a Ms. Lonelyhearts. Whenever she bedded another rising star in UN politics in her climb to power, she dreamed he would love her for who she was for the rest of her life.

Keep dreaming, sister.

His gaze locked on her large brown eyes. "Not quite her usual," he said to the barista. "It's on me."

Her eyebrows arched higher. "No."

Stone smirked and pulled another twenty G from his wallet. Slid it across the counter. To the barista: "Keep the change."

Irani stiffened her shoulders. "I don't know who you are but I know your type. 'Curry fever' you white men call it. You come to a place that plays sitar and tabla jams over the soundsystem—" She flicked her fingers toward the nearest speaker in the ceiling. "—and think any desi girl will fall for you?"

"No. Any woman will fall for me, whether she's South Asian or not. But I'm not here to learn any moves from the *Kama Sutra*. My interest in you is purely professional."

"Is it now."

"Your employer needs to know something."

Her brown eyes jolted wide. "You know who I am?"

"Oh yes."

Her gaze jabbed at him. "How? Why?"

Stone stared back with a faint smile on his lips. It would be so easy to seduce her. A cocksure attitude, some playful mockery of her position in UN headquarters. An hour from now he could toss her skirt suit to the floor next to his bed.

Yet despite Irani's wide mouth and smooth brown skin, his usual urges remained dormant. Uncertain how a tryst would play out with the mission Caitlyn assigned him. Had to be it.

Gas bubbled nearby. The barista pulsed oxygen into Irani's glass of water as if he hadn't heard their conversation. No, he'd heard, but UN employees probably talked shop across the counter from him a hundred times a day. He set down her glass of oxygenated water with a plastic thump.

Stone shoved his thoughts away. "Come with me."

Without looking back, he led Irani to the corner of the lounge nearest the tinted front windows, where lay the pair of beanbag chairs farthest from the other customers. He and Irani would sit with their backs to the street. Not ideal, but the tinting would keep casual observers from identifying either of them, and the angle would prevent anyone from reading their lips.

He gestured to both chairs in turn. Irani took the one closest to the door. He read her intent despite her effort to hide it behind a cool brown-eyed gaze. She sat there for the best chance to escape if Stone proved dangerous.

Stone dipped his head, then sat in the other beanbag without spilling a drop of overpriced water. He rested his glass in a deep cupholder embedded in the knee-high curved wall. Reached for the helmet, hesitating only a moment when the memory of his consecration on Minerva came back. He pulled the helmet halfway down, then with a glance beckoned her to do the same.

"Don't activate the noise cancelling, the music, or the binaural beats," he muttered.

Irani lowered the helmet over her eyes and ears, then he did the same. He shut his eyes and asked with minimal movement of his lips, "Can you hear me?"

"Yes." Her voice carried through the circular pads rimming the earcups. "Who are you?"

"A friend with the UN's best interests at heart."

"I doubt I shall find 'Friend, A' in the UN employee directory."

"I guarantee you won't."

"I need to know who you are," Irani said.

Stone blindly sipped fizzing, limestony water. "James Smith. ITB. Have you heard of Minerva?"

Caitlyn shouted in his mind's ear. [You're giving her my agency?]

[Couldn't give her mine. Your boss Holbrook is on your side, isn't he? If she investigates me, he'll know what's going on and confirm James Smith's existence.]

She needed a moment. [Makes sense.]

"—world," said Irani. "Newly acceded to the Dubai Convention. Surprisingly advanced technology."

"You don't know the half of it."

Her glass clunked in its cupholder. "Go on."

"I recently returned from that world." His whisper turned harsh. "Resist the urge to check employer's database about me."

"Why?"

"I'll get to that. While on that world, I collected intel that its technology is a hell of a lot more advanced than my employer has relayed to you."

"How advanced?"

"Think of it as Hawking Station number two."

The sound of Irani's sharp inhalation reached through Stone's helmet. She understood his reference. "Impossible. The Goldberg-Chen Colonial Technological Development Model predicts—"

He flicked his fingers up and she fell silent. "I don't care what some Ivy League profs predict. The proof is in my pocket. And—"

"A Haw—a place like that. What are they doing with its products?" Irani's tone told him she'd already guessed.

"Building vessels. As you'd expect. Proof of that is in my pocket too."

"Your superior never relayed such intel."

"I provided it to him on my return. Yesterday I found out he never provided it to you. Guess why?"

Irani took heavy breaths. "He wants to throw in with that colony against us? Even more impossible."

He chuckled out a breath. "Whose poli sci model predicts that power brokers never plot coups?"

More heavy breaths. "True, I know how this town works. But your employer couldn't keep so great a secret for so long. We would have found out."

"Would you?"

The front door chimed. Footsteps and the echo of rain on concrete and glass overwhelmed the lounge's ambient music for a moment. Stone kept his head from jerking up toward the door. Hopefully Irani had the same self-control.

Behind the counter, oxygen jetted into water. Irani said, "You said you have proof."

"You'll find it on the beanbag next to your left hand when you end your daily meditation." Hard leather soles clapped on the concrete floor toward them. "Shh."

She didn't reply. Good. Stone listened to the new arrival. The footsteps stopped. The beanbag on the other side of Irani rustled as the new arrival plopped into it. A metallic creak meant the articulation on the helmet over the new arrival's seat needed maintenance. Give the person thirty seconds to pick a program and start meditating...

Stone pushed the helmet above his eyes and ears. He squinted and looked at Irani. The ends of her brown hair peeked out from her helmet. Her trim figure sank into her beanbag. She breathed slowly and deeply, her lush lips parted.

If she wasn't entranced by a meditation program, she put on a good act.

Stone forced his legs off his beanbag to the floor like a man not fully returned to Manhattan. He dug into his pockets and found the memory stick with false intel.

And left it in his pocket. He wanted more cover in case someone noticed a memory stick on her beanbag.

He padded toward the barista. On his way, he pulled another twenty G from his wallet. Rested the bill on the counter. "Pen and paper?"

"You have an insight? You're right, getting it down the old-fashioned way captures aspects that subvoking and virtual sketching just can't." The barista palmed the money, then peered under the counter. Cabinet doors slid back and forth.

The barista set a sketch pad sheet and a thick black pencil on the counter. "Not a pen, but here you go."

"Namaste." Stone carried the paper and pencil to a standing-height table near the window. With unpracticed hands, he wrote *I'll be here M W F 10-10:30 to answer questions.*

The pencil hesitated over the paper. Add something flirtatious?

No. He rolled his eyes and folded the paper. Once, twice. He then walked back to Irani.

On his way, he glanced sidelong at the new arrival. A man, wearing a loosened tie and a suit flipped back from a paunchy belly. His snores clashed with the sitar and tabla music over the soundsystem.

If he worked as a counterintel agent from the Secretary-General's office, he did a poor job.

Stone halted to Irani's left. He slipped the memory stick from his pocket and sandwiched it between the paper's folds. Gently he tucked the open side of the folded paper under her fingers. Her hand stirred slightly but her eyes and ears remained under the helmet.

Keep dreaming, sister.

4

Three days later, Stone approached the meditation lounge five minutes before ten. An Indian summer filled the concrete canyon of 44th with a warm wind and gold lozenges of sunlight reflected off skyscrapers' mirrored glass faces. The breeze off the river smelled fresh for once. He wore khakis and a green-gray short-sleeved polo tight over his upper arms. His biceps drew smiles from young women as the wind swished their hems around their knees.

Inside, three people meditated under helmets. Behind the counter worked a slender girl, kinky brown hair and round eyes, wholesome-looking except for the ring piercing the right side of her nose. She blinked when his usual turned out to be Missouri cave water and four pumps of oxygen.

He took his drink to the standing table near the window and sipped. Pedestrians flowed both ways along the sidewalk outside. Pretty girls caught his gaze, but his usual train of thought never left the station. The handful of women with traces of innocence struck him now like the little sister he'd never had. Women to protect, not seduce. And the more typical women, Manhattanettes exuding wantonness, now filled him with more pity than lust. He could give them a night's worth of memories that would fail to relieve their underlying unhappiness.

And his?

"Damn you, Caitlyn," he muttered under his breath, but the curse lacked any fire.

A carrier tone sounded in his mind. [You want to talk?] Caitlyn asked.

[I want you to leave me alone.]

[I'll stay quiet, but I'll stay on the line until after Irani leaves.]

[Assuming she even arrives,] Stone said.

Caitlyn made no reply. He ignored the carrier tone and scanned the crowd for his contact and any potential threats. No one thronging the sidewalk, male or female, white or black or Nuyorican, old or young, looked familiar from his previous trips to the meditation lounge. No one acted like a counterintel operative skilled in tradecraft.

And, since no one had tried to kill him in the last three days, Gray had not learned of what he had done.

Through a break in the crowd Nina Irani glided toward the door. Wide amber sunglasses hid her eyes in the instant she passed through his gaze. She went to the counter without seeming to give him a glance.

Moments later, soft steps and the fizz of oxygenated water behind him heralded her approach. She stopped next to him at the table. "May I?"

"Sure."

She slid her sunglasses to the top of her head and gave him the same interested look as a thousand other women on a thousand other days. "Haven't I seen you around?"

Irani wanted to play this as strangers flirting. Which meant she feared observation. He gave her a smile he didn't feel and watched from the corner of his eye for counterintel operatives on the street.

"Maybe," Stone said. I've been here a couple of times. Looking for a good place to meditate."

"The back corner is especially good for that." She picked up her glass. "Join me?"

"Sure."

They settled into beanbags chairs. Far from the windows, but facing the street. Stone pulled the helmet down over his eyes and ears, then lifted his glass from the cupholder. He raised the glass to shield his mouth from view. "I find holding the water under my nose enhances my oxygen intake. Try it."

"I never thought of that." Irani inhaled. "Thanks for the suggestion, ah...?"

"James."

"I'm Nina." She sounded delighted to be playing this game.

Stone dropped his voice to a murmur. "We set up enough of a screen. Time to get down to business."

"Very well. I'm a busy woman with no time for chit-chat." Her whispering reply sounded mostly businesslike, but a hint remained that her flirtation with Stone had been more than a cover. "You gave us quite a surprise the other day."

"Us?"

"I shared your report with a select handful of others inside headquarters. Do not fear, I did not identify my source."

"I knew you wouldn't." Stone sipped fizzing water. "Who did you share it with?"

"An expert on exotic matter production. Another expert on warp-drive ship design. A third expert on intelligence and counterintelligence operations."

His mouth suddenly felt parched. Her *third expert* might have been Gray. "These experts must have names."

"Not identifying my sources is a two-way street, James." Irani sounded amused.

"Don't toy with me. Was one of them my supervisor?" He whispered raggedly. "If you told him then I've got a red dot on my chest—"

"Relax. He is not one of the experts I consulted."

He drew and expelled a deep breath. "Good."

Irani went on. "I also sought background on that world from a fourth person with whom I didn't share your report."

"Anyone else?"

"No."

"What did they say?"

"They found the report compelling. However, as one says, extraordinary claims require extraordinary evidence."

"What the hell does that mean? They want more intel? I can't go back to that world to gather more. My supervisor would reject my request and then investigate me."

Irani's whisper sounded peeved. "I am aware of that. What the experts want is to question you in person."

"That's foolish. If the report is compelling they and you should insist the Sec-Gen sends in the peacekeepers before it's too late."

"Oh? Do you have something to hide?"

"Not a damn thing. Meeting me is a waste of time. Time we may not have. I don't know how close that world is to launching the Time of Troubles 2.0 on a galactic scale. I'm damn certain your experts know even less."

"We can only take this to that person you mentioned if you meet with the experts."

Stone drank oxygenated water and clunked the glass into the cupholder. "You desk jockeys are all the goddam same. Gossiping and back-stabbing because you think your ivory tower can't be toppled. I'm trying to tell you it can, and it will, if you don't do something."

"We will do something. Namely, judge the validity of your evidence after the experts meet with you."

Stone clamped his lips into a thin line. [You hearing this?] he asked Caitlyn.

[You know I am.]

[If her third expert is Gray, I'm dead. After they scan my brain in Gray's interrogation facility in New Jersey.]

[Unless you kill him first. You could smuggle a concealed handgun into the meeting, couldn't you?]

[Of course... but that won't help if Gray is not the third expert.]

His forehead crinkled in sympathy with the puzzled feeling she sent through the quantum computer link. [Explain.]

[The bone morphing nanogoop gave me enough of a disguise to fool NYPD automated facial recognition software. But human beings check video of everyone entering UN headquarters. If one of Gray's people sees me and decides I look familiar, my disguise could be blown without me even knowing.]

[That's a chance we'll have to take—]

[We?] Stone snapped his head back. The edge of the knee-high horseshoe wall around his beanbag clanged against his helmet. He winced.

[My neck would be on the chopping block the same as yours.]

[Not the same,] he said. [You'll know instantly through this damn quantum computer interface if Gray grabs me. You'd have a chance to escape to Minerva and blow up the wormhole. Live to fight another day.]

Irani's whisper sliced through the air. "If you refuse to meet with the experts, you are a scam artist, and I will act accordingly."

"Of course I'll meet you. But not at headquarters. Too many cameras and suspicious eyes."

"Where?" Irani asked.

"You must have a discreet location for sensitive meetings. A place away from headquarters. Away from the Upper East Side. Tell me where and when."

"I'll write it down. You'll find it after you finish meditating."

He drank the rest of his oxygenated water, then set the glass in the cupholder and nestled into the beanbag. A last adjustment of the helmet and he pretended to meditate. To Caitlyn, he said, [Happy?]

[Why wouldn't I be?]

[You were gung-ho on me entering headquarters.]

She sent mild exasperation over the embedded interface. [I want you to advance the mission. You found a way to do that without entering UN headquarters. Commendable use of initiative. One of the things I expected when I recruited you.]

[When you inducted me into your conspiracy at gunpoint, you mean.]

She replied with a lilt in her voice. [Let's let bygones be bygones, shall we?]

5

The next day, a Saturday, the nondescript blue sedan drove through the Bedford-Stuyvesant neighborhood in Brooklyn, down Rudolph Giulani Boulevard. Poured concrete buildings lacking straight lines flanked the street. His mother's latest boyfriend, the tanned architect with tiny ears, could tell him the vintage down to the half-decade, if he cared to know.

One block north of the T-intersection at Fulton Street, Stone said, "Stop here."

The blue sedan pulled up to the curb on the right and popped its doors on that side. Stone emerged. The coupe rolled away, waited to turn right.

A mild breeze rustled the leaves of maples rooted between the streets and the sidewalks. A young man, skinny but with a doughy face, pushed a stroller like the blinking escape pod of a spacecraft. His hatchet-faced East Asian wife criticized him over some minor domestic transgression. Her harsh voice clashed with the Haydn melody spilling from stereo speakers inside the stroller. Her husband bore the nagging like an overworked mule.

Stone smiled to himself. He would make a lousy husband, and he wanted it that way.

His gaze took in storefronts: an organic butcher closed today, a handcrafted wooden toy shop, a vape parlor and a nanobrewery crowded with men like the stroller pusher taking a breather from their fishwives. He checked tiny studio apartments above the shops, where bicycles and herb gardens crammed foot-wide balconies. No sign of hostiles.

He leaned against a bus stop. An advertising server with a proximity sensor pushed audio through his transcranial magnetic stim interface—an ad for a men's yoga gym three blocks away at Decatur and Stuyvesant. He ignored the announcer's soft voice and looked across the street.

Excelsior Building 1595 Fulton St Bkln. Tomorrow at 1pm. Northwest entrance, suite 240, Nina Irani's note had read.

Behind a stippled concrete exterior, and above two lower floors of small shops and offices, the Excelsior lifted balconied apartments eight stories into the sky. Two entrances visible, the northwest one across the street from him and a main one at the southwest corner, facing the T-intersection.

Stone dug in the pocket of his khakis for a small object, a flattened hemisphere the diameter of a quarter-G coin. Hand still in pocket, he peeled the backing off the object. Yawned and stretched his arms. Stuck the object high on the bus stop's metal frame. Walked toward the intersection with Fulton Street.

Activate, he subvoked through his old implantable computer to the object. A window projected by transcranial magnetic stim appeared in his vision, projected onto blue sky above two- and three-story mixed-use buildings lining the far side of Fulton. Startup diagnostics. Green *OK*s. Video of the northwest entrance of the Excelsior.

He opened a connection with Caitlyn. [Northwest camera on.] He changed permissions on the camera feed to include her.

[Got it. Piping to body recog database.]

Stone waited at the crosswalk next to two tattooed white women jogging in place behind strollers. He assessed them as not counterintel, then ignored them. When the light changed, Stone crossed to the south side of Fulton.

He opened the door of the Bed-Stuy Historical Society and rested his hand high on the frame on his way in. A cramped space, walls hung with photos of African-American ladies in wide, ornate church hats and spittle-flecked protestors screaming at NYPD patrolmen. Behind the protestors, graffiti tagged faded brick walls.

Stone shook his head. He'd heard his grandparents' stories about the old Bed-Stuy, before gentrification. Unemployment, crime, street violence between blacks and Hasidic Jews. Nothing like the neighborhood outside.

A scrawny white man stinking of marijuana came up to him. "This was once a vibrant community, just like Harlem. We have to preserve that. Photo prints are for sale and we do take donations."

Stone arched an eyebrow, then pulled a twenty G bill from his wallet. "It is a good cause."

On his way out, he activated the camera he'd placed on the door frame. A burly man emerged from the Excelsior's southwest entrance. Stone smiled to himself and walked east on Fulton.

At the next corner with Lewis Avenue, he took the crosswalk to the north side of the street. Eight-year-olds played augmented reality tag on a lawn while their parents sat at the outdoor tables of a café, eating egg white omelets and sipping mimosas and bloody marys. The café's kitchen and order counter were inside the Excelsior, with a dedicated door ten feet from the building's southeast entrance.

Stone stretched his calves by extending each leg backward one at a time. For balance, he pressed his hands against the grooved trunk of a maple.

[Will that stick?] Caitlyn asked.

[I've placed cameras on rougher surfaces a hundred times. You're seeing both the café door and the building entrance, right?]

[I see both. The last thing you need to cover is the loading dock.]

[North side, off—] Stone checked the map for the name of a street that dead-ended at the Excelsior's freight entrance. [Bainbridge.]

[Don't be obvious.]

[Trust my skill in tradecraft. And my desire to avoid capture.]

He went inside the café. The brunch crowd shuffled forward, giving him time to peruse the old-fashioned menu screen. He ignored the pastries and opted for a ham-and-cheese omelet cup and a bottled water. Outside, he strolled along the east side of the Excelsior. Clouds drifted across the sky from the north and the breeze felt a touch cooler than it had when he'd arrived. Indian summer soon to end. Today would be the last warm day for months.

Stone finished eating the omelet by the time he reached Bainbridge. The street narrowed as it snaked to the right around the Excelsior. He jaywalked to a row of retro brownstones. A real estate agent's sign pinged him. The second brownstone in the row, eighteen hundred square feet of central air and heat, could be his for the low price of two billion dollars.

He leaned with an outstretched arm against the pole of a streetlight, then walked back toward the Excelsior as if the brownstone seller asked too much. The camera on the lightpole showed the full length of the alley to the Excelsior's loading dock.

[That's all.]

[Yes,] Caitlyn replied.

Stone went toward the cafe's outdoor seating area. He tossed the empty omelet cup into a recycling bin and checked his watch. 1220. [Now we wait.]

He slipped through the chattering crowd until he found an empty seat at the end of a table. At the other end, two women combining the glowing skin of a recent rejuvenation treatment with the crow's feet wrinkles of early middle age conversed intently. Stone put on a lazy smile. "Is this seat free?"

Both looked his way with sparks of interest that failed to ignite his urges. "It is for you," one said. Her coy expression clashed with her baggy sweatshirt.

He sat and dialed back his charm. His gaze wandered to the lawn where eight-year-olds fled invisible dinosaurs, while the women's conversation returned to the high price of children's violin lessons and their husbands' begging for missionary-position sex twice a month.

Stone's earlier thought echoed. Though he might make a lousy husband, most women proved to be lousy wives.

While his eyes took in the playing children, Stone opened the camera feeds in his mind's eye. Four videos arrayed themselves like the screens at a rent-a-cop's security desk. Even though the ITB body recognition database Caitlyn borrowed today logged thousands of employees at scores of UN agencies and allied non-government organizations, no database could guarantee completeness.

And if anyone could keep his personnel out of body recognition databases, it would be Gray.

Not that Stone knew every one of his fellow operatives by sight. But most people in his line of work revealed their profession through roving gazes, the faint bulges of handguns concealed under clothing, bland exteriors barely covering a skill for swift violence.

Twenty minutes. Sixty people passed through the Excelsior's three doors and one truck parked at the loading dock. No spies, no UN employees—

[Nina Irani,] Stone said.

[Where?]

Irani stood near the curb on the south side of Fulton. Only a sharp angle of her face showed to the camera at the historical society, but the rigid shoulders in her pale brown skirt-suit and the haughty black mass of her hair gave her away. She crossed at the light and entered the Excelsior at the southwest corner.

[Face and posture give a 98% confirmation,] Caitlyn said.

[Twenty seconds after I gave you 100%.]

Caitlyn ignored his jibe. [Southeast corner. Eflorio Vasquez. Five Eyes liaison to the Sec-Gen's staff.]

Though the man passed within twenty yards, Stone kept his eyes aimed toward the playing children. The camera showed a stoop-shouldered man with bushy black beard and eyebrows. Despite Vasquez' affiliation with the intelligence agencies of a US-led five country bloc, he seemed more bureaucrat than spy.

[Irani's intel ops expert?] Stone said.

[Leading candidate.]

Not Gray. Stone might walk away from this meeting alive and without a tail.

Ten minutes later Stone's gaze briefly landed on a man waddling his way on Fulton from Lewis. The waddling man plucked a vape pen from behind his ear and puffed while admiring the maples. Stone yawned and looked away.

[Walter Silverblatt,] Caitlyn said five seconds later. The camera mounted on a tree caught a closeup of widely-spaced eyes and thick hair on the back of the hand holding the vape pen. [ITB's guru on exotic matter physics.]

[He belongs to you and Holbrook?]

[No. He answers to the head of ITB. He would think of Holbrook as the man who hires armed guards for wormhole sites and wouldn't know me from Eve.]

[Eve who?]

Caitlyn sighed. [It's a figure of speech.]

The camera tracked Silverblatt into the Excelsior's southeast entrance.

Time ticked on. At 1258, Stone said, [Did you miss our third expert?]

[No.]

[You can't be certain. Maybe Irani recruited a post-doc from Cornell as her ship ex—]

[Southwest entrance. Charlotte Wang. Space operations advisor to the Security Council.] At least half-Chinese from her surname and her appearance. Silver hoop earrings dangled from her ears and an underbite gave her a face like a fish. The Excelsior's doors slid open for her. A man, loose trousers and a mustache over pointy chin, followed her in.

[Who's that?]

[The man? The database doesn't have him.]

Stone drank the last sips of bottled water and stood. The women now complained about their elderly parents. He left the table without giving them a glance.

[You're going to be late,] Caitlyn said.

[Fashionably.]

Stone took the sidewalk along Fulton and up Giuliani Avenue. Once inside the Excelsior's northwest entrance, he looked around to match what he saw with the map. An innocuous office building, but operatives had died in places like this. Elevators down that hall. Stairwell to the left—

He took the stairs to the second floor. His docksiders' soft soles gave no echo off the stairwell's concrete walls and treads. Suite 240 would be five offices down on the left. He quietly turned the handle and eased open the stairwell door.

Stone entered a carpeted hallway with small professional offices... and the mustached man with the pointy chin. He stood at a door on the left, that of another office midway between Stone and suite 240, with his head turned toward Stone's destination.

The stairwell door wanted to clang shut. Stone controlled it and turned the handle before the bolt clanked against the door frame, watching the mustached man as he did.

A hunch flickered across the mustached man's shoulders. Not expecting someone to come up the stairs? He slipped into the door of the other office. Smooth—he might well be a civilian who happened to be here.

[Still no clue who that was?]

[No,] Caitlyn said. [But I'm as suspicious as you are. I'll inquire.]

Stone padded down the hallway. The office the mustached man had entered bore a sign reading *Suite 270. Soeur du Coeur Au Pair Services*.

Au pairs were girls who lived with a foreign family for year, providing child care and taking language classes. How many women would let their husbands take any action in picking a live-in nanny without them? Next to none.

[Check if that business is a front,] Stone said.

[Already on it.]

Stone continued on, his hearing focused on the door to suite 270. No sound. The mustached man remained within.

He reached the door to his destination and paused with his hand near the knob. No one had tailed him or tried to kill him on his way here.

Now came the hard part.

6

Inside, an office sparsely furnished, but with enough touches—art posters of Manhattan at night, a curtain over the window instead of the usual slatted blinds—to give the space permanence. Stone remained alert, but with shifted focus. No one tries to murder you in his or her living room.

Four people in a semicircle of ergonomic mesh chairs. From the left end of the semicircle rose Nina Irani. She extended her hand and said, "Mr. Smith—"

Stone raised a finger to his lips and glowered at her. He pulled a scanner from his pocket and thumbed it on. Swept it along the wall to the right of the door.

Irani locked the door's deadbolt and turned to him. "I assure you, we've monitored the room for listening devices."

Stone ignored her and continued the scan. The scanner found only the expected, power to the light switch. He extended the scanner's telescopic arm. Power to the ceiling lights. No bugs in the climate control vent spilling central heat.

The numbers in the digital display jumped near the window.

He pulled back the curtain. Held by a suction cup in the lower right corner, a rattler the size of his thumb drew power from its battery. It looked to be a standard model, and the *active* LED glowed green.

Stone relaxed a bit. No one outside the building could listen to their conversation by picking up vibrations in the window caused by their voices. The rattler smothered those vibrations with white noise.

Unless Irani had modified the rattler to appear active when it wasn't.

Stone finished by passing the scanner over a table of liquor bottles. All clear. "Now we can talk," he said.

Irani came toward him, skirt swishing, heels dimpling the plush carpet. "What will you drink?"

"No thanks. We've got work to do." He pointed to an empty chair facing the semicircle. "That's my hot seat?"

"You needn't be hostile. We're all on the side of truth."

Stone rounded the semicircle. The three experts entered his peripheral vision. "All of you?" He sat. "Including the man who followed Ms. Wang into the building and to this floor?"

Charlotte Wang started. The silver hoop earrings swung like pendulums. "No one followed me," she said in a shrill voice.

"Pointy chin? Mustache? Baggy clothes? He walked into the building right behind you. He lurked in the hallway when I came up."

Wang's voice sounded even sharper. "I don't know who that was. If there even was a man and you're not making this up."

"Charlotte, we believe you," Irani said. "Mr. Smith's line of work requires him to be suspicious of coincidences."

Wang glared at Stone. "And how do you know my name?"

"My line of work gives me some advantages. But formal introductions are good manners." He began at the left of the semicircle. "I've already met Ms. Irani."

Next to Irani, Silverblatt sat with legs crossed, his fingers interlaced around his lifted knee. His voice warbled. "Walter Silverblatt."

Charlotte Wang continued to glare. "You already know me."

"Eflorio Vasquez." Vasquez' voice was almost as high as Wang's, but thankfully less shrill. The lower sides of his crossed legs pressed together.

Stone's heart thudded. Even if the mustached man who'd ducked into the au pair office merely needed a nanny, and even though this meeting could not kill him directly, one misstep could bring his scam to Gray's attention. "And I'm James Smith. ITB."

Silverblatt scowled. "I'm going to slice through the horseshit. I'm ITB. We don't have espionage agents in our org chart."

"If you were certain of that you wouldn't be here." Stone stared at Silverblatt. "I'm ready. Let's get started."

"I will," replied Silverblatt. "I flicked through this report. The exotic matter factory specs in here look like copies of the specs of Hawking Station."

"They are what they are."

"Not perfect copies, sure, but like when my nephew downloads his class paper from the worldforum and changes a few words and phrases here and there to avoid plagiarism."

"Would those changes work?" Stone asked.

"What do you mean?"

"All I know about exotic matter factories is sunlight goes in, waste heat and some magical particles that make warpdrive ships and wormholes come out. If I copied the specs of Hawking Station and changed a few things at random to try to fool you, my changes would probably foul things up. Right?"

"Unless you have an expert on your team who modified the specs."

"Where could I find an exotic matter expert smart enough to fool you?"

"You have a point there." Silverblatt scrunched up his wide-set eyes. "I'll make a second examination of the specs."

"I'll wait."

Silence ensued. Silverblatt pulled the vape pen from behind his ear and puffed, looking thoughtful. A sour cherry stink floated through the room.

Wang wrinkled her nose. "I need more jack-and-soda-pop," she muttered on her way out of the semicircle.

Silverblatt puffed again, once more. He moved the vape pen towad his mouth a fourth time but his hand stopped and his wide-set eyes jumped. Under his breath, he said, "That's a clever trick."

He turned off the vape pen and tucked it back behind his ear. "These specs should be about two percent more energy efficient than Hawking Station. Unless you've got a Ph.D. up your sleeve, and I know you don't because I know every professor whose students are capable enough to do work like this, these specs look genuine."

Stone acknowledged Silverblatt's words with a dip of his head. "Who's next?"

Wang returned to the semicircle with a glass of brown liquid fizzing over ice. Her nose wrinkled again at the remaining traces of sour cherry vape. "Nina, can you turn up a fan or something?"

"I'll see what I can do," said Irani. She looked at the far wall without seeming to see it, presumably subvoking commands to the office's climate control system. The stink of Silverblatt's vapor lost its edge.

Wang turned to Stone. "I read with interest your report about the Minervan fleet. Built in the outer system, mining a gas giant's moon. Why so far away from their planet?"

"It's not my job to speculate."

"Make it your hobby," Wang said.

Stone rolled his wrists, flashing his palms. "Concealment. The gas giant is in the part of its orbit almost directly behind Minerva's sun as seen from Minerva and Earth. The Minervans assumed UN ships would come straight into the system toward their planet and not bother exploring."

Wang's head jittered like a communication dish locking on a source. Reflected lights glimmered in her silver hoop earrings. "When did the Minervans start building this fleet?"

"The earliest date I found in the intel is in February '31."

"That's after the scout ship left Minerva on its Earth return." Wang's head jittered again. "They built this entire fleet in eighteen months?"

"The intel suggests that."

"Impossible. It takes us that long to build three ships. A colony world with fewer inhabitants than, than—" Her hands plucked at the air like a harpist's. "—than *Staten Island* cannot build ships twenty times faster than all of Earth."

Stone said, "The Minervans have levels of technical skill and social cohesion beyond Earth. I saw it. Nina's other sources would agree."

"They do," said Irani. Her large brown eyes lingered on Stone's face before she turned to Charlotte Wang. "Do you have other questions for Mr. Smith?"

Wang scrunched up her underbite mouth. "You saw these ships?"

"No," Stone said.

"You saw the crew training facilities in the Minervan's—churches? temples?"

"I never entered the basement of a Center for Alignment with the Universe." Stone blinked. His impassive face hid a spark of childish glee. Always fun to lie to a target.

"All this intel is taken from reports made by the ship builders to their space force superiors back on Minerva?"

"Yes."

"Might the ship builders have lied to their superiors?"

The answer immediately came to Stone. "No."

"No? The Minervans are human like us, no more and no less. If a supervisor fails to watch her underlings like a hawk, they will be lazy. If the supervisor asks if they are on schedule, they will lie and say yes—"

"No."

"Why do you believe the Minervans are different?" Wang's voice became even more shrill. "Because they are all roundeyes with pale skin like you?"

Stone gave a smile that left his eyes untouched. "Because their churches or temples give them social cohesion far beyond Earth's."

Wang blinked, then gulped her whiskey-and-cola. "Maybe you are right. If you are, given the ship designs you acquired…."

Nina Irani raised her eyebrows at Wang. "Have you more questions?"

Light danced in her hoop earrings as Wang shook her head.

"Good," Eflorio Vasquez said from the right side of the semicircle, "because I do." Slouched in his seat, Vasquez nibbled at his bushy beard with his two front teeth. "Smith, where did you pick these up?"

"The ship designs?"

"The whole kit and kaboodle. Ship designs and exotic matter factory plans can't have been in the same place. How many sources did you acquire?"

"Two."

"Two people who didn't know each other?"

"Yes."

Vasquez' top leg tapped air like a metronome. "Minervans have a lot of team spirit, you said. I believe you. And it's not just the usual stuff, the founders' enthusiasm, the small town aspect. Their cult knows how to brainwash people to stay on the path. Am I on target here?"

"You've described the Minervans accurately," Stone said.

"But somehow you found, not one, but two Minervans who betrayed the agencies they worked for to give you intel?"

"Social cohesion far beyond Earth's is still incomplete. Minervans still have personal agendas. And I'm good at—" His gaze slid over to Wang. Lingered a moment before her ugly face impelled his eyes to Irani. Stayed on her large brown eyes and smooth dusky skin as he said, "—seducing people."

Irani matched his stare.

Vasquez snorted. "You rolled three sixes for charisma? I might buy that, but the huge percentage of people under 18 suggests women on Minerva are barefoot and pregnant. And even in our advanced society without gender role stereotypes, there aren't many women working for military and physics agencies. On Minerva I'm sure those agencies are even more of a sausage party. So there aren't many women on Minerva who could provide you this intel, and you seduced them both?" His high voice took on a campy edge.

Stone's eyebrows rose. Vasquez' bushy beard and eyebrows had fooled him into thinking Vasquez was demasculinized like the henpecked dads shuffling like rented mules along Rudolph Giuliani Avenue. Not the case.

His eyes turned steely with amusement around the edges. "Did I say they were both women?"

Vasquez gasped.

Stone turned to Irani and cocked his head, angled his eye, making his words a joke and his interest in women undeniable.

The tip of her tongue peeked between her lips and pulled back. Stone effortlessly read the expression. She wanted to give her body to him.

And he wanted to take it... unless he only found Irani alluring now in contrast to Wang.

A problem for another day. He looked at each of the experts in turn. "I'll field any further questions you might have."

"No questions," said Wang in her shrill voice.

Silverblatt slipped the vape pen from behind his ear. "I'm satisfied with the information you provided."

Vasquez' fingers fiddled with the top button on his shirt. "The tech is all greek to me, but when it comes to tradecraft," he said, and a wistful tone came to his words, "I know what you can do in the saddle."

"Then I'm done here." Stone rose to his full height.

Irani turned up her head toward him. "Will you be available if I need you?"

"For more intel?" he said innocently. "You know where to find me." He strode to the door and turned the deadbolt.

Back in the hallway, Caitlyn said over the embedded quantum computer link, [That went well.]

[I know.] He approached the au pair office. His limbs tensed for action. [Where's the mustached man?]

[The cameras you placed didn't catch him walking out the doors.]

[He could have caught a ride on a delivery truck.]

[No deliveries in the past hour.]

[So he's still inside Soeur du Coeur.] Stone passed the au pair office. He kept his gaze on the stairwell entrance while listening for opening doors or padding footsteps. [Is the au pair agency legit?]

[Soeur du Coeur has paper and electronic tails corroborating its existence], Caitlyn said.

[Which Gray can fake.] Stone flung open the stairwell door. His gaze darted ahead. No one lurked inside. He started down. [Can Holbrook fake those things too?]

A sharp inhalation came over the link. [You think my boss is playing a double game?]

[No. I have no evidence. But when it comes to double games, in our line of work, anyone can play.]

7

Caitlyn's voice in his head woke him. [Time to get up.]

Stone parted his eyelids. Pale gray light leaked around the blinds. [You get boring when you repeat yourself.]

[When you lack routine you get soft. Get up.]

He subvoked to his implantable and a clock appeared in the lower left corner of his vision. [I can sleep for another two hours and still make it to Three Eyes Open by ten o'clock.]

[Galen Heinrichs needs to work out.]

He tossed the top of the sheet toward the footboard and swung his feet to the floor. [Wait. I don't need that long to work out.]

[Traffic will be bad today. US President Goldbaum visited the Sec-Gen yesterday.] Her voice sounded like she smiled and tossed her long blond hair.

[Say no more.] Motorcades and extra security around the President's hotel and UN facilities. Wait. [Presidential visits always make the front page on worldforum. This one didn't.]

[You read and watch worldforum? I'm surprised.]

[It gave me current affairs to tease earnest young women about.]

[Gave?]

[These days I'm focusing on our mission. And not getting captured by my old boss.] Stone grunted.

Pre-workout routine. Exercise clothes, flat-soled sneakers, a gritty shake of creatine and powdered vegetable extract. His black coupe met him at the curb outside his building and took him up Lexington. Emergency roadwork snarled traffic on the FDR. The presidential visit would make traffic worse than usual.

What brought the US president to the city yesterday? Such visits usually only happened when a secretary-general needed something US public opinion wouldn't want the president to give. The worldforum would spin the visit as the president agreeing that the world's needs outweighed any minor inconvenience the American people would suffer. Typically this meant the UN needed peacekeepers, and a thousand white boys from flyover country—did flyover country still exist? Did white boys still exist?—would die.

Maybe those doomed white boys would traverse a wormhole first.

A steely sensation straightened his back and lifted his head. Those doomed white boys deserved better. The refugees generated by their peacekeeping efforts deserved better. The colonists ordered to take in those refugees deserved better.

His current mission would help all of those people.

An atypical thought for Stone and he hurriedly shoved it aside. Focus on the mission.

On the president's visit to the secretary-general. Stone opened up the front page of worldforum in his visual field and scanned headlines. Nothing about President Goldbaum.

He jumped to the local page. Still nothing.

Stone's eyes crinkled. He subvoked to his implantable, *Most recent article on Kwame Goldbaum.*

Monday, two days earlier, he'd spoken at a campaign rally in St. Louis for his party's US Senate candidate. Then silence.

What would bring Goldbaum to visit the Sec-Gen outside of the public eye?

Stone chuckled. Secretely planning a preemptive military strike based on false intelligence would do the trick.

In the locker room at the Iron Horse, he lifted to his eye the retina scan lock at number 19. The door clanked open to reveal a blue gym bag on the locker's bottom, twin to the bag he carried over his shoulder.

Stone dumped his bag on top. The lower bag slumped. Nothing in it?

Almost nothing, more likely. He shut and sealed the locker.

Forty-five minutes later, a warm ache in his arms, he stripped and opened the retina scan lock. He shoved sweaty clothes into the lower bag. His fingers brushed crinkly plastic. Pressed harder and felt something rigid.

A sniff sounded in his mind's ear and he visualized Caitlyn wrinkling her nose. [I'm glad I wrapped it.]

He pulled his electronic liquid-dispensing loofah from the bag he'd brought. [You like spying on naked men?] He grinned and gyrated his hips.

[There's that alpha game crap. I'd missed it.]

He showered, then let the array of air dryers howl water from his skin.

Back at the locker, dampness in his hair and fake beard, he pulled his post-workout clothes—deep green trousers, pastel lime-green henley shirt, denim blazer—from his bag and dressed. Strapped the holster holding his snub-nosed .38 to his ankle and pulled his pants leg over it. His toiletries joined his workout clothes in the lower bag. Last check. Everything.

He walked out with the lower bag into a cloudy day. His black coupe pulled up before he reached the curb. The warm interior would help keep his muscles loose. "The parking garage."

The coupe joined traffic creeping down 2nd. Invoke a traffic control priority code and force cars out of his way? Bad idea. Thanks to Caitlyn's early wake up call, he had enough time… and any investigation into a black coupe racing downtown might lead Gray to the rigid object in the blue gym bag. And him to Gray's brain-scan facility out in New Jersey.

Or a shallow grave.

At the parking garage on 58th, he slid one of his fake credit cards into the payment kiosk. The gate lifted and he spiraled up to level 18. The bland blue sedan waited alone in the corner.

He switched cars. As soon as the blue sedan shut its door behind him, Stone reached into the gym bag.

A rectangular object, half an inch thick, fit in his palm. He peeled off the plastic wrap. A black plastic case revealed itself. A peelable rectangle on one side covered what had to be an adhesive strip. A pinhole-sized yellow LED on one edge barely caught his gaze.

[It's mostly battery,] Caitlyn said. [Induction charged by placing near any flowing electrical current.]

[Skip how it works and tell me what it does.]

[It's a modified version of the quantum computers embedded in our skulls. It identifies people in its input stream and outputs their hidden secrets.]

Stone twirled the device between his fingers. Its black plastic and small size camouflaged its vast power.

And something more mundane. His twirling fingers stopped. [Where does it receive inputs and outputs? Radio frequency?]

[Exactly. To activate, press the pressure-sensitive button on the right side of the top edge—]

Stone scowled. [Which edge is the top?]

[Huh? Ha. I'm reading off the instructions from Simon Bale's people on Minerva. The LED indicator is on the right side of the bottom edge.]

[Got it.] He cradled the black device in his right hand. Tapped with his index finger. [Nothing.]

[Hold for one second.]

He did. The LED turned green.

Stone said, [It won't work its magic from a parking garage in Midtown, will it?]

[No. Turn the device off. We want to save battery until you deploy it.]

He pressed again and the indicator returned to yellow. [Where?]

[The streaming control center in UN headquarters.]

Stone's hand fell to the car seat. [You want me to be seen by Gray?]

[I understand your concern, though it strikes me as excessive—]

[If you knew Gray, you would know it isn't.]

The sound of her breath came over the quantum computer link. [There's no other way to deploy the device. To reduce power consumption, the device's range is only four meters.]

[And I thought Minervans were engineering geniuses.]
[They are.]
Stone mulled. [Even if I slip by the cameras at the entrances, is the streaming control center restricted access?]
[You can easily defeat the SCC's security—]
[And where is the SCC? The basement under the General Assembly chamber?]
[Good guess.]
[Hundreds of people will see me. I hear the hallways down there are a maze.]
[I'll provide a map, and you use your skill in tradecraft to go unnoticed,] Caitlyn said. [There's no other way.]
[And soldiers from the Minervan mission's security detail will hunt me down if I refuse. Fine, I'll do it.]
[Your volunteer spirit warms my heart.]

Stone's early morning musings returned. He would take these risks for a good cause. An actual good cause, not the smokescreen of *peace* and *international community* shielding corrupt power grabs by the wealthy and influential.

[Back up. How do I even get into the headquarters complex?]
Caitlyn sounded disappointed. [Isn't it obvious?]
[No.]
[Get your new girlfriend to invite you in.]
He blinked. [Irani?]
[She can give you access. She probably has spare security passes to minimize the scrutiny you'll receive. And I could tell you found her more attractive after the meeting in Brooklyn.]
[Only in contrast to Charlotte Wang.]
[Really?] Caitlyn asked. [Irani's not beautiful?]
[You're jealous?]
Caitlyn went on as if his words had sailed by. [Oh, it's more alpha game crap, *I only bang 9s and 10s*?]
[That's not it.] He envisioned her long blond hair and hazel eyes. The corners of his lips curled up. [I've seduced plenty of 8s.]
[Then what's holding you back?]
He scowled at the parking garage's gray concrete wall. [What you

and your friends did to me on Minerva.]

[Really? Consecration and convocation made your life of sexual adventure less appealing?]

[Wasn't that your plan?]

[My plan? Do you think I care how many women you've had sex with or will have sex with?]

[As a matter of fact—]

[We subjected you to consecration and convocation because we wanted to recruit you to our cause. You can remain a spy and assassin—and a seducer—while being part of a healthy society for the first time in your life.]

Her words summoned echoes of his earlier thoughts about white boys and refugees. He grunted. [I'll get Irani to sneak me into headquarters.]

[Where's your enthusiasm? Is your head in the game?]

He chuckled. How many times had he said that to her on New Moravia and Trinity? [On missions, I've seduced women uglier than Charlotte Wang and led on men gayer than Eflorio Vasquez. Don't worry. I'll rise to the occasion.]

[You better.]

[I'm talking about Nina Irani, not you. Remember, I don't shit where I eat.]

[Don't flatter yourself,] Caitlyn said. Her tone shifted. [Almost time for you to leave for the meditation lounge. One last thing.]

[What's that?]

[You need to deploy the device today.]

[Today?]

[Events are moving forward rapidly. Fortunately for your concern about Gray, this means he will have a shorter time window to disover you visited headquarters today. Or do you doubt you can rise to the occasion?]

Perceptions of Irani mingled in his subconscious with pages from his seduction playbook. He smirked at the concrete wall. [I have a game plan. And no doubts at all.]

8

Stone strode around the corner toward Three Eyes Open, then hunched his shoulders and hurried. The brim of a New York Giants cap touched a pair of whiskey-brown sunglasses, both newly purchased twenty minutes ago and three blocks away. He ducked into the meditation lounge, glancing up on his way in.

Nina Irani glumly sipped water at the standup table near the door. Her brown eyebrows jumped and the corners of her mouth lifted when she saw him enter.

He ordered his pricey cave water and joined her, standing to her left.

Irani rested her drink on the table next to her sunglasses. "You're late, James."

"Have to be careful in my line of work."

Her wide eyes darted from side to side. "You were followed?"

"Possibly. I ducked into a bodega on 47th and bought—" He tapped his cap's brim and the outer frame of his sunglasses. "That shook the tail."

"I almost didn't recognize you."

He sipped fizzing water. "You didn't come on Monday."

"I had too many commitments at the office. Couldn't slip away."

"Commitments?"

"I shouldn't say."

He rested his hand on her left arm. Her smooth wool suit sleeved soft muscles. "Yes you should."

Irani glanced down at his hand, but her arm remained in place under it. "You're right. It's something you'd like to know."

"I would?" Stone slowly pulled his hand away.

"The issue that brought you to me? We're taking action on it."

He smiled. "That's wonderful." His hand landed on the back of her shoulder.

"My employer had a visitor yesterday. You wouldn't have heard about it. The visitor agreed to provide some resources to address the issue."

He drew back his hand. "I knew I came to the right person with my issue." Time to shift gears. "I'll stop coming here."

Her wide brown eyes drooped. "I won't see you again? Why?"

"You can resolve the issue without anything more from me."

"I don't know that. I may want you to meet more experts—"

"That's the reason? Please."

"Please what?"

Stone drilled his gaze into her wide brown eyes. "Tell the truth. To me and to yourself."

"What truth?"

He chuckled, then brushed the backs of his fingers over her cheek. She trembled slightly. "If you don't see it," he said, "then go back to work and home to a cold and empty bed." He walked around her and to the front door.

On the sidewalk, the hiss of automobiles and the tramp of a thousand footsteps echoed off concrete and steel. He took four steps west toward 3rd—

"James!" Irani's voice rang out like a mezzo-soprano trying to fill a concert hall.

Stone halted and slowly turned. He crossed his arms and arched his eyebrows. The corners of his mouth rose.

Irani's brown pumps clacked the sidewalk. "I don't know what kind of woman you think I am—"

He gripped her upper arms and pulled her into his bearded kiss. Her forehead pushed up a corner of the Giants cap.

She turned rigid for a moment. Then her lush lips softened and her body melted toward his. Pedestrians flowed around them, grumbling and cursing.

Stone whispered through mashed lips. "I want you. Now."

A tiny nod. "We can find a hotel—"

"No." He gestured with his head east on 44th, where the concrete canyon opened up to the line of flagpoles fronting the windowless, domed UN General Assembly building. "Take me to headquarters."

"Headquarters?"

He leaned back and poured intensity into his gaze. "For years you've given them long days and late nights. In return they've given you nothing. We'll go in there and share a dirty secret and they will never know."

Irani's eyes fluttered shut. She exhaled a plaintive breath. "But—security—"

"You can get me past security, can't you?"

"Not all the way to my office."

"Then we'll find another place. I hear the basement of the General Assembly building has a thousand places to hide. Unused conference rooms. Wide couches. Soundproofed walls."

Irani leaned toward him. "Yes," she whispered. She broke away from his grip and walked east toward the line of flagpoles.

He reseated the Giants cap, then caught up with her. They strode side by side, Stone on the right between her and the street. Pedestrians swerved around them. Stone reached for her hand but she adjusted its swing away from his reach.

"We'll keep it our secret," she said while looking straight ahead.

Stone nodded. His gaze flicked over parked cars. Faces in the crowd on both sides of the street. Polished surfaces reflecting the sidewalks behind them. No tails.

The concrete canyon along 44th opened up to gray sky at United Nations Plaza. Ground-level floodlights cast a white glow on the curved white wall and low central dome of the General Assembly building. To the right, the Secretariat tower loomed over the Hammarskjöld library. Concrete and steel and glass clad all the buildings. Some twentieth century architect's failed attempt to build a secular cathedral.

What design would come from the drafting workstation of a Minervan architect aligned with the universe?

Irani's gaze swept up to a window forty stories up the Secretariat building. Her lush low lips pressed together and she looked straight across the crosswalk at the General Assembly building.

The light turned. Vehicles rumbled through the 1st Avenue Tunnel beneath their feet.

On the headquarters side of United Nations Plaza, Irani turned left, toward the north end of the complex. Stone sidestepped to her left, again between her and the avenue, for a better view of the vehicle lanes and both sidewalks.

"You're quite chivalrous," Irani said.

His gaze scanned cars sliding past. "That too."

Behind a hedge and guardian ranks of concrete bollards and Czech hedgehogs, metal caltrops like a giant's jacks, a breeze toyed with the ends of member nation flags. A Japanese tour group, burdened with purses and camera bags, clotted around a tour guide. Irani veered to her left. Her shoulder brushed Stone's upper arm and her breath caught. They passed the tour group and she put ten inches of space between their bodies.

They drew even with the north end of the General Assembly building. Stone angled toward low steps, where a line of men and women in suits and national costume, UN employee badges dangling from lanyards around necks. His arm touched Irani's again—

She raised her left hand to waist height and pointed up the sidewalk. "Not here," she muttered.

"It's the main pedestrian entrance."

"Exactly." Irani's pumps clacked a faster tempo on the sidewalk. They passed the line of UN employees. Under an awning at the top of the steps, one security guard aimed a laser scanner at a QR code on a badge while the other waved a metal detector wand over the next person in line.

Between his plastic 9 mm pistol in his ankle holster and his bluff confidence, he could've entered with her there. He looked ahead, saw security fence screen by a line of maples. "Where do we get in?"

A smile played on her lush lips. "You'll see."

They walked on. A drone the size of his palm descended and hovered eight feet above the sidewalk in front of them. Close enough to see the UN logo and the wart-like camera on its undercarriage. The drone pivoted to Irani, then to Stone. It seemed to monitor him for longer. It buzzed backward at a pace matching theirs.

Stone's blood ran cold. Could the drone pick up his hidden pistol, or the device provided by Caitlyn now riding in his back pocket?

Had someone made him?

The drone's motors buzzed louder. It zipped up and over their heads, patrolling down the sidewalk. Irani seemed undisturbed by the encounter. Probably an everyday occurrence right outside headquarters, but asking her would spoil the mood.

They neared a driveway into headquarters. Irani said, "You're here on official and secret business."

"I'm good at keeping secrets. Especially when they're dirty."

A smile pushed at her low, wide mouth. "I'm serious. Stay quiet unless he asks you something."

"He?" Stone grinned. "Your other lover?"

"Shh."

At the driveway, a blocky guard shack stood between the inbound and outbound lanes of the entrance. A male figure in a navy blue security uniform looked up through the window. Misaligned brown eyes widened in a face two shades darker than Irani's.

The guard shack's door flew open. The guard crossed the inbound lane, his body rocking side to side with each measured step. He bowed his head. "How may I help you, memsahib?" His voice slurred, and not from his South Asian accent. *Cognitively challenged* might be the polite phrase these days. Which meant his parents were either too poor to have diagnosed and treated him, or so well-off that they could demonstrate their wealth and power by squandering some of both on a retarded child.

Given the odds against an impoverished child from one of the Indian statelets finding work with the UN, Stone assumed the latter.

"Thank you, Ajit. Have you a spare pass for this gentleman?" She turned up her hand toward Stone.

The guard's head jittered, giving each eye a moment to look straight at Stone. His body rocked and his eyes darted over Stone's cap, glasses, beard. "Is he a good man, memsahib?"

"The security of Earth and all her inhabitants relies on this man's testimony."

"I have a pass. Wait, please." The guard returned with his slow, rocking gait to the shack and rummaged inside.

Stone lowered his mouth near Irani's ear. "Don't make me wait as long as he is."

"Ajit has a good heart. Forgive him his weak mind."

The guard emerged and came to them. From his pocket he pulled a diplomatic visitor pass on a lanyard. He held it up, fingers pinching the hard plastic, and regarded Stone with his right eye. "You must return this to me."

"He will," Irani said.

The guard bowed and handed over the pass. Stone looped the lanyard around his neck to hide the face of the pass against his shirt.

"Memsahib, sahib." The guard led them to a black, chain link walk-through gate next to the inbound lane. He pressed his thumb to one scanner, aimed his right eye at another, spoke low words to a third, and punched buttons on the lock's mechanical keypad. He turned the handle and held the gate open for them.

This end of headquarters wedged concrete structures around small gardens and allegorical sculptures, like the campus of a college that tripled enrollment in a decade. Irani led the way down a path shaded by a parking garage and a chiller tower, then past an abstract sculpture of a knight with its back to—stacks of eggs?—and its sword and shield raised against a coppery blob. She glanced cautiously at each intersection and every open space and steered their path away from others. When a blind corner brought them face to face with an African man clad in a green dashiki and an Asian woman in a flowery yellow qipao dress, Irani ducked her head.

Stone glanced at the others as they passed. Unfamiliar faces. [Can you make them?] he asked Caitlyn.

[They're on the staffs of their countries' missions. Lobbying to expel more of their political undesirables to Trinity, in fact.]

[That mission was over a year ago.]
[It's still a reminder of how evil the Dubai Convention—]
[I don't need a political officer to tell me about the righteousness of my cause,] Stone said.

Caitlyn fell silent for the rest of his walk through the north grounds with Irani.

Soon, Irani led him past a ten-foot high concrete slab tagged with German-language graffiti, then around the northeast corner of the General Assembly building. A cool wind off the East River rustled through a line of trees screening their view of Brooklyn. She led them to an unmarked door near a loading dock. Held her grounds pass to the lock. A buzz.

They entered an empty hallway of off-white vinyl tile and LED panels in the ceiling. A camera's tiny half-dome enclosure jutted laterally from high on one wall like a dirty white wart. Stone palmed the small of her back.

She writhed away and turned her large brown eyes to him. "Not yet."

Down a stairwell, through basement corridors, down another stairwell, more corridors. Near the middle of the building, under the General Assembly chamber itself. Doors on both sides under more camera enclosures. Plates mounted on the wall identified conference rooms with the names of donors from almost two centuries before. Displays in e-ink showed the day's conference schedule.

Voices and footsteps echoed down twisty halls. Irani's shoulders hunched. Her gaze darted from door to door.

From around the corner, two voices grew louder and more distinct. Suddenly Irani grabbed Stone's hand and tugged him to the right. A green LED glowed on the door handle's baseplate. She shoved the handle down, the door open, and pulled him inside.

Stone rested his hand on the backrest of a black ergonomic mesh chair, duplicate of the ones at the meeting in Bed-Stuy the previous weekend. Five other chairs ringed a birch table shiny with waterproof lacquer. A side table with a water pitcher and a coffee urn. A loveseat upholstered with a roughly-textured blue fabric lurked along the far wall.

No cameras.

The door thumped against the frame. He turned. Irani locked the door and a crisp clack echoed. A moment later, shadows crossed the sliver of light under the door.

Irani waited, her hand on the door handle. Her large brown eyes on his face.

Stone strode to her. He grasped her upper arms. "Now." He pulled her into his kiss.

Her lips mashed warmly against his. Her hands slid up his shoulders. Her body softened into him. "Now."

He walked her backward, around the table, toward the loveseat.

Irani glanced over her shoulder. "No." She tapped her fingers on the tabletop. "Here."

He rapped his knuckles on the birch surface. "It won't be comfortable."

"The table can bruise me. I don't care. I want bureaucrats to spread their papers where we've made love."

His ardor cooled. If she wanted love, she wouldn't get it from him. The case in all his trysts for the past two decades, but now his conscience panged him.

Thanks, Caitlyn.

Despite his thoughts, the fire in his loins flared back up. A month since he'd last slaked his urges. That Eurasian girl in the sleeper berth on the space elevator, her name forgot—

Annika Kim appeared in the corner of his mind's eye. Text unrolled below the words, a dossier on the woman compiled from data pulled from his brain by the embedded quantum computer and unforgeably stored in a blockchain. *Employed as an exotic matter monitor in the wormhole placement branch of the UN Interstellar Transport Bureau/ITB—*

Stop.

The text vanished.

Thanks again, Caitlyn.

Irani stopped with her blouse on her arms over her head. "What's wrong?"

Stone's thoughts pivoted effortlessly back to the task at hand. "The table might be tough on my knees. Old football injury." He closed to her. Rested his hands on her bare flanks. "But for you, it'll be worth it."

Her large brown eyes flared. "You're damn right."

They attacked each other's clothes, tossing them into a growing pile on the floor. Her fingers brushed over the device in his back pocket without seeming to notice. He kept her hands away from his ankle holster. He unbuckled the holster himself and draped it over the top of a chair.

His pistol's hard plastic grip caught Irani's gaze. Half-frozen in fear, half-melting in lust.

Stone landed his fingers on the side of her chin and gently nudged her face in line with his. "My pistol isn't the only thing I know how to use." He wrapepd his hands around her upper arms. Guided her backward to the table. Joined her. Joined with her.

Most men worried too much about the mechanical aspect of a woman's pleasure. True, a touch with just enough pressure here, a lick at the right time there, helped the process. But a greater part of a woman's pleasure came from being desired by a strong and confident man. Being used by him for his pleasure.

Stone used her until their grunts and moans ceased echoing from the gympsumboard walls.

He climbed off the table and picked his boxers from the mingled pile on the carpet. The scent of their tryst filled the room.

Irani propped herself on one elbow. "Why are you going?"

"I'm a busy man."

"See me again."

"You know where and when to find me. In case you have more questions about the intel." He grinned at her.

"Or you have more about the Kama Sutra?"

His grin widened, showing teeth. Stone put on the Giants cap and the cheap sunglasses. He strapped on his ankle holster.

"Can you find your way out of headquarters?" she asked.

Stone pulled up his pants. The device in his back pocket pressed against his backside. His heart beat a little faster. He shrugged. "I'll manage."

9

Outside the conference room, Stone looked left and right. The hallways looked the same, and far enough in either direction might lead him into a dead end. People jokingly compared the basements of the General Assembly building to a hedge maze on some old English country estate. [Which way to the streaming center?]

[Left,] said Caitlyn.

He headed that direction. He smirked. [Enjoy the show?]

[I didn't listen.]

[Really?]

A silence, then, [Turn right. Take the stairs up.]

Stone pulled the handle. The stairwell door thumped against a round rubber stop. He climbed the stairs, his cheeks tight. Caitlyn protested too much. She'd eavesdropped on his tryst with Irani and didn't want to admit it.

At the next landing, he glanced at a door, then up the stairwell. [Which way?]

[This level.]

He pushed open the door. Another winding hallway, more conference room doors. More people, too. To his left, voices blurred together, cut through with the high notes of forks clinking on plates and an espresso machine frothing milk.

[That way.]

The hallway widened. Plush chairs and a stand-up table screened a display case of pastries and the espresso machine behind a counter. A Nuyorican girl from somewhere out on Long Island, a hat like a black mushroom on her head, took an order from three African men in checked blue suits. No threat there. Stone scanned the rest of the crowd—

At the stand-up table, a man with a pointy chin brushed potato chip crumbs from his mustache. The man's gaze rose.

Stone twisted his head away. [Catch him?]

[Who?]

[The mustached man who followed Constance Wang into the meeting last weekend.]

[Good eyes.]

[It's my carcass on the slab if I have bad ones. Who the hell is he?]

[I haven't found him in my database.]

[Not a random civilian who happened to be near the meeting,] Stone said. [A UN employee. Security?]

[I'll dig deeper to identify him. Is he following you?]

[Can't tell.]

[Maybe your hat and glasses fooled him.]

[My carcass if they didn't. Help me shake him.]

[Will do.] A corridor branched off. [Turn right.]

Stone did. Restrooms on opposite sides. The curved bowls of stainless steel water fountains in an alcove on the left.

He glanced down at the reflective curve. A man-sized figure rounded the corner behind him.

[He's tailing me.]

[I'll look for places on the map where you can shake him,] Caitlyn said.

While Stone's legs walked at his normal pace, his mind sprinted. A smoky white wart high on the wall caught his gaze. [If he's security, he can access video from internal cameras.]

[I'll route you away from those the best I can.]

The hallway ran straight. A chatter of polyglot voices ahead and to the left hinted at an open area. A jumble of acrid scents trickled to Stone's nose. Vents in the ceiling sucked up white clouds streaming through the air.

He gritted his teeth and turned left into a crowded vape lounge.

Men, mostly, in suits or national outfits. Two South Asian men, one with his legs wrapped in khaki fabric like a long skirt, the other buttoned up in a Nehru jacket, scrutinized each other while a soft-faced blond man played mediator. A white man with kinked black hair and playful eyes chatted in a Portuguese accent with an earnest young African woman.

Those conversations wouldn't work. Stone slipped further into the crowd. He sensed the mustached man approached the vape lounge, but he didn't look back. Someone yammered about exclusive economic zones and islands he'd never heard of.

Perfect. He sidled that way.

[What are you doing?] Caitlyn asked.

[Watch and learn. And give me background on these people.]

Two men. Their features struck him as Southeast Asian. Both draped in gray suits. At least their ties differed in color.

Red-gold Stripes said, "If it were up to me, I'd let you have those two islets."

"I know." Solid Blue puffed on his vape pen.

"My defense and economic development ministers are blocking me."

"I know."

Red-Gold Stripes shot a quizzical look at the New York Giants cap on Stone's head, then spoke as if he weren't there. "It's all because the contractors have promised them kickbacks."

[I've got them,] Caitlyn said. [The one in the striped tie is....]

Stone listened to her with half an ear.

"I wish only kickbacks held me back from resolving our dispute," Solid Blue said. "If it were just money, every man has his price, and it's often lower than you think. But my defense minister wants his star to rise over my foreign minister's—"

"I can help with that," Stone said quietly.

Solid Blue said, "Have we met?"

"No." In the corner of Stone's eye, the mustached man with the pointed chin pretended to listen to the South Asians' conversation.

Stone refocused his attention on Solid Blue and Red-Gold Stripes. "I'm with ITB."

"ITB?" Red-Gold Stripes peered at him. "The islets aren't big enough to put a wormhole on."

"Our scouts recently found a colony that terraformed a lifeless iceball world into an ocean world. Our preferred wormhole site there would best match with your disputed islands here. But we can't place a wormhole end here while there's a boundary dispute."

"A wormhole site is not a good thing," Solid Blue said. "Sarawak spent heavily on security to keep resettled from jumping off the train, and then lost thousands of square kilometers of forest to a fire caused by a wormhole containment failure."

"A partial failure," Stone said. "And over the lifetime of the Trinity wormhole, the Sarawak government received more from us than it spent to build and operate the transport links to the wormhole. But if working with ITB doesn't interest you…"

Solid Blue and Red-Gold Stripes shared a glance.

In the corner of Stone's eye, the mustached man now listened to the Brazilian man and the African woman.

"What can you do about our problems?" Red-Gold Stripes asked around his vape pen.

"The money coming in should lead your country's contractors and officials to agree with us." Stone turned to Solid Blue and raised his voice a notch, for the benefit of the mustached man now smoothing down his hair three feet away. "We know how to troubleshoot situations like yours."

"How so?"

"Sometimes a man like your defense minister can be bought by a promise to keep his secrets."

Stone continued the conversation while the mustached man eavesdropped. He dropped hints that intel services and the Secretary-General's office supported ITB.

[You've explained away your meeting with Irani, Vasquez, and Silverblatt,] Caitlyn said. [But not the woman your tail followed into the meeting.]

[I'll work warpdrive ships into the conversation. Forcing the topic will raise a bigger red flag than silence would.]

Red-Gold Stripes exhaled a peppery vapor cloud. "Why is the Sec-Gen involved?"

"His office benefits. He brokers a lasting peace and gets his statue out in the garden." Stone hooked his thumb to the north.

"You're calling in favors," Solid Blue said. "Your agency desperately wants a success after the wormhole failure."

"Partial failure," Stone said, "and since then the world of Minerva acceded to—"

"Was wormhole containment the problem?" Red-Gold Stripes waggled his vape pen at Stone. "There's a rumor you must have heard."

"Rumors fill the air around here."

"This rumor says a ship ran the wormhole from Trinity."

Stone raised his eyebrow, angled his head. Then he burst out a laugh. "That's ridiculous. Whoever started that rumor can't do simple math."

Solid Blue said, "Math?"

"All of our ships are wider than the aboveground half of a deployed wormhole. It's impossible."

"Impossible," said Red-Gold Stripes, "for an ITB ship."

"Who else has a ship these days?"

Red-Gold Stripes lowered his voice. "It wasn't from these days. An antique design from the Time of Troubles."

A grin filled Stone's face. "Our counterintel team did great work on this. I didn't want to say it, but our counterintel team started this rumor."

Red-Gold Stripes squinted. "So no old ship from the Time of Troubles ran the wormhole last year?"

"No old ships survive," said Solid Blue.

Stone leaned closer. "Our counterintel team says the exact same thing."

Solid Blue rocked backward. Red-Gold Stripes gave a self-satisfied grin.

A few feet away, the mustached man stroked his pointed chin.

"Gentlemen," Stone said to the two diplomats, "You understand our interest in settlng your boundary dispute. I won't take more of your time."

He stepped back and went around Solid Blue. Sidled past the mustached man. "Excuse me."

"No problem." The mustached man had a gravelly voice. Not what Stone expected from the sight of his pointed chin and a gold clasp holding his plaid necktie to his starched white shirt.

Stone passed the ventilation ducts and entered the hallway. He sucked in deep lungfuls of clean air. [Which way?]

[Left, then left,] Caitlyn said, voice chipper.

He set out. [You sound pleased. In awe of my ability to improvise?]

She responded with two seconds of silence, then said, [I found the mustached man in my extended database.]

[Don't tease me.]

[Evan O'Brian. He's on the books as a manager in headquarters' maintenance department.]

[Maintenance?]

[I don't believe that either. Did he buy your story?]

[He'll check on it. That gives me enough time to find the streaming center.] Stone came to the left turn. He glanced back toward the vape lounge. No sign of the mustached man. O'Brian remained in the crowd.

But before Stone could relax, he noticed a smoky white camera wart hung from the ceiling ahead.

O'Brian had a thousand eyes inside headquarters.

Would that matter? Assume that O'Brian would eventually reconstruct his movements and find that he went from the vape lounge to the streaming center. If he could deploy the quantum computing device in his back pocket unseen by cameras and streaming center employees, O'Brian probably wouldn't find it.

O'Brian also wouldn't stop him from walking out of headquarters. In five minutes Stone would get lost amid the crowds walking the middle 40s.

[Also gives me enough time to exfiltrate after I deploy the device,] Stone said. Then a thought came to him. [Will you order me back to headquarters before this is over?]

[You don't need to know. Why are you even asking? You know operational security requirements as well as I do.]

[If I have to slip past O'Brian, I damn well want to know.]

Caitlyn chuckled coldly. [Think of it as another chance to put me in awe of your improvisational skills.]

10

Caitlyn's directions led Stone up to ground level. The hallways were a little wider and UN employees better dressed, scented with more delicate cologne and perfume. Their faces showed more cheer, either from proximity to power, the white marble floors, or the knowledge that less than a hundred feet away a window let in daylight.

Proximity to the illusion of power. The hundreds of ambassadors and officials in the Secretariat, all the way up Secretary-General Sayyid himself, only considered, debated, acted on information provided them by Gray.

How much control would Gray lose if the Minervans succeeded?

Not the time to mull that now. The streaming center occupied a roomy space between the General Assembly chamber and the Secretariat tower. Stone walked a dozen paces past the glass doors. No cameras before he ducked into a men's room.

Sunglasses into his pocket. He left the Giants cap on the counter under a dispenser which whirred out a paper towel at the motion. He wetted his fingers in the sink and smoothed down disarrayed hair on his temples.

Looking more like a UN desk jockey, he pulled the floor-level sanitary handle with his toe and emerged from the restroom.

Inside the streaming center's glass doors, a reception area of angular leather chairs sported potted plants so green and shiny as to look plastic. Plush carpet cushioned Stone's feet.

[Streaming control is through the door next to the reception desk,] Caitlyn said.

[Don't state the obvious.] Only one door led off the room. [Who's in charge here?]

[What does that matter?]

[Answer my question.]

[The streaming center's chief is named Mehmet Ozcan.]

[Male, right?]

[Now you're stating the obvious. *Mehmet* is the Turkish form of—]

Behind the reception desk's dark granite countertop, a blonde swiveled to face Stone. The tracery of wrinkles at the sides of her blue eyes placed her within a couple of years on either side of thirty. Some things no amount of rejuve could smooth away. She wore a silk scarf, a blue two shades lighter than her eyes, knotted loosely around her neck.

The receptionist asked, "May I help you?"

Stone smiled. "I'm Mr. Ozcan's eleven o'clock."

"You must be mistaken. He's in a meeting off-site until eleven-fifteen."

Stone scrunched his mouth and scowled at a potted plant near the door to streaming control. "Damn those bastards. Damn."

"Sir?" the receptionist asked with a waver in her voice.

"Not you, ma'am."

Her lips mashed together for a moment at the implication she was old.

Stone lightly punched his left palm with his right fist. "They called in behind my back to cancel."

"They?"

He clamped his hand over his fist hard enough for his arms to shake. "Right, now I have to back up and explain everything. Sorry, they've got my blood pressure up with this stunt." His subconscious tossed up a name. Stone extended a hand over the countertop. "Victor Fitzgibbon. I'm with ITB."

Soft skin and a softer handshake. The wrinkles around her blue eyes deepened. "I bet that's exciting, but why do you want to talk to

Mr. Ozcan?"

"My role isn't exciting. I just try to keep the back office in order so the scout ships and wormhole tugs can do their jobs. Enough about me. We have a streaming center of our own, but it's a waste of money. My boss and I have agreed on this for months. The head of our streaming center is a conniving little f—person who'd rather scheme for a bigger budget than do what his job title says and I'm running my mouth...."

"Go on."

"Where was I? Yes. On paper, we could trim our budget by entering a streaming facilities share agreement another agency. That's why I'm here to meet Mr. Ozcan. But somehow the head of our streaming center found out and sabotaged us."

The receptionist brushed a stray hair from her forehead with a fingertip that never touched her powdered skin. Stone added two more years to his estimate of her age. "I understand your situation."

"Oh thank you so much."

"I'll put you on Mr. Ozcan's schedule for next week." She looked away from Stone and at whatever calendar app her transcranial stim unit projected onto her optic nerves.

"Next week? Please. He must have at least ten minutes after his current meeting. Heck, five minutes to get the ball rolling. All I need."

She drew in a breath. He read her as wanting to reject his request. "I can't promise anything, Mr. Fitzgibbon."

"I understand. Maybe one more thing while you contact him?"

"Yes?"

Stone angled his head toward the door to the streaming center. "Can I take a look inside?"

"Standard protocol is that someone accompanies you."

"No one's working?"

"We have employees inside now, but, computer people, you know how they can be?"

Stone nodded. "I deal with my share. I know how to talk to them, don't fret."

"We have a lot of equipment—"

"Which I've seen in ITB's streaming center. Plus, I don't know any of the passwords."

"Very well, Mr. Fitzgibbon." The receptionist rose and came around the counter. Her three-inch heels dimpled the carpet. Her skirt swished over saddlebagged thighs. She probably wore the blue scarf to cover jowls or a double chin. With luck she would find an adequate husband before it was too late.

At the door, she pulled an access card on a retractable lanyard toward a scanner, showed her retina, uttered a phrase. A scanner of a common design. A bag under his bed held all the tools he needed to hack it.

The door swung open with a mechanical whirr. Chilled air billowed around Stone. The receptionist led him through the field of view of a ceiling-mounted camera down a hallway.

[Get ready to feed me some technical jargon,] Stone said to Caitlyn.

[Already on it.]

The first door on the right. A green LED glowed on a scanner. The receptionist knocked, then a second later opened the door.

To the left, a long curved wall of video screens lit the streaming center more brightly than a full moon. Live shots of the General Assembly chamber, the Security Council meeting room, and a dozen other UN facilities. Reporters from media corporations posed like mature adults and kept their press passes hidden from view. Text scrolled in fourteen languages.

Two tables, matching the video wall's curve and laden with monitors and control devices, filled most of the room. Cooling fans whirred, background for a burst of high-pitched mechanical clicks like a robotic cricket.

When the clicks fell silent, the receptionist said, "We have a visitor. Mr. Fitzgibbon from ITB."

At the table nearest the video wall, a chair creaked. A pale face under shaggy black hair leaned out of the shadow cast by a desk-mounted monitor. "What do you want?"

"I hear you guys are good," Stone said. "I want to see you in action."

"We are good. You can look, but don't bother me. And touch nothing."

The receptionist smiled at Stone. The dim light softened the wrinkles around her eyes. "I'll talk to Mr. Ozcan and put you on his schedule as soon as we can."

"Take your time. And sorry to vent at you."

"We all have to get things off our chests sometime." Her gaze probed his. Obviously she sought signs of romantic interest.

Stone dipped his head and looked up from under his brows. "Tell me about."

The receptionist left. Behind her, the door let in a shrinking trapezoid of light from the hallway. Stone squeezed his eyes shut until the door clicked closed.

When he opened his eyes, the technician with the shaggy black hair stared at his monitor. The technician's fingers raced over a clicking keyboard, like a gamer character in an old-time movie engrossed in some shooter game.

[Looks like I don't need to know any technical jargon to hold up my end of a conversation.] Stone's gaze darted to fuzzy shadows. He noticed the quantum computing device in his back pocket for the first time in minutes. [Where do I deploy it?]

[See the access panel on the back wall?]

Behind the rear curved table, in the middle of the wall. [You mean that closet door?]

[All I have is the label on the room schematic. About halfway along the wall?]

[That's the one,] Stone said.

[Inside that closet is the outgoing server. Everything streamed from headquarters to the worldforum goes through there. Deploy within four meters of it. The closer the better.]

Stone made his way around the rear table. Along the base of the back wall ran a line of waist-high metal storage cabinets broken only by the closet door. He couldn't read the labels on the cabinet doors in the dim light.

He didn't need to. Smaller than his palm, black, and with an adhesive, he could stick the device in a back corner of even the most-accessed cabinet and no one would notice.

The cabinet next to the closet door would be ideal. The tech with the shaggy hair remained at his station, his shoulders hunched toward his monitor and keyboard, his back to Stone.

Stone leaned against the front of the cabinet. The bull-nosed edge of the plastic countertop creased his lower back. He peered through the gloom pervading the room.

No cameras.

Where was the second technician?

Stone's eyes fully adjusted to the low light. No human form visible at any monitor or workstation in the room. And the only breaths or sounds of a shifting body came from the tech with the shaggy black hair. By *we* the receptionist and the tech meant all the streaming center's employees.

Stone's heart thudded. He let out a breath. Faced the cabinet. Squatted. Slipped the quantum computing device from his pocket. Gently pulled the handle.

With only the faintest noise, the cabinet door opened.

One shelf. On top, plastic tags labeled coiled, zip-tied data cables arrayed in stacks specific for types of connectors. Below, spare backup power supplies stood in a row like obsolete airplanes at a desert airfield.

Perfect. Stone picked up the device. Held the power button. Rotated to bring the LED into view. Green.

He peeled the cover off the adhesive and silently extended the device into the back corner of the bottom shelf. By feel through the edges of the device he found the cabinet's bottom and back wall. Pressed the adhesive layer to the side of the cabinet for a two-count.

[That should do,] Caitlyn said.

Stone lifted his fingers an inch from the device. The adhesive held.

He pulled out his hand. Closed the cabinet door as quietly as he'd opened it. Stood up.

"I said, touch nothing."

Stone snapped his head around. Shaggy black hair on the back of the technician's head. The tech remained hunched over his keyboard, hands on the home row. Eyes on the wall of text on his monitor.

"I didn't."

"I heard you open a cabinet."

"And I didn't touch anything. You can learn a lot about how a place is run by seeing how well it organizes its storage spaces."

The tech grunted. "What did you learn about us?"

"You guys would do a great job handling ITB's streaming needs."

"We're overworked already."

"I'll tell Mr. Ozcan you need a raise."

The tech's head tossed. Probably rolling his eyes. The rapid-fire clicking of keys echoed around the room.

A sour feeling filled Stone's belly. Would the tech inspect the cabinet?

Only to make sure Stone hadn't stolen a cable or rearranged one of the power supplies. Stone slumped in one of the empty chairs near the cabinet. He shook out his arms and waggled his neck.

[How can you relax?] Caitlyn said. [Aren't you going to do more?]

[I deployed the device and now have to wait for the receptionist to come back. There's nothing more—]

[The tech caught you doing something suspicious—]

[The more you tell someone you didn't do nothing, the more they'll suspect you did something. Looks like he bought my story. If he didn't, the only thing he'd look for in the cabinet is whether I took something, not whether I left something.]

Caitlyn said, [I suppose you're right.]

[No need to suppose. Besides, won't the device alert you if it gets removed?]

[It will, but we'd have a challenge to replace it. Plus we'd have provided a lot of intel to O'Brian and others.]

Stone grinned. [You already have a back-up plan for that case, don't you?]

Her voice shed some tension. [How did you guess?]

Five minutes of white noise from cooling fans and bursts of key clicks like a battle among crickets. Suddenly, a widening rectangle of light made Stone squint. He rose and went to the receiptionist.

An apologetic look deepened the wrinkles at the corners of her eyes. "Mr. Fitzgibbon, I did impress on Mr. Ozcan the urgency of your request. Unfortunately, he can't fit you in until next Tuesday."

"That's disappointing, but I know he's a busy man. What time on Tuesday?"

"Two o'clock?"

Stone looked to the side, where a desk jockey's transcranial stim unit would pop up his calendar. [Any objections?]

[No,] Caitlyn replied. Her tone told him something important lay behind the monosyllable.

Stone said to the receiptionist, "I've got something for that time already. No no, I'll reschedule it. This is more important. I'll see you Tuesday at two."

"You mean Mr. Ozcan."

Stone dipped his head and looked up from under his eyebrows. "Him too."

Minutes later, Stone retrieved the New York Giants cap from the men's room. Sunglasses on, he strode the corridors of the ground floor. A pop up in his field of vision showed him the receptionist's contact information.

[You don't have time for a date this weekend.]

[Just giving my cover story legs.] He followed more data popped into his vision by his transcranial stim unit, a compass and a map of public spaces inside the building. He headed northward toward a burble of voices. He veered to the east at the sight of uniformed guards and a plethora of cameras outside the General Assembly chamber.

[Wrong way,] Caitlyn said. [You can take the western doors to the main entrance. They won't scan you when you exit headquarters.]

Stone tapped the pass dangling on the lanyard around his neck. [Time to return this.]

[Keep it.]

[I can't. Irani promised the cognitively challenged security guard, what was his name?]

[Ajit.]

[—That I would return it. I will. Unless you want me to burn her?]

[On Friday at the meditation lounge, you can tell her you forgot to return it in the throes of passion.]

His cheeks tightened in the beginning of a smile. [I know why you want me to keep it. You're going to send me back to headquarters. This—] He tapped the pass again. [—makes it much easier.]

Especially if she needed him inside headquarters on a different day or time than his meetings with Irani.

[Order you back to headquarters? Maybe I will. Maybe I won't. You don't need to know.]

A laugh burst out of Stone's mouth. [You don't need to tell me. I've already figured it out.]

He strode toward the building's north exit. The chatter outside the General Assembly chamber echoed down the hallways. He counted the white warts of ceiling-mounted cameras and mentally mapped out their blind spots for his return.

11

The clouds had thickened while he was inside, smothering headquarters with gray light. A breeze moaned between parking garages and swirled around abstract sculptures.

He grinned despite the cool weather and the ugly architecture. His heart pounded. He'd played the game well so far and would have a chance to play at an even harder level sometime very soon.

Stone strode on. He hesitated when he passed a coppery blob. The knight remained resolute in his defiance.

The stacked eggs behind the knight resolved into a woman and child. Odd he hadn't seen them before.

He picked up his pace and set aside thoughts of the knight defending the weak.

The walk-through gate opened at a turn of the handle. The hinges squeaked when he pushed it open. A line of three cars waited at the blocky guard shack. Two figures inside, Ajit and an older white man with gray sideburns.

Stone crossed his arms and eyed the passengers of each car in turn. Movers and shakers in each one. Silk suits spilling down paunches and two or three assistants perched on the front seats facing their bosses. No one gave Stone a glance.

He looked up from the last car to find Ajit rocking side-to-side as he crossed the inbound lane. Stone smiled and unlooped the lanyard from his neck. "Thank you, Ajit."

Ajit snatched away the diplomatic pass. "You have made the Earth safe, sahib?"

"I've done my best to help all mankind."

He fixed one of his brown eyes on Stone. "Memsahib Nina said you would. It is good you did not let her down."

Stone found a crosswalk and slipped into the crowd heading west on 46th. He checked glass surfaces and stopped at a smoothie cart. While the blender growled on pomegranate seeds, whey powder, and kale, Stone glanced sidelong back toward UN headquarters. No familiar faces. He'd shaken Evan O'Brian.

At least for now.

Sipping his smoothie, wincing at the bitter aftertaste, Stone called the metallic blue sedan to meet him on the other side of 2nd. Two identical cars passed him before his vehicle pulled up to the curb and popped its doors.

His gaze darted around, seeking hostiles, finding none. He ducked into the back seat, pulled off the cap and sunglasses.

Thirty minutes later, after switching cars in the garage on 58th and dropping the cap and sunglasses in a trashcan on Madison in the lower 70s, he rode up the elevator to his apartment. He pushed the door shut. Locked the deadbolt. Crossed the living room with barely a glance at its three pieces of sterile minimalist furniture. Entered the bedroom.

[You don't have a date,] Caitlyn said. [Taking a nap?]

[Getting out of Gray's line of sight. Even with the osteo-whatever nanogoop and that silly cap, he could make me from surveillance video.]

[He orders a human analyst to backstop facial recognition software, just in case one of his operatives underwent plastic surgery and went rogue?]

[No. He probably does it himself.]

Stone went to the closet. The scent of cedar oil bit his nose as he approached. Eight floor-to-ceiling storage cubbies filled the space like caskets standing on end. Each cubby held a roller carryon case, a pair of shoes, and a change of clothes hanging from a bar. The third cubby from the right held the best match for early autumn weather in Manhattan.

From the bar he pulled dark blue trousers with hidden zipper pockets, plus a long-sleeved shirt of a lighter blue shade tailored to his waist and arms. A black leather jacket completed the outfit... and Gray might know that.

Stone reached to his right and brought down a khaki trenchcoat. A poor match for the shades of blue, but well worth it to stay below Gray's radar. He tossed the trenchcoat onto the bed and changed into the blue trousers and shirt.

He kneeled beside the bed. Reached under. Slid fingers onto the keys of his firearm safe. Entered the combination.

The drawer hissed open, then the motor hummed as it pushed the drawer into view. Stone slid two magazines for the 9mm into zippered pockets of his trousers. Twenty rounds to add to the ten already loaded. He'd have to make them count.

Trenchcoat on, handle of the carryon case up, he left his apartment.

[Find me a hotel,] he said to Caitlyn.

[What do you want? Five stars with a rooftop bar?]

[Skip the sarcasm. I don't want to abuse my expense account. Find one where a small businessman from the Midwest would stay. Think six thousand dollar bottles of water that would make him nervous that he might open one in a moment of weakness.]

The elevator's descent pressed in his ears. He subvoked to his old implantable a request for a rideshare service. Another trip in his black coupe might be enough for Gray to track him.

On the street, a beige Vietnamese sedan with a Roboride sticker in a corner of the windshield pulled up. Stone couldn't remember the last time he'd used a rideshare. He climbed in.

"Where ya going?" the sedan asked in a girly voice.

[Good question.]

[Got it.] Caitlyn gave him an address half a block off Broadway north of Union Square. The Solstice. Stone relayed the name.

"A hotel. Meeting your girl there?" the sedan said. "I'm jealous."

Stone frowned. Oddly programmed, or fishing for data to sell to an advertiser.

Or use for blackmail.

"You're nosy," he told the sedan.

"I'm just trying to lighten the mood. Roboride wants you to have fun while we safely and quickly drive you to your destination."

"Consider it lightened. I'd like silence now."

"Whatever ya say." The sedan took him downtown without another word.

Wedged between a high-rise apartment building and an office tower, the Solstice resembled most of the other thousand hotels where he'd stayed on missions. A lobby with cheap artwork, here photoprints of the Flatiron Building a few blocks up Broadway. A dry smell from the heating vents. A pair of elevator doors.

A video monitor on the wall opposite the elevators showed a reporter in front of a sculpture of a handgun with its muzzle tied in a knot. *Non-Violence* was the sculpture's name. On UN headquarters. Reporters usually posed in front of it when peacekeepers would be deployed. The words "impending announcement" and "galactic security" came from speakers turned down low.

Stone's gaze snapped to the monitor. He strained his ears to listen.

"Next, please," a matronly voice said, her tone insistent. He hadn't heard her the first time.

He turned to her. A South Asian woman with incipient jowls and black hair in a bun. Her family might have owned the place for six generations. "Sorry," Stone said. He waved at the monitor. Put on a slack grin. "I've seen reports from UN headquarters all my life, but to finally be in Manhattan, only a mile from it in real life...."

"Welcome to New York. How long will you be staying?"

[Another good question.]

[Reserve for a week,] Caitlyn said. [I'll update you if you need to stay longer.]

"Check out next Wednesday. I want to do some sight-seeing after my meetings."

"I need your name and a form of payment."

Stone gave her a false name and a matching credit card from the stash Caitlyn gave him weeks ago. The clerk pursed her lips at the piece of plastic, then rummaged under the counter for a card reader.

A minute later Stone rolled his case toward the elevator. He glanced at the video monitor and halted. The reporter's words remained too quiet to distinctly hear, but the headlines across the bottom of the screen told everything Stone needed.

Security Council closed door meeting tomorrow 9am

Sec-Gen Sayyid speech to Gen Assembly tomorrow 11am

US Pres Goldbaum to attend Sec-Gen speech

[I'm on-duty tomorrow.]

Caitlyn said, [I can't confirm or deny that. You don't need to know.]

Stone's heart thudded. A smirk came to his lips. [Don't worry. Either way, I'll be ready.]

12

[Time to wake up,] Caitlyn said.

Stone's eyes slid open on his bedroom. His implantable projected *8:02* in the lower right corner of his vision. Light seeped around the blinds, bright enough to suggest yesterday's clouds had broken. He kicked the covers to the foot of the bed. [What's my agenda today?]

[You need to be at the streaming center by 11. Armed.]

He sat up, stretched his arms toward the ceiling. [I'm always armed. Who am I killing?]

[Ideally, no one. Are you disappointed?]

[I'll be in position. Out.]

Stone pulled workout clothes from his roller case. The Solstice's fitness room lacked kettlebells. He made do with a circuit of weight machines. A video monitor blared with talking heads speculating about the galactic security crisis to be the subject of Secretary-General Sayyid's upcoming speech. A newly rediscovered colony world. Riots on a world long ago acceded to the Dubai Convention, an outburst of racism and xenophobia from original colonists now outnumbered by resettled thirty-to-one.

"You're both wrong," said another, an older Caucasian man, with frizzy gray hair and eyeglasses, a ridiculous anachronism heightened by round lenses. "My sources inside UNHQ tell me that we've discovered intelligent aliens."

Stone snorted out a breath and pushed the handles of the chest press machine away from his torso. The pundits would be proven wrong in a day, but next week they would spew more nonsense, as credible and respected by the public then as today. Ten seconds of websearch could remind the public of the truth and puncture the inflated egos of the talking heads.

His arms softened. The weight plates crashed onto the stack.

Or the public knew the truth about the pundits—about everyone who appeared on video streamed out of UNHQ—and didn't care.

[Is this going to work?] he asked Caitlyn.

[It will. If you're in the streaming center by 11am.]

[Not what I mean. We'll activate the quantum computer I deployed yesterday during the Sec-Gen's speech and everyone in the General Assembly chamber gets their vile secrets revealed to the world. Will the world care?]

[The billions watching will know the truth.]

[What good will that do? Of those billions, the tens of millions with even a little power benefit from the current regime. A man can overlook a lot of unpleasant truths if his livelihood depends on it. Now flip it. The hundreds of millions with no power at all already know the truth. They talk about it all the time when they're smoking weed in their trailer parks or praying to their gods in their shantytowns. But without power, they can't do a damn thing about it.]

Caitlyn chuckled. [Do you always have doubts about the cause you're fighting for right before an operation?]

He finished his set of chest presses. A truth pushed at the back of his mind. He rested the weight paltes on the stack and the truth formed into words he couldn't avoid.

[I've never had a cause before.]

She gasped in a breath, then spoke as if she hadn't heard his last words. [Only a few will have both the power and the desire to act, at first. But those few will be enough instill the desire into those hundreds of millions in those trailer parks and shantytowns, and neutralize the power of those tens of millions.]

[Really?]

[Really. Now finish your workout. You have ninety minutes to get into position.]

Stone did three sets on the pullup bar and the squat machine while the talking heads competed to out-praise the Secretary-General's leadership and moral bravery. On his way out of the fitness room, he drank water and crushed the paper cone with his fist.

Back in his room, he showered and dressed. Ash-gray plaid suit, no tie, he'd look like a low level headquarters employee. He snapped his 9mm into his ankle holster a moment before room service arrived with breakfast steaming under a stainless steel bowl.

He gulped down a spinach omelet and smeared almond butter on whole-grain toast. Spilled the last crumbs in another Roboride he climbed into on Broadway. This one chatted in a woman's gosh-wow Southern voice about the big city. Trying to take his mind off clotted traffic, flowing as sluggishly as an old man's blood.

The Roboride pulled up to the curb at the corner of 48th and United Nations Plaza. Stone pulled one of his fake credit cards from his wallet, waved it. "Hon, I sure hope you have a good day. Come ride with us again. We'll sure treat you—"

Payment approved. The Roboride's door popped open. Stone scrambled out. A short walk under clear but cool skies brought him to the parking garage entrance.

He came up short. A line of cars, most of them multicolored siblings to the metallic blue sedan he'd ridden on previous days, backed up from the blocky guard shack halfway to 46th.

[Is this usual rush hour traffic?] Stone asked.

[No,] Caitlyn said. [Look there.] Another head seemed to turn within his.

Stone shut his eyes and rocked on his feet for a moment. [Careful.] His equilibrium snapped back into place and he looked where she bade.

A long black car. A corpulent, balding man on the rear seat faced assistants. Some agency chief coming to headquarters for the Secretary-General's speech.

Stone ducked his head. Hunched his shoulders. Gray could ride in one of the column of cars. He would need no facial recognition software to see through Stone's false beard and morphed facial bones.

Another problem. How long would it take Ajit, the security guard, to let all the cars through?

Time to cut the line. He strode across the empty outbound lane toward the blocky shack. No one inside the window.

He went around the front. Near the gate stood a solitary man clad in navy blue: the older man with gray sideburns seen yesterday.

"Morning. Where's Ajit?"

The security guard scowled. "Wish I knew. He's a retard, but he knows how to read a goddamn clock."

"A shame he isn't here. Can you help me? I need to get through."

"Pedestrian entrance is the other side of 46th." The guard turned his back to Stone. "Next!"

A smile played on Stone's lips. Maybe he would get to kill someone today after all.

The smile faded. Murder on the street in broad daylight, in front of witnesses in the waiting cars, would bring every armed guard in headquarters after him. Find a better way.

"Can't do that. My role is best served staying off the entry log."

Over his shoulder, the security guard said, "Pal, that b.s. might work on Ajit, but I'm not buying it."

"Ajit doesn't know me from Adam. But he trusts someone in the Sec-Gen's office who vouched for me yesterday."

The guard pivoted. "And I'm the heir to the King of England. Pal, it's the pedestrian entrance, or I call you in." His right hand drifted to a taser in a hip holster.

Stone lowered his voice. "How's a hundred K sound?"

The guard's eyes darted. He licked his lips. "Double or nothing."

"Deal. I'll duck into the shack and leave it on the counter—"

"Where I can see it." The guard turned to the next car in line.

Stone entered the guard shack through the open door. Chips marred the plastic countertop under the dusty window facing the nanotube-alloy highrises across United Nations Plaza. Spare passes on lanyards hung from a hook on the wall to the left of the door.

Stone sat on a round metal stool. Pulled his wallet from the inside pocket of his suit jacket. Counted out ten $20,000s under the chipped plastic. Fanned them enough for the initial *20* to show on each one.

Hid his hand inside his jacket and got on his feet in the doorway.

The guard stood at the open window of the car at the head of the line. "Snap inspection. Today of all days. I gotta do what I gotta."

The gate arm rose. The car rolled forward. The security guard pivoted and took a step alongside the car, then looked into the shack.

Stone slipped his hand from his suit jacket just far enough to reveal the fanned-out 20Ks.

A sidelong glance from the guard, followed by a single curt nod. The guard then turned to the line of cars.

Stone piled the money on the counter. Slipped a headquarters grounds pass off the hook. Looped the lanyard around his neck. He walked around the gate arm and tucked the thick plastic pass inside his jacket.

He grinned at the cluster of plain buildings and abstract sculpture ahead of him. This pass he wouldn't return.

The grin died. [Any word on Ajit?]

[He's on the work schedule—]

[Obviously.]

Caitlyn went on, her voice mildly peeved. [He didn't call in sick. Traffic was worse than usual between his home address and here this morning, but even with the expected delay, he should have been here three hours ago.]

Stone waited for a car to pass him. Not Gray inside. He let out a breath and crossed the inbound lane to the footpath trod by him and Irani yesterday. [O'Brian is questioning him.]

[We have to assume that.]

Stone mashed his lips together.

Caitlyn said, [Ajit can't tell him anything he doesn't know already. O'Brian will conclude Irani is the contact in the Secretary-General's office you alluded to in your chat with the diplomats in the vape lounge.]

[I'm probably in his facial recognition database.] He rubbed the backs of his fingers over his fake beard. Should he have shaved this morning? Facial recognition software would still find him in a crowd, but a clean shave might fool the human eye.

[Elude O'Brian for about an hour is all I ask.]

[I'd like to complete the mission by leaving headquarters when it's over.]

Caitlyn spoke with mock puzzlement. [You said you had a cause.]

[That I'd rather live for than die for.]

He pressed on. Yesterday's travels guided him through the maze of buildings between him and the General Assembly. He avoided cameras where he could, turned his face where he couldn't. The sculpted knight still defended the weak with sword and shield. Yet even if the knight slew the evil coppery blob, wouldn't another threat arise?

The boy behind the knight might become a man before then.

A faint, high-pitched whine jerked up Stone's head and widened his eyes. A drone, nearby. Where?

The whine echoed between buildings and faded below audibility. A routine patrol. Not looking for him.

Excess tension bled from his shoulders. Enough remained to charge him for action. The 9mm put just enough weight at his left ankle to remind him it waited for his touch.

The last of the plain concrete buildings fell away. The General Assembly building's white marble wall loomed above him. Camera domes of matching color dotted the edge of the roof. The footpath crossed a narrow strip of grass to a door tiny against the building's two-century old majesty.

A wave of the grouds pass at a security scanner let Stone in.

A glance back showed a guard, brown hair slicked back from an oval face, trudging toward the same door.

Stone's heart thumped. A tail or a coincidence?

Either way, shake him.

Stale warmth from an overworked climate control system surrounded Stone. The corridors echoed with voices and the clack of leather soles on marble tile. He strode through crowded halls, giving a nod here or a *good morning* there when his gaze happened to meet that of a scurrying headquarters employee. No witness O'Brian might question would rememeber him, and passing figures might obscure his face enough for facial recognition software to mismatch and anyone watching live the output of the cameras to lose sight of him.

Hope is not a planning factor. Stone wound his way through the mass of UN employees. His arms and legs tingled.

The crowd slowed and merged into a single file. Stone approached the heightened security zone near the General Assembly chamber. Guards in dark blue uniforms waved scanners and checked passes.

He veered toward a hallway leading to his left.

The guard with slicked-back borwn hair still followed him.

Stone entered teh hallway and looked up.

Fifty feet away, two guards stood behind and to the sides of a suited man. A gold tieclasp glinted between the sides of the man's baggy suit jacket. Above his pointy chin, a mustache covered his lower lip.

Evan O'Brian locked his gaze on Stone. He lifted his right hand toward the inside of his jacket. He started forward and the two guards behind him followed.

13

O'Brian's gravelly voice carried down the hallway under the high, echoing chatter of the security line. "Don't try anything stupid, 'Fitzgibbon.'"

Stone's right arm wanted to reach for the 9mm. He resisted. Gunfire in the General Assembly building would bring dozens of armed guards after him. Worse. The Sec-Gen's speech would be postponed until O'Brian secured the site.

Flee? Footsteps and hard breaths behind him. The guard tailing him blocked his escape. He would have to turn his back on O'Brian and the others, yet could probably overcome the guard—

Another footstep. More breaths. Make that two guards.

Stone held his hands wide, palms out. [My best play is a get out of jail free card,] he told Caitlyn.

[Gray will find out… in a few hours. Do it.]

Stone waited until O'Brian stopped just outside the reach of his fist. "I invoke Protocol Eleven-J."

"I'm sure you do," O'Brian said.

"Allow me to transmit my authentication." Stone subvoked to the implantable computer under the skin of his chest. O'Brian accepted the transmission an instant after Stone sent the request.

"Come with me."

Stone squinted. "Didn't it authenticate?"

O'Brian's gaze stayed on Stone's face. "Somebody else gave you Eleven-J clearance. Not me." The guards boxed Stone in, two in front and two behind, close enough for thick cologne and the creamy smell of hair pomade to reach Stone's nose.

Fight through the two behind him? Then run down hallways dotted with cameras. Bad idea.

Caitlyn's voice sounded in his mind's ear. [You have forty minutes to get to the streaming center.]

[I'll talk my way out. Do you know where they're taking me?]

[O'Brian's office is in the upper basement. Northeast corner.]

[In this building?]

[Yes.]

The guards trailing O'Brian led Stone that direction, further from the streaming center with each step.

Five minutes later they brought him to O'Brian's office. The e-ink sign by the door labeled the space *Headquarters Security Officer*. Normal people would read the sign and think of rent-a-cops like the man with gray sideburns at the drive-in gate.

Inside, Stone squinted at bright ceiling lights. They illuminated a wide space permeated by the smell of coffee and artificial creamer. Wood-grain plastic desks shoved against the walls.

Four doors in the far wall. To the left, one labeled with O'Brian's name. Banked video monitors in the next room, feeds from all the cameras around headquarters, no doubt. Next, a conference room. On the right, a steel slab contained a thick window criss-crossed with reinforcing mesh.

"Holding?" asked one of the guards.

"Conference room," O'Brian said. "Make yourself comfortable, 'Fitzgibbon.'" He tapped the air in the direction of the two lead guards. "Both of you stay with him. You other two, return to your normal duties." O'Brian went to his office.

Stone scowled at O'Brian's back.

"You heard the man," one guard said. He set his fists on his hips, right hand near his taser. Under a low forehead, his thick, dark eyebrows knitted.

Stone jerked his thumb toward a water cooler near the coffee pot.

"I'd like a cup of water."

"Conference room."

"Chief said he could make himself comfortable," the other guard said around uneven teeth mashing a piece of chewing gum.

Stone went to the water cooler. Extended his hand around a large plastic cup. Just the right size for what he had in mind. He held the cup under the spigot and pressed the blue dispense button. [Can you give me a diversion?]

[What do you need?]

[I'm flexible. Flip a circuit breaker. Lock O'Brian in his office. Anything.] Stone took a sip. [Bonus points if you can block their minds from controlling their bodies.]

[Bonus points?]

[Because I wouldn't have to kill them.]

[I'll see what I can do. You have thirty minutes to reach the streaming center.]

[Then stop talking, woman, and get working.] He put a playful tone in his voice, the same tone that could send a conquest to her kitchen to make him breakfast.

[Alpha game crap,] Caitlyn said. She cut the connection.

Stone took another sip. Still twelve ounces of water in the cup. He caught the guards' attention and nodded toward the conference room. "There?"

The second guard paused his gum chewing. "That's what chief said."

Stone went in. A motion sensor undimmed the lights. Ten black plastic mesh ergonomic chairs waited in precise rows along the long sides of a brown wood-grain table. Stone sat near one end of the table and slid a coaster into position for his cup.

The guard with the low forehead and thick eyebrows stood against the far wall. "I got this," he said to the gum chewer. "You wait outside."

Defense in depth. They feared what Stone could do.

The gum-chewing guard stepped out. He left wide the door to the main room.

A clock on the far wall ticked each second. Stone kept his poker face while his stomach churned. What took O'Brian so long? Researching something? Or making him cool his heels?

Stone took a calming breath. The latter, obviously. O'Brian played a power game. He wouldn't fall for it.

Even though he had twenty-five minutes to reach his position.

A door rattled in the main room. O'Brian's gravelly voice said something to the gum chewer. Inaudble reply. O'Brian then entered the room and took a seat across the conference table from Stone. His loose-fitting suit draped off his arms and down his torso.

"I'm free to go?" Stone asked.

"Think so, 'Fitzgibbon?' "

"You don't have to enunciate so much. It's an easy name to pronounce."

O'Brian smoothed down his mustache. "Except it isn't yours and you know it. I checked ITB's records. That agency doesn't have an employee by that name."

"If I have Eleven-J status, I wouldn't be on the books under my real name."

"I could almost believe you. That story you gave Vu and Tungsiripat sounded good when I heard it."

[Who?] he asked Caitlyn.

[No, Vu. He and Tungsiripat were the two diplomats you improvised with yesterday. I told you their names, remember?]

"But then I followed the threads backward and forward. I know you met with Irani and her cabal last Saturday out in Bed-Stuy."

"Who are you saying I met?"

"Jesus Mary and Joseph, stop playing dumb. I know she's conspiring against the Sec-Gen—"

Caitlyn's voice burst in. [What's he talking about?]

[Diversion first. Figure out Irani's game later.]

O'Brian kept speaking. "—recruited Wang, Vasquez, and Silverblatt. You're obviously part of it."

"The only thing I'm part of is ITB's effort to place a wormhole on that island Vu and Tungsiripat were talking about. I met with Irani and the others to facilitate that. I haven't a clue what Irani might be plotting against the Secretary-General."

O'Brian smoothed his mustache again. "If all you're involved in is siting a wormhole, why the detour to the streaming center?"

Stone blinked once.

"I followed you on camera from the vaping lounge to the streaming center. I went there and talked to the receptionist. A nice enough girl even if she has a little too much meat on her thighs. She told me about the man from ITB who wanted to set up a meeting with her boss to rent streaming services from their office. How does that tie into wormhole siting?"

Stone kept on a lazy smile. "I multitasked yesterday."

O'Brian slapped the table. Thick eyebrows jumped on the guard behind him. "You're here today to help Irani embarrass the Sec-Gen on a live worldforum stream to a billion viewers. Your visit to the streaming center was a scouting mission, wasn't it, to figure out how to keep it on the air? I don't give a good goddamn if you have Eleven-J status or not. Your part in this is over."

[Caitlyn.] Stone's voice carried a sharp edge.

She spoke hurriedly. [Working on it. Almost.]

Stone rested his hand on the table near the water cup. He gave O'Brian a wry grin and slowly shook his head. "Here's the truth. I'm investigating Nina Irani, not conspiring with her."

The guard along the far wall furrowed his brow, trying to keep up. O'Brian's expression showed he udnerstood Stone but didn't believe him. "Are you now?"

"She put out feelers to ITB. She wanted false intel about a colony world. My boss, Holbrook, strung her along and assigned me to infiltrate her conspiracy. I scounted the streaming center because Vasquez assigned operatives to keep it transmitting. I'm going to neutralize them."

O'Brian lifted his pointy chin. "If that's true, you should have come to me. My team can secure the streaming center."

[Everything is in place,] Caitlyn said. [I can't hack their implantables to neutral—]

[Less talk. More diversion.]

[In 3…]

Stone turned his palms up for a moment, then closed his right hand around the water cup.

[2...]

"You never know," Stone said, "who to trust."

[...1!]

The lights failed. The basement's deep darkness blinded Stone.

He threw the water cup into the gloom where he'd last seen O'Brian's face. Jumped back from the table. Landed in a crouch, right hand near his ankle holster.

O'Brian grunted. His chair wheels sounded, rolling backward.

"Huh?" The guard. He hadn't moved.

Stone yanked free his 9mm. Aimed into darkness at O'Brian's chest. Squeezed the trigger twice.

The shots echoed off the gypsumboard walls. Stone's ears rang. Propellant tang bit his nose.

Two more shots at the guard's chest.

He stayed crouched. Ran out the door. Collided with the second guard. The second guard fell backward. Rows of uneven teeth snapped shut.

Two more shots.

Stone stood up, gun still in hand. Only the ringing in his ears filled the silence. He pulled in a long breath. The thick metallic smell of blood told him he'd scored hits. But enough? [I'll attract attention in the halls if there's blood on my hands from checking their pulses. Can you pull telemetry from their bodies?]

[No. Their implantables are only hooked up to the worldforum. I'll restore the lights. Maybe you can tell by sight if they've been neutralized.]

[Call an entrenching tool a space. If I've killed them.]

The lights snapped on in the main room. The guard lay on the plastic tile floor in a seeping puddle of blood. Two chest wounds. Blank eyes stared at the ceiling and mismatched jaws would never again close.

Stone turned. In the conference room, the guard with thick eyebrows slumped against the wall. Blood streaked down the gypsumboard and soaked his blue uniform from his collar to his lap. More blood pooled on the carpet under him. Neck and chest, fine shooting in the dark.

O'Brian's head lolled back in his chair. His eyes showed whites in a pallid face damp with sweat and the water flung by Stone. Two chest wounds, enough for him to have already bled out, just like the others—

O'Brian's tongue dabbed at a drop of water trickling down the side of his face.

Stone snapped the 9mm up to aim at the man's face.

"Damn you." O'Brian's voice burbled. Blood dribbled from between his lips.

"I was going to hell long before this," Stone said.

"Worth it? Bring down—" O'Brian stiffened, his chest fighting for breath. "Sec-Gen?"

"I'm playing a much bigger game. You should have let me go."

"Damn you—" O'Brian mouthed. His chest heaved. His face contorted. Then the tension fled his body. His last breath rattled in his throat.

Poor bastard. Doing his job. Just like his men.

Just like Stone.

No. Stone finally did something more than a job. More than play a game he was good at. He had a cause. Something to die for, if he had to. And until then, something to kill for.

He checked the time. 10:50. Ten minutes to get to the streaming center, or else these three deaths—and the hundreds more on his convocation profile and on his conscience—would mean nothing.

14

The hallways near the General Assembly chamber echoed with a few hurried footsteps. The building seemed to hold its breath, lick its lips, check its wristwatch. Five minutes till the Secretary-General's speech and everyone was in position.

Everyone but Stone.

He approached the glass doors of the streaming center, then looked up and down the hall. He expected no disturbance after he went in. Not before the speech.

But after? Oh yes.

[Can you remotely lock the doors?] he asked Caitlyn.

[Wish I could.]

[You cut the power and wireless network near O'Brian's office.]

He expected an explanation. Instead, she said, [Get into position.]

Stone pulled open one of the glass doors and went inside. Same potted plants and angular leather chairs between him and the door to the control room. Perhaps he could lock the outer doors unnoticed by—

The receptionist looked up from her desk. Wide eyes brightened, for a moment smoothed out her crow's feet. "Mr. Fitzgibbon. What brings you here today?"

"The Secretary-General's speech will put you to the test. I want to see how you handle it. Because if you can, I'm even more certain that we should move our operations to you."

She brushed a blond strand behind her ear. "That's a great idea. But Mr. Ozcan and the techs won't want to be disturbed."

"I wouldn't dream of that. I want them to do their jobs as if everything were normal. They're in the control room now?"

"Yes. I'll take you there." The receptionist came around her desk with a swish of her skirted thighs. She passed him, hips swaying to keep her balance on high heels, and gave a coy smile. Hoping he would ask her out, not angry that he hadn't yet. She waved her prox card at the sensor and bent her eye to the retina scanner.

"It's great power to be the gatekeeper," Stone said.

"Confirm," she said to the security panel. She straightened up. "It's not that great. All of us have access." The door swung open and she led him through.

[Hurry,] Caitlyn said.

[Almost there.] "Just a second," Stone said. He knelt and moved his hands to his left shoe.

"Certainly." The receptionist turned back to face him. Behind her, a camera dome on the ceiling watched them. Feeding video to a room full of dead men. A mechanical whirr came from the door closing behind him.

The receptionist glanced at his shoe, where his hands flapped the tight loops in his laces. Her forehead furrowed.

The door sealed itself with a thud and a click.

Stone drew his 9mm from his ankle holster. Stood and aimed in one motion. "Cut your wireless access now or else."

She gasped. Her body froze. Her blue eyes locked on the muzzle.

He subvoked to his implantable. It pinged hers, reported the result. She remained on line, but hadn't sent a message.

Yet.

"I've killed three people already today. Don't make me kill four. Cut your wireless access."

Her mouth worked but no sound came out. She managed a faint nod. She went off-line.

Stone told his implantable to keep pinging her. A denial of service attack: occupy her implantable's transceiver bandwidth enough to prevent her from sneaking a message past him. "We're going to the control room," he said. "Now."

"Don't hurt me—"

"I won't if you do what I say."

She turned. Her back arched as if her spine wanted to leap out of her chest. With heavy steps she trudged down the hallway. Stone kept the 9mm aimed at her spine. His gaze darted and his ears strained for any sign of interruption.

They reached the door to the control room. A green LED showed at the scanner. Her hand reached for the handle, stopped. She looked back, a question in her eyes.

"Open," he said softly.

She turned and pushed the handle in.

He shoved her with his free hand. Burst into the pale, washed-out light of the control room after her. Elbowed the door shut. Aimed the 9mm at a tall figure standing at the front and clad in a dark suit and a tie the color of dried blood.

"What's going on here?" said the tall figure, a man sporting a trimmed beard. His face looked pallid in the video screens' light. Brown eyes stared at the pistol in Stone's hand.

"Cut your wireless access now." He continued speaking, taking in the three other figures in the room. "All of you."

They did.

Stone subvoked. *Denial-of-service everyone in the room.*

In his vision, local network icons showed his implantable devoted most of its procesor cycles to the task.

But the techs had another route to send messages. Each one sat at a keyboard, and he had to allow data to flow from this room to worldforum.

[Can you stop them from typing a warning about me to someone outside?] he asked Caitlyn.

[I can't stop them, but I can alert you if it happens.]

[Have to do. And keep me informed if the speech is on air?]

[Yes.]

"Here's what we're going to do," Stone said aloud. To the tall figure: "You're Ozcan?"

"I am."

"Your people will be fine if everyone does as I say. The techs will keep the Secretary-General's speech streaming. And nothing else. Don't try to type and send a message behind my back. We're monitoring network traffic out of here."

Two of the techs—the one with shaggy black hair and another, face long and forehead furrowed—nodded trembling heads. Tiny rectangles of reflected light jittered in their eyes.

A moment later, the third tech, seated at the back table, held up thick-fingered hands. "Yes sir, we will, don't hurt us, please—"

"Quiet," Stone said. He beckoned the receptionist to move next to Ozcan. She frowned at the tech at the back table, then to her boss. Ozcan extended his hands toward her and pushed his palms down on air.

Ozcan calmed her, but what did the third tech have to do with it?

Stone locked the door. Sidestepped to his left, in front of the left side of the curved video wall. Held his 9mm at his side. From his vantage point, he could take in all five of them at a glance. Even if the third tech were just as he seemed, you never knew when a desk jockey might decide to be a hero.

The third tech's gaze jerked like a rabbit's back and forth from the receptionist to Stone's pistol. A man might be foolishly brave against an operative with a handgun if he deluded himself into thinking he could win a woman's affection.

The long-faced tech's forehead creased even deeper. He strained his upper body to look through Stone at the monitors behind. "I can't see."

"Deal."

"You said I have to keep streaming but if I can't see—"

Ozcan's voice sounded firm yet kindly. "Do the best you can."

The long-faced tech sat back. His chest still heaved. High strung. Have to watch him too.

Stone took a breath of chilled air tanged with sour sweat. Gaze still on Ozcan and the others, he asked Caitlyn, [Ready?]

[Yes. With ten seconds to spare.]

The video monitors behind Stone bathed the faces in front of him with light. [Can you give me a window on the stream?]

Her voice lilted. [I can do better than that.]

The walls and floor turned to glass and the control room teleported two hundred feet away and twenty feet in the air. Behind the third tech, at the far end of a large chamber, a gold rectangle climbed up between incurving halves of a wooden wall. The gold rectangle bore a single decoration—a UN seal fifteen feet in diameter. Olive branches extended their reach, almost encircled the globe.

The General Assembly chamber. He blinked, took a long breath. If he didn't know better he could believe the sight around him was real.

[How?] he managed.

[The Minervans have made great advances in virtual and augmented reality.]

[This is constructed from the outgoing stream?]

[Yes. You'll see what a billion viewers around the world will see.]

The green marble rostrum behind the speaker's podium—fifty-foot video screens flanking the gold rectangle halfway up the wall—two banks of windows running almost the full width of the incurving wall, from which the interpreters watched and worked—the tables where the diplomats sat, arrayed from the podium back behind and under his feet—Stone resisted the urge to look around.

Ozcan and his people watched the video wall behind Stone, rendered invisible by the Minervan VR tech. When they didn't cast nervous glances at him.

Expand the local connectivity icons, he subvoked to his implantable.

Two long seconds, then the icons lurched into glowing red orbs, each projected onto the chest of one of the streaming center employees. Denial-of-service packets from his implantable showed up as yellow bursts impacting each orb.

No one tested his warning—through their implantables.

[Anyone sending out a warning through the computer system?]

[None that I can track.]

Stone's gaze returned to the black-haired tech and his long-faced partner. They clacked keys at their stations along the front table. [Good.]

Behind the third tech, the video screens on the sides of the gold rectangle switched to a closeup of the rostrum. An Asian man in a baggy suit rapped a gavel. A white noise of chatter subsided. Another rap brought silence save for the motions of over a thousand people crammed into the chamber.

The Asian man held the gavel at the ready, then nodded and set it down. He leaned into the microphone. "The chair recognizes Secretary-General Abdullah Sayyid."

The Secretary-General rose from one of the white chairs flanking the podium. Applause broke out, as polite as a symphony audience. Among those applauding were US President Goldbaum, his afro like a black dandelion, and from the end of the row, Nina Irani.

The closeup panned down. Despite the descent from Muhammad asserted by the surname *Sayyid*, the Secretary-General looked Italian at first glance. Dark hair receded from a broad forehead and his sharply-tailored suit and tie might have been hand-sewn in Milan. His tan suggested long hours on the tennis court. His small eyes flicked over a few faces in the crowded chamber, then landed on the teleprompter in front of him.

Sayyid raised his right hand to his chest. His dry voice said in a posh English accent, "To your Excellencies, honored guests, and all citizens of Earth and her daughter worlds: *as-salāmu 'alaykum*. In particular, I welcome the delegation from the most recent daughter world to return to Earth's embrace. The delegation from Minerva." He gestured with his right hand toward the back left of the chamber.

The crowd applauded. The video screens zoomed in on a table. Five men and a woman, all wearing intense colors that stood out against the backdrop of dark suits around them. A blond woman in a long red dress—not Sheila van Bentum—Stone's heart slowed. The costume of a facilitatrix of Alignment with the Universe, Minerva's state non-religion. A man in a blue suit, one of her male colleagues, sat next to her. The other four men wore shades of yellow. The ambassador and an aide were two. A third had blue eyes and a short, thick scruff over his lower face. Simon Bale, High Councillor of Minerva's Security Directorate.

[What's he doing here?]

[Bearding the lion in its den,] Caitlyn said. [He's not defenseless.]

Stone squinted, then noticed the youngest-looking man of the Minervan delegation. Alert green eyes studied the crowd and did not smile when Bale and the others raised their hands to acknowledge the applause. A special operations soldier in the Minervan military, assigned by his superiors to the conspiracy spearheaded by Bale. Skilled enough when equipped with an invisibility suit to capture Stone on Minerva, but what good could he do exposed to a thousand in this chamber and ten million in the city outside?

Never mind him. [Where are you?]

[Offsite.]

[Don't state the obvious.]

[Don't ask for information you don't need to know.]

The applause faded away. The Minervan delegates lowered their hands.

Sayyid resumed his speech. "As Secretary-General, my position is one of great honor. This honor comes, not in the trappings of office, but by carrying out the responsibilities of office. Paramount among those responsibilities is the maintenance of peace.

"Those of a certain age know far too well what disasters may strike Earth and her daughter worlds if peace is not maintained. Last century, disorder ravaged all the nations of Earth like a cancer. Disorder destroyed billions of lives. Our predecessors had to work as surgeons, excising diseased flesh from the body of humanity. Only then could they work as healers, restoring wholeness to that body."

Stone remembered the frightened shouts from the back cars when the train passed through the wormhole to Trinity. Hundreds of Africans ethnically cleansed from their home country and dumped on an overwhelmed colony so men like Sayyid could add to their hoards of wealth and power. Hundreds then, a drop in a stream of tens of millions over decades. Tens of millions ripped from their alignment with the universe.

He sniffed out a breath at the urbane sophisticate at the speaker's lectern. Sayyid wasn't aligned with the universe either. How much did he hide? His Swiss bank accounts and his Swedish mistresses, of course. But something lurking behind his small eyes told Stone he hid much more than that.

"Our predecessors did not work as surgeons lightly," Sayyid said. "When excising a cancer, one must sacrifice healthy flesh around the cancer's margin to ensure no disease remains to reinfect. Likewise, when our predecessors wielded the scalpel of peacekeepers, some innocents perished. Our predecessors regretted the need, but those innocents knew that they set down their lives for the good of all mankind, and they were content."

Like hell.

"Yet just as cancer may recur in a body once cured, so too may the cancer of disorder return to the settled galaxy. It is with deep regret and heavy heart that I must say not only that it can, but that it already has."

Near the front and center of the General Assembly chamber, heads turned to launch hundreds of conversations. Murmurs broke out. The high ceiling and central dome mashed the words into an uneasy rustle.

Stone glanced down and to his right. He oculdn't see the Minervan delegation.

[How are our people reacting?]

[The ambassador, his aide, and the facilitators are as confused as anyone else. Bale is telling them this is all according to plan.]

Stone drilled his gaze in turn into each of the streaming center employees. The receptionist shrank away from him. Ozcan looked like he had heartburn. The techs hunched their shoulders.

Behind the third tech, the Secretary-General remained in closeup on the General Assemlby chamber's giant screens.

"One of our daughter worlds," Sayyid said, "has turned against us."

The murmurs heightened, like waves crashing against a beach at high tide.

"We have incontrovertible intelligence, gathered at great personal risk by one brave agent, that the colony world of Minerva has mastered exotic matter and space combat technologies. We have incontrovertible evidence that the colony world of Minerva plans to unleash a fleet of warpdrive ships against Earth."

Murmurs erupted into an outcry. The monitors showed another closeup of the Minervan delegation. The ambassador leaned on the table and mouthed *No*. Next to him, Simon Bale folded his arms and eased back in his chair.

Sayyid raised his voice. "Therefore, as we speak, peacekeeping forces generously provided by President Kwame Goldbaum of the United States are deploying through the wormhole to neutralize the Minervan government's threat. Swiftly and surely, we shall allow the Minervan people to establish a new government aligned with the principles of the United Nations charter, and we shall expunge the threat of war from the entire settled galaxy."

A gruff voice shouted, "Proof!" More voices around the chamber echoed the call in a dozen languages. At the rostrum, the chairman banged the gavel.

"Proof!" came the call again. Sayyid's supporters hissed and whistled.

The chairman banged the gavel three times, called for order.

Sayyid raised his voice. "The extraordinary situation before us demands proof. We have that proof. We now show it to the world." He extended his hand toward Nina Irani.

The gigantic video screens switched away from Sayyid's closeup. A title slide and an introduction slid by. Up popped an animation of an exotic matter factory.

"The Minervans have built a duplicate of Hawking Station. They hid it from UN ships by masking its solar panels and aiming away its radiators. Both the specifications provided by our brave, solitary agent and the analysis of experts confirm what they have done."

A video interview came on screen. A man with widely-spaced eyes. Stone needed a moment to recognize him without the vape pen behind his ear. Walter Silverblatt, Ph.D., Interstellar Transport Bureau.

From off-camera, Irani's voice. "You have reviewed all the intelligence gathered by the operative regarding the Minervan exotic matter factory?"

"Yes." Silverblatt's voice lacked its usual warble.

"What is your conclusion?"

"It's total and absolute falsehood."

A new murmur rippled through the General Assembly chamber.

"You make a bold statement. On what basis do you conclude the intelligence is fabricated?"

"It's an irrefutable matter of physics. Exotic matter factories generate terawatts of waste heat. If the Minervans operated one, it would glow like a red dwarf star. Any UN ship, coming in from any angle, would have detected it."

"In summary, it is your expert opinion that the colony world of Minerva has not built an exotic matter factory?"

Silberblatt stared into the camera. "Yes."

The ripple through the General Assembly chamber turned into shouts. Cries of "Liar!" and "Fool!" burst through the noise, aimed at Sayyid.

The Secretary-General stiffened his back. "My presentation has been tampered with by Minervan agents—"

A shrill voice pierced the General Assembly chamber. "Warmonger!"

Inside Stone's mind Caitlyn called out, [Convocation!]

15

The chamber's hubbub lessened. Notes of discomfort burst out. On the video screens, Secretary-General Sayyid's left eye twitched. He raised one hand to his forehead, steadied himself against the lectern with the other. A wave of similar reactions passed over the thousand diplomats.

Ozcan sagged back againt the front table like he'd been punched in the gut. He breathed heavily and pressed his fingertips against his forehead.

The receptionist's eyes clamped shut. She groped blindly for the table, then slumped to the floor. Behind them, the long-faced tech grimaced and balled his hands into fists.

A euphoric wave flowed through Stone's chest. The drones sent by Bale and the other Minervan conspirators had delivered their payloads of medical nanomachines against the designated targets. The nanomachines had built quantum computers in their targets' skulls, just as they had to Stone a few weeks earlier on Minerva. He'd expected they would, but now, to see success—

"What the hell?" The shaggy-haired tech stared, mouth slack, at the video wall. The nanomachines must have missed him when they circulated through the ducts and pipes of UN headquarters.

Stone refocused on the control room. "Keep streaming." He lifted the pistol in front of his chest. "Your lives depend on it."

The tech swallowed. His Adam's apple hung up at the top of his throat. He stared at Ozcan as if his eyes could bring the streaming center chief out of a seizure. "Sir. Sir!"

Not a seizure. An altered state of consciousness induced by the quantum computer embedded in Ozcan's skull accessing Ozcan's mind and linking him with the public blockchain of formerly hidden secrets of everyone on Minerva and, now, thousands on Earth.

The tech should know. And so should the tech on the back row—

—who wasn't there—

Stone crouched and rolled to his right. A gunshot from his left screamed and flashed in the dark room.

"Kill the damn stream." The grim voice of the third tech came from the left end of the room.

Not a tech. An operative.

For whom?

"But," said the shaggy-haired tech. "But—"

"He's trying to bring down the Secretary-General. Kill the goddam stream. Now."

Keys clicked from the shaggy-haired tech's position. The virtual reality fell away. The video wall turned into a tilework of test patterns, red green blue black white.

Gun in hand, Stone peered through the nest of cables and table legs between him and the far end of the room. A glimpse of flexing legs in gray trousers. Too far a shot in dim light and with civilians in the way.

The legs disappeared from view.

Feet clomped the far end of the rear table. Out of sight, above Stone's crouched view.

The operative's footsteps came closer. Light steps and soft soles. He'd have his handgun drawn—

Stone slid between the end of the rear table and the control room wall. Popped up. Fired. Two rounds. Ducked. Moved silently back toward the front table.

He gulped a breath. The operative must have fired. How many muzzle flashes?

How many gunshots?

Over the ringing in Stone's ears, ragged breaths from somewhere. "Oh god oh god oh god."

The shaggy-haired tech cowered under the front table. The other tech, the receptionist, and Ozcan wrestled with the emotional storm unleashed by convocation Ignore him.

A shadow cast by the test patterns lurched on the back wall. The front table clattered. The shadow aimed a handgun at the spot where Stone had just fired—

He popped up. The operative filled his sights. Stone fired. One shot in the back. One round left in his 9mm.

The operative spun his body. His pistol turned even faster. He fired toward Stone.

Stone raised the muzzle. Fired.

The round smashed through the operative's cheek. He toppled backward. Tumbled off the edge of the table. Crashed into the cowering technician's empty chair.

"Ohgodohgodohgod."

Stone went around the table, pistol ready in his hands. The tech gasped. Stone ignored him.

Lying in a spreading dark stain, the operative twitched once, then lay still.

Stone checked the operative's neck for a pulse. None.

Stone pulled back his hand. Blood on his hands now, but at this point, his work was done.

No it wasn't. The test pattern glow still filled the room.

The operative's handgun lay on the floor, near the feet of the cowering tech. Stone picked up the handgun. A German model, heavy and precisely engineered. No UN agency's standard issue.

His gut sank for a moment. He willed the sensation away. To the tech, he said, "Get the stream back on."

"Oh god, oh god."

Stone ejected the empty magazine. Slotted home a full one from his zippered pocket. Nudged the tech with his foot. "Back online. Now."

Motion at the other side of the table. Ozcan bent at the waist and said under the table, "Come on out."

Stone stepped back. Blood squished on the tile. Careful, don't slip.

He cleared the pool of blood and met Ozcan's gaze.

A black rectangle ringed with a thin gray bezel floated over Ozcan's shoulder.

```
Mehmet Ozcan
Public-facing profile (algorithm: esb-2078.34.113;
block: 7005264)
++++++++++
Kindly, scheming, dedicated to his work.
Director of [United Nations Headquarters Electronic
Communications Center/UNHQECC] since 2125-03-21.
Formerly assistant directior of same. Acquired position
by spreading rumors of prior director's cocaine
addiction and affair with former receptionist.
Perception of [UNHQECC] has improved during
his tenure.

In professional settings, others consider him "a
father figure" who "should pay more-"
```

Stone skipped the rest. More information about the man in front of him, a link to a deatiled profile on all of Ozcan's good and evil. Information gathered by the newly-activated quantum computer in Ozcan's skull and shared over the convocation blockchain.

Ozcan's eyes scanned the air above Stone's shoulder, where Stone's public profile must be hanging in the man's vision. Ozcan gulped. Probably at the link to the fullest known list of all the people Stone had killed.

The tech crawled out from under the table. He shied away from the dead operative. "Sir?"

Ozcan's gaze returned to Stone. "This is happening in the General Assembly chamber?"

"Yes. Definitely to Sayyid. Probably to a majority of the delegates."

Ozcan faced the tech. "It's our duty to stream what's happening. And there's a hundred thousand dollar bonus if you get us back online in thirty seconds."

The tech went to the far end of the table. He sat next to his long-faced partner. Keys clicked. A moment later, the long-faced tech shook off his confusion and joined in.

Stone jerked his head toward the dead man on the floor. "Who was he?"

"I don't know. He came in and showed a badge. He showed me your photo and told me you went by the name of Fitzgibbon. You posed a threat to the UN and your plot involved the control room. He said he would pose as an employee and surprise you."

"Name? Agency?"

"Jackson Schmidt. UN Intelligence Agency."

Stone went around the table. He kneeled and reached into the dead man's torn and blood-soaked suit jacket. Pulled out a badge holder. Flipped it open.

The name and photo matched. A frigid nugget lodged in Stone's gut. [Can you read this badge number?]

[I need more light. Hold it above the table.]

Stone raised it. Willed his embedded quantum computer to share what he saw with Caitlyn.

[Got it,] she said. A moment later she added, [He shows up in the UNIA database.]

The cold feeling in Stone's gut exuded thick dark tendrils. [You're one letter off.]

[UNICA? He's one of yours?]

[No. One of Gray's.]

Stone dropped the blood-smeared badge holder on the table. A bank of brightly-colored test patterns silhouetted both Ozcan and the receptionist.

```
Albertina Wrigley.... Lost her virginity at age 14 to
[Ivan Sotomayor] and has had 31 sexual partners. Suffers
genital herpes well-controlled by antiviral medications...
```

Her gaze landed on Stone. She shrank back and peered up at him. Out of fear at how many people he'd killed or shame at her sexual history?

The latter. The only thing worse than discovering the truth about others is discovering the truth about yourself.

"Got it!" said the shaggy-faced tech. The test pattern vanished. The video wall filled with an image of the General Assembly chamber. One monitor showed a closeup of the lectern.

Sweat dotted the face of Secretary-General Sayyid. Though his hands still gripped the lectern, he pushed his body away from it. His eyes looked impossibly wide. His gaze darted over the crowd inside the chamber. Then he twisted his shoulders, looking for something hanging in the air behind him.

Something he couldn't see, but everyone else could.

```
Abdullah Sayyid
Public-facing profile (algorithm: narrat-2107-11-03;
block: 7005264)
++++++++++
Abdullah Sayyid is the [Secretary-General] of the
[United Nations], holding office since 1st January
2127. Prior to his current office, he worked as
[Foreign Minister] of the [Republic of Persia]
after rising rapidly through lower positions in
that country's government <link>.

Sayyid's rapid rise was facilitated by membership
in a [global secret society of Muslim politicians]
<list of members> who record one another engaging
in rituals in which they freely declare Allah is
not the one true god, freely declare Muhammad is a
false prophet, and freely worship pagan and
Christian idols. <[link to rituals reconstructed
from memories of secret society members] [list of
locations where audio/ video recordings of rituals
are stored]>....
```

Ozcan braced his hand on the table. "*Siktir*." He drew out the word. His tone made clear it was a profanity. "I've heard of such dark rituals that one must do to rise in the deep state. But to see it confirmed...."

On screen, Sayyid hunched the shoulders of his expensive suit jacket. He shifted his weight as if deciding whether to flee to stage left or stage right.

"I don't get it," Stone said. "He doesn't believe the religion he professes. That makes him like every Christian politician in the US and Europe."

"No," Ozxan said. "A million imams will condemn Sayyid and the other members of his secret society to death for apostasy. They will fire up five hundred million naive Muslims to carry out the sentence."

[Did you know this?] Stone asked Caitlyn.

[I knew UN headquarters was built on dirty secrets its insiders wanted to never see the light of day. I didn't know the details. Like Goldbaum.]

The US President sat, blinking, puzzled, while his dossier unspooled above his shoulder.

```
...major financial backers include a [consortium
of real estate developers] desiring [removal of
African-American and Mexican-American populations
from small Midwestern cities]. In exchange for
campaign contributions and employment for Goldbaum's
extended family, Goldbaum has given speeches urging
these minorities to `take back' the South and
Southwest, and changed Federal regulations to
encourage these minorities to leave the Midwest...
```

Stone rolled his eyes. New York's real estate developers did the same over a century earlier. [You can't be surprised by *that*.]

[Maybe I shouldn't be. Good god.]

[What?]

From her tone, he pictured her face drained of color. [Look at Kroebel.]

No face came to mind, but Stone knew the name. The director of UNICA. The man above Gray on the organization chart.

The name *Karlheinz Kroebel* labeled a lanky man seated between Goldbaum and Nina Irani. He folded his arms over his chest and regarded the chamber with flat eyes.

```
...sexually exploits African girls aged 9-11. Spends
1-2 hours every weekday reviewing photos of girls
from refugee and resettlement camps and ordering
transfer of desired victims to isolated compound
in northeastern Pennsylvania <[latitude- longitude
coordinates]>...
```

[Good God,] Caitlyn said in a ragged whisper.

Stone's gaze slid away from Kroebel. Nina Irani sat with tightly crossed legs and held her fingers over her mouth. Stone skimmed her dossier.

```
...her marriage ended when her husband discovered
nude selfies sent to her affair partner...
```

A saint compared to those around her.

```
...seized on false intel provided by [Stone Chalmers]
of [UNICA] as an opportunity to discredit [Secretary-
General Abdullah Sayyid] and force his resignation...
```

[Hey! How did my name get in this? You moved me to a private blockchain—]

[No.] Caitlyn's lecturing tone. [Your role in our conspiracy is kept in a private blockchain.]

[I never gave her my name.]

[After accessing her memory and the public lockchain, her embedded quantum computer calculated that *James Smith* and Stone Chalmers were the same person.]

The chill feeling from when he'd guessed the dead operative worked for Gray came back. [Did Gray undergo convocation?]

[Check yourself. Don't worry, he can't know if you look at his public profile.]

By thought, Stone entered the search term. The top hit came to mind. *Martindale Gray* with a head-and-shoulders portrait. Gray eyes above a long, narrow nose. A dossier of dirty secrets which Stone lacked the time to investigate.

Stone's limbs tingled. His heart thumped. [He knows I went rogue.]

[Get out.]

[But the mission—]

[Is accomplished. Ozcan will keep streaming.]

His mind raced. [I can't go back to the hotel. Public cameras everywhere.]

[Not in the First Avenue tunnel below UN Plaza. I'll send a car down there to pick you up. It will take you to a safe house.]

[How do I get into the tunnel?]

[There's an accessway from the lower basement to the tunnel. I'll give you directions. Now get out.]

Stone returned his attention to the room. Video light washed the receptionist's face. "Sir," she said to Ozcan, "someone's in the lobby, trying to get back here."

"Don't let them," Stone said.

Ozcan raised his hand and made a calming gesture. "I won't stop streaming until they drag me away. I don't know what is going on, but the truth being revealed about these people is too important."

"Can you direct a camera in the chamber?" Stone asked. "The Minervan delegation knows what it means."

Ozcan regarded Stone. The video wall silhouetted the man's profile. Ozcan turned then to the shaggy-haired tech. "Do it."

"Back to the people in the lobby," Stone asked. "Their purpose isn't to stop you. They're coming for me."

The receptionist started at something projected to her by her old-fashioned implantable. "They're prying at the lock."

Stone asked, "Is there another way out?"

"Go back to the hallway and turn right. Second hallway to the left. Follow it around until you see the exit sign over it."

"Got it," Stone said. Behind Ozcan, one screen on the video wall jumped. The camera panned across the rear tables of the General Assembly chamber. It stopped and focused on Simon Bale and the facilitators from the Center for Alignment with the Universe. "Thank you."

"Go with God, Mr. Fitzgibbon."

Stone nodded. He had more faith in his 9mm and the twenty

rounds he still carried, but he would take all the help he could get.

16

Stone left the control room. The lock clicked home behind him. The click echoed down empty hallways.

A simple lock, but better than nothing. Once Gray's men got through the secure door from the lobby, a deadbolt jutting an inch into thin steel framing wouldn't delay them long. But every second the video streams from the General Assembly chamber flowed, thousands, perhaps millions of people around the world would see the truth about the power brokers who sucked like ticks on streams of money and blood.

He turned away from the lobby and followed Ozcan's directions to the rear door.

But even though he hurried away from Gray's men, Gray could still track him. He subvoked to his implantable, *Full shutdown.*

Flashing red letters bloomed in the center of his vision. *Warning. You have requested full disconnection from worldforum. This is a violation of UNICA protocol. Confirm? Y/N*

"Yes," he said aloud.

The usual array of icons across the bottom of his vision disappeared. He was as disconnected as he could be while awake. Hell, even asleep. Gray could force a message to him any time day or night. Now he was truly alone—

He turned left and shuffled to a stop. His implantable might not be truly silent. It could be transmitting his location to Gray even now.

Stone pressed his chest, upper left, just under the collarbone. The round disc of his implantable resisted his fingers. [When you send that car, I need a first aid kit, a sharp knife, and some high-proof alcohol.]

[Now's not the time to take up drinking.]

[It's a field antiseptic.]

[You're going to do surgery on yourself?]

[With our embedded quantum connections,] Stone said, [I don't need an implantable any more. Especially since Gray might pick up a signal from it even if I shut it down as fully as I could.]

[I'll see what I can do.]

Stone halted near a door under a red and white exit sign. [Here's the back door. Which way to that accessway?]

[Turn right. Twenty yards to the nearest stairwell. Take it all the way down and I'll guide you from there.]

Stone turned his ear to the door. Gray would have a detailed floor plan of the General Assembly building. Operatives could be waiting outside even now.

[Do we have visitors at the back door?]

[I can't tell.]

He raised his pistol. If Gray's men were positioned outside the door, he had ten rounds and the element of surprise.

Stone turned the doorknob and yanked in a swift motion. He slipped through the half-open doorway and ran to the right.

Warm white LED light. The cracking sound of footsteps on marble. Two men in khakis and untucked shirts blocked the hallway between the streaming center and the stairwell to the basement. One man had red cheeks and sweat matted his brown hair to his forehead. The second man's hand lay on the first man's shoulder. Cool blue balls rotated over both their shoulders. Icons projected into Stone's vision by his embedded quantum computer. Minimized public profile windows. Both men had undergone convocation.

The second man looked up from under crinkled eyebrows and a furrowed brow.

Stone kept running. They'd undergone convocation, but would they take his side?

A deep voice shouted from behind. "Hybrid!"

Stone ran forward. No need to look over his shoulder. At least one man, probably two. The tone of the shout made clear the Minervan nanomachines had missed the deep-voiced man.

More. They knew his UNICA code name.

Gray's men.

Five yards to the two men in front. Closing. The second man reached for the small of his back, where he could carry a holstered handgun under his untucked shirt—

Stone lowered his shoulder. He barreled into the second man. The man staggered backward. His handgun clattered to the marble. The first man didn't move.

He ran to the stairwell. An urge came to tell them to embrace convocation, to heed the Minervans, to turn against the UN and against Gray. No time. He yanked open the stairwell door. Pounded down, left hand on the rail, two and three steps at a time, footsteps echoing off concrete walls.

"Goddammit," sounded the deep voice down the stairwell, "your assignment was to stop him!"

The stairwell door thumped close, smothered any excuses from the two men.

Stone reached the lower basement landing. He grabbed the door handle and pulled.

A burst of sound echoed down the stairwell. Gray's lead operative must have opened the door from the ground floor.

When he'd opened the door just far enough, Stone went through sideways. He tugged on the handle to close the door.

The automatic closer at the top resisted his pull.

Damn. He stepped back, picked a direction, and ran to the nearest corner. His shoes slapped vinyl tile. He had to get out of sight and earshot by the time Gray's lead operative and the others opened the door.

He rounded the corner. No sound behind him yet. Breaths coming hard, he slowed to a jog. [Where to?]

[Straight, then second left, a right, then down. Keep running.]

[They're behind me?]

[I assume so. But also, I can't find a route that won't lead you past cameras. Those are Gray's men?]

[Absolutely.]

[Can they access the cameras?]

[Assume yes.] Stone ran. His feet slapped the floor. Stone dashed left, right.

A narrow hallway. Off-white walls stark under LED panels. An acoustic tile ceiling lacking the half-domes of cameras.

His chest rose. Out of camera view.

Then cold ran down his spine.

No door.

[Where?]

[Keep going. Around the corner. Remember, all I have are schematics. I don't know what the accessway door looks like.]

"I hear him," called one of Gray's men. Protocol failure. A team should only communicate through their implantables over a private channel.

Stone turned the corner. Still no cameras.

A steel panel at floor level, painted white. Two feet wide and three tall. A flange like the sanitary handle on a public restroom door jutted out at floor level.

[This better be it.]

[It is.]

Stone crouched. Grabbed the flange by hand. Tugged.

Puck lights activated, dimly lighting a dark space. The puck lights clinged to the left-hand wall near the floor and extended downward in a stairstep pattern.

He entered, still crouching. His hair brushed rough concrete. He ducked further, turned, pushed the steel panel shut behind him. A clang echoed away into the darkness behind Stone.

Assume it echoed down the narrow hallway back to Gray's men.

A thick steel bar lay in a track across the panel. An enclosure mounted on the concrete wall waited to receive it.

A giant deadbolt. Stone slid it home.

He descended the stairs. The ceiling remained at the same height until he could stand straight and raise his hand to stippled concrete.

His footsteps echoed downward.

Gray's men scratched at the steel panel above him.

At the bottom of the stairs, the passageway turned left, out of sight. A rumble came to him through the final steps. Traffic in the First Avenue tunnel under UN Plaza. Not far now.

[Car ready?]

[Three minutes away.]

Stone breathed more easily. Gray's men didn't have enough time to force open the steel panel. He reached the landing and turned.

Puck lights lit up in two lines running straight ahead to a metal door. [That's the way out?]

[Yes.]

The line of lights on his left had a gap. He approached. More strings of lights activated, marking a side tunnel extending toward the Secretariat building. He angled his head for footsteps coming from that direction. None.

Stone kept walking. [What are these tunnels for? I haven't seen any utility stations a worker would need to access.]

[Escape,] Caitlyn said. [Like the tunnels out of a medieval castle that a lord could use to flee invaders.]

[That's why the panel could be locked from the inside.] His eyes jolted open and he sharply inhaled stale air. [Does Gray know this tunnel exists and where it leads?]

[You know his capabilities better than I do.]

[In other words, yes.] How long would it take Gray's men to go from the General Assembly basement to the Secretariat building, find the entrance to the side tunnel, and come after him? Or send a team by vehicle to block the exit? [How's traffic on First?]

[The car will be here in under two minutes.]

Stone reached the metal door. Full height. No need to stoop. He put his eye to a peephole. Fisheye glass showed a narrow walkway ran alongside two lanes of flowing traffic. No sign of Gray's men.

He pulled the door toward him. The hum of electric motors echoing off tile spilled past him. He brought his gun hand to his side and went through.

A four-inch-high mass of crumbling asphalt lay under his feet. A delivery van in the right lane veered away from him. Stone jumped back. The muzzle of his 9mm clacked against a wall of subway tile.

[Hell of an escape route.]

[The assumption is that an escaping Sec-Gen would have a loyalist in a vehicle waiting for him.]

[Lucky him.]

Stone pushed the door shut. More subway tile, yellow, faded and dingy from years of passing traffic and city air, covered the outside of the door. The seams around the door matched in size the grout lines between tiles. Ten million people passing in vehicles never noticed. Excellent camouflage.

He headed north, along the one-way flow of traffic. A rectangle of daylight showed the tunnel exit under 47th. But the tunnel to get there felt like a prison. Subway tile and pavement pounded him with noise. A sheaf of electrical conduit ran horizontally along the wall like cell bars at head height. Harsh white bulbs made it impossible to hide. Camera domes bulged from the ceiling like gun turrets on ancient bomber aircraft.

[You have a new car for me somewhere Gray is blind?]

[Three identical ones in a parking garage in sight of a malfunctioning camera. I know what I'm doing.]

Which could involve throwing Stone to the wolves. No, that would gain her nothing now. She would help him leave the scene. He had too much value as a bargaining chip, if she could gain something by surrendering him to Gray that would offset the hit to her reputation when the details of their conspiracy came to light.

Stone scowled. Hadn't she earned his trust by now?

Not in his line of work.

He glanced over his shoulder. The escape door blended in with the wall of dirty subway tile. No one on foot. Vehicles hummed toward him on autopilot from the tunnel mouth at 42nd.

He squinted past blue-white headlights. A faceted sedan, metallic blue? Yes.

The sedan pulled into the right lane and flashed its hazard lights. Cars behind it shifted lanes. The sedan slowed next to Stone. Stopped. The *clunk* of its door opening carried through the noise.

Stone let out a breath. He took four brisk steps and hopped in.

The door thudded shut and the metallic blue sedan accelerated back into traffic. Stone lay on his left side on the mid-cabin floor. Blue carpet scratched his cheek above his false beard. [I never thought I'd miss this car.]

[You've never ridden in it before,] Caitlyn said.

[How many of these do you have?]

[Enough.]

[The Minervans have quite a budget. Or do you have blackmail on a car dealer out in Queens?]

With a smile in her voice, Caitlyn said, [Need to know.]

Stone grinned. If only for a minute, he had a chance to relax.

Something buzzed. Stone rolled onto his back. Eyes alert. Sounded like—

A drone smaller than his palm hovered an inch below the ceiling. Its rotors turned invisibly fast, like a dragonfly's wings.

[Damn.]

[What? Oh. Headquarters site security. Must have sneaked in when the door opened.]

Must have? Even if she played a double game, he couldn't do anything about it until he saw her face-to-face. Right now, the drone took priority.

The light from the tunnel exit grew stronger. He reversed his grip on his pistol. The drone held its position. A standard model, with a swift evasion program, but its image processing would poorly handle lighting changes—

The sedan burst into daylight. Stone sat up and clubbed at the drone.

Plastic crunched. The drone smacked off the window and fell to the carpet at his feet. He pounded it three times more with the butt of his pistol.

The last rotor spun down. Clear plastic splinters of the camera cover littered the carpet.

[Five minutes to the car exchange,] Caitlyn said. [Stay out of sight.]

Stone flattened himself on the floor. He returned his pistol to his ankle holster. The blue sedan merged with traffic from UN Plaza. By the sound of electric motors around the sedan and the feel of the sedan's pulses of acceleration and braking, traffic flowed normally away from headquarters.

Autopilots had no idea how the power structure of the UN—of the world—had just been rocked.

[Can I access worldforum through the quantum computer link?]

[It will be slower than you're used to, but yes.]

Stone thought at his quantum computer to give him the live feed from the General Assembly chamber. All he got was a still image of the Secretariat and GA buildings overlaid by the words *Technical Difficulties - Please Stand By*.

[Gray's men shut down the stream,] he said. [Do you know what's happening?]

[I'm checking.] The sedan slowed to turn left on 51st. [Sayyid, Goldbaum, and Kroebel left the podium and front seats. No. They left the chamber.]

[How did they get out?]

[To both sides of the rostrum there are stairs to the upper basement.]

The sedan turned left. [They're trying to escape.] He imagined Gray's men pounding at the steel panel with a battering ram or attacking it with a blowtorch. He grinned. [I blocked their path...] The grin dried up. [...out of the GA building. The bolthole from the Secretariat building is still open. We've got to publicize the exit door in the First Avenue tunnel.]

Caitlyn said, [I'm already on it. My bots are filling social media. Some locals are on their way to shut down all the escape routes from UN headquarters.]

[You're instigating a riot.]

[I'm crowdsourcing extralegal regime change. You have a better idea?]

The sedan slowed, turned right. A grate clanked under the tires. The sedan started up a ramp into a shaded, echoing space. Stone's view out the windows showed only concrete splashed with the headlights of other vehicles. A parking garage.

The sedan spiraled up five or six levels. Finally it pulled into a spot.

[Your car is to the left. Inside are the first aid kit and other items you asked for. You'll also find an electric shaver. The car won't drive out of the garage until you put on the shave off your beard.]

He rubbed his hand over his chin. [Glad to get rid of it.] His hand went up to his cheekbone. [When do I revert the osteogoop and go back to being the real me?]

[After we send you through the wormhole to Minerva.]

17

A chill ran down his arms and tried sinking him into the cloth seat. He sat taller. [You want me to go to Minerva?]

[No. I'm ordering you. Get in the other car.]

The two sedans popped their side doors. Stone took two crouched steps on the concrete, face down and hidden by the door panels. Caitlyn might have neutralized all the cameras she knew of, but a drone with a zoom lens might happen to photograph him from the distance.

He entered the second car. A duffel bag lay in the middle of the floor. He pushed it out of the way and lay down, knees bent and pushing at the front seats, back hunched against the seats in the rear.

Stone reached into the bag. He pulled out the shaver and touched the blades to his cheekbone. [Wait. I'll generate fibers that will get in the carpet. Hell, some of my hair will be with it. I'll leave DNA—]

[There's a fully charged wet/dry vacuum in the bag. Clean up as best you can. I'll send the car to a hand wash facility after it drops you off.]

[Where are you dropping me?]

[A safe house. You don't need to know the location yet.]

Stone grunted and ran the shaver over his beard. At least she was consistent about keeping him in the dark. But sending him to Minerva? [I should stay in the city.]

[Your mission is complete. You fulfilled the objective.]

[I revealed the dirty little secrets of a million power players. What happens next? Lynch mobs are already on their way for Sayyid and Kroebel. Far more powerful and organized forces will react to the situation soon enough. You've unleashed chaos.]

[Bale and van Bentum have strategized—]

[They increased the number of people monitored by the reputation blockchain by twenty-fold in an instant. Without prepping them with the consecration ritual and the other work Alignment with the Universe does. While billions more are outside of convocation and don't fully understand what they saw on the worldforum stream. No strategy can account for all those variables.]

Caitlyn's voice turned snippy. [Our team can handle it.]

[You and a few Minervan soldiers disguised as Bale's bodyguards—]

[And my boss, Holbrook, and all the ITB assets he can deploy—]

[You fired a silver bullet but only wounded the werewolf. You need all the help you can get. Here in New York.]

[We can't use you. Your cover's blown.]

Stone turned off the shaver. Under his fingertips, his bare face felt like a stranger's. [No one's seen me with my new bone structure and clean-shaven.]

[The beard or lack of it would only fool a casual observer. Your new bone structure has been logged by a facial recognition database. Anywhere you go in the city—anywhere you go on Earth—Gray will find you.]

[Hats, sunglasses, I can disguise myself—]

[You know that won't fool Gray's facial recognition database—]

[It will for long enough to take one shot.]

Her breaths sounded over the link. [We'll talk more after you get to the safe house.]

Stone grinned but kept silent. He brushed beard clippings off his shirt. Not yet time to clean the floor. Save that for later. And wise of her to include a wet/dry vacuum in the duffel.

From the bag he removed a first aid kit and a paring knife wrapped in flexible foam. Two inches long and keenly edged. Closest thing to a scalpel she could have found at short notice.

He rummaged inside the duffel and touched flexible plastic. The item sloshed as he pulled it out. A plastic jug of 190 proof grain alcohol with an inebriated farmer on the label.

He grimaced. His father's drunken descent to an early grave involved cheap vodka in bottles like this.

Stone shook his head. His father was dead, but he wasn't. And he wanted to stay that way.

Also unlike his father, he had a purpose in life, and wanted to keep it too.

He lay the bottle on its side next to him and reached into the duffel. His fingers touched fabric. Some rags, a heavy towel, and a change of clothes. He returned the towel and the clothes to the bag, then took off his shirt. Soaked a rag in grain alcohol. The medicinal odor filled the car.

Stone wiped the rag over his hands, then the faint bulge of his implantable. Evaporating alcohol tingled his skin. He dipped the knife blade into the bottle. Moved the tip near his chest. Made the first cut.

No pain for the first moment. Then it stung. Burned. Stone gritted his teeth and kept cutting around the implantable's outline. Cut between skin and muscle. Damn it stung.

Yes, but remember that time in a dirt-floor hut in Venezuela, sterilizing a knife and tweezers over a candle flame to pull a bullet from your thigh?

After cutting three-quarters of the way around his implantable to yield a flap of skin, he set down the knife on the soaked rag. Blood oozed out of the cut and down his chest. A civilian would freak out at the sight, believe they were dying, clueless how large a stain could be left by a tiny amount of blood.

He grunted and lifted the flap. Reached in with his other hand. The implantable slid, held only by viscous body fluids to his muscle. He plucked it out. A two-inch disk like a giant plastic coin. Set it on another rag.

Neutralize the implantable in a moment.

Stone opened the first aid kit. Took out what he needed. Biosafe glue around the edges of the flap. Press down, smooth out. Pain throbbed in his chest. Seeping blood outlined the cut. Fairly straight and clean. Still should leave enough of a scar for women to trace with fingertips in his bed on mornings after.

A numbing spray dulled the pain. Tension escaped from his body.

[Why didn't you use the local anesthetic to begin with?] Caitlyn asked.

[Pain would've told me if I'd made a mistake.]

Stone tore open a sterile dressing. Put it in place, taped it down. Reminded himself to use numbing spray on his chest hair when he changed dressings.

He shook out his arms, then wrapped the implantable in the rag it lay on. Reached for his 9mm. Reversed his grip. Smashed the implantable repeatedly with the butt of his pistol. Plastic crunched.

He unwrapped the rag. Broken halves of the implantable's housing parted to reveal chips, wires, the battery.

With the butt of his pistol, he ground the implantable's interior components into fragments.

He grinned. Impossible for Gray to track him now.

—through his implantable. He still had to keep his head down, literally, and lie low at the safe house until he set out on his next mission.

[Tell the car to start driving,] he said. [I'll clean up as we go.] He grabbed a trash bag from the duffel and shoved the shaver and blood-soaked linens into it.

The car backed out of its spot. The hum of electric motors reached him. Outside the windows, red and white lights bloomed. A glimpse showed the brake and reverse lights of the sedan he'd ridden here in. Two more identical sedans parked down the row.

Stone lowered his head. He vacuumed up beard clippings and drops of blood as the sedan descended the ramp. The headlights of the sedan behind him glinted off the door pillars of his car.

[That's good enough,] Caitlyn said.

Stone turned off the handheld vacuum. Scowled at a quarter-inch-long hair clinging to the carpet weave. [It is?]

[We'll strip and clean the interiors of every car you ride in.]

[We?]

[ITB personnel. They won't ask questions. Even if convocation caught them, I'll communicate over my implantable. They'll think they're cleaning up after official ITB business.]

She could be setting him up. Leave evidence in this car to lead Gray to him in the safe house. But he eyed more beard clippings, and drops of drying blood. He lacked the tools to clean up beyond Gray's ability to extract evidence.

[I suppose you keyhole kops can do the laundry,] Stone said.

The sedan reached the bottom of the ramp. Driving through the city, pedestrians and drones passing close to the car might notice him sitting on the floor, eyes open, and wonder why someone would ride so uncomfortably.

And the cabin already stank of grain alcohol.

He set the bottle on its side, then crawled onto the rear bench seats.

[What are you doing?]

[Someone walking past the car won't be surprised to see a drunk sleeping it off.] He lay on his side, face toward the backrest, hand on the side of his face to shield his eyes from daylight. [Good enough?]

The car turned right onto 51st. [I can't see you on public cameras.]

[Didn't think you would. How long till I switch to the next car?]

[Next car?]

[You said ITB people would strip the interiors of *every* car I rode in. Not *both*.]

She sounded like she smiled. [Good catch. About forty-five minutes.]

Hours of action weighed down Stone's limbs. He yawned. [Give me some peace and quiet.]

[Sure. You've earned it.]

The car turned left on Lexington, heading downtown. He snoozed for a time, then fell into a deeper sleep.

The echoing hum of a thousand electric vehicles woke him. Outside the windows, brake lights cast a red glow on walls lined with subway tile. The Brooklyn-Battery Tunnel or the Holland Tunnel to New Jersey?

The car emerged into cloud-dappled daylight. Balconies curved in a turn-of-the-century style jutted from midrise buildings on both sides of the street. The tires whispered with a resonance indicating solid ground, and not an elevated expressway deck, lay under the roadway.

New Jersey, then.

The car turned right onto a side street. Two more turns brought it into a parking garage. Up to the fourth level, where the car parked beside two other metallic blue sedans with faceted surfaces.

He reached for the door handle.

[Wait,] said Caitlyn. A two-seater buzzed past toward the down ramp. [Now you're clear.]

Stone climbed out. The clank of a nearby train yard came to him between the garage's concrete pillars. The open door of the next car welcomed him in.

He crawled onto the back seat, lay down on his back. A comfortable place to take a nap, maybe that's why family men with hour-long commutes from Long Island bought this make and model. This car waited for the other two to drive away before it backed out of its spot.

A few turns between more gentrified apartment buildings brought him to a line of cars waiting on a wide patch of potholed asphalt. The Holland Tunnel toll plaza. [Back to the city,] said Stone.

[You have amazing powers of deduction. What's this?]

Red and white lights strobed through Stone's rear window.

Stone hunkered lower on the back seat. [Got a camera?]

Caitlyn fed him an image. Four SUVs with Port Authority police markings blocked the entrance to the toll plaza. A pudgy, mustachioed cop climbed down from one. More doors opened.

Stone reached for his ankle holster. He could take out three or four cops, but eight?

His car crept forward. The pudgy cop turned away from the toll plaza and spoke into a shoulder-clipped handset. His growling voice squawked over a loudspeaker. "—security issue. All vehicular routes between New York and New Jersey are closed until further notice."

Stone raised his eyebrow. [Did your team account for this variable?]

[We knew there would be chaos.]

[I almost got cut off from the safe house.]

[We have others, outside the city. On the way to the Minerva wormhole. Which is where you should be going.]

Traffic crept toward the toll plaza. Stone's car rolled forward twenty feet. [Looks like I'm heading back to Manhattan and staying for a while. Unless you want me to fight my way through the half-dozen Port Authority cops behind me?]

[Go to the safe house. We'll find an alternate route for you to Minerva.]

[Or you'll decide I'm right.]

The car approached a toll booth. Stone rolled back to his side, away from cameras. A pause while the transponders communicated, followed by a creak and clank as the gate arm swung up.

The car accelerated into the tunnel mouth. Midday, inbound traffic should be light. Yet the car trudged along. Brake lights pulsed arrythmically off the subway tile.

Stone smirked. [More chaos at the tunnel exit?]

[Checking. Tribeca's quiet.]

The tunnel exited into one of the wealthiest neighborhoods in the city. Many of Tribeca's residents would have been targets of the Minervan plan. Prominent actors and artists concealed secrets as dirty as any politician's. Those who'd undergone convocation would hide behind closed doors and stay off the worldforum until someone reestablished order.

Caitlyn went on. [Civil disorder in Chinatown. Protestors are blocking Canal and Beach at Lafayette. That's backing up eastbound traffic from the tunnel exit. The car will reroute.]

[Chinatown doesn't seem the kind of place for rioting.]

[No riots.]

[Yet,] Stone said.

[They're just protesting. Calling for the resignation of their local state Assemblywoman.]

[No big deal. Your strategy accounted for that.]

She ignored his sarcasm. The car merged right and climbed out of the tunnel. It joined the clotted traffic taking the exit lanes to Hudson. A right turn sent it northbound. Stone stretched out as far as he could across the car's rear seat. After a time it turned right. Maybe onto Houston. No, traffic flowed too quickly—

[Traffic's lighter than usual.]

[People are off the street, making sense of what happened.]

[Plotting their next moves.]

The car continued heading crosstown on Houston. Traffic thinned out even more and not once did the car pulse its brakes to avoid jaywalkers. Part of him marveled at his good luck, but he knew better. Half a million people living or working on Manhattan had undergone convocation, and millions more knew what had happened in the General Assembly chamber. They were quiet now like martial artists gathering their energies to strike.

More turns brought him to the Lower East Side. Another ramp into another parking garage. But instead of spiraling up, the car took another ramp down, to a basement loading dock. Its motor whined to a stop.

Stone peeked out the window.

A freight elevator's dented steel doors faced him.

[Wait in the car,] Caitlyn said.

Machinery clanked. The freight elevator's doors parted.

[Take it to the seventh floor. Room 702. The room keys are in the glove compartment.]

Stone reached in. His fingers found thin metal and points like a cat's teeth. He pulled out a ring with two keys and the glovebox closed.

The freight elevator waited for him. The car popped its door.

Stone crouched, covering his face, and ran up steps to the side of the loading dock. The metal box wobbled under his last pounding footsteps. He waited in the back corner, facing more dented steel, until the doors closed.

A clank below, then a deep hum. The elevator rose.

The doors opened to a hallway of dingy carpet that might have been yellow before thousands of dirty shoes trod it. [Left.]

Stone followed the hallway around a bend. Two mechanical locks on door 702. He guessed the correct keys the first time. Moments later he entered. Lights came up behind him, revealing a living room he ignored for the moment.

He locked the door from the inside. Let out a breath.

[I'm at the safe house. Now we can talk.]

18

Stone stood with his back to the door. In front of him, the sharp white light of dozen motion-activated table lamps illuminated a living room with mismatched furniture and flattened beige carpet. Throughout his career, he'd whittled away a thousand hours in a hundred rooms like this.

[Settle in,] Caitlyn said.

His heart thumped. He felt like an electric charge seeking ground. [I don't want to settle. I want to do something.]

[Which is?]

Of course she spoke truth. Acting without intel would get him killed. For nothing.

Caitlyn said, [We've stripped the new clothes from the emperor, but we don't know who's going to try to dress him again and with what—]

[You made your point.]

Her voice softened. [There's food in the kitchen, a first aid kit in the bathroom for when you need to change the dressing, and some clothes that might fit you in the closet.]

He took a step. [Usual safehouse features?] He tilted an armchair onto its front legs. Heavier than it looked.

He eased it all the way onto its back and poked his finger at the flimsy white fabric covering the underside. A rigid material hidden by the white fabric resisted his push.

[Kevlar?]

[It's lighter and cheaper than bulletproof steel.]

[Bullet resistant. Nothing's bulletproof.] A standard feature of Gray's safehouses, Kevlar or steel panels in the bottom of furniture allowed chairs and tables to be turned on their sides and used as shields. ITB or the Minervans had learned from the best.

He reached for the arms to reset the chair on its feet. A slit along one edge of the white fabric caught his eye.

In went his hand. His fingers curled around the stippled plastic of a pistol's grip.

Stone let go and put the armchair back in place. [How many more weapons?]

[I'll show you.] She popped cutaways into his vision. Handguns hid in the bottoms of almost every table and chair. [And all the lamps have magnetic snap-away cords and weighted bases for throwing.]

[You know how to make a man feel at home.]

[Don't expect me to cook for you.]

More at ease, he explored the apartment. Curtains over video monitors recessed in the walls. The monitors awakened when he pulled back the curtains. A bright view of a tropical islet made him squint until he dropped the curtain.

To the right, past the only climate control vent, he went around a corner to a dining room. One round table, four chairs. Farther brought him to a narrow kitchen decades out of fashion, with an induction cooktop inlaid in a cultured stone countertop. He opened cabinets, verified the presence of hidden pistols, rapped on doors and listened for Kevlar layers sandwiched by wood.

Back on the other side of the front door, a doorless passageway led to the bedroom. An accordion-folded room divider decorated in an East Asian style screened a double mattress lying on a futon frame. A closet off the bedroom held a few shirts and pants in nondescript shades of gray. Also off the bedroom, a three-quarter bath with, surprisingly, a glass shower door and floor tiles separated by crumbled grout.

Stone scowled. [Front door's the only exit.]

[Two boltholes.] She popped up more cutaways. Crumbled grout masked the edges of a square hatch under his feet. Another hatch glowed in the kitchen, a false bottom on an empty cabinet.

Caitlyn said, [They open to catwalks in warehouse spaces below. Also, the lights will blink when someone is coming this way in the corridor. The blink rate will increase with proximity to the front door.]

A one-bedroom apartment, no exterior windows. Caitlyn could charge ten million a month in rent, but he got to stay here free.

His stomach growled. How long since breakfast?

To the kitchen. Frozen meals stacked high in the freezer. He pulled off the top one and microwaved it. In the refrigerator, bottles of still water, cartons of ultrapasteurized milk. The cabinets held pouches of carbs six ways and dried fruit.

The microwave beeped. He took his pot roast, a compostable fork, a bottle of water, and a pouch of dried pineapple to the round table in the dining room. He peeled back the plastic wrap from the pot roast and steam and a beefy smell billowed out. To Caitlyn: [Can you give me a news feed?]

[Done.]

A smaller version of the streaming center video wall covered his view of the living room like a translucent curtain. Reporters of different races and sexes, but all with ideologies conforming to a narrow band of acceptable pro-UN opinion, stood in front of official backdrops—studio sets, a slice of the Secretariat building, the entire headquarters complex from across the East River. Their lips moved silently, their facial expressions attempting to calm and reassure the public yet failing to mask their own confusion and fear.

Red and white pulsed in the window to the lower left. The window zoomed in on police SUVs blocking First Avenue two blocks south of headquarters, just upstream of the tunnel's entrance ramp and the surface lanes to United Nations Plaza.

With a thought, Stone enlarged the window and unmuted the audio.

A nasal tone leaked through a male reporter's voice. "—blocking off vehicular access to and from UN headquarters. I asked the NYPD's on-scene commander if their intention was to keep people out or to keep people in. His only answer was that NYPD wants to maintain order until the situation can be resolved."

Stone flipped to another view. Another tunnel mouth, this time near where First Avenue reemerged at 47th. Similar line of police SUVs and officers clad in dark blue milling around. A different shade of blue marked headquarters security on the sidewalk along UN Plaza. Somewhere off-camera, a crowd made restive sounds. Not a riot, yet, but a skillful agitator could encite the crowd to throw rocks and try to storm headquarters.

A man's voice, falling back on the elocution lessons they must teach at the Columbia journalism school, said, "Police officials confirm that at least twenty or thirty members of a local mosque have barricaded the First Avenue tunnel and the FDR tunnel in both directions under UN headquarters. They refuse to disperse until the apostates, we presume that means Secretary-General Sayyid and others, are handed over for justice under sharia law. The police are treating the situation as a hostage situation and are negotiating accordingly."

Stone's jaws mashed a tasteless chunk of overboiled carrot while his gaze went from window to window. External views of headquarters, a wavy-haired anchorman—Steele Roberts, Robert Steele, the man's name always eluded Stone—in a studio with a here's-what-you-should-think window over his shoulder. The window showed an icon of a wormhole and a raised fist, captioned with the words *Colony World Terrorist Plot*.

Stone enlarged and unmuted.

"—UN spokespersons have identified the hackers as being agents of the Minervan government. The hacking attack was an attempt to discredit UN and national government officials who recognized the Minervan military threat—"

Between the anchorman's wavy hair and the terrorist plot caption floated an icon of a wise cartoon owl. A symbol of Minerva. [He underwent convocation.]

[We targeted media figures, remember?]

[Can the general public see that icon?]

[No. It's not in the stream, it's projected by the embedded quantum computers of those who've undergone convocation. But we are mirroring public profiles over the worldforum at minerva.gov.colony. The general public will find out his truth soon enough.]

Stone opened the anchorman's public profile. Steele Roberts—he'd been right the first time. Bachelor's and master's from two different Ivy League universities. Forty-six years old. His stock portfolio outperformed the market average for the last decade, thanks to inside information received at yacht parties with US senators and social media billionaires. Addicted to cocaine and college boys with hairless chests.

A swig of cold water. A jerking image with a tall golden rectangle flanked by giant video monitors caught his gaze. Stone switched away from the tawdry anchorman and enlaged the new image.

The General Assembly chamber. A crowd gathered around the Minervan delegation, jostling for a better view. The image was recorded by someone's implantable tapping into his or her optic nerves. Simon Bale's mustard-yellow suit, close-trimmed brown beard, and piercing blue eyes dominated the scene.

"—we have revealed to the world the truth. The UN's leaders are inept, corrupt, and evil. The UN's aiders and abetters, in national governments, at giant corporations, universities, and the media are also inept, corrupt, and evil. They have proven their unworthiness to lead the settled galaxy."

He dialed the harshness in his voice back one notch. "But everyone is worthy of at least one small role, if he is aligned with the universe. We from Minerva can help you truly know yourself and find the role that best fits who you are and best serves all mankind." He gestured to his left, to man and woman clad in blue and red. "The facilitator and facilitatrix can better explain—"

A reporter cut in. The video remained on-screen, but muted. "That's footage recorded about an hour ago from the optic and auditory nerves of a diplomat inside the chamber. The man with the beard was Stephen Bell, the Minervan ambassador to the UN—pardon me, Simon Bell. Bale. As you just heard, Bale claimed responsibility for this event. You also just heard his scurrilous attacks on journalists—"

[That's Morgan Hinojosa talking,] Caitlyn said.

[What secret is he trying to hide by staying off-screen?]

[In college, he drunkenly threw a chair of the roof of his dorm. Hit someone in the head, brain damage the rejuvenation techs couldn't repair. His family settled with the victim for six hundred million and bribed the district attorney to prevent a criminal prosecution.]

Morgan Hinojosa. Probably more Anglo-looking than Stone's conquistador-American great-grandfather Plutarco Blanco. *Viva la raza.*

Time for another video feed. This one came from a young Asian woman, pink-dyed hair and affected eyeglasses, in a waterfront park in Brooklyn. The upright blue Secretariat building and the low marble dome of the General Assembly looked small against the backdrop of black nanotube alloy skyscrapers across the river.

Another wise cartoon owl showed above her shoulder.

The reporter spoke. "—despite the lockdown, unconfirmed reports are streaming in from inside. Four security personnel killed by the Minervans. Revolver fire at the Secretariat building from a location near us—"

Stone laughed. From a thousand yards away, a revolver would drop rounds in the river far short of the target. Reporters.

Another laugh, over the video feed. The usual crowd gathered near a reporter. Out of sight behind the camera crew. Surprising that any man off the street in Brooklyn would know enough about firearms to laugh at her ignorance.

"—Minervan delegation is performing an occult ritual inside the General Assembly chamber—"

More laughter in a throaty burst from multiple voices. Laughter gave way to a chant. "Fake news! Fake news!"

Behind the glasses, the reporter's dark eyes flickered to the left of the camera. Her shoulders hunched for a moment. Then she threw back her shoulders and leveled her chin. Perhaps she remembered she wielded the weapon of the video media, more powerful than even a magic revolver capable of firing across the East River.

Despite standing tall, uncertainty trickled into her voice. "—as you can hear, Minervan co-conspirators are harrassing me, and no doubt all reporters, as we bring you the truth—"

The loudest burst of laughter yet. A grinning frat-boy voice led the chant in a new direction. "Blowjobs for promotions! Blowjobs for promotions!"

The rest of the crowd joined in, male voices and female, the latter rediscovering the sharp edge of slut-shaming lost from the modern era since before the Time of Troubles. "—for promotions!"

A tremble crept into the reporter's lip.

Stone didn't bother opening her public profile. Some of the aerosolized medical nanotechnology released by Simon Bale's drones must have floated across the river to Brooklyn. People in the off-camera crowd had undergone convocation.

The chant repeated three times more. The reporter crumbled. Tears streamed out of red eyes. She dropped her oversized microphone, a prop as fake as her glasses, and waved the camera to her left while she bent over to the right, sobbing. A moment later, her camera feed went dark.

By muscle memory, Stone stuck his fork into a corner of the pot roast tray. The coated paperboard rattled on the tabletop. He looked down. Empty.

He guzzled the rest of his water bottle, then threw the residue of his lunch into the compactor to the left of the kitchen sink. He closed the heavy lid and electric motors ground away. The smaller the volume of trash that had to be disposed from the safehouse, the lower the chance of discovery.

Back in the dining room, he swept his hand at air. His embedded quantum computer read the gesture and removed the virtual video wall from sight and hearing.

[Based on the mainstream reporters,] he said, [you generated the chaos you expected.]

[We're getting a lot of posts on social media now. People are desperate for understanding. Even those who haven't undergone convocation know the Farah Chongs of the world are inept, corrupt, and evil.]

Stone took another bottle of cold water from the fridge, then found a plush chair facing the door. A table near his right hand bore a throwable lamp and carried a handgun secured by hook-and-loop fabric on its underside.

He settled into the cushion and opened up the worldforum.

He needed half an hour to learn the dynamic. The aiders and abetters Simon Bale had spoken of, the people with recognizable names and validated by blue checkmarks and curated posts, were united in condemning Minerva. Whoever coordinated their public pronouncements hadn't imposed any greater consensus than that. That the social media stars of the status quo had even that much conformity told Stone they were like a school of fish, or a flock of sheep, acutely sensitive to the actions of their crowd. Their peers tested the edges, then backed away if no one followed. Sec-Gen Sayyid bravely followed his freedom of conscience. President Goldbaum sought to extend the blessings of diversity to the last small all-white towns of the rural Midwest. The sexist bigots who interrupted Farah Chong's report should be identified and punished. Those views got some traction as the afternoon wore on. Kroebel proves that love has no age boundaries, and girls raised outside the patriarchal strictures of the western world can give consent at much younger ages. No one echoed that post, a few criticized it, and the author apologized ten-fold.

People outside the orbits of the aiders and abetters who'd undergone convocation diverged in opinions. A few agreed wholeheartedly with the unofficial official line. More agreed, but with doubts. Can our leaders truly be comitted to social justice if their motives are so base? Generally, those posters dropped out of the main channels after blue checkmarks condemned them as racists or fascists.

Thousands more who'd undergone convocation just wanted to know what had happened to them. Links to the Minervan public profile database and Alignment with the Universe's guidebooks appeared on a thousand worldforum sites, like mushrooms after a rain, in threads soon deleted by site moderators. The frequency of those posts fell off as users learned how to use their embedded quantum computers and the blockchain to communicate privately and without censorship.

The same dynamic happened among the hundreds of posters who hated the UN and the elites from the start. The four hundred, not twenty or thirty, Muslims blockading headquarters to prevent Sayyid the apostate from escaping sharia justice. A political science student at the JFK School at Harvard calling out the corruption and hypocrisy of his professors. A cop with the NYPD, matching a hundred open cases, from petty vandalism in the Upper East Side to garrotted hookers found half-covered with autumn leaves in the woods in Central Park, to unwilling confessions plucked from the subconscious minds of UN officials by convocation.

Tens of thousands, representative of the billions untouched by the aerosolized medical nanotech who'd only seen convocation and its effects in official video, could only post on the worldforum. Lines of posts appeared on Chirrp and Threddit, using an ever-evolving jargon to squirm away from the censors. *150E6* stood in for Alignment with the Universe, *120 sec* for the anti-Minervan line parrotted by the establishment media.

Helping them were people from Minerva. A quadrillion-terabit trans-wormhole fiber link connected the colony to the worldforum. Through senses granted him by his embedded quantum computer, Stone felt half the colony's adults turning their attention to Earth's billions, like a warm wind at his back. Minervans added their voices to Chirrp and Threddit. They quoted profiles from the public database and added links to more, accessed by millions every second. Over four hundred million people on Earth tuned in and out of a live broadcast of a service inside the cathedral-like main Center for Alignment with the Universe in downtown Euler City, Minerva's capital.

Stone smiled warmly when a tall woman in a long red dress, blond hair piled high on her head, stood with other facilitators and facilitatrices on the dais. Sheila van Bentum, the oldest woman he'd failed to seduce in his days before convocation. Tears streamed down her cheeks, past her wide smile, as she sang along with hymns from the songbook, *Evening Star* and *Closer to the Heart*.

His smile broke up on a question. [The UN hasn't shut down the data link to Minerva. Why?]

[They have,] Caitlyn said. [The Minervans deployed a fleet of drones carrying wireless relays through the wormhole. The drone fleet ties into worldforum infrastructure at Los Angeles, Las Vegas, and Phoenix. The UN cannot silence the Minervan people.]

The service continued. A straight-backed facilitator delivered a sermon in a resolute voice. His manner reminded Stone of photos from a twentieth-century history class, non-violent resistors facing water cannons and piano wire meat hooks, King, Gandhi, Bonhoeffer.

All of whom ended up dead.

The content of Sayyid's speech echoed in Stone's mind. [What's the peacekeeper army doing?]

[It's still in its starting position in the Mojave Desert surrounding the wormhole.]

[Dissension in the ranks?]

[The soldiers and junior officers who'll actually do the fighting are under radio silence. We should assume they have no clue what happened. Presumably they're wondering why their commanders haven't given the green light.]

Through the quantum computer embedded in his skull, Stone queried the blockchain. [A hundred generals and admirals based at the Pentagon underwent convocation.]

[So did a hundred more at major military bases around the United States. They're debating now about whether to follow Sayyid and Goldbaum's orders or to stand down—wait a minute.]

[What?]

[US military activity.]

Stone rubbed the backs of his fingers on his jaw. Minerva had a military, freshly raised after the UN rediscovered the colony, well-trained and bolstered by convocation. No man would want his fellow soldiers, and his family and friends back home, to think him a coward. Yet the Minervan military was unblooded, and probably had no more than a thousand soldiers. Against them, the US armed forces, though bloated with rear echelon mofos, tied down by rules of engagement and political correctness, and demoralized by constant deployment wearing the blue helmets of UN peacekeepers, still had ten times the military strength Minerva could field. [If peacekeepers establish a beachhead on the Minervan side of the wormhole—]

[No, not against Minerva.] A chill touched Caitlyn's voice. [Against New York.]

19

Sweat oozed in his armpits. He checked the lights but they hadn't flickered. He remembered a cramped flat in a Southeast Asian city, tidy and clean and the taste of rice noodles and fish sauce before, a wreck of splintered plastic furniture as if the two rooms had explosively decompressed out the shell hole gaping in the concrete block wall, after. Every officer in every armed force in the settled galaxy talked about precision munitions and surgical strikes, but when high explosive munitions started flying, they ripped the mask off the talk.

Maybe she had it wrong. [What's your intel? The generals and admirals wouldn't give orders over the quantum computer net.]

[This isn't talk out of the Pentagon. People are in action. Soldiers at Fort Bragg and Fort Campbell are hurriedly prepping. Transport aircraft near those bases are spinning up. JFK shut down its longest runway and is diverting flights to Newark and LaGuardia. Word out of the mayor's office and 1 Police Plaza is that NYPD will open the bridges and cede control around UN headquarters to US forces.]

[Are those prepping soldiers receiving blue helmets?]

[Hmm.] Her forehead must be creasing between her blond locks and her hazel eyes.

[Hmm?]

[I hadn't thought about that. I'd assumed the US military was deploying under the UN banner, to lift the blockade on headquarters and extract Sayyid and Goldbaum.]

Stone asked, [How is Goldbaum giving orders?]

[Let me investigate.] Her attention dropped off the line.

The incision in the skin of his chest ached. While she worked, he went to the bathroom and found a field medicine kit. He lifted his shirt. Deep red spotted the dressing. A corner of the tape floated free from his skin, riding the mat of his chest hair. He yanked the dressing free, wincing.

More red, spotted with green and yellow lymph, showed on the skin-side of the dressing. The incision itself was an ugly red U under his collarbone.

The things he did to avoid Gray.

He applied antibiotic, procoagulant, and a numbing agent, followed by a clean dressing. Better tape, which meant it would hurt even more the next time he changed the dressing. Then he saw inside the medicine kit a squirt bottle of adhesive remover, *remove tape from skin and hair the pain-free way*, and laughed.

The laugh dried up.

Did the orders to the US military come not from Goldbaum, but from Gray?

Stone drifted back to the living room and dropped onto a yellow couch's lumpy cushion. He rested his feet on an oval coffee table, then swung his legs up and stretched out on the couch. Shut his eyes.

Glimpses of O'Brian, Gautam and Merrill on Minerva, Ulrich, Teresa Benavides bubbled up from memory like tar globs on the river. Dying or dead, which pained him more to see?

Answer failed him before he drifted…

[Wake up.]

Stone blinked groggy eyes. Dug heels into the cushion and scrambled upright. Adrenaline trickled through him, rendering him half-alert, like a drunk person drinking coffee. He took deep breaths. [How long did I sleep?]

[Forty minutes.]

He yawned. [Should have told you to wake me sooner.] He squeezed shut and forced open his eyes. More deep breaths. The nap-fog broke up. [What did you find out?]

[US military action confirmed. An operations officer at Fort Bragg underwent convocation and he's consciously pushing details to the blockchain. Two battallions of mechanized infantry will arrive at JFK by seven tonight. Four hours. One battallion will surround UN headquarters by two o'clock and occupy it by four tomorrow morning. The other will seize three targets around Turtle Bay and the Upper East Side.]

[That's an ambitious timetable. What's their objective?]

[Mass arrests. Sayyid, Goldbaum, the list has over six hundred names.]

He squinted at the bare white walls. Only more questions came up. [They're going after Goldbaum? Violating the chain of command to arrest their commander-in-chief?]

[When the soldiers move into UN headquarters, the Secretary of Defense will proclaim that everyone ahead of him in the line of presidential succession is guilty of at least one impeachable offense. The draft of his speech has a lot of rhetoric about the national will and the original intent of the constitution making him the true President.]

[How good is his argument?]

[He's cleaner than everyone he wants to arrest,] said Caitlyn. [The hardest drug he uses is gin and he's been faithful to his wife for thirty years of marriage. He's gone along with weapons procurement decisions that enriched some retired generals but gray looks white next to black—]

[Gray. He's behind this.]

[Looks like it.]

Stone leaned his head back on the yellow couch's backrest. [Maybe we should find some evidence.]

[I have. UNICA's office building is not a target. Gray's off the arrest list. Both thsoe aren't conclusive, though. From the UN organization chart, Gray's official title at UNICA looks so bureaucratic that an outsider might think him too unimportant to be worth arresting. But there's other evidence.]

[I'm listening.]

Caitlyn said, [In their internal communications, the Defense Secretary and the senior generals refer to 'a friend at Turtle Bay.']

[An insider in the UN hierarchy. Maybe not located at headquarters.]

[Right. The friend ordered all UN personnel to stay at their work locations until further notice. Who has the authority to do that?]

[Somebody high up at the UN Interagency Coordination Authority. And with Kroebel trapped inside headquarters...]

[Exactly. One more thing. The Defense Secretary's proclamation also condemns Sayyid, Kroebel, and hundreds more of crimes that void their moral authority. Gray's record on those matters is about as clean as the Secretary's.]

[It is?]

[Haven't you checked his public profile?]

[I've been busy.]

[Take a few minutes and read it.]

Stone pulled a breath into a chest suddenly tight. A thousand times he'd wondered how much the old man's true self differed from the veneer he showed his subordinates. A grin pushed up the corners of Stone's mouth.

He thought his request to the computer embedded in his skull. Up unfurled the truth of UNICA's Assistant Director of Operational Planning, Martindale Gray.

Eighty-seven years old and in the second highest priority group for rejuvenation treatments. He'd held his bureaucratic job title and its true power as the UN's leading spymaster since before Stone's birth. From an old money New York family possessed, by the time of his youth, with far more old than money. Scholarship to Columbia. One ex-wife, one son, two daughters, seven grandchildren. Memberships in a racquetball club in the city and a sailing club in the Hamptons.

Stone chuckled. Behind Gray's desk, the painting on the wall, two sailboats racing. A tell all along, and Stone had lacked any idea.

Gray lived cleanly. He collected whiskeys and whiskys from around Earth and the settled galaxy. Apparently the spelling difference provided a clue to origin.

Collected, but didn't abuse. In Gray's thoughts, captured by the quantum computer in his head, each day the old man abided by a two-drink maximum.

Little in the way of sex kinks, either. Five million-dollar sessions with a call girl in the months after his divorce. In the decades since, a steady habit of overlapping casual girlfriends and brief exclusive relationships with women older than his eldest daughter.

Bile rose in Stone's throat. His mother, prowling Manhattan for prominent men, could have bedded Gray—

Stone opened the link to the list of Gray's sexual partners, searched for her name, blew out a breath. His mother's name was off the list. Which fit with the woman Stone knew. She might be aroused by Gray, puppet master of the settled galaxy, but she'd politely dismiss an assistant director of some boring logistics department inside an alphabet-soup agency around Turtle Bay.

His stomach settled, Stone read further. Gray lived a clean personal life. No live boys, no dead girls, no drunken mug shots.

Yet Gray the man hadn't cajoled or threatened US generals to occupy UN headquarters.

Time to learn more about Gray the puppet master.

Stone turned to the section of the old man's public profile relating to his profession.

Gray, recruited by the UN's spymasters while still in college, in the waning years of the Time of Troubles. Infiltrated the exotic matter factory built in Venus' orbit by a libertarian billionaire, later renamed Hawking Station, and returned to Earth with the keys to the galaxy and a trail of blood behind him.

Holy hell. When order reestablished itself after the chaos of this day, when a million people were assembled in public convocation, Stone would read every word.

He took a breath. Reestablish order first.

Stone read more. Gray rose quickly through the ranks of the UN intelligence services after his triumph at Hawking Station. He unearthed the secrets of bureaucrats, diplomats, even Secretaries-General.

Forget live boys. Dead ones. Dead girls too. Bribes taken to pardon mass murderers. Thefts of trillions of dollars by thieves disguised in three-piece suits. Ethnic cleansings and wars aided and abetted to engorge insiders with more wealth and power. A hidden dark history of the last fifty years.

Gray knew all the crimes. Blackmailed half the perpetrators. Allied himself with the other half. Including... he searched for military titles. American generals and admirals, at the Pentagon, at Fort Campbell and Fort Bragg....

Stone abruptly noticed the lumpy cushion under him, the plain white walls of the narrow apartment [Engrossing reading.]

[Surprised?]

He angled his head for a moment, then straightened. [No.]

Nervous energy ran down his limbs. He pushed himself off the yellow couch, took a leak, went to the kitchen for a bottle of water. Under the LED panels, he guzzled half of it. [No surprises, but his profile doesn't tell us his plan after his pet generals make the mass arrests. Does your source know?]

[No. What are you thinking?]

He returned to the yellow couch. [Gray might try to strike a deal with the Minervans. He acts on the knowledge pulled out of the heads of the power brokers and offers to kingmake.]

She took thoughtful breaths. [Problem. The arrest list. Simon Bale, the ambassador, and all other members of the Minervan mission are on it.]

[He would want to negotiate a deal from a position of strength. Holding the Minervans at gunpoint would do that. Or possibly he's already struck a deal with Bale and would arrest the Minervans to cover it.]

[You believe that?]

[It's possible.]

[So are his pet generals ordering their men to perform summary executions.]

Stone checked the time. Four o'clock. Transport planes were being loaded in Kentucky and North Carolina right now. He smacked his fist against his thigh. [We need to find out his plan.]

[I'll keep digging for intel from the army bases and the Pentagon.]

Stone folded his arms in front of his chest. [I'll work up a plan for getting to Gray.]

[Did I say you were still in play?]

[I can't get to Minerva before Gray's pawns roll through the streets in their armored fighting vehicles. I'm in your hand whether you wanted me there or not. I'm your trump card for one trick. Do you want to make the best possible play?]

[Do it.]

She left him alone in comfortable silence. Stone went to the kitchen. Puffy, airtight pouches of almonds and dried pineapple opened with a whispered exhalation of nitrogen.

Munch and think. Sip water and think. The UNICA garage entrance and the pedestrian entrance on the west-east street. A freight entrance off an alley. Exits from three fire stairs, one opening on the alley, two on the street.

The fire stairs! His elation faded like a child's balloon the morning after the birthday party. One-way doors and alarms screaming the instant he forced one open from the outside. If Gray had even thirty seconds of warning, he could button up his office and turn the approaches into a kill zone for Stone.

Walk in through the main doors? Break and enter through the freight entrance? Cameras, alarms. No.

Drive in? The face recognition software at the entrance wouldn't open the gates. Hide on the floorboards? Security might let an empty car into the visitor level of the parking garage. Then get out and stroll in the lobby door. Of a building on lockdown. With Gray's people undoubtedly backstopping the facial recognition cameras. Dammit.

The parking garage....

A common design. Incomplete walls to let in air and light and save on construction costs. Facing both the street and the alley. Rappel in. How? Toss a grapple on a rope up from street level. High chance of being seen, though.

A possibility quickened his heart. Did the building next door have windows opening onto the alley—?

He continued planning the approach. He knew where the visible cameras and microphones were, and could guess at the location of the invisible ones. If his face were seen, though....

But Gray would make a stranger strolling through UNICA's offices with sunglasses and a ball cap even faster.

His stomach growled. Six-thirty. Stone stretched and went to the kitchen. He transferred a tray of chicken cordon bleu with asparagus in garlic sauce from freezer to microwave.

Six-thirty. Two formations of transport planes descending the night sky. Two thousand men, dozens of armored fighting vehicles. Hours to offload the planes, hours to fuel and supply vehicles and men and brief junior officers on their objectives.

Arrest the corrupt UN leadership. Restore American sovereignty. Smoke screens for Gray to kingmake in both Washington and New York. Nothing would change.

No. A million people knew themselves and one another in a way that dispelled smoke screens and unmade kings. Even if the blockade of Minerva continued, data links would remain intact.

The microwave pinged. A cold hunch seeped down his chest. [Caitlyn.]

Silence responded.

[Caitlyn.]

[I'm here.] Her voice sounded thousands of miles away.

[What are Gray and his pet generals planning to do about Minerva?]

Nervous dark humor edged into her tone. [They won't invade.]

[They'll blow the equilibrator ring on the Earth side. The wormhole will self-destruct in a burst of gamma rays.]

[How did you—]

[I know Gray,] Stone said. [He'll want to neutralize all the threats to his plan.]

[The evidence points that way. The generals' friend near UN headquarters asked them to *quarantine the infection*. The units blockading the wormhole on the Earth side pulled back twenty miles. Traffic control is diverting aircraft from a forty-mile radius too. Every US government agency maintaining a satellite received a high-priority request to confirm orbital positions.]

If a wormhole's equilibrator ring failed, the gamma ray burst would be heaviest on the tangent. On the Earth side, ITB sited wormhole mouths with the equilibrator rings positioned vertically. A containment failure on Earth would send most of the gamma rays into the crust or the sky. Molten rock, unlucky airplanes destroyed in flight. A disaster, but not a catastrophe.

On the colony worlds, though, equilibrator rings lay horizontally at ground level. The gamma ray burst would scour thousands of square miles with lethal radiation. Anything flammable would ignite, unleashing a firestorm that would make the nuclear strikes of the Time of Troubles look as tiny as the firebombings of Tokyo and Hamburg two centuries ago.

[That fits.]

[There's more. A cruise missile unit at Camp Pendleton in California is in operational readiness.]

Guide a missile at the equilibrator ring. Safer than having a demolition crew place explosives wired for remote detonation. Ten minutes for the launch sequence, ten minutes in flight.

Steamed smells of garlic and breaded chicken pushed from his nose into his brain. His dinner, cooling in the microwave. He no longer felt hungry.

Forget that. Eat. You need all the strength you can muster. [Have you warned the Minervans?]

[First thing. Civilians are getting to cover. Most people on Minerva should survive. But Euler City will be destroyed. Years to rebuild.]

His next words tumbled out of his mouth. [Why hasn't the cruise missile unit launched yet?]

Caitlyn's voice lilted. [Some US government agencies haven't yet complied with the request for orbital positions.]

[Some US government agencies are run by Friends of ours?]

[Not friends, but fellow seekers of alignment with the universe.]

[How long can you stall?]

[Five hours, I think.]

[You think.]

The dregs of the lilt drained from her voice. Her words sounded hollow, as if she spoke in a drained swimming pool. [That's the best I can do.]

[No. You can do something even better. Play your trump card.]

[To do what? Kill Gray? His pet generals will still follow his orders even if he's dead.]

Stone pictured the old man at his antiquated computer. A

standing-height desk held video monitors and an alphanumeric keyboard. His grin was audible in his voice. [Gray can send new orders after he's dead.]

20

The window of the empty studio apartment let in a narrow trapezoid of faint, sterile light from the distant street. The light glowed on the right-hand wall, opposite the kitchen area to the left. A reflected glint on synthetic granite and pressed stainless steel. Outside the window, the fire escape down to the alley showed a similar sheen. A musty smell of weeks of disuse and dust in the corners.

Stone eased the front door shut behind him. Quietly worked the locks. The deadbolt snick echoed off bare walls and a deep brown ceramic tile floor grained to look like hardwood.

He listened for sounds out in the hall or alarms triggered when he broke into this apartment. Silence. A night for civilians to hunker down. In the morning, they would find out which flag to salute, and in front of which sovereign to kneel.

Bag over his shoulder, Stone went to the window. Thick paint sealed half the apartment windows in the city. Not this one. A dark seam surrounded the lower sash.

Stone ducked into a dark corner between the window and the bathroom door, opposite the glowing trapezoid on the far wall, and set down the bag. He pulled out three garments. Stripped to his underwear and ankle holster. Stepped into blue pants from the safehouse closet. Light yet stiff synthetic fabric. A shirt hand-delivered to his metallic blue sedan by a nose-pierced girl at a resale shop in the East

Village. He buttoned the shirt. As best he could tell in the dim light, the shirt's color and fabric matched perfectly to the pants. Caitlyn had a good eye for color when ordering online. The only thing that might lead someone to give him a second look was Esteban's sewn-on nametag on the breast pocket,

But the people most likely to give him that second look worked in the building across the alley.

He put on a cap, also from the resale shop. A darker blue with an Islanders logo, bill with a frayed edge. A pair of workboots, two sizes too large, spare socks wedged in the toe. A second 9mm, this one taken from the safehouse. He moved it toward his waistband over the left side of his abdomen, then shook his head. Swap it for his pistol in its ankle holster. He knew his pistol better than any woman's body. Every week at the range he practiced targeting from the hip. The new 9mm looked a twin to his, but even minor differences between the two could throw off his aim.

Two extra magazines went into the back pockets of his pants. The tail of his untucked shirt covered them. Forty rounds total. He stuffed a set of burglar's tools about the size of one of the magazines and wrapped in waterproof plastic into his left front pocket. Rappel line in his left hand.

Stone released the catch and opened the window. The sash rattled up the side grooves of the frame. Cool night air, laced with a rotten egg stink from a dumpster, trickled into the apartment.

He backed his legs out the window and tested the metal grill of the fire escape landing with part of his weight. It held.

He emerged from the window. Bolts squeaked as the fire escape bore his full weight. The landing was six feet by eight, with metal mesh stairs angling down from the upper left and a hole to his left to access the next flight down.

Not going that way. He ducked under the stairs from above and kept his feet clear of the reflective bee-striped strip marking off the hole for the descending stairs.

The air felt cooler and denser, as if half the city held its breath. A glance to his left showed no traffic on the street. A glance seven floors down. No winos in the alley. Across, UNICA headquarters blocked half the sky.

His embedded quantum computer showed he had two hours before the cruise missile team in California would receive clearance to destroy the wormhole.

More than enough time. The clock wasn't his enemy.

The people across the alley were his enemy.

Stone took the end of the rappel line with the adhesive anchor in his right hand. Directly opposite him, the UNICA parking garage showed bands of starkly-illuminated concrete above the low walls of each deck. This high, this late at night, even with Gray's order that UN personnel remain at their posts, the garage level across from Stone held only a few cars, clustered near the elevator in the center of the builidng. Far from the gap between levels through which he would infiltrate.

He aimed and flung the adhesive anchor. The rappel line hissed as it slithered out of his left hand. The anchor splatted three inches below the top of a wall. A tug confirmed the adhesive held.

Time to make fast the other end. Stone tied a timber hitch at his eye level around a length of black pipe supporting the next landing up the fire escape. Tugged. The knot held, but more bolts fixing the fire escape to the concrete wall squeaked in the silent alley.

He glanced down. Seven floors. His gut clenched. If a safety inspector took a bribe to overlook bolts unable to hold his weight—

His gut eased, relaxed by the slow pounding of his heart. The most important mission ever. He gripped the rappel line in both hands. Crouched with both feet on the railing.

Set off for the UNICA parking garage, hand over hand. The bolts behind him squeaked each time he grabbed the next stretch of rappel line. The line rubbed against his palms. Should have thought of gloves. His upper arms smoldered. Keep your elbows bent. Man up. Don't look down.

Stone reached the parking garage. He pulled down with his right arm, lifting his body toward the rappel line. He reached his left hand up. Rough concrete nibbled at his palm. Reached over the lip of the wall. Held tight. Swung his left leg up. Banged his knee. He stifled a curse and got his left leg over.

His center of gravity cleared the wall. Both feet touched the solid concrete of the parking deck.

Stone turned away from the alley. He left the rappel line's anchor stuck to the outer wall of the garage. If he had to leave in a hurry, he wanted as many escape routes open as possible. He strode toward the elevators, catching his breath as he went.

[I'm in the UNICA garage,] he told Caitlyn.

[Roger that.]

At the elevator lobby, he punched the down button. While he waited, he worked on his posture. Hunched shoulders, downcast eyes. Bob your head like your implantable is piping to your auditory nerves your favorite song when you were a teenager. Move your throat muscles to practice a Nuyorican accent. *Ai, vato....*

Ping. The UNICA logo on the elevator doors split in half. In. Down.

The elevators opened to the lobby. Dim lights shone like distant moons from the ceiling of the double height atrium. His workboots thumped on cream-colored marble. Take the building's main elevators down to the basement, find a janitor's cart—

"Hey, man" came from the information and security desk, squatting and underlit like a UFO crossed with a convertible.

Stone trudged along. Eyes half closed. Head bobbing to a song full of thrashing guitars and operatic vocals he'd listened to in the locker room before games. *Across the storm-tossed sea, we come a-viking—*

The voice echoed around the atrium. "Yo, dog, talk to me!"

Stone blinked, looked up, eyes shaded by the bill of the Islanders cap. The security guard on duty was African-American. White hairs salted both his trimmed beard and fade haircut. Old enough he might remember Bedford-Stuyvesant before gentrification. He splayed his width across a chair behind the security desk. Stone could outrun him, but not the dozen reinforcements he could summon.

"*Qué?*" Stone asked.

Brown eyes with yellowed sclera glanced at the nametag on Stone's shirt. "You ain't Benificio. Where Beneficio at?"

"Beneficio? Ai, I don't know, man. My boss call, say I work here tonight. This day all mess up, man."

The security guard nodded sagely. "Damn if you ain't got that right. Hell, Beneficio might show up anyway, huh?"

"I don't know, man."

"Aight, I won't keep you."

Stone nodded, then resumed his trudge to the main elevators. Three steps later, he halted. "*Chinga,*" he said to no one. He turned to the guard. "Ai, man, this day all mess up, my boss no give me access card."

The guard heaved a heavy sigh. "Damn." He flipped an *on patrol* sign up on the counter, then waddled out of the security desk. Keys jangled and he breathed hard after four steps. "I get you down the basement. Don't stop here on your way up."

"You give me card to go in offices?"

"I can't do that, dog. Look, most everybody still at work. Knock on doors and they let you in. And if an office is locked up and nobody there, just skip it. Your boss ain't gonna find out. Like you say, this day all mess up. Com-pren-day?"

Stone nodded as if he didn't comprehend. "*Sí. Gracias.*"

The guard unreeled an access card from his belt, waved it at a scanner. A green light, a beep. The elevator door opened. The guard waved inside. "Aight, go on."

Stone trudged on. He pressed the down button and kept his shoulders hunched, his gaze on the marble tile, even after the guard turned away. If someone monitoring a camera saw him break character before he got close enough, he would never get within pistol range of Gray.

In the basement, past a break room full of the cough syrup smell of energy drinks, he found the janitorial store room. A rolling trash cart. Empty container, fully-charged battery. He clipped the cart's control tag to his collar. Pressed *start*.

The cart followed him out of the storeroom and to the elevator. The simple computer in the bottom housing next to the battery and the motor could not question his legitimacy. After the UNICA logo on the doors split down the middle, the cart followed him in.

Stone's heart thudded. Adrenaline wanted to split his lips apart in a grim smile. He willed his face blank and his finger to move slowly. He pressed 27.

The elevator shot upward. He bobbed his head to remembered music. 23, 24, 25... The elevator slowed. Stone's stomach floated into his throat just before the floor indicator flashed 27 and the elevator stopped with a mechanical clunk.

Across the storm-tossed sea, we come a-viking, kept on beat by the pounding of his heart.

The doors parted. Stone trudged out. The cart's motors hummed behind him. He turned left without thinking. His right hand rose three inches from his side toward the handle of a door with a frosted glass window and the etched words *Operational Planning*.

Remember your role. The office's security system won't recognize you.

But you still have to knock. He put his hand back in motion, aiming for the space between *Operational* and *Planning*. His knuckles tapped twice on the frosted glass.

No answer.

He rapped the door. Glass rattled in the frame.

From inside, muffled voices spoke. Heavy footsteps sounded through thin carpet. Coming closer.

Stone lowered his gaze. The bill of the cap further shielded his blue eyes. A moment later the door swung open.

A woman glimpsed in his peripheral vision. Long face framed by brown hair parted down the middle, no makeup. A solid figure, but slender enough to surprise him after her thudding walk. He'd seen her a dozen times but never learned her name.

She craned her long neck back and forth, looking over his mismatched uniform and the robotic cart behind him. Tendons popped in and out of relief. "Don't you have an access card?"

"Car...?" Stone jammed alarm into his voice. "Señora, soy substituto, hoy muy loco, mi no tarjeta."

"You're a substitute? Loco, crazy, today?"

"This day all mess up."

"You have that right." She rubbed her eyes and stepped back. "Come in."

The cart followed him. He reached for the door but she shut it first. She tromped past him to her station.

A cubicle farm stretched out, like a hedge maze lined with rough slate-colored fabric. Gray's analysts worked here, reviewing each day's field reports from the three hundred UN member nations and the fifty rediscovered colony worlds. The analysts remained here now, while the distant windows mirrored the overhead LEDs, but none of them worked. Voices muttered in clumps around cubicle entrances or at wider spaces filled with couches or conference tables. Confusion settled on the room like a heavy gas contaminating the air.

He worked his way around the cubicle farm. The cart rolled loyally after him. A few faces glanced up from their cubicles, usually with a guilty start before ignoring him a moment later.

How many had undergone convocation? How many digged through all the information at hand, either through the quantum computer network if they were joined to the blockchain or over the world-forum if they hadn't, trying to understand their place in the universe?

Even if everyone in the cubicle farm had undergone convocation, they couldn't help him. Analysts. Their strongest weapon was presentation software.

Only he alone could stop Gray.

Stone trudged on. He left the cubicles behind and went down a corridor. The offices of analysis managers and operational staffers to his left, along the exterior wall. Stone stayed in character despite the urge to stride past before anyone saw him. Some of these people would know him by sight, would know he reported directly to Gray.

But now light seeped under closed doors. All of these middle managers engrossed in private struggles. Trying to make sense of the summaries provided by their analysts. Rebalancing their friend and foe accounts based on the convocation blockchain. Or feverishly deleting all the copies of their child pornography collections.

Stone rounded the last corner. A sitting area to the left of the door. Chairs and a sofa in black leather and steel, glass-topped table. Gray's personal secretary sat behind the low walls of her station, hunched forward more than usual for her aged back, fiddling with her engagement and wedding rings. Her lower lip trembled. She didn't even glance at Stone.

Past her station, a single office had its door open. The e-ink label bore no name, only the title *Director of Operational Planning.* From inside came the hum of computer cooling fans, overridden briefly by a quick rattle, a burst of typing on a computer keyboard.

Head down, heart slamming, Stone trudged into the open doorway. He glanced over his shoulder. The cart rolled in. He gripped the free side of the door and slammed it toward the jamb. In one motion he pivoted and drew the new pistol from his waistband—

Behind his cherrywood desk facing the door, the glow of his computer monitors on the left side of his face, Gray held a blue steel .38 in both hands, aimed at Stone's chest.

"I've been expecting you, Hybrid."

21

With his 9mm aimed at Gray's chest, Stone laughed. "Hi, boss. What do you want to talk about?"

Gray, A tall man in a three-piece suit the color of ashes. Eyes matched his family name. He looked down his long, narrow nose and over the barrel of his pistol. "What makes you think I wish to talk?"

"You haven't fired yet."

Gray arched an eyebrow. "You know as well as I that even if I put a bullet through your heart, you would have ten seconds before you would bleed to death and enough training to put me at grave risk."

"And vice versa." Stone kept the muzzle unwavering on Gray's chest, his gaze, on Gray's eyes. He reached behind him with his left hand. The door handle should be—yes. His thumb pushed the lock button. His left hand rejoined his right in gripping his 9mm.

"Very well," Gray said. His pistol's muzzle remained a dark eye staring at Stone's chest. If he raised the muzzle a fraction of an inch, he could fire at Stone's head, possibly dropping him instantly. But Gray would know Stone knew that. Gray would know Stone would fire first if he tried a headshot. The older man kept his pistol level. For now.

"I would ask you a few questions," Gray said.

"You could have sent me a message over the embedded computer network."

"Which you would have ignored."

Stone said, "You know me well."

"Not well enough."

Caitlyn's voice sounded in his head. Her breath sounded as if she hurried someplace. [What are you doing?]

[I was a hostile when you recruited me.]

[You want to turn him?]

[Why not?]

She sputtered, then her words spilled out. [You couldn't blow a wormhole when we recruited you.]

[If he's alive, Gray will have that power. Would you rather the man with that power be a friend or a foe?]

"Give my regards to Ms. Fredriksen. She is your handler, I take it?"

[Hush,] Stone said. "I'm working solo."

"Don't lie to me, young man." The floor-to-ceiling windows to the left reflected Gray into Stone's peripheral vision. "You've never had an independent plan in your life. You have been nothing more than a killing machine I've wound up and pointed in the right direction. Now someone else has pointed you in a different direction."

Stone grinned. "Insulting me to distract me? I'm too good a killing machine to fall for that."

"How did they turn you?"

"You want to allocate percentages to the different MICE factors? You have more in common with the Center for Alignment with the Universe than I thought."

The MICE factors. Once per year, Stone sat through a counterintelligence training led by a rabbitty guy with a black buzzcut and clipped mustache. He'd stayed awake through enough of them to pass the test. Operatives get turned in one of four ways. Money. Ideology. Compromise, usually blackmail, the same currency of live boys and dead girls Gray had dealt in for half a century. Ego, the victim's belief that he could take control of the situation from his handler.

"There's no need to quantify it."

"Compromise is the most apt description. They activated the embedded quantum computer—"

"Convocation."

"Yes. I didn't take any pleasure in lying to you about it the last time I was here."

"Focus, please." Gray yawed the muzzle a millimeter to the right. As if Stone had forgotten the old man aimed the handgun at him.

Gray would want to wrap up the conversation—either with Stone dead or bending the knee—as quickly as possible. Holding two and a half pounds with a steady aim would eventually tire their arms. So far, only a faint ache trickled over Stone's forearms. Gray would feel worse. Stone held the advantages of youth and strength.

Keep him talking. Outlast him.

"They subjected me to convocation," Stone said, "then press-ganged me into their conspiracy. To keep me loyal, they monitored my actions through a private blockchain, and would send a hit squad after me if I revealed the conspiracy's objective or my membership in it."

Wheels turned behind Gray's eyes. Time to throw sand under them, to give them more traction across the old man's icy mind.

Stone went on. "Yes, even though every adult on Minerva is connected to the reputation blockchain, you can set up private blockchains for limited times and purposes. People with high reputations are somehow selected to validate—"

"A Venetian election. Cycles of vote and random draw. Facilitatrix van Bentum posted a thorough explanation of it."

"I'm sure," Stone said. He swallowed once, dryly. "So there's plenty of room for you."

[Hold up,] Caitlyn said. [I lack the authority to induct him into High Emprise LLC and Friends.]

[I'm not talking about him joining our private club. I'm talking about working in concert with him. Can he help us rebuild the UN and the Dubai Convention to be more aligned with the universe?]

[Yes, but—]

[No excuses.]

[It takes time to set up a Venetian election,] Caitlyn said, [then time to validate a private blockchain.]

[Get started.]

[I'm busy.]

He refocused his attention on the tall man behind the cherrywood desk. The wheels behind Gray's eyes turned with assurance now, like the sailboat crew winching up lines in the painting on the wall behind the old man. "What role could I play?"

"The same role you play now. Gather intel, color the options to the honest politicians, and lean on the dishonest ones to give you the results you want."

"Is that possible? Many of my intelligence sources, and most of the political figures whom I advise, have undergone convocation. Their secrets are public knowledge."

"A million and a half people on Earth could have undergone convocation today," Stone said. "Billions on Earth, and millions on almost fifty colony worlds, did not. You can be fully employed for decades to come."

Gray looked thoughtful, but his .38's muzzle remained steady.

"Think of the world your grandchildren will grow up in. Which one do you want? The same as we have now, with Sayyid, Goldbaum, and Kroebel replaced with people as corrupt and venal? Or a world where leaders can't hide their crimes?"

"You make a strong case." He slipped his finger out of his .38's trigger guard. "What would you have me do next?"

"Tell the missile team to stand down."

"I'm curious how you learned about the plan to isolate Minerva."

Stone smirked and gave his head a minimal shake. "Need to know."

"You also have intel on my joint venture with the US military?"

"Yes. That can go ahead. But remove the Minervan delegation from the arrest list."

Gray lowered his .38 an inch. "I will do these things."

Heart slamming, Stone pulled his finger from the trigger of his 9mm. Lifted the fingrtip far enough for Gray to see. Mutual expressions of good faith.

The older man nodded. He quarter-turned to his left, to his computer monitors and his keyboard. His right side faced Stone. He lowered his .38 with muzzle down toward the cherrywood desktop, on a trajectory to land next to a squatty glass of whisky.

The peaty smell reminded Stone of meetings here. He licked dry lips. He lowered the 9mm a few inches. Sparkling water with a lime wedge would quench his—

A swift upward motion of Gray's hand. Stone acted immediately, unthinking, out of well-grooved habit. Pivot on his right foot. Finger on trigger. Move his pistol into position, no need to aim with his eye.

Gunfire. Stone squeezed the trigger. More gunshots, Gray's and his. He counted four of his own. Ringing ears. Stinking propellant. Joyous dark energy surged through Stone.

Gray's legs folded under him. Crimson splotched the chest of his ash-gray suit. Mouth gaping, he collapsed. The wheeled ergonomic chair near his cherrywood desk rolled to the side with a lazy half-spin.

Stone felt no wounds. A glance down his body showed no blood. He crouched and duck-walked around the desk. He yanked the wheeled chair out of the way with his left hand. Held his 9mm ready in his right.

Gray lay on his back. The heels of his polished black wingtips dug at the carpet. Trying to sit up. The .38 lay under the cherrywood desk, a foot from his open right hand, muzzle aimed somewhere under the computer workstation. Must have tumbled like a football when Gray dropped it.

Gray grimaced. Blood trickled from his mouth. Sweat ran down his pallid face. His heels dug in again. Pushed him scant inches toward the back wall. The metallic stink of blood mingled with an acrid odor coming from a wet stain soaking the old man's crotch.

A chill washed down Stone's arms and legs. Killing Gray was like striking down a king. A fault line deep underground had slipped and soon an earthquake would rock the foundations.

"Why did you try to take me down?" Stone asked.

Shallow breaths. Tight lips pulled back from teeth. "Had to."

"Why?"

His heels stopped digging into the carpet. His legs straightened. "Grandchildren. Would have prospered. If I remained kingmaker. And kingbreaker. You took that power from me. They won't prosper in this new world. New—"

Blood gushed from his mouth, dribbled down his cheeks, stained the ash-gray woolen collar of his suit. His eyes bulged. His chest convulsed, his back arched, his body scrabbled for one more inhalation.

Gray's torso fell slack. Cold eyes looked at Stone. Through him. Through everything. Through nothing.

Stone rocked to the side. The cherrywood desk held him up. Filigreed brass drawer pulls jabbed into his upper arm. [He's dead.]

Caitlyn didn't reply.

Stone pushed himself to his feet. Stepped over Gray's arm. Left foot between Gray's unmoving legs, right foot between Gray's right leg and the desk. [You there?]

[Yes.] She sounded even more hurried than earlier.

[Where are you? Where are you going?]

[Nevermind that now. Are you at his computer?]

A tray mounted on the underside of the workstation held a keyboard. Letters, numbers, punctuation, and a bunch of keys with funny labels. When you're the most powerful man in the galaxy, you can keep using archaic computer inputs, instead of subvoking to an implantable like a normal person. On the workstation surface stood three curved monitors, horizontally spaced bezel-to-bezel, covering 120° of arc. The monitors showed a blue circle that shaded to green and grew four corners as it crossed a deep black background from left to right.

[You can see this from my optic nerves? What is it?]

[Screensaver. Tap a key.]

[Which?]

[Any!]

He set his 9mm on the workstation surface, then reached down and jabbed *k*.

The green square vanished. The black background remained. *This session was locked by user gray. Enter password to unlock.*

[Damn,] Caitlyn said. Stone couldn't tell if she swore at what Stone saw or at something around her.

He remembered a past mission. Files encrypted on a computer disconnected from the worldforum. Highly secure, except for a password needed by a foreign minister with too many other things to remember.

A cursor blinked in the appropriate space. Stone's index fingers hunted for and pecked out the character string *p@$$w0rd*. Moved toward the enter key.

Tap tap tap on the door. Barely audible in his still-ringing ears. Dainty knuckles.

He jerked his head to his right. The roar of gunfire would have alerted everyone on the entire floor. Jagged holes in gympsumboard marked where Gray's .38 had missed. Probably punched through the soundproofing and out the gypsumboard on the other side of the wall.

Another *tap tap*. "Mr. Gray?" A timid female voice. Probably the old man's secretary.

Stone glanced down. The door's lock button remained pushed in.

Did Gray's secretary have a spare key?

Deal with that problem later. He returned his gaze to the monitors. The cursor blinked at the end of *p@$$w0rd*.

Stone hit enter.

The lock window remained on the black background. A line had been appended to the message.

Incorrect password. Four tries remain.

Four tries? Until what? A security team received an alert of a possible intruder in Gray's office? The gunfire and Gray's secretary sounded the alert a minute ago.

He hunted and pecked on the keyboard. *pA$$w0R—*

[Stop! He may have it configured to wipe his computer after too many failed unlock attempts.]

[He could do that? I'm not thinking straight. Of course he could.]

[Even if he didn't, if he has it configured to lock him out for an hour or two....]

[Got it. I'll try plan B.] Stone found the backspace key, held it down until the cursor blinked at the left edge of a blank line. Then he bent down and looked at the underside of the workstation.

Plan B. A password written down the old-fashioned way, pen on paper, and hidden somewhere obvious. He'd never needed to find a password this way on a mission, but he'd passed a training exercise by remembering it.

Not under the workstation surface. Or the keyboard tray. He lifted the keyboard. No alphanumeric gobbledygook. Maybe the keyboard model number? Try that if nothing else came up.

The back of a monitor? No, a visitor to the office could see the monitors' rear panels from the drinks table to the right of the door.

Not all the monitors. The leftmost monitor on the workstation aimed its rear panel at a bookcase and the office's back wall. He reached around the side, groped over the top. Nothing.

Try the desk drawers—

A fist pounded on the door. Stone lurched. Not the old man's secretary.

"Gray!" A coarse male voice. One of the operations staffers, Conrad, Conway, something like that. Conaway. Ruddy cheeks and eyes swaddled by fat. Probably a frat house date rape in his public profile.

The fist pounded again. "Gray, what the hell's going on?"

Couldn't he smell the propellant? The stink of the old man's piss and blood?

Of course he could. But the only violence Conaway dealt with happened far from this nanotube alloy skycraper, meted out by field operatives. Conaway's mind couldn't process the evidence of swift, deadly action taking place down the hall from his office.

Conaway's voice spoke something muffled. He'd turned away from the door. Talking to Gray's secretary.

Stone held his breath and listened for traces of sounds. No noise reached him over the ringing in his ears. But had a shadow passed one of the bullet holes made by Gray's .38?

He picked up his 9mm. Finger in the trigger guard. Muzzle pointed at the door. His left hand reached to his back pocket and slid out the spare magazine. His thumb checked the top cartridge. Rim here. Rounded hollow point there. He would slot it in correctly the first time, saving a second by not inserting the magazine backward.

Behind the door, metal jangled. Then scraped into the key slot on the handle. The handle slammed down, the door flew open—

A massive thump pounded the wall fifteen feet to the right of the door—

22

A rectangle of gypsumboard and foamed insulation collapsed into the room, revealing a hole wider and taller than a man. White dust and curling green tendrils of foam. Wisps of smoke from the edges of the hole.

In the sitting area outside, male figures. Body armor bulked under their shirts. Assault rifles, short black barrels, curved magazines as long as a child's arm. Poor accuracy but hundreds of rounds.

Instant knowledge ran down Stone's limbs. The men outside couldn't fire into the office until they knew Gray was dead or wounded.

Aim the pistol. Head shots. Fire. Fire. The man on point staggered. His assault rifle dropped to the floor and his hands went to his neck. Blood spurted through his fingers to the carpet.

A hand from behind grabbed the wounded man by the waist and tugged him backward, out of the hole.

Stone kept firing until he counted the tenth round. Duck under the desk. Eject. Slot in the fresh magazine. Rack the first round into the chamber.

Assault rifles barked like a pack of wild dogs. Rounds smacked gypsumboard over the desk. Glass tinkled on the desktop. The peaty smell grew stronger. More bullets pounded the privacy panel and the rest of the desk facing the hole. Steel and Kevlar layers sandwiched by the wood stopped them.

"Hold your fire!" shouted a resonant male voice in the sitting area.

Another cried out, "Man down! We need medical!"

"Is Gray—?"

Over the ringing in his ears and the roaring of his breath, Stone listened for footsteps coming in through the hole for a second try. Nothing.

"Hey!" The resonant male voice again. "Hostile! I'm talking to you!"

Did they not know who he was? Or did they not want to reveal to the desk jockeys cowering in their cubicles and offices that the man who'd engaged in a gun battle with Gray was one of UNICA's own operatives?

Something lightly touched the back of Stone's leg. He jerked it toward his body, bringing it fully under the desk, and whipped his head and the pistol around.

Brown liquid dripped from the edge of the desk to the floor. Whisky from the smashed glass.

"You're good but you're outnumbered. Come out with your gun down and your hands up. You'll get a fair trial. But if we have to go in there, you're a dead man."

A sudden urge made Stone shift his body under the desk. From his new position, he could see Gray's face. Sightless eyes. Slack cheeks. Mouth and jaw slick with blood. Stone had to look, for reasons he couldn't understand.

He shook his head. Those reasons would get him killed. Think of a way out.

"You hear me? If you're playing possum to get us in there, so you can down another of my men, you might hurt a lot before you die."

If they stormed the room, he might get one, two if he were lucky. But trapped under the desk, they couldn't miss.

He needed time. Maybe a futile need, doomed to fail, like Gray trying to push himself to a sitting position in hopes of drawing more breaths. Doomed to fail but he had to try.

"You said fair trial?"

"I did."

"I need a guarantee."

"Of what?"

"That you won't shoot me when I've got my hands up!"

No answer for a moment. Stone imagined him checking the playbook on how to fool a hostile into surrendering during a standoff.

"We can find a third party whom you trust and have them assure you of our intentions."

"Maybe." Stone peered out from under the desk. Could he sprint for the floor-to-ceiling windows? He might be able to shoot enough cracks in the bullet-resistant multi-layer glass to kick out a hole. Then somehow climb over two hundred feet down seamless glass and carbon nanotube alloy before a street team could pick him off. Fat chance.

"Work with me. Name a name."

Stone could buy more time, if nothing else. He dredged up a name from memory. Which Southeast Asian diplomat, Solid Blue or Red-Gold Stripes? Didn't matter. "Tungsiripat."

"Who?"

"A diplomat. I helped him and Vu resolve a border dispute the other day."

Somebody chuckled without humor. The male voice said, "Pal, if you're jerking my chain…."

"True as can be," Stone said. "Hand to God."

Even with Gray's corpse next to Stone, even if he escaped, the missile team would destroy the Minerva wormhole and the US military would impose a new world order. Stone twisted his upper body. Looked at the underside of the keyboard tray on the standing height desk. Almost close enough to touch.

Even if he knew the password, if he stood at the keyboard, the combat team on the other side of the wall would gun him down before he could change Gray's orders.

"I'll start making calls. But I lack patience for games, pal."

Stone's breath caught. Delay worked in favor of the combat team, too. Delay gave them time to deploy in a skyscraper across the street a high-powered rifle to punch through the window. Or a man-portable missile with a high explosive warhead carefully tailored to obliterate the contents of the office with minimal collateral damage.

Or throw in through the hole in the wall a canister of nervous system suppressant. Stop breathing, pal. We'll drag you out after you fall unconscious. Or die.

The ringing in Stone's ears faded now. Voices muttered in the sitting room. Medical equipment beeped. Men shifted their weight and made equipment belts creak.

A faint clod. A boot on a surface harder than carpet. The gypsum-board slab lying inside Gray's office. Echoes off the intact walls. One man or two?

Just trying to dupe you, pal. Talking out of one side of my mouth and ordering in a fireteam with the other.

Two men made more sense. One covers the other.

Stone licked his lips. His finger rested on his 9mm's trigger. Spring up, fire, hope you can get them both before covering fire through the hole in the wall struck him.

He took a breath. His muscles tightened like a coiling spring—

"Stop!"

A woman's smooth voice. A voice heard a thousand times in his mind's ear over the past weeks. Now live, no more than fifty feet away.

"Who the hell are you?" the team leader said.

"Caitlyn Fredriksen. Interstellar Transport Bureau. This is my superior, Robert Holbrook."

"Going to introduce the rest of your entourage?"

Stone's breaths came rapidly. Caitlyn had come. She'd guessed right that he could use help. [Glad you're here.]

[Can't talk.]

Entourage, the team leader said. An ITB combat team? A grin pushed at his mouth. Help, only fifty feet from him.

But still two men in Gray's office, no more than ten feet away, creeping closer.

[Hostiles in the office, coming for me.]

[Got it.]

The team leader said, "This is a UNICA matter."

"Gray plotted to destroy the Minerva wormhole. That makes it ITB business."

Murmurs on the other side of the hole. A creak of body armor on the other side of the desk. Had the gunmen come one step closer?

"Who's the ITB operative you sent to kill Gray?"

"ITB? That's one of yours. Hybrid."

Confused words blabbered on the other side of the wall. The team leader spoke to his men, a waver in his resonance. "What the hell does that matter? Men turn traitor all the time, sometimes for a blond piece—"

[Get down,] Caitlyn said.

Assault rifles barked again. Rounds punched through gympsumboard, spanged off Gray's desk. A pained grunt, a high scream, just on the other side of the desk. More screams, further away. More small arms fire, echoing off the walls, impossible to tell if the UNICA team overcame its surprise and returned fire, or if Caitlyn's squad kept going.

After an eon, ten seconds at the most, silence and the stink of hot metal, propellant, and fresh blood settled over Gray's office and the sitting area. A relative silence, carrying agonized groans and the frightened words "I surrender" like baseline static on an old-fashioned radio. [Sitting area secure. What have you got?]

Stone creeped out of his hiding place. Head below the desktop, he crouched in the pool of blood next to Gray's chest. Peered arond the corner. A lower leg, black pants and boot with toe down, heel up. Immobile.

He crept to the next corner. Peeked. A view of most of the office. The open door. The hole in the wall. The black pants belonged to a corpse lying face down, head turned away. The other man stretched out face-up on the carpet. A low moan escaped from his mouth. At his side, his hand trembled in a pool of blood.

[Office secure. How many casualties did we take?]

[One dead,] Caitlyn said. [Four wounded. Holbrook has a broken rib where a round dented his body armor.] Her next words sounded with the faint exertion of movement. [He'll take charge of the prisoners and the wounded.]

She stepped through the hole, a tall lithe feminine shape in black. A blond ponytail showed under the back of the visored helmet covering her head, face, and neck. The helmet pivoted. Hesitated over the dying man and the dead one.

She came closer, then lifted her helmet off and set it on the corner of Gray's desk. Her hazel eyes—good god, she was beautiful—

"Glad you could come to the party."

"A real blowout." Her legs wobbled a bit. She shut her eyes and sucked in a breath. "Less chatter. Let's find that password, or far more blood gets spilled than this."

Stone went around the desk. Careful steps over Gray's corpse. She followed him and only gasped once.

He turned to her. Grabbed her shoulders and tugged her off-balance. She took a stumbling step into the pool of Gray's blood. Soil her as much as he was soiled. "We'll clean your shoes later," Stone said.

"Right. It's just, he was, to you, like a father.... Head in the game," she told herself. "Password."

"I checked the workstation, including the backs of the monitors and the underside of the keyboard, for a taped-on piece of paper. Nothing. Maybe he used the model name on the bottom of the keyboard."

She shook her head. "The model names and serial number ranges of all computer equipment since the 1990s is in the dictionary files hackers use to crack easy passwords."

"He would know that. Okay. No password copy on the workstation. I didn't have time to check the desk."

She moved closer to Stone, squeezing him between her upper arm and the edge of the workstation. She smelled of soap and a dab of floral perfume, of life in the midst of a battlefield. "I'll take these drawers."

He stepped around her and over Gray's legs. The bloody carpet squished under his shoes. "I'll get the rest."

No need for subtlety. Gray would never know if they ransacked his desk. Pull out the drawer. Lift and tug to get the drawer free of the track. Dump the drawer contents on the desktop. Check the drawer, inside and out, for a piece of paper taped in place or wedged into a crevice between drawer panels. Only bare wood smelling like an old English library.

Throw drawer away with a tumbling thump onto the carpet near the windows. Paw through the items dumped on the desk. Letter opener, binder clips, a torn-open plastic wrap holding disposable pens. Sweep those to the floor. A block of sticky yellow notepaper. Peel notepaper off, sheet by sheet, look at both sides. Not just for ink, but for the imprint of a cheap plastic pen pushing down to write on a sheet above.

Nothing.

Invisible ink? That worked in mystery stories for children. An imprint of a pen, or a sheen of dried chemical, would give it away. Stone tore off sheets of notepaper and flung them aside until the block evaporated. The yellow notepaper blanketed Gray's face like confetti at a parade fallen onto a passed-out drunk.

Stone reached down. Next drawer.

Caitlyn tossed away the last of a stack of business cards. "Anything?" she asked.

"No." His voice sounded strange, speaking to her aloud after weeks communicating through the quantum computer networkd. "You?"

"No luck."

"Keep going."

Five more minutes. Every other drawer came up empty. Two more minutes to check the interior of the desk. A sheet of paper at the bottom, looking as if it had fallen behind a drawer.

"What's this?" Stone said. He grinned and pulled out the paper, then stood up with his prize.

Notes from a meeting two decades ago. Names Stone recognized and English words or obvious abbreviations. No gobbledygook string of letters, numbers, and punctuation. Dammit.

"What do you think?" he asked, not expecting much.

"Sounds like you already know the answer." She turned back to a heap on the desk, sifting through itsems she'd already reviewed.

Stone turned around. He pressed his rump against the bullnosed edge of the cherrywood. Spilled whisky put a damp line across his pants as he cast a tired gaze downward. The yellow sheets from the sticky pad over Gray's face now reminded Stone of a corpse in a gutter in a polluted shantytown outside São Paulo. The password could be locked up now in two pounds of rotting meat.

No. Gray had a sharp memory, but would've been too cautious to trust his secrets to his memory and nothing else. Everyone had a brain fart once in a while. Touch typists sometimes rested their hands on the wrong keys. People forgot things after being away from work for vacations.

Stone's gaze tracked upward. Only two bullets had struck the painting of the sailboat race, both high, puncturing clouds. The boat in the foreground turned its right side to the viewer, showing a blue stripe running horizontally on the white hull, just below the registration code in black letters and numbers near the back end.

He frowned.

Did sailboats have registration codes of twelve character strings?

Look closer.

That slack rope made an S look like a $, didn't it? A hand reaching over the railing covered the top of a W, making it lowercase. And didn't that splash of water across the bottom of an I made the letter look like a !?

And what regulatory agency, on land, in the sky, or at sea, would permit any vehicle's registration code to have an ambiguous character in the first place? No *I* or *l* or *1*, no *0* or *O*.

"Found it."

She jerked her head up, a blond and pink blur in his peripheral vision. "Where?"

Slowly he turned to her. His left hand pointed at the registration code on the side of the sailboat. "There."

She angled her head to the painting, showing him only two-thirds of a hazel eye. A moment later her eyebrow rose, and her eye glinted like an agate under a jeweler's lamp.

Caitlyn turned to the keyboard. "Read it to me."

He read off the twelve characters. She tapped the keys. Hit enter.

She looked over her shoulder. A colorful panorama of autumn leaves and rolling hills appeared behind her. But the color seemed bleached compared to the intensity emanating from her hazel eyes.

"We're in."

"Don't look at me," Stone said, though part of him wanted those hazel eyes to stare at him forever. "Give the orders."

"Stone Chalmers, voice of reason." She grinned and turned back to the workstation.

Men from the ITB force came in through the door. A stretcher clattered. Bodybags unzipped. The ITB men slapped an oxygen mask on the wounded man and wheeled him out on the stretcher. Others carried out the dead man on the other side of the desk, then came for Gray in his shallow grave of yellow sticky notes. Someone set up an air scrubber in the corner, plugged it in, turned it on.

Stone barely noticed the work being done in the corner of his eye. He watched Caitlyn. She adjusted the keyboard tray and worked with proud posture. Her gracile fingers flew over the keyboard. She composed lines, asked him to look over her shoulder. "Would Gray say that?"

"Close. Change the beginning of that sentence to 'A change in circumstances requires....'"

The orders went out each with a swoosh over the speakers. Missile team in California to stand down. Strike all Minervan personnel from the New York arrest list. She prepared five new communications, to the US Vice-President, the leaders of the two houses of Congress, and the two cabinet officials ahead of the Secretary of Defense in the presidential line of succession, informing each of them of the planned military operation in New York.

"Stirring the pot?" he asked.

"The more people know, the better."

After sending the last message, she looked around, blinking, as if she'd forgotten where she was. The scrubber chugged in place and the thickening stench of blood lacked its former edge.

She glanced into the corner near the door, where liquor decanters and bottles of sparkling water stood on a table of cherrywood with gold inlay. "We've earned a drink, wouldn't you say?"

Stone nodded. He turned to step out of the L-shape formed by the workstation and the desk. A jolt ran through him. He'd half-expected Gray's corpse to still lie there. Now, only a few sticky notes rested on a reddish-brown splotch of dried blood.

He led the way to the drinks table. Caitlyn scooped a short glass into the icemaker and poured amaretto over the collected cubes. He cracked the seal on a bottle of sparkling Italian mineral water, drank it warm, lips on the bottle's mouth and hand throttling its neck. He had to will his hand to relax its grip.

The ping of an incoming message sounded. She went back to the workstation. Stone drifted over while her fingers rattled out her reply. He stepped over the pool of Gray's blood and hitched himself up on the desktop. Instead of watching her, his gaze landed on the pool of blood and he couldn't pull it away.

He became aware that her fingers left the keyboard some time ago. He looked up. Her hazel eyes roped him in. "What are you feeling?"

"He was the nearest thing I had to a father for the past twenty years."

"You did what you had to."

"I know."

"You gave him the option. He made the first aggressive move. You acted in self-"

"I know," he said, more insistently. "Why are you trying to ease my conscience?"

She swept with two slender fingers a blond lock behind her ear. "The world still needs you."

"What about you? Do you need me?"

Caitlyn winced. "Part of me has wondered if it could work between us."

"But you know it wouldn't."

"I knew before Sheila van Bentum consecrated you in her basement on Minerva. What we learned there, and what I already knew about myself, confirmed it wouldn't work. I'm an adult, motivated by faith, a warrant officer instead of a knight-errant, with above-average suitability for a monogamous relationship. Maybe you can change...."

"But the odds are against it. I know that as well as you. I already knew it before I underwent consecration." Emotions churned in him, like cross-currents ripping past a beach, but his core was a jagged volcanic boulder rooted in bedrock and jutting above the ocean's surface. "After this is over, find a good man and live happily ever after. Till then—" He set down the fizzing bottle of sparkling water. He extended his hand to her. "Maybe we can keep working together."

Gray's computer pinged again. She shook his hand. "I wouldn't want to work with anyone else."

Epilogue

Fat flakes of snow drifted down the evening sky, past the hundred-foot-high stained glass windows of the new East Harlem Center for Alignment with the Universe, the naked branches of maples, and the rocky hill jutting up from the middle of Marcus Garvey Park. Behind the park's brick walls, children shrieked with delight as swing chains creaked in rhythm. A street vendor on the Madison Avenue sidewalk sold hot chocolate from a cart. Whipped cream shirred out of canisters hooked to the side of the cart. The iron gates into the park stood open under the awning of solar panels powering them.

Stone picked up a cardboard cup of hot chocolate from the street vendor. He raised his hand in toast. The street vendor scratched at a week's worth of white beard as he glanced over Stone's shoulder. The public profile would tell the vendor that Grid Wentworth had more than enough reputation points and credit score to settle his tab in good time.

Stone skipped the whipped cream. The sugar and molten chocolate would do enough to damage to his belly despite his daily kettlebell routine. The half-decade off active duty since the very public convocation of Sayyid, Goldbaum, Kroebel, Gray, and a million others hadn't made him fat. Age had.

Into the park and down the foamed concrete walkway. Near the playground, breath streamed from the mouths of parents bundled in jackets and scarves. Of course, an operative could notice a child alone in the park and pretend to be the parent. A couple jogged by, both with the scrawny look of people who ran too many miles every week. Headbands thick enough to hide radio receivers and earbuds covered their ears.

Over almost every adult shoulder swirled a globe of gray, green, blue, red, and yellow, a marker, visible to all those who'd received a quantum computer embedded in their skulls and undergone convocation. Look at the globe, think it open, and read that person's public profile.

Stone didn't bother. His targets would have public profiles as false as his. An exercise, two trainees would exchange an encrypted memory stick, two others played counterintel and would try to stop them in the act. All he had to do was identify them. An easy way to earn his consulting fee of twelve galaxies an hour.

He still had to convert the currencies in his head sometimes. Call it half a million of the old, pre-convocation dollars to sip hot chocolate and observe the park's visitors.

The fat flakes fell one by one from the city-washed sky. He ambled through the park. Sips of hot chocolate kept him warm. Easy to watch people over the cup's rim. Lanky men of some Southwest Asian origin, black hair and bushy eyebrows, tossed a flying disc and jabbered in an unfamiliar language. Three old Chinese men, wisps of black hair over bald scalps, moved in slow-motion through a tai chi routine. Near the basketball courts, a South Asian woman in a brown suit, dark brown hair dabbed with gray at the temples, sat with her ankles crossed on a bench.

The woman looked up from a bottle of oxygenated mineral water. A wide, low mouth, accentuated with lush lips and rust-red lipstick. Large brown eyes locked on his.

"Stone?" she said softly.

He blinked. Memories wrapped around him, like a shed skin fitting itself back on a reptile.

"Nina?" He glanced above her shoulder. The first lines of the public profile confirmed it. Nina Irani, once employed by former Secretary-General Abdullah Sayyid, now an associate director of an intergovernmental consortium representing about half of the independent states of South Asia.

A basketball thumped on the court surface. A boyish voice whined for a pass.

"I'm surprised you remembered me," she said. Her voice carried an operatic power, though the intervening five years had dented it and rejuve treatments had failed to buff the dents away.

"Remember you? Who can forget, these days."

Her mouth tightened for a moment. She'd been nothing special, another notch on his bedpost. Then she forced a smile. "We both used each other, those days. Have you time to talk?"

"Can't. I'm looking for someone."

"Four someones, I should think?" Her smile reached her eyes. "Earn your consulting fee. I'll be here when you're done." She looked away and sipped mineral water.

Stone continued his circuit of the park. He made the trainee bringing in the encrypted stick before he finished his hot chocolate. She stuck it to the bottom of a drinking fountain basin when she took a drink.

He tossed the empty cup into a recycling bin, turned, identified the counterintel team. A different pair of joggers. What appeared to be sweat matted their hair to their scalps, a sign of a long run on a cold day, but all the water bottles clipped to their jogging belts were full. They jogged twenty yards past the drinking fountain, then did cool-down stretches while keeping the fountain in sight.

Stone reported what he'd seen to Schrenk, ITB's interim head training officer now that Caitlyn had taken maternity leave. She'd contracted Stone for this consulting job a week before she went into labor.

He strolled toward the drinking fountain. A man who looked about twenty, pale skin and jug ears, came from the opposite direction. He carried an antique camera on a neck strap and craned his head. A student photographer working with an archaic medium, looking for subjects. He stopped at the drinking fountain. Took a long drink, left hand holding the camera to keep it from bumping against the steel bowl, the thumb of the right hand pressing the button while wide fingers groped underneath.

Easy to make him, but the joggers looked too interested. The photography student walked away from the drinking fountain, continuing his path past Stone. The joggers disentangled from their stretches and hurried after him.

[Found the fourth,] he sent to Schrenk. [I'll write up my report tomorrow.]

Schrenk had a voice that reminded Stone of maintenance men and beat cops. [How'd the kids do?]

[I made them, didn't I?]

[Yeah, but you're damn good.]

[I know,] Stone said. Memories from the roster of past foes, living or dead, forced themselves up. Teresa Benavides. Laclede. Simon Bale. Caitlyn. Gray. [But so are the people they'll go up against.]

A thoughtful pause. [Thanks, Chalmers.] Schrenk cut the connection.

Stone ambled away from the drinking fountain. Over the squeak of sneakers, the same kid on the court whined for the ball. On the bench, Nina studied the stained glass mural looming over the park while her hands unscrewed and rescrewed the cap of her empty water bottle a quarter turn at a time.

"Mind if I sit?" he said, like one stranger to another.

"Sure."

He thought at his embedded quantum computer to relay a message to her. [Talk privately?]

[Sure.] Her hands tightened the cap one last time, then laid the water bottle on the bench between them.

A snowflake floated down past his left eye. [Your public profile is a fake?]

[Yes. I'm authorized to tell you the truth. I'm with the Transgalactic Intelligence and Operations Consortium.]

He'd kept his ear to the rumor mill. Investigating Kroebel's sex crimes had led to the discovery of thousands of abused minors, thousands of unidentified corpses and missing persons, and trillions of embezzled dollars, with all clues pointing at a dozen of UNICA's top people. Gray had been fairly clean, guilty only of being an accessory after the fact. But without the old man to crawl out on his thousand strands of spiderweb to manage the story, the twin waves of revulsion at Kroebel's crimes and the restoration of national sovereignty that had crashed over the UN had led UNICA to be disbanded. TIOC had succeeded Gray's operation as the primary intelligence agency on Earth, Minerva, and the other colony worlds. [You should have come up with a better acronym.]

[All the good ones were taken.]

Stone sniffed out a chuckle. [I'm happy to consult with you just like I'm doing for ITB. My standard rate is twelve galaxies per hour—]

[No.]

[Then what?]

[South Asia remains a worrisome region for those who seek a peaceful and just order where all are aligned with the universe. The states there are wealthy enough to support weapons development and belligerent enough to make thinkable their use. We encourage the spread of Alignment into the region.]

[The locals have other plans,] Stone said.

[Which is where you come in. We seek an operative of great skill and experience to go under cover to the Ganges Republic as an Alignment facilitator. Your long history with Alignment indicates that a hypnogogued cover story would more effectively be implanted into your brain than into the brain of a lesser operative.]

[I can't be the only operative you could use.]

[No,] she said, then switched to speech. "Our previous work together made you stand out among the candidates." Her tone was unmistakable. Redolent of memories of their tryst in the General Assembly basement. Craving another opportunity.

"I'm flattered you think so," he said. He smiled gently. She was enough of a woman of the world to accept what he had to say next. "But I'm retired."

About the Author

Raymund Eich files patent applications, earned a Ph.D., won a national quiz bowl championship, writes science fiction and fantasy, and affirms Robert Heinlein's dictum that specialization is for insects. In a typical day, he may talk with biochemists, electrical engineers, patent attorneys, epileptologists, and rocket scientists. Hundreds of papers cite his graduate research on the reactions of nitric oxide with heme proteins.

Connect with the author at **www.raymundeich.com** or scan the QR code below.

Sign up for his mailing list to receive exclusive, pre-release content about his upcoming books. Your email address will never be shared and you can unsubscribe at any time. Go to **www.raymundeich.com/mailing-list** or scan the QR code below.

Other Books by the Author

Available wherever books are sold.
    Learn more about these titles at our website, **www.cv2books.com**, or scan the QR code below.

Stone Chalmers

Earth barely survived the 21st Century. Biotechnological and nuclear terrorism, civil war, famine, and ethnic cleansing killed billions. Thousands fled on warpdrive ships to colonize planets around distant suns.

In the 22nd century, after the United Nations established control over Earth, it opened wormhole links to the distant colonies, to prevent a repeat of the previous century's chaos on a galactic scale.

Enter operative Stone Chalmers. Spy. Assassin. Instrument maintaining the UN's order on the settled galaxy.

Opposing him are hostile forces on colony worlds... and within the UN itself.

When Stone clashes with those forces, the UN—and every human world—will be transformed forever.

Learn more about the Stone Chalmers series at **www.cv2books.com/stone-chalmers**, or scan the QR code below.

The Progress of Mankind (#1)

To maintain order in the 22nd century, the UN relocates undesirables through artificial wormholes onto colony planets. Everyone benefits... except the planets' original colonists.

Now, the newly rediscovered colony of New Moravia learns the UN's plan and fights back.

The Greater Glory of God (#2)

Thousands fled the chaos of the 21st century on rogue warpdrive ships to settle colony planets. When Earth reunified in the 22nd, its fleets rediscovered the colonies and hunted down the warpdrive ships.

Every warpdrive ship but one.

To All High Emprise Consecrated (#3)

After unifying Earth, the UN has rediscovered the colony of Minerva. Prosperous and technologically advanced, Minerva quickly submits to UN supremacy.

Surprisingly quickly...

In Public Convocation Assembled (#4)

After unifying Earth, the UN controls all human colonies scattered through the galaxy by means of wormholes, warpdrive ships, and ruthless operatives. Operatives working to strengthen the UN.

Or destroy it.

The Confederated Worlds

The purpose of all other combat arms is to put the infantryman in sole possession of the battlefield.

A thousand years from now, while Earth sleeps in virtual reality, three polities—the Confederated Worlds, the Unity, and the Progressive Republic—strive to connect the scattered, terraformed worlds of humankind by artificial wormholes. When they meet, they clash, in a decades-long struggle of arms that will embroil every human world, in which dedication to duty liberates worlds—and oneself.

Learn more about the Confederated Worlds series at **www.cv2books.com/the-confederated-worlds**, or scan the QR code below.

Take the Shilling (Book 1)

The Confederated Worlds implanted in his brain the skills to make him a soldier. Tomas Neumann had to learn for himself how to survive interstellar war.

Operation Iago (Book 2)

The Confederated Worlds lost the war. Can Lt. Tomas Neumann win the peace against elusive, deceptive foes out to turn the Confederated Worlds against itself?

A Bodyguard of Lies (Book 3)

Assigned to the halls of power, only Capt. Tomas Neumann can save the Confederated Worlds from the ultimate treachery.

Novels

The Blank Slate

Neuroscience entrepreneur Clay Shieffer must stop a tyrannical president... because he unwittingly gave the tyrant power over the human mind.

New California

After New California's founder committed suicide, two men vied to rule the colony.

Ashwin George, supported by the colony's elite and the Chinese company dominating half the settled galaxy.

Against him, Desmond Park, nanotechnology engineer, armed with the most formidable weapon of all.

A single idea.

The Reincarnation Run

Solitary spacejock Landry Krieger smuggled people past the watchful eyes of interstellar governments, in hiding spaces he built in his ship, *Midnight Angel*.

When the priests of Tao Pacem sought his services, he resisted. Brown robes? Yin-yang symbols? Dreams of sparking a rebelling by sneaking the reincarnation of their spiritual leader to their oppressed homeworld? After Landry's earlier experiences with religious leaders, he needed more reason than money to say *yes*.

He got that reason, when an arrogant agent of the oppressors tried to scare him off the job.

Short Novels

The ALECS Quartet

He had a month to learn the planet's mysteries—and Juliette's.

His cover story: return to Elard to dismantle his sect's missionary work to the planet's natives.

His true mission: investigate decades-old mysteries of love and death.

His objective: return to Earth with his discovery.

If he can.

A Mighty Fortress

Theodore and his team from the Lutheran Interstellar Terraforming Society would transform a barren, rocky world into a refuge of faith and life.

Or die trying.

Collections

The First Voyages: The Complete Science Fiction Stories 1998-2012

From 21st century asteroid settlements to World War II Romania, from an Earth dominated by immortal aliens to Christ's empty tomb, a fresh, distinctive voice in science fiction will take you on journeys to the photosphere of the sun, the coding regions of DNA, and the complexities of the human psyche.

Stage Separations: The Complete Science Fiction Stories 2013-2018

In these pages, you can...
...race against time to solve mysteries hidden in a planet's vast desert—and in a woman's heart ...learn the true story of a president's assassination ...journey 14,000 miles to a high-tech fountain of youth ...win or go "home"—to an Earth you've never seen

and explore six other worlds created by a distinctive voice in twenty-first century science fiction.

Lightning Source UK Ltd.
Milton Keynes UK
UKHW021052050520
362811UK00013B/743